A loveable old woman who seems to know more than she should.

A child's diary ... a bloody rag.

A mystery that only Alexandria Dumont can solve with a little

BLACK MAGIC

"A spellbinding novel by a bright new talent. Don't miss it!"

"Absolutely captivating! Brenda Jernigan has another sizzling, suspenseful hit with Whispers on the Wind."

"It's a fresh change of pace and picked number 1 in my book."

"If Brenda K. Jernigan's name is on the cover of a book, I guarantee it will be a good read."

Books by Brenda Jernigan
THE DUKE'S LADY
THE WICKED LADY
LOVE ONLY ONCE
CHRISTMAS IN CAMELOT

The Misfit Series
DANCE ON THE WIND
UNTIL SEPTEMBER
WHISPERS ON THE WIND
SOUTHERN SEDUCTION

BLACK MAGIC

BRENDA JERNIGAN

DELLARTE
PRESS

Dellarte Press books may be ordered through booksellers or by contacting:

Dellarte Press™
1663 Liberty Drive
Bloomington, IN 47403
www.dellartepress.com
1-877-217-3420

ISBN: 978-1-4501-0018-2 (e)
ISBN: 978-1-4501-0020-5 (sc)
ISBN: 978-1-4501-0019-9 (hc)

Printed in the United States of America

Dellarte Press rev. date: 8/2/2011

Prologue

Heaven or hell?

She wasn't sure.

The ground chilled her feet as a prickling feeling crept over her.

She'd been in this place many times before. The air, thick and heavy, prevented Alexandria from seeing a foot in front of her.

Uncertainty squeezed her heart.

She wanted to run.

She always ran from the things she didn't understand, hoping one day to find the answers she so desperately needed.

Afraid to move any farther, she waited.

She knew he'd come …

He always came in the wee hours of morning.

Her heart drummed faster as the cloaking mist separated just enough for her to see him.

She didn't know his name.

She wasn't sure she'd ever seen him, yet there was something familiar about him that nagged at her.

He is my destiny.

He stood tall, a powerful man exuding sensuality in the way he carried himself. She sensed something strong, unyielding, and for once she wanted to let her guard down and take a chance, but risk wasn't in her nature.

What would happen if she touched him?

He never came close, but merely stood staring at her.

But this time was different. She could feel him reaching out to her as he raised his arm.

He needed her.

Someone needed her.

She grew tired of the game and started to move in his direction, watching his dark, languorous eyes. Just before she reached him, he smiled and said, "You don't belong here."

In the blink of an eye, he vanished, and she stood amid the misty darkness, left alone with ghosts and shadows.

Black Magic, she thought for one crazy second.

While she lingered, staring at the spot where he'd stood, an emptiness like she'd never known sunk hard as a rock in the pit of her stomach.

Trembling, she wrapped her arms around herself. Sadness filled her as she murmured, "I don't belong anywhere."

*C*hapter One

Alexandria Dumont jerked straight up in bed. Her gown clung to her sweat-drenched body. Gulping for air, she took several deep breaths until she calmed herself down.

The dream.

Always the unfinished dream.

"Damn, damn, double damn," she swore as she slid out of bed. "You're a doctor, Alexandria. You should know better than to think so much about a dream."

But this time I almost saw his face, her subconscious told her.

Snatching her jeans off the overstuffed chair in her bedroom, affectionately known as her spare closet, she slid into her jeans and pulled a sweatshirt over her head.

She was going to be late.

Again, her conscience reminded her.

"It's not like I have rounds at the hospital," she muttered. "I'm just going to the flea market with Carol."

Speaking of Carol ... Alexandria peeked out the window and saw her friend waiting in the driveway. She grabbed her purse and headed for the door.

"Sorry, I overslept," Alexandria said as she slid into Carol's slate-gray BMW.

"You look like hell, Dr. Dumont," Carol Dennison commented as she backed out of the driveway.

"Thank you. Direct and to the point—that's what I like about you."

"Well, somebody needs to say something," Carol told her. "You're working way too much. You need a break from school and work. Like an honest-to-goodness vacation. Look at you!" Carol waved her hand down the length of Alexandria's side. "You've run yourself into the ground studying late at night, not to mention the extra duties at the hospital."

Carol's disapproving expression told Alexandria that her best friend wasn't through with the lecture.

"I thought that trip we took to Mexico would have helped you relax, but you've worked twice as hard since we returned. You need several weeks away from the grind."

"That would be wonderful, but I have patients and I need to take a couple of tests." Alexandria paused in thought. "But I'm going to bed early tonight. Maybe it will help some, but not if I have that dream again."

"You had it again?"

Alexandria nodded. "Last night."

"Did you get to see your dream man?"

"Almost. But there were shadows on his face. He's so mysterious, I find myself wanting to meet him." She looked at Carol. "Get that—I want to meet a man who doesn't exist. Sounds stupid, doesn't it?" She sighed. "Maybe I should have studied mental health. At least that would tell me why I've had the same dream every night for the past two months. Anyway, this time he spoke to me."

"And?"

"He told me I didn't belong there."

Carol laughed. "I think you're a hopeless romantic, looking for something that doesn't exist. But I'll admit you sure have kept me entertained with this dream of yours."

"I don't know if I'd say it's exactly entertaining ..." Alexandria broke off and gazed out the window.

More like scary.

Once they arrived at the flea market, they entered a big white archway leading to the buildings. A variety of booths lined several rows. Each vendor hawked his items as one-of-a-kind, and some of the little nooks held garage sales without the garage. The two women passed a stall filled with beautiful paintings and another packed with candles of many colors and fragrances. Alexandria loved to stop and buy miniatures for her shadow box.

Finally Alexandria saw what she'd come for. Hattie was hard to miss today with her hair wrapped in bright red and yellow scarves. "I'm going to see Hattie. Join us later," Alexandria told Carol.

She had just taken a step forward when a stabbing pain shot through her temple, and she had to stop and massage it. Ever since they had come back from their short trip to Mexico, she suffered with sudden headaches. Maybe it was stress, she wondered while she walked toward Hattie, realizing how much she had come to love the old Cajun woman. She had only known her for a couple of months, yet it seemed like a lifetime.

"I like your scarves," Alexandria said, then gave the big woman a hug. Hattie wasn't old, though her wisdom gave the impression she'd been around for a hundred years. She was a stout woman with bronze skin and hazel eyes that shifted between hues of green and blue. Her high cheekbones set off her beautiful, well-defined face.

"Ah, my Alexandria. How have you been, Cher? I've missed you dese past two weeks. What kept you from comin'?"

"I had a very difficult case. A child who I could have helped walk again, but her mother didn't believe in doctors and took her out of the hospital before I could stop her." Alexandria slumped down in a folding lawn chair beside Hattie. "I could have helped her. I know I could have."

"I can see from de dark circles under your eyes dat you put your heart into dis. But sometimes we cannot help those who cannot help themselves. Dere will be other children."

"I just hate to lose one."

Hattie gave Alexandria's hand a squeeze. "I found sometin' for you."

"You found the painting that I described."

"*Oui.*" Hattie nodded. "You're goin' to love it, to be sure." She rose and skittered to a wooden crate where she pulled out a large cardboard box that stood waist-high from the ground.

Propping the box up against a wall, Hattie backed away from the painting. "I done and had dis shipped up from *La Maison*. Found it about a year ago and save it all dis time. Just didn't know what I was savin' it fo'." She gathered her long skirts and sat down on the aluminum folding chair. "After we talked so much about de Old South, I knew de paintin' was meant fo' you."

"*La Maison?*" Alexandria tilted her head sideways while she deciphered Hattie's Cajun French dialect. "The house."

Hattie nodded.

Alexandria approached the mysterious box, her stomach churning with butterflies as she started stripping off the cardboard until she could grasp the wooden frame. She tossed her auburn hair over her shoulder and out of her way as she tugged and finally freed the painting. Turning it around, she grew thoughtful.

The wind's breath surrounded her, blowing wisps of hair against her cheek and engulfing her in its warmth. Alexandria took a few steps back to examine the painting in its entirety.

The faded brown frame was cracked with age, but the oils appeared as vivid as the day they were first applied to the canvas.

Hesitantly, she reached out to touch the painting. The moment her slender fingers brushed the surface, a prickling sensation crept over her. She felt cold yet intrigued that a mere piece of canvas could evoke both happiness and sadness at the same time.

Several minutes passed as she stared at the newfound treasure. Inhaling a deep breath, she swore she smelled the magnolias hanging in the trees beside the mansion. Behind her, Hattie cleared her throat and asked, "How do you like de paintin', Petite?"

"I'm not sure." Alexandria returned to her seat beside her friend so she could observe the picture from a distance.

As she studied the landscape, the paint and canvas took on a life of their own ... a life that somehow encompassed Alexandria and tugged at her.

A magnificent southern plantation sat high atop a grassy knoll overlooking a lake. A woman, who appeared young and beautiful, stood in a regal ball gown beside the lake. The dress was in true Southern-belle style with ruffled peach-colored satin and lace that fell in layers over a big hoopskirt. The low-fitting bodice displayed daintier frills of peach lace, with just a hint of small white flowers mingled in the design of the material.

Such a beautiful gown, Alexandria thought as her gaze traveled up the woman's body, wondering who this intriguing person could be. The answer eluded her, for the mysterious lady wore a big, white hat trimmed with a touch of peach, orange, and white flowers around the center. The floppy hat tilted to the right side completely hid the lady's identity. But the most startling thing about the whole picture was the woman herself. Sadness radiated from her bent head as she stood by the lake, gazing at her reflection.

A horrible reflection ...

The dark water didn't reflect the mystic beauty of the plantation. Instead, it revealed the charred remains of a home that was no more.

The girl's image showed her once-beautiful gown now torn and tattered, hanging in rags from her shoulders. A single tear lingered on the bottom of her cheek, and the hat was now gone, but most of the woman's face still remained hidden in the murky waters of the lake.

Good versus evil, Alexandria thought, then shivered as a profound sense of foreboding ran up her spine. However, strange as the painting made her feel, this was the home she'd always imagined living in--providing she'd lived in the 1800s. She shook her head, freeing herself from the sad trance.

She turned and affectionately placed her hand on the Hattie's arm. Again Alexandria wondered why she felt so close to a woman she hardly knew. But there was something in Hattie's eyes ... a secret ... a knowing ... something that Alexandria couldn't explain.

"I'll always cherish this painting because you gave it to me," she said, then paused as her throat tightened with emotion. "Do you know the plantation's name?"

Hattie hesitated as if she were trying to decide what to say. "*J'sais pas.* But it was once a magnificent home, wouldn't you agree?"

Alexandria nodded, wishing Hattie knew more about the painting. "The South back then was a time of elegance."

"Dat it was, Alexandria, but they had their hardships, too."

"I think I'd truly love to have lived in that time."

"Mebbe." Hattie paused, causing Alexandria to look at her. "Dere is somet'in' in your fortune dat will brin' you some excitement."

Alexandria wanted to laugh at Hattie's matter-of-fact tone. "Are you still thinking of telling my future?" she asked, hiding her amusement. "You know I don't believe in that stuff."

Hattie frowned and grew serious. "Sometimes, you have to put aside what is logical and dare to dream, no." Hattie looked deep into her eyes. "You keep such a check on your emotions, and dat is not good. You can't learn everyt'in' from books ... sometime you have to experience life."

Carol strolled over and dropped her packages by a chair. "Excuse me," she interrupted. "Tell me you're not having your fortune read. I bet you're still looking for that knight in shining armor?"

"Sarcasm doesn't become you," Alexandria said. "And no, I'm not having my fortune read."

"How do you like de painting?" Hattie tactfully changed the subject.

Carol moved closer to get a better look. "It's beautiful! Do you have any idea where this plantation is?" Not waiting for an answer, Carol pulled the painting forward and peeked behind the canvas. "Oh, look. You must have ripped the backing when you pulled it from the crate," Carol said as she bent down. "There's something here."

"What is it?"

She handed Alexandria a small, leather-bound text that had been hidden under the backing. "Looks like a book of some sort."

Alexandria opened the cover. A musty smell tickled her nose and she sneezed. She tapped the book on her hand several times to rid it of dust before trying again. "Seems to be a diary," she said, noticing the beautiful penmanship. "Maybe it will tell me something about the painting." She wanted to sit down and read it now, but her throbbing headache did a good job of killing her enthusiasm.

"Mebbe," Hattie said, coming up behind her. "De next time I see you, you can tell me what you've discovered."

"I'll look at it tonight and let you know what I find next week." Alexandria massaged her left temple. "It's time to go. My head hurts, and I really don't feel well."

"Wait, Petite!" Hattie rummaged in the bottom of her bag and brought out what appeared to be a very old blue tin a little bigger than a fifty-cent piece. "Take dis." She placed the tin in Alexandria's hand and closed her fingers around the cool metal. "It's an herbal tea dat will do wonders fo' your headache."

Alexandria slipped the tin into her purse. "I've always liked hot tea when I'm feeling under the weather. I'm sure I'll be better next week."

"You will be feelin' much better, Petite. I guarantee," Hattie promised before adding, "When tomorrow comes, Alexandria, you'll feel like a new person."

Alexandria waved goodbye to Carol and went into her small apartment, thankful she didn't have anywhere else she needed to go. The dark clouds gathering in the sky promised to drown everything in their path tonight.

She placed her keys on the small butler's table by the door, then flipped on the light, hoping that when she started her own practice, she could throw out the hodgepodge of furniture she'd accumulated over the last several years. She strolled into the bedroom. The bright lemon-yellow decor welcomed her as she propped the painting against an old oak chest at the foot of the bed and laid the diary on the nightstand.

In the kitchen, she placed a copper teakettle on the burner and set the temperature to medium-high, then returned to the bathroom.

She sank down into the tub. The water felt good, and the heat did wonders for her tired muscles. After drying off in a soft terry-towel, she slid on a pink satin nightgown and relished in the silkiness caressing her skin. Stepping back in the bedroom, she pulled back the green-and-yellow-striped comforter on the bed.

"I'd better check my bag," Alexandria mumbled to herself as she placed her black doctor's satchel on the bed, making sure everything was there for tomorrow's rounds. Coughing several times, Alexandria remembered her previous bouts of bronchitis, and hoped she wasn't coming down with something. She didn't bother to put it back on the floor. Instead, she placed the bag on the other side of the bed--the side where no one ever slept.

There were times when she wondered if a man would ever share that side of the bed, especially since she'd become so independent ... perhaps overly so, but she'd had to. This fast-paced world waited for no one, especially orphaned medical students. But sometimes, she would like to be able to let her guard down and lean on a strong man's shoulder and have him wrap his protective arms around her.

Carol was wrong about her being a hopeless romantic. There had to be someone out there, someone who'd take her breath away, someone who would be strong and caring. Alexandria slumped just a little. Sometimes, it felt as if the entire world rested on her shoulders.

The teakettle sounded its usual sharp whistle. She blinked and found she was still staring at the bed. "God ... I'm pathetic."

She turned and padded barefoot across the soft white carpet to the kitchen. Filling her cup with the herbal tea Hattie had given her, Alexandria decided it smelled a lot like sassafras as the steam rose from the tiny cup and tickled her nose.

Just as she reached for the kitchen light switch a sharp clap of lightning made her flinch, causing a little tea to slosh out on the saucer. Licking her finger, she walked over to the dining room window and peeked through the blinds. The night had turned dark, but she could see the pine trees bending under the street lights. In the far distance, lightning streaked across the blackness, turning the sky an unusual purple color. Just as she'd predicted, an electrical storm was fast approaching.

Back in the bedroom, she placed the teacup on the nightstand and lowered the temperature on the electric blanket. Even though it was spring, the cool nights could produce a chill. Thankful for the toasty covers she knew she'd find, she climbed into bed. Placing a couple of pillows behind her head, Alexandria picked up the diary. Eager to read, she took a sip of tea and sighed as the warmth penetrated her body.

Again she gazed at her newly purchased painting and smiled at the crazy feelings she'd had this afternoon. A sharp boom of thunder made her breath catch in her throat. She laughed at her jitters, but opened the nightstand drawer and grabbed a flashlight in case of power failure.

A dull, aching pain behind her eyes told her she should probably go to sleep, but the lure of the diary won out. This would be like a trip back in time, reading the private thoughts of someone she didn't know.

The rumble of thunder surrounded the apartment, and the bushes outside her bedroom window scraped the building.

Good thing she wasn't easily spooked by storms because this one threatened to be a real hair-raiser. She finished the last of her tea, then opened the small, leather-bound book to the first page.

> *May 1, Dear Diary,*
> *Today is my birthday. I am nine years old. I had a lovely birthday party, and best of all my brother was there. I heard several of the older girls whispering how good looking he is, but he just looks like a brother to me. He teases me, saying that I was a mistake, because he is fifteen years older than I am. But I tell him he was the mistake. When I was born our parents were trying to correct it. He always laughs when I say that. He gave me this book for my birthday and had my name written on the front.*

Alexandria shut the book to look at the cover, but the name had long since worn away. In the bottom left hand corner, she spied a faded one and eight, so she assumed the journal was written sometime in the eighteen hundreds. Reopening the journal, she continued to read, noticing her headache had eased a little.

> *I will treasure it always, because my brother loves me very much. Mother looked sad today. I wish she would smile more.*
>
> *May 15,*
> *Mother said we are going for a ride in the carriage to see an old friend of hers. She told me not to tell anyone, but I can tell you, Diary.*

May 25,
Mother is dead. I cry all the time now. I don't understand what
happened. We were only going for a ride.

My legs are numb. I've tried over and over again to make them
move. But I can't! They don't work! The doctor said I'll not be
able to walk again. That makes me sad, Diary. I can't ride my
pony, either. I couldn't even go to Mother's funeral. Brad said she
would have understood. I sure do miss her. Now I only have Brad.
It's so lonely lying here in bed--at least I've got you, Diary.

Gulping back a lump of helpless anger, Alexandria curled her knuckles around the book, dying to know why and how all this had happened. The frustration of her own parents' death surfaced unexpectedly; tears trickled down her cheeks. The painful emotions she thought she'd successfully buried twisted in her stomach. She knew exactly how the child felt. Never would she hear the sound of her parents' voices or experience the comfort of her mother's arms.

She shook herself and dabbed the tears from her eyes, then safely stored her own painful memories back away and focused on the book again.

Had the accident occurred before they met the mother's friend?

June 8,

I heard Brad telling Edmund they had found a bloody cloth on the
seat and bloody handprints on the outside of the carriage. I wonder
what he means? Brad doesn't smile much anymore.

He asked me what happened, but I don't know. I should remember
something, but I cannot. I was asleep on the carriage seat, and
don't remember anything else until I woke up in my bed.

Diary, do you suppose Brad blames me for Mother's death? I am
so lonely, I wish I had a friend … someone to talk to. Someone
who will understand how lonely I feel. I'm scared, Diary.

The room filled with light as a bolt of lightning struck a tree outside the window, leaving everything bathed in darkness. Alexandria jumped, but she was too consumed by the diary to let the storm bother her, and too tired to use the flashlight.

Tears burned her eyes. If only she could have helped the poor child. Laying the book across her chest, Alexandria sighed. She was tired and wanted to read more, but her eyes refused to cooperate. It was probably a good thing the electricity had gone out. She could feel the weight of her eyelids as they grew heavy.

Alexandria shivered. Even wrapped in the blankets, she still felt a chill ... a cold she'd never known before. The coolness penetrated her bones and dulled her headache. Yet, it wasn't an uncomfortable sensation. A peacefulness settled over her, and she began to relax.

She'd been driving herself too hard, that's all. And, yes, she was lonely ... so lonely. She definitely knew how the child in the diary felt.

As if a long-awaited peace settled upon her, she gave in to the pulling sensation. In the distance she could see a light. The closer she got to the bright glow, the warmer she felt and the more peace she found.

And when tomorrow comes she'd feel better ... much better.

Yes, tomorrow she'd feel like a new person.

Chapter Two

The rich aroma of coffee filled the air, tickling Alexandria's nose as she stretched lazily in bed.

Her headache was gone.

She felt wonderful!

Still half asleep, she sat up, then blinked several times at the bright sunlight filtering in through the window. Her leg bumped a lump under the covers. She slid her hand beneath the sheet and retrieved the diary, a small reminder that she'd been reading last night. As she laid the book beside her medical bag, she caught a movement in the corner of her eye.

Her breath caught in her throat.

She wasn't alone.

"Damn, you scared me! How did you get into my bedroom?" Alexandria demanded.

Hattie sat in a corner chair, rocking slowly back and forth.

Had she come to take the painting back? Alexandria's gaze traveled desperately around the bedroom. Where was the painting?

Wait a minute.

This wasn't her bedroom!

Her eyelet drapes were gone. Instead, a porthole displayed a clear blue sky.

"A porthole?"

Okay. She held her hands up like stop signs. She was having another dream ... an honest-to-goodness nightmare ... except she was wide awake. Something was wrong.

Very wrong.

A strange, apprehensive shiver crawled from her toes all the way to her neck. "Where am I?"

"*Bonjour*, Petite. Well now ... dat's a question. How do you be feelin' dis morning?" Hattie asked.

"I--I'm not sure. This has to be a dream. Either that, or--or I've finally gone off the deep end because you shouldn't be here, and at the moment I'm not quite sure exactly where here is." Again Alexandria glanced at the unfamiliar room. "Where am I?"

"You're in a cabin aboard de steamboat, *Magnolia*," Hattie explained. She yawned, then stretched. "You needed a vacation. I simply arranged it."

"Are you crazy?" Alexandria's voice cracked with emotion, and she had to clear it. "I have a job to do. I have bills to pay." Again her voice grew louder. "And I want to know one thing right now ... how in the hell did I get here?"

Hattie clicked her tongue with disapproval. "Such language fo' a lady. I see my job will be cut out fo' me." She chuckled.

Alexandria leaned back with an exasperated sigh, folded her arms across her chest and waited. "This explanation had better be damn good."

Hattie frowned at her again. "We're sailin' down de Mississippi River."

That was it! Alexandria didn't want to hear anymore. She jumped from the bed and ran to the door where she fumbled with the doorknob before she finally unlatched it, then ran outside--straight into a rail.

Okay, she really was on a boat.

And she was on a river. Hell, she could be in China on the Yangtze River for all she knew. What kind of drugs had she taken last night? She went back into her cabin.

"You told me you'd like to have lived in dis period, and I've merely granted your wish." Hattie's expression reflected pure innocence.

"I'm afraid to ask, but what do you mean by 'live in this period?' W--what period?"

"1835, of course." Hattie acted as though it were the most natural thing in the world.

Alexandria slumped down on the bed. "Impossible! Everyone wishes they were someplace else. That's human nature. But the absurdity of this situation is way too much. It's true I love the antebellum period, but I never expected to be a part of it."

After several moments, Alexandria managed to pull herself together.

She needed her wits about her, that was, if she had any left. "I get it. This is a joke, isn't it?"

"No, Petite."

"Then tell me I'm dreaming."

Hattie shook her head.

"But how? I don't' understand. You drugged me, right?"

"Dere are many t'ings dat are unexplainable. I'm not certain even I'll be able to explain, but I will try." The heavyset woman got to her feet and slowly moved across the room. "To be sure, I'm not as young as I used to be, Petite, and a cup of chicory coffee is just what I need before continuing dis mornin'. I've been busy getting you here, and I'm just a little tired. Mebbe, a cup would do you good as well."

Alexandria rolled her eyes, but didn't bother to answer.

"Black Magic is powerful. I simply use it to get what I want."

"And you wanted me?"

"*Oui.*" Hattie nodded. "You have no family and your childhood was very unpleasant. Yet you have a special talent dat is needed here. However I cannot tell you why. Everythin' will be revealed to you later. For once in your life you'll have to trust someone and believe dat I do have your best interest at heart."

"Yeah, I know. You're my fairy Godmother." Alexandria shook herself mentally. "I've only known you for a little while. How do you know so much about me?"

"Sometimes the scars show thorough, Petite," Hattie said softly. "But I understand."

Stunned, Alexandria couldn't say anything. The mention of her youth made her eyes sting, but she wouldn't cry. She hadn't cried in a long, long time. Thinking back, she remembered her painful days with her aunt. Alex had never felt like she belonged there.

And she hadn't.

She was always the outsider. The one without a family. So she'd become a loner, trying hard not to let her emotions show. *If people get too close, they'll hurt you,* her inner voice told her. It was better to feel nothing than to risk getting hurt. She could still hear her aunt's last words, "You'll never amount to anything, Alexandria Dumont."

Well, she had proven her aunt wrong by holding down two jobs to get a medical degree. Hattie was right; that was behind her. Alex must be concerned with the present.

Except the present had disappeared overnight, if Hattie was to be believed. None of this should be happening. This couldn't possibly be real! However, she was wide-awake and Hattie was here. "Just how did you manage to get me back--back to this place? Did you wave a magic wand? Twitch your nose?"

"You make fun o' things you know nothing about, but Black Magic is powerful ... more powerful than you know. Black turns to white, death becomes life." Hattie sighed. "Fo' some strange reason, fortune has put us together."

Alexandria still didn't believe her, but the wise old woman had said some peculiar things. She searched her mind for possibilities. This wasn't logical. She frowned. After all, she'd only had a headache ... Then again, maybe she had died.

Could heaven be a boat on the Mississippi? She smiled at that peculiar thought.

This had to be a dream or a joke. A joke, she thought, that's it. Carol! This had to be another one of Carol's jokes. And Hattie was in on the prank.

For now, what choice did Alexandria have, except to play along and figure out how she could return to the *real* world. After all, she had patients who depended on her. When she worked at the hospital, she was needed. She'd learned long ago she could give her love to children because they wouldn't hurt her.

But what if by some quirk she had slipped back in time? Hattie had to be the link for Alex to return home, so she'd make sure to remain with her friend. Everything would straighten itself out, she told herself.

"Well, I simply refuse to believe I'm not going home, so don't even try to convince me." She held up her hand, then slid off the bed and straightened her gown. Moving over to the porthole, she looked out.

Hattie slowly sipped her coffee. "You really should have some *café au lait* and toast, Petite."

Oh, what the hell, Alexandria thought as she moved over to a corner table, where she poured a hot cup of coffee and laced it generously with cream. "Where is the bathroom?"

"Over dere." Hattie pointed to the corner of the cabin.

"Where? I don't see a door?"

"De *pot de chambre* is behind dat screen."

"A chamber pot!" Alexandria groaned, then laughed. "I must say, Hattie, you've done a damn good job with this hoax. Just look at all these antiques." *Rather new-looking antiques*, Alexandria thought as she moved over to the light green partition, mumbling under her breath. "They never mentioned this in the books I read."

Hattie shook her head, chuckling. "I think you will miss your, ah, how you say, conveniences, but you'll ...."

"I know, Hattie. I'll adjust," Alexandria finished for her. But when she tried to squat on the small pot, she wondered if anyone could adjust to *this*.

After Alexandria had eaten her toast, smeared with a delicious grape jam, and downed a cup of very strong coffee, she was ready to attack the day. 1835 ... the year kept running though her head. Hadn't she always wondered what life would be like back then? She knew she'd wake up tomorrow morning to find this had all been a dream, but for now she would enjoy her so-called adventure. It wasn't as if she'd left a family back home. She'd left an empty apartment. So who would miss her other than Carol? If Carol wasn't part of this joke, that is.

Alexandria walked over to the wardrobe, opened the door, and found old-fashioned clothes hanging inside. Two day dresses and one dinner dress hung there. She turned and looked over her shoulder. "Are these mine?"

"*Oui.*"

"Where are the others?"

"Dat's it, cher."

Poor in this age was not good, Alexandria thought as she chose a lemon-yellow garment made of dotted swiss with a simple top, short sleeves, and a wide, white satin sash to complement the waist. Since she didn't see any undergarments, Alexandria slipped the dress over her head, thankful that she'd slept in her underwear.

She bent over and brushed her hair, removing all the tangles from the night before. She straightened and shook her head, letting her hair cascade down her back.

Looking into the mirror, she scrutinized her face, then pinched her cheeks for added color, wishing she had the makeup still at home on the bathroom counter. In fact, she wished she had her whole bathroom. A chamber pot would be hard to get used to. She wondered if Hattie had gone so far as to hire a bunch of actors to carry out this ruse. Alex was ready to find out. She turned around. "Do I look like a true Southern belle, Hattie?"

"Like a breath of fresh air."

"Let's go up on deck." Alexandria smiled and thought to herself, *so I can ask some questions.* "I want to look around."

"I think I'll lie down. I'm a bit tired. Remember, you are in a different century, and t'ings are not de same."

"How can I forget?" She saw Hattie frown at her remark. "I'll remember."

Once outside the cabin, Alexandria noticed that she had to walk up a flight of stairs to reach the main deck. She walked over to the railing to glimpse the vast Mississippi River, which stretched as far as she could see. The water was as smooth as canvas and the sun shimmered across the translucent, olive-green surface.

Majestic bluffs overlooked the river with charming grace and soft beauty. At the base of the slopes near the water's edge were broken, turreted rocks of rich brown and rust. This is breathtaking. Maybe she would enjoy this trip, after all. She was sure they would stay here for an exciting adventure and then she would return to reality.

Hattie had to be kidding.

And the more she thought about it, Carol couldn't afford anything this elaborate.

Alex leaned over the rail and looked down river, noticing the many twists and turns ahead. She tried to recall what she knew about the Mississippi River. Very little, she realized. Geography had not been her best subject. "I wonder what part of the river we're on?" Aware that she had been talking to herself, she quickly glanced around to make sure no one was near.

Evidently it was still early, because she had yet to see anyone, so she decided to explore the boat. Behind her loomed two tall, fancy-topped chimneys, belching black smoke that drifted in the wind. She could hear the splashing of the trundling paddle wheel, but couldn't see it from the spot where she stood.

The pilothouse sat in front of two smokestacks. White-painted, gingerbread work adorned the cabin promenades, suggesting an opulent, Southern hotel set afloat. Glass fronted all four sides of the rectangular cabin, providing the captain with a panoramic view. A big, wooden steering wheel stood regally in front of the windows. Alexandria raised her hand, shading her eyes to get a better view of the structure.

The captain saw her and waved in cheerful greeting. She waived back and left the railing to walk over to one of the many chairs that sat scattered about the deck for the passengers. The *Magnolia* was very clean with its whitewashed walls and navy blue trim.

Two gentlemen strolled toward the bow of the ship and nodded in greeting as they passed her. How dignified they appeared with their polished silk hats, elaborate shirtfronts, diamond breast pins, and carrying kid leather gloves. Their patent leather boots glistened in the sunshine, making Alexandria feel plain in comparison.

"Excuse me," she called to the men.

They politely stopped and tipped their hats. The tall one said, "Can we be of some assistance, ma'am?"

"I--I wonder if you could confirm the exact date." Alex felt herself blush under their quizzical stares. "It's just that I've been traveling so much that I've lost track of time."

"Yes, ma'am. It's May fifth," the shorter one answered.

"And the year?"

"Are you feeling ill, ma'am?"

"Just a little, but indulge me with the year."

"Why, it's 1835."

"Thank you." She managed a nod, even though her head had started to spin. "Good day, gentlemen." Alexandria didn't need these men asking her any questions, and she didn't want anyone to think she was daft though she seriously questioned her own sanity at this moment.

1835? Impossible.

She just needed to think. She stumbled over to a group of chairs and was about to take a seat when she heard rapid footsteps pounding across the deck. Before she could turn to see who was in such a rush, something hit her arm, and she was shoved headfirst into a nearby rocking chair.

"Damn it," Alexandria swore. "Just how rude are these people?" She was trying to straighten up when a second person came around the corner and roughly hauled her up out of the chair. Hard fingers dug painfully into her arm, but she couldn't see a thing for the hair in her face.

"My dear, you'll regret being part of this scheme!" The accusing, cultured voice held a slight Southern drawl.

Pushing the hair away from her eyes, Alex wanted to see who was dishing out this abuse. She'd had more than enough. She might not be dressed as nicely as everyone else, but that was no reason to be treated so badly. Then it dawned on her what the man had said. Had he just threatened her?

She found herself looking directly at the chest of a rather large gentleman. Slowly, her eyes traveled up to the face of the man who held her imprisoned within his arms.

"Now, wait just a minute..." She almost wished she hadn't looked at him. His was a face she'd not soon forget. The stranger appeared arrogant, his features chiseled and hard, and no smile lingered on his lips. Yet she sensed his coiled power, waiting to be released.

Tawny brown hair streaked with blond highlights brushed his forehead. A square jaw proclaimed his stubbornness. He had a close-clipped mustache, and a glint of contempt lit his ice-blue eyes. Something vaguely familiar about him poked at her memory.

She shivered. What a man. His chest was wide and his shoulders muscular. Surely, all his clothes had been made especially for him because no ordinary man could wear them. But his clothing definitely fit the style for 1835.

Could Hattie have been telling the truth? By some quirk of fate, could Alexandria have truly slipped back in time?

The man's very size silenced her. Hadn't she just recovered from the first assault when this gentleman had grabbed her? She felt like a rabbit caught in a snare. Where was that spunk and courage she'd used to get through med school? Finally she managed to find her voice. "I--I beg your pardon?"

"I said you'd regret being a part of this ploy," he repeated, his voice a harsh growl.

"Look bud! I don't know who licked your lollipop, but I don't know what you're talking about, and I would appreciate you letting go of my arm."

"I bet you would, darlin', but I have no intention of letting you get away." He pulled her closer and made no attempt to loosen his grip. She could feel every inch of his body pressed next to hers. Unexpected warmth surged through her, and Alexandria stared at him in astonishment.

"What? No excuses?" he asked.

"What the hell are you talking about?" Alexandria challenged him with her eyes while she took a measured breath. *Be calm*, she told herself. A calm person can handle any situation. Don't let him get under your skin. It wasn't like her to lose her temper or composure.

His eyebrow arched. "Such language for someone who is *supposed* to be a lady. I'll tell you what I'm talking about ... I'm talking about this." He bent down, retrieving a wallet from her chair. "Your partner picks my pocket and you hide the loot." His hold tightened as he jerked her up on her toes, bringing her face to within an inch of his. "Do you think I've not seen this ruse before?"

"Supposed to be a lady?" Alexandria spat back. "You wouldn't know a lady if she fell at your feet. Let go of me!" she muttered through gritted teeth, then kneed him in the groin.

Immediately, he released her arm. He took a step backward, grimaced, and swore under his breath.

All right, so she wasn't in control, but she'd be damned if she was going to let this high-handed jackass falsely accuse her of thievery. What had happened to the genteel Southern manners these men were supposed to have?

"I came up here for a quiet morning walk," she informed him in a clipped tone. She noticed that he was still bent over but assumed he could still hear her. "I was simply enjoying the view when a man dashed around the corner and rudely knocked me down." She pointed to the chair behind her. "I've no idea who he was because I didn't get to see him. Before I could get straightened out, *you* appeared and accused me of being his accomplice. Unless you would like a lawsuit on your hands, you'd better come up with more evidence than a wallet thrown in a chair. I doubt that would stand up in any court of law."

Her breath came out in short gasps of outrage, and she didn't care for the man's amused expression now that he'd recovered, and the murderess gleam in his eyes was quite unsettling.

"Oh, you think to take me to court, you little minx. I don't think you'll get very far. After all, you don't belong here."

You don't belong here.

My God, he was the man in her dreams. She'd truly slipped into some niche of her imagination. God help her, she'd gone off the deep end!

Brad Wentworth had barely recovered from the vicious blow the hellcat had inflicted. He stared at the lady, suddenly seeing her as a woman instead of a criminal. And what a beauty, he thought. Crazy as hell, but still beautiful.

She stood before him, her copper-colored tresses in wild disarray around her lovely shoulders. Her hair reminded him of a fine burgundy wine with its perfect mixture of browns and reds. He watched the sunshine reflect across her hair, noticing the shimmering highlights that begged to be touched. Wasn't she aware that ladies wore their hair pinned neatly upon their heads?

Come to think about it, everything about this woman was strange. For one thing, she talked funny, and she didn't possess the pasty white skin of most of the females around here. Instead, her skin had a touch of light bronze, which was most unusual for a redhead. The captivating green embers in her eyes were framed by the longest black lashes he'd ever seen. But ... he shook his head. The fact remained, she was still a thief, no matter what kind of pretty package she presented.

Finally tearing his gaze away, Brad noticed the rest of her attire. She wore a nice dress, and she most certainly looked lovely in it, but it wasn't the dress of a wealthy lady. He glanced around for her companion, but found none. It appeared she was very much alone. Perhaps her partner had deserted her. Or maybe she was to meet him later with the loot.

Though she was unaccompanied, she stood before him not in the least bit intimidated. And just now she had threatened him with what she called a lawsuit. He was sure she meant legal action. This woman did use some strange words. But a woman taking *him* before a judge when *he* was an attorney--now that was good for a laugh. The lady was obviously educated, but absolutely crazy.

"You proclaim your innocence, Madam, and you possibly could be telling the truth. Would you care to tell me who you are?"

"My name is Alex ... Alexandria Dumont."

"Dumont. The Dumonts from St. Louis?"

"No."

Brad waited for her to elaborate. When she didn't, he asked, "Where are you headed?"

"I don't think that's any of your business. And I don't believe I caught your name." Alexandria's attempts at sounding haughty went very much against her nature. But she wondered just what he would say if she told him she didn't have the slightest idea where she was going, or the fact that she had no idea where she was now.

They stood in silence, glaring at each other, when a rich, vibrant voice sounded behind them.

"Is there some trouble here, Brad?"

"I don't know, Tom. That's what the lady and I were just discussing," Brad said to the man.

"Well, perhaps I can help."

Alex could tell this was the boat's captain by his dress. He looked like the colonel at Kentucky Fried Chicken--except his hair was red instead of white.

"A thief picked my pockets, and when I chased him around the corner, I found this young lady with my wallet. A young woman, I might add, that I do not know, nor have I seen before this morning." Brad raised a questioning brow at her, as if he dared her to dispute his story.

Her temper flared. She curled her hands into tight little fists as he challenged her patience. Hadn't she always been a mild-mannered person ... until now? But this man! This pig-headed stubborn fool made her lose control. And that she didn't like--nor him, for that matter. She'd liked him better in her dreams when he didn't speak. All men should be quiet unless spoken to.

"Well, I've never seen you, either, and furthermore, I wish I still hadn't laid eyes on you," Alexandria uttered dryly before turning the tables. "How do I know you didn't set me up? Perhaps this was a plan of *yours*."

Brad could see Tom Leathers was enjoying the little display of heated sparks and knew why his friend smiled. Hadn't Brad always boasted of his cool indifference in any difficult situation? Well, that truth ended as of now. He had never had a female speak to him like this before, and he damn well didn't like it one bit. The little fool didn't know her place.

Leathers cleared his throat. "You haven't seen her before because she just came aboard at our last stop. I think you can rest assured that she's an innocent bystander," Captain Leathers defended. "I have had some other reports of thievery, and I've got my eye on someone. It could be the same person who accosted you."

Brad noticed how the woman stared at the Captain, her eyes wide with amazement, then she asked, "And what is your name, sir?"

"Captain Tom Leathers, at your service."

Brad rubbed his chin. What was it about this woman that made her stand out from all the others? She was definitely different. For now, he decided, he would let the matter rest.

"I believe, Miss, or is it Madam?" Brad found he wanted to know if some poor fool had married her. Of course, he wasn't interested, just mildly curious. Something about her intrigued him. Was there a man in her life who could calm those angry sparks he saw? He couldn't help but grin as he wondered what it would be like to tame her. But, right now, he saw nothing in Miss Dumont's eyes, no recognition, only displeasure. Why, he hadn't impressed her at all! That was both surprising and refreshing.

She still looked like she wanted to do him bodily harm, and she had damn near did him in a moment ago.

"It's Miss." She arched an eyebrow, mocking his previous actions and daring him to make a smart comment. She had a good mind to tell him it was Ms.

"Miss Dumont, I believe an apology is in order. I mistook you for a thief, but I think if the situation were reversed, you'd feel the same way." He bowed graciously.

That was an apology? He might be good looking, but he was extremely arrogant. Perhaps he was used to women falling all over him. Well, she surely wouldn't be one of them. The only thing she wanted to do was get as far away from this man as possible.

"I believe you've forgotten to introduce yourself," Alexandria reminded him.

"You're quite right, Miss Dumont. My name is Bradley Wentworth."

Bradley. A most unusual name, she thought, then she recalled the captain had called him Brad. The diary had mentioned that name. Could he be? No. Impossible. She shook her head. This was just a coincidence--nothing more.

As he introduced himself, Alexandria remembered that she was in another age and should try to get along with him.

"Mr. Wentworth," she said in a smooth, cultured, and somewhat sensual voice. "If that was an apology, then I accept." She stared at Brad and, for just a second, became captivated by his vivid blue eyes. They were as blue as the Mediterranean Sea, and she wanted to look away but could not. For one brief moment, a drowning sensation overwhelmed her, and she found she could quickly become lost in his stormy eyes.

Captain Leathers tugged on her arm. "I believe, Miss Dumont, I offered to show you my boat." He crooked his elbow, and when Alexandria placed her hand on his arm, he expertly moved her down along the walkway, leaving Brad behind.

She felt relieved to be out of that mess. But just why had the Captain come to her rescue? She didn't get a chance to ask.

"I thought it was better to put some distance between you two before Brad exploded again. I've never heard him apologize to anyone, except you, young lady. And you had the nerve to act as if he'd truly insulted you." Captain Leathers chuckled. "I just hope this boat is going to be big enough for the two of you. Perhaps I should put you both at opposite ends of the *Magnolia* and dare either of you to cross the center line."

Chapter Three

"Why did you help me, Captain?" Alexandria asked.

"Were you guilty?"

"No."

"I didn't think so. I saw you earlier from the pilothouse," he explained.

"That was you I waved at this morning!"

"Sure was, ma'am." He laughed good-naturedly. "And now that I've rescued you, would you like a tour of my boat, Miss Dumont?"

She nodded. "Please call me Alexandria."

"I'd be so honored. Alexandria is a good Southern name." He smiled down at her, then stopped and turned to face her. "Before we go any farther, I'd like to ask you a question."

Alexandria hesitated. She wasn't too sure she wanted to answer anything. However, the captain didn't wait for her consent.

"You didn't realize who you were talkin' to back there, did you?" Instead of putting his hands in his pockets, he grasped his lapels.

"He introduced himself as Brad Wentworth. Other than that, I don't know anything about him. Except the fact that he's rude."

"Then allow me to tell you, ma'am, he's not someone you'd like to make your enemy. Why, he's built River Bends into the largest cotton plantation in New Orleans. Yep." The Captain nodded his head. "It's a grand home, indeed. Once he practiced law in New Orleans, but he rarely takes a case now unless it's for a personal friend."

"Did you say lawyer?" She hoped she hadn't heard correctly.

"Yes, ma'am, best there's ever been. He's never lost a case," Captain Leathers boasted as he rocked back on his heels.

"Well, that's great. I really put my foot in my mouth this time," she said with a disgusted sigh. How embarrassing to threaten a lawyer. Why didn't she think before speaking? No wonder Brad had grinned at her as if she were an idiot.

"Is there somethin' troublin' you, Miss Dumont?"

"When I was arguing with Mr. Wentworth, I told him I would sue him." She smiled at herself, for she'd always been one to jump feet first into anything.

"Tell me, ma'am, you didn't?" Captain Leather's chest rumbled with laughter.

"I'm afraid so."

"Well, I'm sure Brad has been puzzled by your brief encounter this mornin'. Normally, women vie for his attentions; they don't threaten him." The captain stopped to wipe the tears from his eyes. "I can't remember when I've had such a good laugh. Yes, siree, Brad's pride surely must have suffered today."

"Mr. Wentworth isn't married, then?" Alex told herself she was mildly curious.

"No, ma'am. You wouldn't be interested, now would you?" the captain teased.

"Not on your life," she quickly assured him--almost too quickly. "Now, how about that tour you promised?"

She liked this older gentleman. Judging his age to be around fifty, she watched him as he strode heavily but gracefully along the hurricane deck. He loomed nearly as tall as Brad. His broad chest and shoulders appeared massive in his gray coat, and he reminded her of one of the Confederate statues she had seen in the park back home. A dense fringe of dark red beard sprinkled with gray jutted from his jaw and matched his thatch of red hair.

Leathers explained different items on his boat, and Alexandria could tell he was proud of the *Magnolia*. His pale gray eyes appeared full of fight as he spoke. Wide stern lips accented his face, and there was an air of confidence about him. Yes, he was definitely captain of this boat.

His voice penetrated her thoughts. "The *Magnolia* is three hundred feet long, and forty-odd feet in the beam."

"Is that good?"

"You betcha. She's the fastest boat afloat."

They finally stood behind the big wheel Alexandria had noticed earlier.

"What a wonderful view," Alexandria commented. From the high perch, she could see the decks fore and aft. It was a good time to find out her exact location on the mighty Mississippi. "I've spent quite a bit of time in my cabin, Captain Leathers. Can you tell me where we are on the river?"

"Just outside of Louisville. We'll be in New Orleans in about two weeks."

Two weeks, she thought. Somehow that seemed like a life time. When had she ever taken two weeks off from work? Guilt washed over her when she thought of her patients, yet she knew other capable doctors would take over her case load. Would anybody even notice she was gone?

Two more weeks, she thought again. Hopefully, by then she would learn the way of things in this life. She still felt as if she were walking through a very vivid dream, and she wasn't too sure she'd gotten off to a good start this morning. What would happen when they reached New Orleans? She only hoped Hattie had some kind of magic in that bag of hers.

—)—

"Did you sleep well, Hattie?"

"*Oui,* Petite, I feel much better." Hattie stretched, getting the creaks out. She had fallen asleep in the dark green chair. "How did your morning go?"

"I'm not sure you want to know." Alexandria shut the door and proceeded to the over-stuffed chair.

"Not good, I take it from de frown on your face."

"Remember when you told me I'd meet a handsome stranger?" she reminded her.

"I do." Hattie lumbered over to the washstand. "And did you meet him?"

Alexandria frowned. "Maybe there were two handsome strangers, and you forgot to tell me about the second. This morning, I did meet a good-looking man. But this one is arrogant, stubborn, and I hope never to see him again."

Hattie gave her a disapproving stare. "I warned you, cher many t'ings would be different from what you're used to."

"I know." Alexandria waved away her warnings. "But let me tell you what happened." She abruptly stood, then began pacing back and forth, trying to ward off her vexation as she spent the next hour filling her friend in on what had occurred.

Hattie listened, and grunted every now and then, but other than that made no comment. "I'll get dressed, and dis time I'll chaperon you up on deck, then mebbe you can work off some o' dis frustration and quit your pacin'. And men will not get de wrong idea about you walkin' around without a chaperon."

"I'm a big girl, Hattie. I can go out by myself."

"Evidently, not in 1835."

"Well, Cousin, are you going to tell me what has you in such a fine mood this afternoon?" Edmund Lucas asked Brad as they stood at the ship's helm.

"There's nothing wrong. What makes you think differently?" Brad snapped.

"Well, Sir, for the last hour you've been standing here, just staring as you've downed one bourbon after another. I know the Mississippi is interesting, but I don't see anything out there that would hold your attention for this length of time." Edmund waited for a reply. Receiving none, he proceeded. "Therefore, I'll assume your mind is on something else that's troubling you, and you can't find the answer to the problem."

"Did somebody give you a crystal ball and tell you to go looking for problems?" Brad growled. "I don't care to discuss what's bothering me."

Edmund thought a moment before attacking Brad again. "Did you find the person who took your wallet this morning?"

"No, though I did retrieve it and everything was there. I guess the thief didn't have time to take the money."

"Where did you find it?" Edmund propped his right elbow on the rail as he watched Brad.

Brad reluctantly answered. "In the hands of a very beautiful young lady. I can still picture her angry, emerald eyes."

"She stole it?"

"No." Brad shook his head slowly. "At the time, I thought she did, and accused her of the fact. But I was wrong. She just happened to be in the way when the thief ran past her."

Edmund reached out and grabbed his cousin's arm. "Wait! Did I hear you say you were wrong?" He started laughing.

"Yes. And you don't have to be quite so smug about it."

"Sorry. It's not often I hear those words come out of your little ol' mouth. Tell me, what did the lady do when you accused her of stealing your wallet? I bet she broke out in a fit of tears, because, if I know you, you were probably yelling at her."

Brad sipped his drink. His cousin knew him well. "Yes, I was. And no, she didn't start crying." He smiled as he recalled the incident and the defiant young woman. The fact that he still hadn't gotten that redheaded she-devil out of his thoughts irritated him. Hell, next month he planned to announce his engagement.

"Well, what did she do?"

"She threatened to take me to court!"

Edmund laughed so hard, it took several minutes before he could speak. His amusement became infectious, and Brad began to chuckle, too.

"This has got to be a first." Edmund picked his drink back up and offered a salute. "Here's to the first lady you've not completely charmed off her feet. I never thought to see the day. She must be a Yankee."

Brad glared at him. "Remember, I'm to announce my engagement in one month. I don't need to be charming ladies."

"I've not forgotten. That's something else I've been wanting to discuss with you. I can't believe you're finally going to ask Julia to marry you. What made you change your mind?"

"Probably had too much to drink," Brad said with the indifference he felt.

"If you don't mind me saying so ..." Edmund looked at him ruefully. "You don't appear too excited about the prospect of marital bliss with the one you love."

"Most people marry for money, not love," Brad reasoned. "What is there to be excited about? I've known Julia for years, and I'm sure she'll make a proper wife. She comes from a wealthy family, and she seems pleasant enough."

"Oh, please." Edmund sighed. "Sounds like the lady--and I use that term loosely--already has you well-trained."

"Watch out! That's my future wife you're referring to. And I'm *not* trained!" Brad scowled. "And you should know better than anyone. It's just time to settle down and start thinking about the plantation. I think Missy needs a woman around the house, too. There are many things I can't talk about with her that a woman can."

"You could hire a maid," Edmund suggested.

"I have a maid, if she ever comes home."

Edmund turned his back to the river and leaned against the rail. "I know Missy's a child, but do you suppose she'll ever meet any young men, especially since she's in a wheelchair?"

"I don't know, Edmund. It's sad to see her unable to walk and play. She is such a beautiful little girl, even if she is my sister." The fact that he couldn't help his crippled sister stuck like a thorn in his side. And doctors had been useless. "One thing's for sure, I can warn Missy about men like you, Edmund."

"And what, may I ask, is wrong with me?" Edmund sounded offended while he watched the milling crowd.

"Absolutely nothing. From what I hear, you have women hanging on your coattails."

Edmund grunted. "I wish what you said were true. Right now, I'd settle to have that woman over there hanging on my coattails." He chuckled. "Hell, I'd give her the coat. She is absolutely stunning!"

Brad still stared out over the river while he finished his bourbon. "According to you, my friend, all women are stunning and just waiting for your bed. Is this one really worth wasting my time to look at?"

"I've never seen beauty such as this one, and remember I saw her first, cousin."

Brad straightened. "Now, my friend, you've gotten my curiosity up."

As Brad turned, Edmund said, "She has the most beautiful red hair I've ever seen."

In an instant, Brad spotted the hellcat he'd run into this morning. But this time, he grinned. "I've got news for you Edmund: I spotted her first."

"That's impossible!" Edmund looked at his cousin with surprise registering in his eyes. "That Kentucky bourbon has gone to your head. You had your back to her!"

Brad draped an arm on Edmund's shoulder. "Remember when I told you about the little she-devil I ran into this morning?"

"You're kidding." Edmund nodded toward the woman. "That's her?"

"I'm afraid so."

"Brad, isn't that your housekeeper she's sitting beside?"

"Hattie." Brad supplied the missing name. "It's about time she came back home."

"Where has she been?"

"On a vacation of sorts. She told me it was something she had to do, if that makes any sense. As you know, Hattie has her papers and is free to travel. She told me she was going up North. I assume she visited some of her relatives."

"She is *one-of-a-kind*." Edmund shook his head. "Quite frankly, I don't think you've ever owned Hattie."

"I know," Brad sighed. "Believe it or not, I think I've even missed her bossiness." But one thing he couldn't wait to find out was just what in the hell Hattie was doing with his little she-devil. Did this mean he would be seeing more of her?

Alexandria watched all the beautiful ladies. And the good-looking men with their impeccable dress. Out of the corner of her eye, she glimpsed two gentlemen walking toward them. At first, she wondered who they could be until she saw those ice-blue eyes.

"Hattie, that's him!" Alex clutched Hattie's arm. "Look, he's the one with the cold eyes."

Hattie glanced the direction Alexandria indicated. "Are you sure, Petite?"

"Yes."

"Damn."

Alexandria's head snapped around to her friend. "Why did you say that?"

But Hattie didn't answer. Two gentlemen now stood in front of them. The shorter of the two grinned like a cat at Alexandria. He had a boyish air about him and he was nice looking with sandy blond hair and irresistible blue eyes.

Alexandria's cheeks grew warm. Evidently, Mr. Wentworth had told his friend about the incident this morning and that was the reason for the big smile on the gentleman's face. Her eyes cut to Brad, daring him to look at her. She was ready to take him on just like she had several doctors in the past; however, he didn't even glance her way. He was looking at Hattie ... and smiling.

"Hattie, I never know where you're going to show up." Brad smiled affectionately at her. "But it's about time you came home. A little longer and I'd have had to replace you."

"Home!" Alexandria all but shouted. "Wait a minute ... You know him?"

"Do you find something wrong with Hattie knowing me?" Brad now turned his attention on Alexandria.

"Yes, I do." Alexandria told him. "She could have at least told me."

"And would you like me to tell you how I know Hattie?" Brad inquired.

"No!"

"Oooee wait a minute. To be sure, you both done and got your tail feathers in a twist," Hattie sounded like a mother scolding her children as she stood and gave Brad a hug. "It's good to see you, Master Brad."

"Do you know this woman beside you?" Brad arched an eyebrow in question.

"Well now ... dats a question. Dis is Alexandria Dumont." Hattie turned to look into Alexandria's irate eyes. "Petite, dis is de gentleman I work fo'," Hattie said, her hand still on Brad's arm. "I believe you said you met him earlier."

"You could say that I had the misfortune of running into him," Alexandria grumbled, frowned then asked, "You actually work for him?"

"*Oui.* I'm housekeeper fo' River Bends and have raised Master Brad since he was knee-high to a grasshopper."

"River Bends is my plantation," Brad supplied.

She couldn't help but notice the sudden gleam of laughter deep in his eyes. He seemed to enjoy this little charade he and Hattie had pulled on her.

"Hattie, may I speak to you? Alone," Alexandria blurted out. This was too much! Her pulse quickened. Why did she come unglued when this man drew near her?

"We'll talk later." Hattie patted Alex's hand like a mother would a child then she turned to Brad. "I understand dat you and Alexandria have gotten off on de wrong foot. I'd like you both to start over again." Hattie gave them a motherly frown. "To be sure, you both remind me o' children." When neither of them moved, she added. "Well...?"

Brad conceded first, a slight smile on his lips. "I'm happy to make your acquaintance again, Miss Dumont." He bowed graciously, then looked at Hattie. "Happy?"

She nodded.

When Brad smiled, he probably could get anything he wanted. His smile was quite captivating, she thought. And his strong, commanding features gave the unmistakable appearance of sophistication. Once again she couldn't help but notice how broad his shoulders were in comparison to the other men she'd known. He wore a tailored brown jacket that fit him perfectly.

Brad would be absolutely perfect, Alexandria mused--that is, if he weren't such a chauvinist. So absorbed in her assessment of him, she hadn't realized he'd quit talking as he awaited her reply. Hattie poked her with an elbow to gain her attention.

Alexandria glanced up into Brad's eyes and found his smile had broadened. Once again, she blushed. Damn. She was attracted to a man she knew would only be trouble. Worse, he knew she'd been giving him the once-over. The knowledge registered in his eyes.

"It is ... it's ..." She paused without completing her sentence. She wasn't sure it was a pleasure to meet Brad, because she didn't like him. The word she wanted to use was unusual, but that would never do, so she settled for, "... nice to meet you, Mr. Wentworth."

"Please, call me Brad." He grinned at her. "How did you and Hattie meet?"

"Well--"

"Alexandria's mother was a dear friend o' mine," Hattie interjected. "When she died, I promised I'd look after Alexandria for a while. She's a doctor, and I thought maybe she could help on da plantation."

Alexandria couldn't believe the story Hattie had just made up on the spur of the moment. What a perfect liar she was. What else had she lied about?

"A doctor?" Edmund asked. "Brad hates doctors."

"Excuse me for being so rude," Brad said, frowning because he'd completely forgotten that Edmund was standing beside him. "This is my cousin Edmund Lucas, from New Orleans."

Edmund took Alex's hand and placed a light kiss on the back. Just like in the books, she thought. Now here's what she expected from this adventure of Hattie's! "Yes, I'm a doctor," she confirmed. "Let's hope you're never sick if you hate doctors."

"There aren't any women doctors that I know of." Brad laughed sarcastically. "The old sawbones I've seen have been useless."

"You've probably had a bad experience with a physician, but there are some very good practicing doctors."

"Well, you can't prove it by me. The ones I've met are completely incompetent."

"And I suppose you've never been wrong?"

"Never."

"Well, count this a first, Mr. Wentworth. You probably have never heard of any women doctors, but I assure you, Mr. Wentworth, you're looking at one now!" Why did she let him get her temper up? Even in her own time, she'd bumped into doubting Thomas's.

"I insist you call me Brad, Miss Dumont."

"All right, Brad, but you're still wrong." Alexandria smiled, sweetly. She could tell a stinging reply hovered on the tip of his tongue, but Edmund took her by the arm and saved her from having to listen to Brad's parting remarks.

"Let's take a walk, Miss Dumont, while Brad and Hattie catch up on old times."

She left with Edmund. She smiled slightly to herself. She had now met the infamous Brad Wentworth twice and both times another man had dragged her away.

What in the world was going to happen when there was no one with them to intervene?

Chapter Four

Alexandria waited in her cabin for Hattie's return. She moved constantly, talking to the walls, the bed, anything that would listen.

Why hadn't Hattie told her she worked for Brad Wentworth? Now that Alexandria thought about it, there were many things she didn't know about the woman. Only, why did Brad Wentworth have to be one of those things?

In the middle of her pacing, the door opened. Hattie stepped into the cabin.

"Why didn't you tell me?" Alexandria blurted out.

"Should it matter?"

"Of course it matters!"

"Why?"

"Why ... why?" Alexandria stuttered. She really wasn't sure why. "B--because he doesn't like me. And worse he doesn't like doctors. He's impossible!"

By the time Hattie had advanced well into the room, Alex asked at least fifty more questions. But Hattie, never one to get flustered or to hurry, simply let her rattle on while she fixed herself a cup of tea. She walked over to the overstuffed chair, and motioned for Alexandria to sit on the bed in front of her.

"I am de housekeeper at River Bends, Petite. However, I'm not a slave, but a free black woman. Brad gave me my freedom when I saved his sister from a carriage accident three years ago. I have my own home, so you'll not be livin' under de same roof as Brad."

Relief washed over her. What would she have done if Hattie had been living in Brad's house? That would have meant constant contact with the intolerable Mr. Wentworth, and probably more arguments. Thank goodness that wouldn't be a problem. However, another problem she hadn't thought of came to mind. What would people say about her living with a black woman? In this time, it wasn't heard of, but Alexandria didn't much care. She felt safe with Hattie--except when Hattie was getting her into trouble.

Alexandria's attention was drawn back to the black woman as she described the plantation where she lived. She listened to Hattie's stumbling depiction of River Bends and its vastness. It was obvious Hattie found the plantation beautiful, but hard to capture in words. Finally, she just said, "I t'ink you'll like River Bends--and even Master Brad."

"Why do you still call him Master, Hattie?"

"*Parce que,*" Hattie mumbled.

"'Because' isn't much of an answer."

"You forget, cher, I was once a slave."

"But you're free now."

"*Oui,* so let's just say it's out o' respect. I look after Brad like a mother would a son. I thought the world of Catherine, Brad's mother. She'll always have a special place in my heart, just as her children do ... ." Hattie stopped. She wanted to say more, but didn't know if she should. She rarely opened up and talked about herself.

Hattie had tried to convince Alexandria that Brad wasn't like the men from her century. In time, Hattie knew she would see Brad in a different light, because she was going to make a big difference in this family. Hattie had kept her promise. But there were some things she couldn't tell Alexandria. The child would have to find out on her own.

Hattie decided it would be safer to change the subject. "How did you like Edmund?"

"He's all right. I have the feeling he's quite a ladies' man. He does have irrepressible, twinkling eyes and he takes great care to say all the right things."

"Then he impressed you?"

"If you mean in your sly way of asking, could Edmund be the one to steal my heart? The answer is no. I'll know Mr. Right when I meet him; that is, if there is such a person. He'll be gentle and kind. And he'll never raise his voice." Alexandria realized what she'd just said and thought to herself, *and dull as dirt if he's anything like I've just described.* "Maybe I wasn't meant to fall in love." She sighed.

"Ah, Petite, you're still young. Sometimes fate has a funny way of presentin' itself. You might meet de man of your dreams, cher, and never even know it's happened."

"Did anybody ever tell you that you talk in riddles? I know I should understand what you mean, but I don't."

For the next four days, Alexandria stayed in her cabin. She didn't want to take the chance of running into Brad again, and she didn't want to keep wearing the same dresses over and over. But with these few garments, she'd keep the dry cleaners busy--whoops--that wouldn't work, either. The garments would have to be hand-washed. An image of herself kneeling beside a creek beating her clothes on a rock formed in her mind. Alexandria shook her head. She had worked like a dog to pay her way through medical school, and finally when she could start earning money, she once again found herself poor. Poor... it seemed she'd been poor all her life. Did she have to be poor in the nineteenth century, too? And to think she'd fantasized about the eighteen hundreds. They had no electricity.

Thomas Alva Edison, I need you.

Her thoughts turned to Carol. Alexandria missed having her friend to confide in. Carol had always understood her so well. What had Carol though when she'd walked into Alexandria's empty apartment? By now, she'd probably reported to the police that Alexandria had been kidnapped. In a way, Alex supposed, she had been kidnapped, or at least she'd have a lot of explaining to do when this adventure was over ... if it ever was over.

Was there a chance she'd never return? She shuddered at the scary thought. Maybe she'd find someone from this time she could make friends with. Of course, Hattie was her friend, but the woman was also motherly, bossy, and sometimes impossible. And she'd gotten her into this fix in the first place.

Alexandria had been jarred into the eighteen hundreds when Hattie told her she couldn't eat in the dining room because she was black. So Alexandria dined with Hattie in the room.

"That's the stupidest thing I've ever heard!" Of course, Alexandria knew her history, but confronting it was quite a different story.

"I agree." Hattie shook her head. "But, in de eighteen hundreds t'ings are quite different. Remember, cher, in dis time, people are slaves. Of course, the slaves at River Bends are luckier than most for having a master such as Brad, but dat's not true of de rest."

"Why?" Alexandria couldn't think of a reason anybody would be lucky to have Brad.

"Because he treats us like human beings, not dirt, and he believes strongly in families and not separating them. At River Bends, each family has its own house and small garden. Dese are not small rooms with several families staying in 'em, like some plantations have. They're homes. And in return, all de slaves are extremely loyal to Master Brad. Somehow, dey know dey'll be given their freedom one day."

"I do remember reading about slaves being beaten. Brad doesn't do so, does he?"

"No, Petite. He'll not ask anyone to do anyt'in' dat he wouldn't do himself. He's a fair man, but can be stern if crossed."

On the morning of the journey's fifth day the boat slowed down. Walking to the window, Alexandria pressed her forehead against the glass, trying to see what was happening outside. But she couldn't see anything except trees.

"Why are we slowing down?"

Hattie looked up from her sewing. "We're probably approaching Natchez, Petite. We'll stop here fo' a little while and unload some of our cargo."

Alexandria turned from the window. "Good, I can't wait to see some dry land."

"You should be careful on de wharf and not go alone," Hattie cautioned. "I think I'll ask Master Brad to accompany you."

"No!" Alexandria snapped. "I'll be careful, and I promise not to be gone long--I promise," She emphasized, seeing the doubt in Hattie's eyes.

"*J'sais pas* dat it's a good idea. Every young woman needs a chaperon." Hattie shook her head slowly. "But if you must have your way, cher, then go. But be careful."

"I will." Not wanting to wait a moment longer, Alex scrambled into her beige gown and pulled back her hair with a piece of yellow lace ribbon.

Up on deck, she found she still couldn't see anything except for the backs of people's heads as they stood at the rail. There didn't appear to be an empty space, until one gentleman moved away. Quickly, she seized the opportunity and squeezed into the small spot so she, too, could see what was happening.

Natchez was nothing less than an oasis in the desert, sitting high on a bright green hill surrounded by a black forest of papaw, palmetto, and orange trees. Even the air changed as it filled with the fragrance of sweet-scented flowers.

At the bottom of the hill, the wharf extended into the green waters of the Mississippi River where the boat would dock. A collection of faded gray buildings lined the waterway. Like an entryway into the city itself, the wharf was in stark contrast to the city.

A gentleman standing next to Alexandria began talking to his friend. "William, I've heard tell life in this river town is turbulent, raw, and sometimes very brief if you're not careful. You sure you want to go down there?" He laughed.

"Yeah, I've heard all those tales," William said. "I've also heard it's full of gamblers, fleecers, and prostitutes just hovering along the waterfront ready to catch their share of travelers. Hell, yes, I want to give it a try."

As the two joined in a hearty laugh, Alexandria looked at the wharf again and scowled. She didn't see any of what the gentlemen had just described. The scene before her appeared peaceful.

There was little activity around the houses and buildings surrounding the wharf. The area seemed to be sleeping in the spring sunshine. Two men sitting in their splint-bottomed chairs were tilted back against the wall, hats slouched over their faces, asleep. A few men milled about the streets, while others lay sleeping on cotton bales piled high on the dock.

The whistle blew and a sudden change seemed to come over the town as the steamboat drew closer. A Negro drayman raised his prodigious voice. "Steamboat a-coming!" And the lazy town started to come alive. The two men, who had been sleeping in the splint-bottomed chairs, pushed their hats back and lowered their chairs on the porch. They stood up, stretching from their naps as they turned to watch the steamboat docking. People started appearing in the streets. Drays, carts, and men of all ages begin walking toward the wharf, waiting for the steamboat.

And just like the suddenly awakening town, she felt excitement building inside her. Her nerves tingled as she shut her eyes and took a deep breath. However, she stood back, forcing herself to wait for some of the other passengers to disembark. When the gangway was fairly clear, she decided it was time to investigate the wharf. Alexandria didn't noticed that the ladies--all with companions--went straight into town. She needed desperately to stretch her legs.

She walked between wagons stacked high with snowy-white bales of cotton. Many slaves hustled about her, each working at different jobs. Some tended horses while others loaded freight. She watched in fascination as the slaves unloaded the cotton, their black skins glistening in the sun. She was now looking at a time period she had only read about in books. Looking at it--and living it. My God, she was really here.

The slaves had no shoes, and their shirts were torn and tattered, some no better than rags. She longed to tell them that one day life would be better, but she knew they wouldn't believe her. They didn't even bother to look up when she walked in front of them.

Moving along the wharf, she noticed a woman standing in front of a building several feet ahead. She intended to ask the lady the location of the general store, but as Alex drew closer, she saw the woman's gaudy clothes and smelled her cheap perfume. A hooker!

A little too late, Alex realized she had wandered into the wrong section of town. Before she reached the prostitute, a man rushed out of the building and grabbed the woman by the arms. He shook her until her head bobbed back and forth.

"You've been fooling around with them Watsons again!" he accused.

"No, I haven't!" The woman's voice, though shrill, trembled with fear. "I know the Watsons and the Darrells don't get along. Don't involve me in your feud," she screamed at the man holding her.

"Don't lie to me, bitch!" He slapped her hard across the face.

Then another voice cried out from behind the woodpile, "If you want a Watson, I'm over here!" Slowly, a man stood up and drew his gun, pointing it at the filthy man holding the prostitute.

The man shoved the woman inside the building, and started running in Alexandria's direction.

"I'm going to shoot," Watson hollered.

"Omigod!" Alexandria cried. She stood directly in the bullet's intended path. But she couldn't make her feet move. Fear had frozen her to the spot. She needed to do something! And fast.

Stunned, she felt as though she were watching television, and at any moment she could conveniently flip the channel.

But she wasn't watching a western. This was real! She was smack in the middle of a gunfight--with *real* bullets!

An explosion from Watson's pistol came from behind the woodpile came. Alex stumbled and felt the breeze as the first man ran past her, but still she stood glued to her spot.

Finally, when she felt she would pass out with fear, an iron like grip seized and jerked her out of the bullet's path. She heard the man grunt as he hauled her up hard against him. She didn't know who this brave man was, but she was thankful just the same. He swayed against her.

When everything had grown quiet, Alexandria looked around to see who her fearless rescuer had been.

Chapter Five

Brad held Alexandria with an authoritative grip; however, he didn't look at her. He glared down the street. Watson moved away from his hiding place. Instead of putting away his gun, the bastard pointed the barrel at Alexandria's back. Brad anticipated his move and in a split-second drew a pistol from inside his coat pocket and fired. The bullet hit Watson square in the chest. He crumpled to the ground. His death appeared instant.

"Oh, my God! You shot him!" Alexandria gasped. "Someone call a doctor--wait, I am a doctor." She tore out of Brad's grasp and ran to the fallen man. "Call 911!" she shouted to the curious onlookers. Dropping to her knees, the doctor in Alexandria, now that she remembered she was a doctor, took over. Placing two fingers on the side on the victim's throat, she felt for a pulse. She forced herself to forget that Watson had been trying to shoot her. Not finding any signs of life in the man, she stood. "Somebody needs to call an amb--" She stopped as her wits returned. These people stared at her as if she were absolutely crazy. And to tell the truth, she just might be.

"Are you always getting into trouble?" Brad growled as his gaze traveled over her. Alex smiled. How sweet. He was checking to see if she'd been hurt. If it were possible, he looked both irritated and amused at the same time.

"It would seem so," she said, taking a step away from him. A gaping hole in Brad's jacket caught her attention, and the first sign of blood started to seep through. "Good heavens! You've been shot!" She snatched the handkerchief from his shirt pocket and ripped his shirt to apply pressure to the wound.

Then it dawned on her; Brad had taken the bullet that would surely have hit her. Yet he stood before her tall and proud as if he were shot every day.

He'd saved her life.

"It would seem so," he said. She realized he'd used her same mocking words.

Alex slipped her arm around his waist. "Come, let me help you back to the boat."

"I'm perfectly capable of walking, Madame."

"Let's go, then. I've got to take that bullet out," she informed him.

Even though Brad had just stated he could walk by himself, his arm dropped around her shoulder. As they moved up the gangplank, he asked, "What do you mean, take the bullet out? I need a *real* doctor."

"I thought you didn't like doctors."

"I don't. But this is different."

"Well, Mr. Wentworth, you *have* a real doctor, and I intend to remove that bullet at once." She issued the order firmly, leaving no room for arguments.

"Lady, you're dangerous!" Brad announced. Yet, once they reached the deck of the boat he stopped and indulged in a long look at Alexandria. His entirely too-sober gaze traveled over her body. He leaned only inches from her face as he spoke again. "Since I've known you--and I admit for my sake it hasn't been long--you've been involved in a robbery, and just now you were in the middle of a gunfight." He brought his finger up to brush her cheek. His breathing sounded a little harsh, and his voice grew quiet as a faint smile crossed his mouth. "In my opinion, you seem to live very dangerously, lady. How do I know you'll not use your knife to slit my throat?"

His softly-spoken words and gentle touch warmed her with unexpected tenderness. For a brief moment, she had the unbelievable urge to kiss the wretch, but smiled instead. "I guess you're just going to have to trust me."

Footsteps pounded on the planks. Edmund's eyes grew wide at the sight of Brad and herself slowly coming up the walkway.

Without warning, Brad swayed against her. She tried to support him with her body, but his weight was just too much. "Help me with your cousin, Edmund!"

Edmund ran to them. "My God, what's happened?" He looked shocked at Brad's pale appearance. "Surely she hasn't shot you ... has she?"

"Of course not," Alexandria snapped at the absurd question. "If you'll help him to his cabin, I'll go and get my medical bag." She turned to leave. "What is your room number?"

"Two-ten," Brad replied.

Edmund slid his arm around Brad's waist and helped him to his compartment. "Aren't you going a little out of your way these days to impress women?" Edmund quipped.

"You're not amusing." Brad grimaced. His shoulder now throbbed. And the thought of that woman with a knife in her hand wasn't comforting, but he'd never let his cousin know that.

"You're really going to let *her* take that bullet out?"

"I guess. Hattie swears Alexandria is a good doctor, believe it or not, and I trust Hattie."

Edmund yanked all the covers back off the bed, then turned and helped Brad out of his jacket, stripping him down to his waist. "That, my friend, is a nasty hole you've got there. By the way, you still haven't told me what happened." Edmund shook his head as he looked at the open laceration. "It couldn't have been a fair fight, because I've never seen a man alive who could beat you."

"I saw our Miss Dumont leaving the boat unchaperoned. Instead of heading into town as she should, the little idiot went walking around the wharf." Brad moved away from the mirror and sat on the bed. "I still can't believe it! Every woman knows how dangerous the docks can be, and no respectable lady walks around alone. Of course, I knew she shouldn't be there, but before I could get to her, she'd walked into the middle of a brawl. I pulled her out of the way just in time, but somehow I was a little slow in moving my own hide."

"Here." Edmund handed Brad a glass of bourbon and held the bottle ready. "I think you're going to need this."

"Thanks." Brad drained two shot glasses, trying to deaden the pain. "But you know, Edmund, I've never met a woman like her before. She is definitely different from the other females I've met."

Just then, the door opened. Alexandria entered with her medical bag in hand. She surveyed the primitive conditions. "Edmund, get some hot water. And Brad, I need you to lie on the bed. I don't like the looks of this." The wound was still bleeding profusely, so she applied pressure to the hole, slowing the flow of blood.

When the hot water arrived, she sponged off the wound. Brad grimaced with pain. "I'm sorry. I'll try to be gentle, but I'm going to have to dig that bullet out." But she knew it was going to hurt like hell without anything to numb the injury. Taking a small bottle out of her bag, she shook some liquid onto a piece of gauze. "I want you to breathe deeply when I hold this cloth over your nose."

"Are you sure you've done this before?"

"To be truthful, I haven't. But they say practice makes perfect," she teased him, but the horror in his eyes made her regret her jest. "Of course, I know what I'm doing."

"What is that?" Brad inquired, pointing at the bottle.

"Chloroform. It's an anesthetic that'll make you sleepy."

Not giving Brad a chance to protest, she covered his nose and mouth with the gauze. He struggled a little, but was weak from loss of blood and soon closed his eyes. Alex was thankful that she had some modern supplies in her bag. She'd have to work fast before the anesthetic wore off. He was still losing blood.

Taking her scalpel, she made a neat incision. She had to dig deep to find the piece of lead lodged in his shoulder next to the bone. Brad moaned when she loosened the bullet and pulled it free, and the strangest desire to comfort him washed over her. After all, he had taken the proverbial bullet with her name on it.

Edmund had been so quiet, Alex had almost forgotten he was in the room, until he asked, "Did you get the slug?"

"Yes, but it was deep. Pour some of that bourbon in the wound." She nodded toward the bottle. "It'll help disinfect it."

Quickly, Edmund flushed the incision with brown whisky. "I'm fascinated at how well you work. I guess you're definitely everything you claim to be."

She raised a brow at him. "Thank you. Please take a sheet and tear some wide strips so I can wrap your cousin's shoulder when I'm finished." She looked back to the incision, trying to survey the damage and consider the best way to repair it.

Brad's muscle was torn. She wondered if a doctor in this time would even notice. When it came to medicine, Alex was glad she came from another time. She repaired the tear first before closing and sewing him up. Smiling to herself, she remembered how Professor Thomas had teased her about her small, neat stitches. He'd told her she was more a dressmaker than a surgeon, perhaps a talent that would serve a dual purpose now, she thought wryly.

After she'd finished, she stood, stretched her back muscles, and admired her work. Brad would come away with a slight scar, but it wouldn't be bad. Fever and infection were her main worries now.

She checked Brad's pulse and found it strong. A good sign but his loss of blood worried her because his face was much too pale. She walked over to the washbasin, and cleansed her hands.

It was then that she noticed Edmund staring at her. His expression seemed odd, and she wondered if she had grown horns. "Is something wrong?"

He frowned. "I've been present many times when a bullet has been taken out of someone, but I've never seen a doctor perform as you have."

"I merely sewed him up." Alexandria brushed off his praise. Even though she appreciated the compliment, it embarrassed her. "Come over and help me bandage his shoulder." They wrapped the white sheets around Brad's wound, then tucked him under the covers.

"I think I'll stay with Brad tonight," she said, then added, "In case there are any complications."

"I'm not sure that's such a good idea," Edmund stammered. "We wouldn't want people talking about you. It just isn't proper."

"It is very proper for a doctor to stay with a patient." She looked at Edmund. "If Brad started hemorrhaging, would you know what to do?"

"Hemorrhaging?" Edmund frowned. "I don't understand."

"It means uncontrollable bleeding."

"Well ... no." He thought a minute. "I see your point, and quite frankly, I'm relieved. I'd rather have you here with him."

"Will you stop by and tell Hattie I'm staying?"

Edmund nodded.

"And Edmund--" He stopped to look at her before leaving. "I promise I won't compromise your cousin."

Edmund grinned boyishly. "It's not Brad I'm worried about."

Alex smiled. He had such an easy-going personality. She pulled a chair over by the bunk and sat down. Propping her head on the back cushion, she closed her eyes and took a deep breath. She was tired and confused. Everything was much different here. At times she wondered if she would ever adjust. Her thoughts in turmoil, she closed her eyes and drifted off to sleep.

Damn, his head hurt! Brad thought as he struggled to open his eyes. It felt twice the size it should be, and the throbbing pain in his arm reminded him none-too-gentle what had happened. He glanced down at his aching shoulder and found it completely bandaged. Alexandria had taken care of him--just like she'd said she would.

He turned his head, searching for his doctor, and found her asleep in the chair beside his bed. Her tousled hair clung to the sides of her face. He couldn't help the small smile that tugged at the corners of his mouth. Was she an angel, doctor, or demon? He really would like to know this lady better and find out why she intrigued him so much.

Alexa's eyelids flew open as she remembered she had a patient to attend to. When her eyes adjusted, she found herself staring into Brad's warm blue eyes. She frowned. His eyes were not the right color. They appeared glassy, which meant he had a fever. She reached over to touch his forehead and found it hot beneath her fingertips.

"How do you feel?" she asked, her hand still on his forehead.

"Like hell! Did you get the bullet out?"

"Sure did."

"Thank you." Brad's smile was weak, and his feeble effort to keep his eyes open finally exhausted him. Once again, sleep overtook him.

Alex picked up a cream-colored bowl and set it on the table beside the bed. A sponge bath would be necessary to bring his fever down, but first, damn him, the rest of his clothes would have to come off. There would be no blush on her cheeks like a silly school girl--she had seen men naked before--but this one definitely had a fine physique. Dipping a soft cloth in the cool, clear water, she began sponging off his chest. She did this several times, thinking by now she probably knew his body better than he did. What a magnificent physique! Stop it, she scolded herself. A professional didn't ogle their patients. She wasn't supposed to think such things. *But how could she not help noticing? The Greek Gods would be jealous.*

Alexandria felt Brad's forehead again. It was hotter than before, and he had started to shake.

"I'm cold." He reached out and touched her hand.

And again his mere touch shocked her. As chilled as he claimed to be, his hand seared her like a hot iron. "I know," she soothed him. "Lie still. I'm going to get some more blankets."

She piled several quilts on top of Brad, but he still shivered, causing her to frown with frustration. Alexandria didn't give much thought to her next actions. She merely took off all her clothes and climbed into bed with him. What else was a doctor to do?

She snuggled next to Brad's body, hoping to share her body heat with him as she put her arm around him. He trembled. She rubbed his chest in a soothing motion, trying to give him all the comfort she possibly could ... and still feeling horribly helpless. If infection set in, she could lose him.

Something deep inside of her screamed out, *she couldn't lose him.*

The immense heat from his body caused her to sweat, too, but she didn't pull away. Brad needed the warmth from her flesh. It seemed like hours, but finally his shivering stopped and his breathing became regular. She said a small prayer. A fine perspiration covered them both, but at long last the fever broke.

Sometime in the wee hours of morning, Alex wearily let exhaustion claim her, and she fell asleep. She knew lying nude in a man's arms could be dangerous, and she really should get up and put on her clothes. However, she was much too warm and contented, and the long-awaited sleep felt wonderful.

Yet her dreams were anything but peaceful. She dreamed of passionate kisses. Tender lips moved across her ear and then her face. Soft feathery kisses that made her moan with desire. Warm lips nibbled on her neck and caused her breathing to quicken. Possessive lips touched hers ever so softly at first, and then with an unexplained urgency. Her mouth became ablaze and pleasure burned within her.

Alexandria felt things she never thought existed. She floated in sensual passion. She had kissed men before, but never like this--these were the things books were written of. A liquid fire burned in her blood and somewhere deep inside her excitement flared. This dream seemed so real, and she craved the man who held her possessively in his arms. Did he say something about love? No, that was impossible, she thought. She didn't know anyone well enough to mention love. Love ... the one thing that always seemed to elude her

Similar visions seared through Brad's subconscious. He craved the woman he held in his arms with an intensity he had never experienced before. He thrust his tongue deep into her mouth not wanting to stop. But his condition from the fever had weakened him. Drained of what little strength he had left, he marveled about this wonderful dream girl. Who was she? It wasn't Julia. Julia didn't have the wild passion this creature had. Only a dream ... a figment of his imagination. Slowly, he stopped his kisses. His energy spent, Brad pulled his dream partner within his arms like a child cuddling a stuffed animal.

"I could love you," he whispered before he contentedly fell asleep.

Chapter Six

Wrapped in warmth and contentment, at last rested and refreshed, Alexandria felt wonderful when she first awoke. But when she tried to move, she found herself trapped. She opened her eyes and gasped as she came fully awake and found a man's arm thrown possessively across her.

Slowly, a blush swept over her body. Even the tips of her toes heated as she remembered climbing into bed with him last night.

She didn't want to get out from under the warm cover, but staying here, with Brad wrapped around her, would surely spell disaster. She liked being with him too much, and now she had another reason to avoid Mr. Wentworth. Good thing he still slept, or he'd surely accuse her of being a harlot, too. The wretch always thought the worst where she was concerned.

Gently, Alexandria moved Brad's arm, being careful not to awaken him. When she was at a safe distance, she turned and placed a hand on his forehead, making sure there was no fever.

Quietly, she slipped on her clothes, noticing how much softer the lines in Brad's face appeared as he slept. Remembering her splendid dream last night, Alexandria was nevertheless glad it was only a figment of her overactive subconscious. Yet one realization stood clear: To become involved with this man would only mean disaster. The way he awakened her senses made her aware of needs she'd long ago thought impossible.

However, she couldn't help but wonder if Brad really was a good kisser. He had been superb in her dream. A Kevin Costner and Tom Cruise rolled into one.

I guess I'll never know, she mused.

Dear Lord. There she went again. What wicked thoughts! But she was a doctor, and she'd had to do everything in her power to reduce her patient's fever. Still, she bet her professors would have frowned on the particular method she'd used last night.

And what if Brad had awakened? No, she didn't want to think about that. It would have been tough explaining why she was curled up naked in his arms. He already thought she was a pickpocket.

As she straightened her clothing and despite her best intentions, Alex's gaze traveled over Brad's body once more, taking in every inch of his muscular frame. She sighed, forcing her attention back to his face.

A pair of weak, blue eyes stared at her with puzzlement in their depths.

The drugged sleep was slow to leave Brad, and confusion clouded his mind. He could see the beautiful Alexandria sitting across from him. His brows drew together as he thought about last night. Had that been a dream? It had to be. She had only cared for his shoulder ... not the rest of his body. But what a delicious illusion it had been.

"Good morning. How are you feeling?" she whispered.

"I'm not sure," Brad muttered, realizing he was beginning to like the sound of her voice. "Will I live?" he asked, frustrated at the pain he felt in his arm. He hated being helpless.

"Yes, you'll be fine." She paused for a moment. "Mr. Wentworth, I want to thank you for saving my life, and I'm sorry you were hurt." He watched as she placed the instruments in her black bag. "I've removed the bullet. Your shoulder should be as good as new in about six weeks." She grew pensive. "I guess I shouldn't have gone to the wharf by myself."

"You're damn right! That was a foolish thing to do. Do you know what could have happened to you?" Brad's tone was a little sharper than he intended, but the pain in his shoulder put him in a foul mood. Strangely, the fury intensified every time he thought of what could have happened to Alexandria. What if he hadn't followed her?

"Why should it matter to you what happens to me?" she snapped.

Before he could snarl an answer, Edmund entered the room. "Good morning. How is our patient?"

"If being a gremlin means he's well, then I'd say he's recovering nicely." Alexandria snatched up her bag and started for the door. "I don't think Mr. Wentworth needs me anymore, so I'll leave him in your capable hands. That is ... if you can stand him."

After the door slammed, Edmund looked at Brad and shook his head.

"What's a gremlin?" When Brad didn't answer, but instead stared at the door, Edmund said, "I take it you were your usual charming self this morning."

Brad merely grunted, refusing to answer him.

———)———

Back in the cabin, Hattie ordered Alexandria a bath. Yes, a hot soak-- that was just what she needed to ease her tension. However, a hot shower would have been better, but that, too, she'd left behind her.

The warm water felt good as she lowered her body into the small, steamy tub. She began telling Hattie everything that had happened yesterday, intentionally omitting her remedy for Brad's fever. Hattie's obvious concern for Brad touched Alex. She assured Hattie he was fine, but the older woman insisted on seeing him for herself.

"You'd better wear thick armor," Alexandria told her just before the door shut. She enjoyed the rest of her bath in peace.

After drying off, she longed for some fresh air and warm sunshine. She dressed in her beige linen gown and went to the upper deck to find a quiet place to sit.

They had left Natchez and were on their way once again, which was fine with Alex. If she never saw the site of her frightening memories again, it would be too soon. The forest seemed of older growth than before, and the trees wore brilliant varied shades of green. The river, which was remarkably straight, compared to the first time she had looked at it, had put on its loveliest garb. Blossoms deliciously perfumed the air, and birds whistled blithely along the banks. The morning was beautiful as the sun shone in a glory of carmine.

Alexandria searched for a secluded haven. Presently, she spotted a rocking chair in a small nook of shade. It looked inviting and exactly where she wanted to be. Someone was sitting in her place. Perhaps they would not mind giving her the other chair.

As Alex drew closer, she discovered a child watching her intently. When Alexandria smiled, the young girl returned her smile, and for some strange reason, she felt drawn to this little person.

What a beautiful little girl with soft blond curls and stunning black eyes, she was fair of face and certainly not over twelve years of age. However there was a sadness about the child that somehow reached out and touched Alexandria. "Hi. Do you mind if I sit down?"

"I would like the company," the girl admitted.

"Are you by yourself?" Alexandria looked around to see who chaperoned the child, but found her alone. This, Alex thought strange, because the young lady was in a wheelchair.

"No, my brother is accompanying me. But I haven't seen him this morning, so my cousin brought me up here. I asked him to leave me for a while. I get so tired of staying in my room all the time."

"That's the reason I came up here, too," Alexandria admitted as she sat down in the nearby chair. "The cabins can really get stuffy, can't they?"

"Yes, they can," the child agreed. "Where are you from?"

Alex didn't know exactly what to say. "I'm on a vacation of sorts. You see, a friend of mine decided I needed a little time away from work, and she arranged this trip."

"That sounds nice. What kind of work do you do? I don't know many ladies who work."

"I'm a doctor."

"Really!" the child exclaimed. "That's the reason I'm on this trip. We went to the doctors in St. Louis in the hopes they could do something for my legs."

Alex thought it was nice to have someone who finally believed her, but that was the beautiful part of children. They always trusted everyone. "What did they tell you?"

"There isn't anything they can do." A sadness entered the girl's voice and she hung her head.

"I'm sorry," Alex murmured. "Back home, I used to work with children who had been injured. Have you always been in a wheelchair?"

"No." She turned to look at Alex. "Three years ago, I was hurt in a carriage accident."

The color drained from Alex's face. *No. It can't be.* "Has anybody ever tried to exercise your legs?"

A quizzical expression crossed the child's face. "Exercise?"

"It's a means of bending and flexing your muscles. We want to stimulate blood to the areas that have laid dormant." The child still looked confused. "Do you understand?"

"Not really, but maybe someday you could look at my legs and see what you think," she said hopefully.

"Perhaps I can." Alex gave her a reassuring smile. "I'd have to check with your mother first."

"She's dead," the child blurted out. "You'd have to ask my brother.

You'll like him. He's handsome!" A look of admiration entered her eyes. "All the ladies talk about him, but I guess that will stop once he announces his engagement."

Alexandria saw the child's eyebrows draw together into a frown. She didn't look too happy about the future marriage. "That will be nice. Then you'll have a sister."

"I don't want *her* for a sister!"

The blatant dislike the child showed surprised Alex. "Why not?"

"She's mean." The girl leaned over and whispered, "She's only nice to me when Brad is around."

"Brad?" The hair stood up on the back of Alex's neck.

"Yes, he's my brother."

Alexandria grew quiet. Did the child have to say Brad? Did everybody she meet have to know this man? Did she have to find he had an adorable sister and ... and that he was also engaged? And why should it bother her Brad would be marrying soon? She frowned. Maybe this was good. Now, she wouldn't have to worry about him in that way ... not that she ever had. She could, however, offer her pity to the poor woman.

This was too much of a coincidence. Alex had only read a few pages of the diary, but now she wondered if this was the child in that book. A carriage accident, a crippled child, and Brad. Now everything made sense. Hattie had brought her back to this time to help this child. However, Alex had the weirdest feeling that there was a piece missing from the puzzle.

"Ma'am." The little girl touched her arm. "Did you hear me? You know, I don't even know your name."

Alex snapped out of her contemplation. "My name is Alexandria, but my friends call me Alex."

"But that's a boy's name."

"Now ... do I look like a boy?" Alexandria held up her hands.

"No." The child's sweet, carefree laughter touched a place in Alexandria's heart. She noticed how the girl's eyes twinkled, and she found herself smiling back at the child.

"My name is Melissa, and my friends call me Missy."

Omigod! Why did she feel like an invisible hand was guiding her to her destiny? She must remain calm. She didn't want to frighten the child. "Well, I hope you will consider me a friend, Missy."

Melissa reached over and touched Alex. "I'd like that. Are you going to New Orleans, too?"

"Yes, I am."

"Good."

They spent the next two hours talking about all sorts of things. Alexandria learned a lot about Missy. Alex could tell the child needed a friend. Missy talked about River Bends with glorious detail, making it sound too good to be true. It was also quite evident she adored her brother, and Alex was impressed to find Brad spent quite a bit of time with her. They observed the people strolling about and pointed out funny hats, odd walks, and pretty dresses. Giggling could be heard often from their corner, and more than once someone turned to stare at them.

Even before he got close, Brad heard his sister's laughter. Yet he stopped, shocked. It had been a while since he'd heard that happy sound. It took him only a minute to spot Melissa and Alexandria. He stood back watching them, noticing how well they got along together. Melissa's humor sounded good. His heart soared at the happiness he saw in his sister's face.

"Alex, you must come to dinner tonight," Melissa insisted. Her wide eyes shone with hope. "It would be so much fun to have you there."

He watched Alexandria hesitate. "I don't think I should impose on you."

"Oh, you wouldn't be imposing," Missy said eagerly. "We'd love to have you. Wouldn't we, Brad?"

Alex turned in the direction of Melissa's gaze and found him standing behind her. The color on her cheekbones turned a very vivid pink.

"Wouldn't we what, Missy?" Brad asked.

"Brad, this is my new friend, Alex. I just asked her to eat dinner with us."

"Alex?" Brad drawled dryly. "That's a man's name."

"Oh, Brad ... does she look like a man? Alex is what her friends call her."

"No, Missy." Brad shook his head. "She definitely doesn't resemble a man." His mouth twisted in amusement.

The woman glared at him. "You can call me Alexandria."

Laughter burst forth from his lips. This feisty lady didn't like him, and she made no bones about it. Damn, if he didn't like her blazing temper.

"Missy, Alexandria and I have already met, and I think it would be a wonderful idea if she had dinner with us. It will be a small payment for fixing my arm." He patted the sling which supported his injured limb.

"Edmund said you were hurt yesterday, and he told me not to worry. What happened?"

"You might say I had a slight accident," he said with an amused glance toward Alexandria.

"You mean Alex is the doctor who took care of you?"

"The very one." Brad nodded to Alexandria. "How about eight o'clock?"

Reluctantly, Alex nodded her head as Melissa grabbed her hand, imploring her to accept. "How can I refuse?"

That night, Alexandria finally got to wear her royal blue satin with the tacky big flower in the middle of the bustline. The flower had to go. She yanked the blue rose off and slipped it over her left ear. Her mass of auburn curls cascaded down her back, and the vivid blue flower provided the perfect accent. The low-cut dress fit her like a glove and was simple in design, especially when compared to the other dresses she had seen on the boat. After receiving Hattie's nod of approval, Alex left.

Standing at the entrance of the dining room, her knees weakened as hesitation set upon her. The maitre d' had not yet spotted her, so she took the chance to look around the spacious and very elegant room.

Each round table was draped with a hunter green tablecloth, and in the center were bouquets of yellow and green flowers. Elegant crystal and china gleamed in the candlelight. Several huge chandeliers hung from the ceiling, each an April shower of glittering glass-drops, which provided lovely rainbow-lights falling everywhere from colored prisms.

"May I help you, Madam?" The maitre d's haughty voice broke into her thoughts.

"Yes, I'm with the Wentworth party."

"Your name?"

"Dumont." Alexandria watched as he scanned his book.

"Oh, yes, the Wentworth party is seated at the Captain's table. I see your name has been added. Follow me, please."

The swirl of royal blue satin caught Brad's attention out of the corner of his eye. He turned to see who it was. A vision of loveliness moved across the room in his direction. Alexandria's dress was not the most elegant, it was quite simple--but on her the design was more stunning than anything from Paris. She wore no jewelry, nor did she need any. She was all the glitter the dress needed.

Brad, Edmund, and Tom stood when she neared the table.

She greeted them with a smile and took the seat Brad held out for her. The captain spoke first.

"We're glad you could join us tonight. I must say you look very lovely," the captain complimented. "Are you enjoying your trip, Miss Alexandria?"

"Yes, it's been most interesting." She smiled. "It's the first time I've ever been on the Mississippi. Will we be in New Orleans soon?"

"Sometime tomorrow," the captain answered readily.

"Good!" Melissa proclaimed. The child looked very pretty tonight dressed in an apple-green silk dress. Her black eyes glistened, and Alexandria couldn't help but notice the resemblance between brother and sister.

"Are you looking forward to going home, Missy?" Brad asked.

"Yes, I am," she admitted, glancing down at her lap, then looking at her brother again. "I ... I'd like for Alex to see our home." She paused shyly. "That is, if she wants to."

"I think that can be arranged." Brad smiled at his bubbling sister. "You see, Missy, Alexandria is traveling with Hattie."

"Hattie's come home?" Seeing Brad nod, Melissa turned to Alexandria. "Is that true, Alex? Are you really staying with Hattie?"

"Yes, she's a friend of mine."

"That's wonderful! Now we can see each other often, and maybe you can help me exercise like you said." Missy's excitement caused her to talk faster.

"What do you mean by 'exercise'?" Brad inquired.

"You see, Alex is a doctor."

"I know that Missy. She fixed my arm, remember?"

"Oh, that's right. Well, she has worked with children like me before and ... you tell him, Alex."

Alexandria looked at the excited child. This probably wasn't the best time to bring up the subject, but since Missy had left her little choice, she explained, "I've worked with children who've had similar injuries such as Melissa's. I've found that sometimes exercising the muscles can be very beneficial to the patient."

Anger flashed in Brad's eyes. "The doctors have said there is no help, and I don't want to get Missy's hopes up," he said in a deadly calm voice.

"I'm sure they did," Alexandria said patiently, knowing the doctors in this time knew little of rehabilitation. "But perhaps, they're wrong. I won't know until I examine her."

A nerve started to twitch in Brad's jaw, and Alex could tell he doubted she was telling the truth. But his response had been typical of someone who didn't believe that, barring nerve damage, and injured person could walk again. She had a slight feeling they were getting ready to have words, but thank goodness, the steward arrived ... saved again.

Dinner was a gourmet feast of Jambalaya and Creole Gumbo served on a bed of fluffy white rice. After a dessert of Southern pecan pie and hot coffee, the musicians began to play. Alexandria watched as the couples started for the dance floor.

Captain Leathers, never a man to let grass grow under his feet, was already standing. He offered his arm to her. "If you don't mind waltzing with an old gentleman, I would be honored if I could have the first dance."

"Captain Leathers, there is nothing old about you," Alexandria teased. "I would be honored to waltz with you, but I must warn you I'm not a very good partner."

Captain Leathers laughed warmly. "Well, neither am I."

"Have you always been a captain of a steamboat, Captain Leathers?" Alex found the man easy to talk to.

"I've been doing this for thirty years. I've never wanted to do anything else."

"Do you have a family?"

"Yes, a wife and a daughter. Sometimes they sail with me, which I enjoy very much," he admitted. "Tell me, are you and Brad getting along better?"

"Well ..." Alexandria paused. "I wouldn't say it was smooth sailing, but we have had a few civil conversations. I can't figure out why he makes me so mad."

"Perhaps, you're both alike," Captain Leathers pointed out.

She peered at him. "Have you insulted me?"

"No." He laughed. "But, from my observations, I'd say both of you are strong-willed. It's similar to the mighty Mississippi and my steamboat. Both are very powerful in their own rights, but if I take the time to study my charts and learn to navigate the mighty river, it's as tame as a kitten and there is smooth sailing. I hope you two can learn to get along. Melissa seems to like you very much."

"She's a sweet child," Alexandria agreed.

They were quiet as they danced through several more songs.

"May I cut in, Captain?" Brad tapped him on the shoulder.

"Of course, I guess we have had too many dances."

Another waltz began as Brad swept Alexandria into his arms. She'd noticed earlier he'd removed the sling from his arm. His arms ... yes, he had strong arms that probably held her much too close, but at the moment she didn't care. He was such a graceful dancer that Alex felt like she was floating on a cloud. She was prepared to finish her argument from dinner, but he had yet to utter the first word to her. Letting her guard down, she relaxed and enjoyed the music. And though she hated to admit it, she liked being held by this tall, handsome man.

Brad wasn't sure why he had intruded into the captain's dance with Alexandria. It wasn't like him, but he had to confess the feeling of her body pressed next to his was not unpleasant. Not unpleasant at all. Perhaps, the exact opposite ..."I want to talk to you about Melissa," Brad stated, needing a diversion from his thoughts.

"I'm listening."

"I don't want you to give Missy false hopes that she can walk again. I don't want her hurt!"

"You're so sure she can't walk, but what if she can?"

"Christ, Alex, all the doctors we've taken her to say there is nothing they can do." Brad hadn't realized he had slipped and called her by her nickname, but this woman was so hardheaded that she provoked him.

"I don't want Missy hurt, either, but if there is a chance I could help her, then I'd like to try."

Hadn't she heard him? The doctors said Missy wouldn't walk again. Brad was getting ready to stress the point further, but before he could say anything, a piercing scream cut the air.

Chapter Seven

"It's hot ... it's hot!" Melissa screamed.

"You idiot!" Captain Leathers bellowed at the waiter. "How could you be so clumsy?"

"I'm sorry, Capt'n, but I tripped." The waiter had towels blotting up liquid from Melissa's lap. An empty coffee urn lay on the floor beside her chair.

Alexandria clutched Brad's arm. "My God, she's been burned!"

They ran to the table. Alexandria grabbed some dry cloths and lifted Melissa's skirt slightly, so she could place the material next to her skin. "Is that better, Missy?"

Melissa nodded her head just enough for the tears that brimmed in her eyes to escape down her cheeks. "It was s--so hot."

Alex looked at Missy, a little astonished, but said nothing.

Brad ripped the skirt from Melissa's dress, trying to keep the scorching coffee off her, and threw the fabric to the floor. He scooped his sister up in his arms. "Let's go to your cabin and get you out of these wet things." Cradling her head in the crook of his neck, he murmured, "It will be okay, sweetheart." He turned to Alexandria. "Will you come with us? I might need your help."

She watched how gently Brad treated his sister, and for just a moment, Alex's heartstrings tightened. She quickly shook off the feeling as she went to her cabin to fetch some cream for Melissa's burn.

Hattie accompanied Alex. Brad had waited for her to return then left them alone.

Melissa hugged Hattie as the older woman soothed, "Ma Petite, what have they done to you?"

"It hurts, Hattie. But I know everything will be all right now that you're home."

"*Oui*, it will."

Alex and Hattie helped pull the remains of the ruined dress over Missy's head. Hattie took the garment. "While you exam the child, I'll check on Master Brad," Hattie said, moving toward the door.

When the door had shut, Alex asked, "How did this happen, Missy?"

The child wiped her eyes and blew her nose before answering. "The waiter tripped and the coffee urn landed in my lap. It was so hot that I screamed out," she whispered brokenly. "I could just die of embarrassment."

"Don't be upset, sweetheart." Alex cuddled Missy in her arms. "It was an accident and you didn't have any control over what happened." Alexandria held her back and pushed the hair out of the child's face. "You said the coffee was hot. Could you feel it on your legs?"

Missy nodded, causing her blonde curls to bounce and fresh tears to tumble down her face. But Alex wasn't seeing tears. Her mind churned on how she could help Missy.

While applying a soothing cream to Missy's legs, Alexandria observed two red streaks, but they didn't appear too serious. After she covered the burns with the thick white cream she asked, "How does that feel?"

"Better."

"Missy, if you could feel the burning coffee and just now the cream I applied, I think that could be a promising sign. Maybe I can work with you some, since I'll be staying with Hattie."

"I'd love that." The child's face brightened. "Will you talk to Brad?"

"I'll try," Alex acknowledged, but she wasn't sure how far she'd get, remembering well their heated words of a moment ago.

As if on cue, Brad stuck his head in the door. "How are you two doing?"

"She's doing fine. Melissa was very lucky that her dress absorbed most of the liquid." Alex pulled the covers over the child. "There are two small red streaks, perhaps secondary burns, on her legs. But they should fade. It wasn't as bad a burn as it could have been."

Hattie had followed Brad into the room and now sat on the bed holding Missy's hand.

"Good." Brad smiled at his sister. "Missy, I'll walk Miss Alexandria to her room and then come back and check on you before I go to bed."

"I'll be here, cher." Hattie patted Missy's hand. "Hattie will take care of you." The gentle woman soothed, and Alex smiled. Who wouldn't want Hattie caring for them?

"All right. Good night, Alex. See you tomorrow." Melissa hugged her.

"Sleep tight, Missy," Alex said.

Once outside, she turned to Brad. "You don't have to walk me to my room."

"But I insist." He took her hand and placed it in the crook of his arm. "A lady should never walk alone. Or have you forgotten yesterday so soon?"

"Point taken," Alexandria conceded. She decided this would be a good time to talk about Missy, so she suggested a stroll on deck.

The wind had started to blow, a sure indication a storm was brewing. They stood by the rail watching as the wind played havoc with the trees, bending the young saplings down, exposing the pale underside of the leaves. Gust after gust followed in quick succession, waving the branches up and down. She wondered if this storm could zap her back to her own time. As much as she hated to admit it, she hoped not. For the first time since she arrived here, she wanted to stay and help Melissa. Alex wanted to give the child a chance to be whole again. The strong winds tugged at Alex's curls until it whipped them free of their pins, and she shut her eyes while the breeze rushed through her hair.

"You like storms, don't you?" Brad's husky voice sounded strange, causing Alex to look at him. His intense blue eyes held a warmth she'd not seen before, and she fought the urge to reach out and touch him.

"Yes, I do. I don't know why, though. Maybe it's because they're so unpredictable."

"Much like you." He teased her.

"I'm not really that bad--am I?"

"Well, I'm just getting to know you, but I must say you've definitely brought some excitement into my life. You might say much like the winds of this storm."

There was something about Brad, a sort of aura that drew her, as if a magic spell were being woven around her. "Is that so bad?" she whispered, looking up at him, and damning herself for being so weak. A sixth sense warned her that this man spelled trouble. When she was around him, she seemed to come unglued and get that silly schoolgirl feeling like she was falling in love... but when had she ever listened to her sixth sense?

Lost in thought, she stared out into the night. Beside her, Brad did the same.

Finally, she looked up at him. He gazed deep into her eyes, then reached out and touched her hair, brushing the stray strands away from her cheek. His rough male fingers produced an excitement so sudden and unexpected, she quivered beneath his touch. The lines of his mouth grew gentle as he looked down at her with a sizzling stare that became so intimate that he knew she couldn't move.

Much to Alexandria's shame, she didn't want to pull away.

Please don't zap me back to my time right now.

She closed her eyes and rolled her head back, enjoying his gentle touch as his warm fingers caressed the nape of her neck. When his thumb traced a pattern to the front of her chin, she was filled with such a light-headed sensation that she swayed toward him and willingly melted into his arms.

He cupped her face in his hand and tilted her head upward, tracing her soft pink lips ever so slowly with his thumb. He appeared to be fighting for control as he lowered his mouth to hers. However, she'd lost control the minute he touched her. She sighed and shut her eyes as she waited for a kiss. Brad was the man in her dreams; maybe she had been summoned to treat his sister, but somehow she felt there was something more.

His mouth covered hers with an intoxicating caress that soon made the rest of the world slowly fade away. A warm wind whipped around them, but she barely noticed.

Somehow Brad had forgotten he barely knew this she-devil--no, this Goddess who had fused into his body and rendered his discipline nonexistent. He noticed the loose strands of hair dancing around her face. He wondered if she had any idea of her beauty. He needed to deny his attraction for her and hopefully this kiss would satisfy his curiosity, but her tongue brushed his lips and he wanted more. His hand moved to her backside. He drew her next to him.

Parting her lips, he drove deeper, wanting to taste all of her. She was so sweet, so alive. He felt things he shouldn't be feeling. Alex was only a temporary part of his life while Julia would be a permanent part.

Alex's head was puzzled with many thoughts when she finally realized she clung to Brad like a desperate female. She pulled back slightly. "I'm--I'm sorry." She felt Brad's shoulders tense. These longings that he stirred within her body could only spell trouble for her.

He stared down at her from beneath heavy lids, and she wondered what he must think of her. She shouldn't have let him kiss her. Where were the brains that God have given her?

Perhaps she'd left them in the other century. She wanted to convince Brad she was a professional doctor, and falling into his arms wouldn't help her case.

Brad slowly let out his breath, dropping his head and closing his eyes. He ran a hand through his hair before looking at her again. Staring into Alex's passion-filled eyes, he found she felt the same things he did. Her scent still filled his head and her mouth beckoned him for one more kiss, but he knew better than to allow his passion to overrule his common sense. Was this woman a witch, casting a spell over him?

"It was as much my fault as yours," Brad finally admitted. And where had she learned to kiss like that? His head snapped up, thinking of her innocent stroll through the docks.

Alex cleared her throat. "The real reason I walked with you was ... I--I'd like to work with your sister," she blurted out and then continued before he could say anything. "Missy told me she felt the heat from the spilled coffee on her legs. That's a good sign. I think maybe I could help her."

His eyes seemed to penetrate her mind. "You're serious about this?"

"Yes, I am. What could it hurt?" Alex rushed on, knowing she had to convince him. "I'll be staying with Hattie, so it will be convenient."

He grew quiet for a moment. "All right. We will give it a try, but you'll not live with Hattie. You will reside in the main house with me ... and, of course, Melissa."

"With you?" She heard the astonishment in her own voice. Was the man crazy? They were having a hard enough time living on the same boat!

"You have some objection to that? I assure you my home is nicer than Hattie's."

"What will your fiancée have to say about that?"

"My fiancée?" He chuckled. His brow raised a fraction. "You didn't seem worried about her a minute ago."

Alex's cheeks burned. She longed to slap him. However, he'd spoken the truth. She hadn't cared about his future wife one damn minute. In this time period, he must consider her a loose woman--instead of a modern woman with raging hormones. She'd never have stooped so low in her own time--married men, or almost-married men, were definitely off limits.

"I haven't proposed yet, but I'll take care of Julia. I just think it will be best if you are with Missy as much as possible. And I want to monitor what you are doing. I *always* think of what is best for my sister?"

"Well, I don't think it will necessary to live in your home when I can stay with Hattie. Don't they have rules about that sort of thing in your time period."

"Living with a slave isn't entirely proper, my dear." Then, as if like an afterthought, he frowned and stared at her. "My time period? Rules? Your manner of speaking seems odd. What are you talking about?"

Alex reddened. If she told him, he'd put her in a straightjacket. "Never mind. It just wouldn't be proper."

"Proper be damned!" Brad's cheek started to twitch. "I'm not going to attack your virtue, Madam. This is for my *sister!*"

"But--" Alexandria's protest died on her lips; because his scowl was hot enough to burn. The huge man standing before her intimidated her far more than any man she had ever encountered. And unfortunately that intrigued her all the more. Everything about him screamed, "Beware, be careful, I'll get what I want."

"It is my way or not at all!" His brisk tone snapped. "The choice is yours!"

"Oh, really." She stared at His Royal Highness. "Then I guess I have little choice."

Back in her room, Alexandria's thoughts tumbled over and over, about her past, her present, and God knows what the future held. She tried to sleep, but sleep eluded her. An arrogant face with vivid blue eyes kept creeping into her thoughts. She must be crazy to even consider living under the same roof with Brad Wentworth. She'd have to think of some way to make him change his mind.

After getting up and washing her hair, she sat towel-drying the long strands, thinking how she missed her hair dryer and hot curlers. If she had known about this adventure, she would have crammed many of her modern conveniences in her bags.

Suddenly, Alexandria started giggling. "I wonder where I would have plugged in my curlers and hair dryer," she said out loud. "Electricity hasn't been invented yet."

She wiped the tears of laughter from her eyes. At least she felt much better, and decided to read more of the diary. Hattie was staying with

Missy, so it would be a good time. She hadn't given much thought to the little book since her arrival. Now she believed the diary had something to do with her journey. Would it in fact tell her what was going to happen?

She thought for a moment. She remembered the book falling on the bed the morning she'd arrived in this century. However, it wasn't in her medical bag, so she looked under the bed, but still no book. "That's strange, I wonder where it could be?" After completely searching the room with no results, she gave up. Perhaps Hattie had taken the book; Alex would ask her about the diary. Tomorrow she'd figure out how to get home. There had to be a way.

Sleep was welcome, but, once again, not peaceful. Brad plagued her dreams with delicious kisses and an intimacy she had never known. And that scared her. She'd always been careful to have control over any situation she was in. But now she was no longer in control of her emotions or her destiny, but in her dream he held her in his secure embrace while she savored his kisses.

Alexandria shook her head in disgust as she stared into the mirror. She looked like a hag this morning with the dark circles under her eyes and the puffy bags that spoke of her restless night. If only she had some makeup, maybe she could hide these circles. Knowing that was impossible, she resorted to pinching her cheeks and fluffing her hair.

Alexandria and Hattie packed up their few belongings and went up top with the rest of the passengers. If Hattie recognized her lack of sleep, she didn't say anything, for once.

The dock at New Orleans was vast in comparison to the other places Alex had seen. Large warehouses lined both sides of the streets. A variety of ladies and gentlemen milled about the levee, with their fancy carriages lined up, apparently waiting for the passengers to disembark the ship.

Edmund came over and stood beside Alex. "What do you think of our city, fair lady? I believe you told me you'd never been here before?"

"Good morning, Edmund." She couldn't resist smiling at his boyish charm. "I think it must be a very large city if it's anything compared to the wharf."

"That it is. It can be quite festive at times." Edmund took his time describing the docks and warehouses to Alexandria as the *Magnolia* eased toward the wharf.

She heard little of what he said as she became lost in her own thoughts, wondering when she was going to wake up from this dream. She had always wanted to go to New Orleans, but had expected to arrive by plane, not paddle wheel.

Soon they would be leaving the steamboat and heading for River Bends. Then she would actually see her first plantation, and, after last night, she supposed she'd be living in such a house. Why did she promise to be Missy's therapist, knowing this would only put her in Brad's company more. The results would be more arguments. Alexandria sighed, she knew the answer. She was doing this for his sister. She felt sure Melissa could walk again. And for that reason alone, they would learn to tolerate each other, and she damn sure wouldn't fall in Mr. Wentworth's arms again.

Brad approached, pushing Melissa's wheelchair. "Good morning. Is everyone packed?"

"You need any help?" Hattie called. Brad shook his head as he stopped beside them.

"How are you feeling this morning?" Alex asked Melissa, feeling her forehead.

"I do feel better." She sighed. "I'll be glad to get home."

"Did you have de carriage sent out?" Hattie asked.

Brad looked toward the dock. "It's over there." He pointed to a dark vehicle.

Alexandria's stomach had twisted the minute she saw Brad, and the unwanted picture of him holding her flooded her mind, causing more embarrassment than she'd felt in years. She forced herself to forget about last night and looked at the impressive carriage he pointed to. It was dark burgundy with big black wheels, pulled by two perfectly matched white stallions.

Men, women and children began stepping out of their carriages and the wharf soon became crowded as they waited for passengers to disembark. Except for the clothing and the horses and buggies, it reminded Alex of an airport where relatives, no matter what century, were glad to meet their loved ones. Her chest tightened as she realized she really was an outsider. Even at home no one would be there to greet her.

Once the walkway was lowered, Edmund took Alexandria's arm and escorted her to the dock. Hattie helped Brad with Melissa.

The men and women at the foot of the gangplank watched eagerly while they waited. They chatted and smiled and nodded to Alexandria and Edmund as they made their way through the milling crowd to the

Wentworth carriage. Just before they reached it, the door of the coach swung open and a woman stepped out and adjusted her skirt.

Her brown hair was piled high on her head. When her head snapped up, Alex could see cat-green eyes, not the emerald color of her own, but more of a yellow green and very pale. The woman's lavish clothing was made of the finest material, and dazzling jewels hung around her neck and sparkled in the sunshine. The stunning brunette projected an air of sophistication that made Alex wonder how she could ever compete with these well-bred ladies. She had a college education, which didn't mean much in 1835. And she was more a jeans and tennis shoes person. Not that she wanted to compete, she quickly reminded herself.

Other than being a good doctor, Alex couldn't say the same, except that she'd always longed for a loving family. She watched as the lady ran up to Brad and threw her arms around his neck, kissing him intimately. Evidently, they were not strangers. This must be Brad's girlfriend. Alex had to admit he had chosen well. The woman looked completely confident, and gave the appearance she knew exactly what she wanted in life.

"I've missed you, darling," the woman cooed to Brad.

Brad didn't smile as he disengaged her arms from around his neck, which Alex found strange. He asked, "What are you doing down here, Julia?"

"Why, I came to see you, darling."

Brad glanced around. "I don't see your carriage."

"That's because I've been using yours." She laid her dainty gloved hand on his shirt front. "I didn't think you would mind, since we'll be married soon."

Rather rigidly, he said, "I would like you to meet someone." He placed his hand under Julia's elbow and turned her around.

"Julia Tucker, I'd like you to meet Melissa's new nurse, Alexandria Dumont."

Alex raised her eyebrow at Brad, and he quickly corrected his statement. "I mean Melissa's new doctor." If Alex didn't know better, she would have sworn he blushed.

"A doctor?" Julia laughed. "There are no women doctors that I've ever heard of. Why, most women cannot read or write."

"My dear, I wouldn't let your ignorance show," Edmund commented.

Alexandria felt her color deepen as she conspicuously stood out like a sore thumb among these people. "I believe Brad will testify that I am a doctor, and I've taken very good care of him so far." Why did she feel she needed to explain anything to this woman?

"Take care of you?" Julia turned to Brad, demanding an explanation. "What does that mean?"

Brad showed little emotion as he spoke. "I met with an accident, and Miss Dumont kindly removed the bullet and sewed me up."

"A bullet!" Julia's hands flew to her mouth. "You were shot?"

"We'll discuss it later," Brad abruptly answered her, and Alex wondered why he didn't explain. She figured he wanted to wait for some privacy.

Julia looked put out, but thankfully kept her mouth shut. She kept cutting her eyes at Alexandria, and she wondered what the woman was thinking as they climbed into the carriage, providing the woman had a brain.

Edmund made the carriage ride pleasant. He held Alex's hand and attempted to entertain her by pointing out the different sights.

She, Edmund and Melissa were the only ones chattering as they rode through the city. Julia sat next to Brad, her hand possessively resting on his leg.

Alex felt the woman's eyes on her again, but she couldn't understand why Julia acted so jealous. Alex wanted to assure her that she had nothing to fear. As far as Alex was concerned, the woman could have the ill-tempered Mr. Wentworth.

Julia reached over and held Brad's hand. "I've been makin' arrangements for our little ol' engagement party, darlin'. You should see the dress I've bought. Why, it's simply gorgeous."

Oh please! The simpering Southern Bell routine was a bit much. Alex knew she'd rolled her eyes.

"Don't you think you should have consulted me first? We've not set the date--yet," Brad reminded her as he continued to look out the window. Alex thought he looked utterly bored and she couldn't help thinking he didn't resemble a man in love. Maybe things were different in this time, but still she wondered.

"Why, you told me before you left we could make the announcement in a couple of months. And I thought what better way than a party, darlin'."

Brad sighed and turned to her with a faint smile. "I guess that will be fine, seeing as you've already made the arrangements."

She leaned up and kissed him. "It's good to have you home, darlin'. You're right, we will talk more later when we're alone."

Alex wanted to throw up. She felt that Miss Tucker was putting on a show for her benefit, especially the way her cat-eyes kept cutting her way. Evidently, the woman was establishing her territory. Not that there was a need.

"Edmund, do you live near River Bends?" Alexandria asked, wanting to keep her thoughts off Brad and Julia.

Edmund's eyes smiled his approval that she was taking an interest in him. "No, I have a modest house in New Orleans."

"Modest?" Brad chortled.

"Well, let's just say it's comfortable."

"You don't raise crops then?"

"No, ma'am, that never appealed to me," he said, but the way he looked at her made Alex feel very pretty.

She smiled. "What do you do for a living?"

"What an odd expression," Edmund said as he cocked his head to the side. "I presume you mean what work do I do?"

She nodded.

"I'm in shipping," Edmund quipped.

"For God's sake, Edmund!" Brad wasn't sure why his cousin's playful remarks were irritating him, but they were. "Edmund owns the *Magnolia*."

"You're kidding?" Alex turned to Edmund. "Why didn't you say something on the ship? I can't believe you didn't tell me earlier."

"Boat," Edmund corrected. "I thought you might find something wrong with my boat, and then I'd have truly been crushed." He winked at her.

Brad watched as Alexandria laughed at something his cousin said. Edmund had all the witty and charming sayings down pat.

His sister was also taken with Miss Dumont. Once they'd entered the carriage, Missy had asked to sit by Alexandria. The child seemed to trust her, and it had been a long time since he'd seen Melissa so happy and alive. His sister's head was resting in Alexandria's lap. What a wonderful mother she'd make, he thought. Somehow that thought wasn't unpleasant even though he wasn't sure why he was having such thoughts.

He couldn't seem to take his gaze off the woman, and his unexpected attraction to her confused him, so he turned and peered out the window.

"Isn't it unusual for a doctor to take up so much time with one patient?" Julia seemed irked and her remark sounded snide.

Brad had never noticed how rude Julia could be. He didn't like her pushiness. She seemed to be taking liberties and trying to move into River Bends before he was ready. Damn it, he'd said he would marry her, but when *he* was ready, not at her demand.

Alexandria decided right then that she didn't like this woman, not in the least. She had sat here and endured Julia's insults about as much as she planned to. And her irritation had nothing to do with Brad. Oh, no it was Julia's bitchy personality. It probably would make Alexandria's stay at River Bends quite uncomfortable after Brad married her. But, until that time she had no intention of taking her verbal abuse.

"Did you hear me?" Julia demanded.

"You were speaking to me?" Alex watched the woman nod. "I presume that you're familiar with several doctors and you've studied their doctor-patient relationships?"

Julia gave a puzzled frown. "Well, no."

"Then I suggest you butt out of things that don't concern you."

Brad appeared to be staring out of the window, but Alexandria noticed a slight smile.

"Why, I never--Brad are you going to let *her* talk to me like that?" Julia whined, folding her arms with exasperation across her middle.

Brad turned to his future fiancée as if he hadn't heard anything. "What, Julia?"

"You need to teach your hired help some manners."

"Alexandria is not hired help, Julia," Brad spoke in abrupt phrases. "She has agreed to help my sister, and will be a guest in my home. I expect her to be treated as such. If I were you, I'd watch your sharp tongue. "You are not mistress of River Bends yet!"

Chapter Eight

"Time's a wastin', Miz Alexandria."

Alexandria felt someone nudging her, but she wanted to sleep. Wasn't today Saturday? She didn't have to be at the hospital--so why not sleep late?

Once again the voice penetrated her sleepy thoughts. She opened her eyes and found herself staring at Sarah, her wide-eyed maid.

Alexandria yawned. "Good Morning, Sarah. I'll dress myself this morning."

"Good mornin'. Yo' sure is a funny white woman, Miz Alexandria. It's my job to help yo' dress."

"I know, but this morning I'll do it myself. You're dismissed for now."

"Yo' sure, Miz Alexandria?"

"Yes, I'm sure, Sarah." Alexandria stretched, trying to wake up. She had been here for two weeks, but it still felt funny having someone help her dress when she had been dressing herself for years. The short time since her arrival she'd found women did very little in 1835, and that was one thing she certainly didn't care for in this time period. After all, women had brains, too! Thank goodness she would have her work with Missy to keep her busy.

She watched as Sarah closed the door behind her. Alex had dreamed she was back home, and had completely forgotten about her little adventure arranged by her thoughtful friend. Throwing back the covers, she climbed from the high, four poster bed and walked over to the window to look out. She pulled back the lace curtains and glanced across the back lawns of River Bends. At least she was in the same place. With Hattie around, Alexandria was never sure exactly where she might wake up.

She found it hard to believe that the luxury here surpassed any place she had ever stayed in before. Even the rich hotels would be mere hovels compared to this place. This bedroom was as large as her whole apartment back home.

She felt like a princess surveying her kingdom, even if she was merely a guest.

The well-manicured, lush, green lawns reached all the way to the river. The formal gardens located directly under her window presented a kaleidoscope of colorful azaleas in full bloom, and the air carried the faint smell of magnolias. The trees further down by the river were covered in grayish-green Spanish moss.

This was exactly how Alexandria had pictured a grand plantation would be; however, River Bends went beyond any expectations she had ever had. She thought back to her first look at River Bends ...

The house had not been visible when they first made the turn into the driveway.

A three-quarter-mile lane led to the dwelling. On each side of the road live oak trees were planted exactly the same distance apart, and tufts of gray Spanish moss dangled from each branch. The trees reminded Alexandria of soldiers standing at attention, waiting for their master's return. She'd squirmed in the seat trying to glimpse the house.

As they neared the end of the lane, River Bends loomed larger than life in front of them. The house, flanked by aging magnolias, cut a striking silhouette against the pale blue sky. Instead of the customary white, this mansion was made of red brick; that is, all but the front entryway, which was a classic beauty in white. Six massive Ionic columns supported the central portico, and done in a graceful half circle that lent grandeur to the mansion.

River Bends had an elegance all its own. Surprisingly enough, Alexandria felt at home from the moment she stepped foot in the house.

"It's so big." Alexandria whispered her thoughts, embarrassed by her simply worded statement, which made her sound like a child. Ten years of college and med school and those were the only words she uttered.

Julia, of course, pounced on her slip of the tongue. "Big, darling? Is that all you have to say? River Bends is a little more than 'big'. It's a 17,000 acre cotton plantation. And we're very proud of it, aren't we, Brad?"

"Yes, we are. River Bends is a special place," Brad agree with Julia, then said to Alex, "When you're settled in Alexandria, I'll show you around the place."

After receiving no response from Alexandria this time, Julia clamped her mouth shut and only had one more temper tantrum when she found out Alexandria was actually living in the main house.

As Alex had stood in front of the house, she had the oddest quiver in her stomach. This place looked like the house in the painting, and when she'd walked through the door she felt very much at home--which was absolutely absurd. There was no way she could have ever been at River Bends before, but deep down she knew she was glad to be here, if even for a little while.

That had been a week ago ...

A distant rider caught her attention. Immediately, she recognized the wide shoulders. Brad sat astride his beautiful white stallion, and perfectly fit the role of plantation owner. He appeared to be supervising the unloading of a flat-boat.

Fascinated, she watched as he pointed to some supplies. Though she couldn't see his finely chiseled mouth, she could imagine him issuing orders with calm authority. She liked that about him, except when he was issuing orders to her.

That's when their two centuries collided.

If she were a princess, Alexandria thought with a smile, Brad would be the frog who would turn into Prince Charming. However, he was Julia's Prince Charming. To Alexandria he was just an odious toad. But a recklessly, handsome toad, she had to admit.

Turning from the window, she made her way to the clothes closet to choose a dress. Swinging open the doors, she noticed her wardrobe hadn't changed. "I wonder which of the three dresses I should wear today? I wonder if I will ever have more than three?" Alexandria had to chuckle at herself when she remembered looking in her closet back home and thinking the same thing. She made a promise to save the money Brad paid her for being Missy's doctor, and when she had enough, she'd definitely go shopping.

Today Alex planned to begin Missy on her exercise program. Tying her thick hair back with a ribbon, leaving its silky length hanging down her back, she headed for the child's room, which was located two doors down from hers.

The maids had just finished dressing Melissa when Alexandria entered the room.

"Good morning," she called cheerfully.

"Hi, Alex. Have you had breakfast?"

"No, as a matter of fact, I haven't."

The child patted the side of the bed, a big smile on her small face. "Good, you can eat with me."

Together they enjoyed delicious French toast sprinkled with cinnamon and sugar. Alex inhaled the aroma of her tantalizing coffee. The Creole coffee, flavored with equal amounts of strong coffee and rich thick cream provided an appealing diversion from anything she had ever tasted before.

As they talked over breakfast, Missy told her small things about the work on the plantation. Alex discovered that River Bends produced bricks as well as cotton. All the bricks in the buildings, walls, and walkways had been manufactured here. River Bends also had the world's largest pecan grove, according to Missy.

"My goodness, how does Brad manage so much?" Alexandria found just one more thing to fascinate her about the man.

"He has a foreman who oversees the cotton fields, but mostly Brad takes care of everything himself," Missy said before taking a sip of hot chocolate.

Alexandria, not wanting to talk about Mr. Wentworth, changed the subject. "Well, young lady, are you ready to start your exercise program?"

"I think so."

"Good." She cleared away the dishes, then brought her medical bag over to the bed and put it on the nightstand. She took out a small rubber hammer, and bending Missy's legs slightly, tapped each leg just below the knee. There was no response. Alexandria then ran a wooden spoon up the center of Missy's foot. Missy wiggled her toes, slightly. Perhaps the muscles in her legs were just lazy from inactivity, Alex thought. At least, that's what she hoped.

"Before we start, I want you to know this might be painful because you'll be using muscles you haven't used in a long time. Just remember, the more pain you feel, the better. It means the circulation will be returning to your legs."

"I promise I won't complain, Alex. I just want to walk again."

Missy looked so full of hope. Alexandria prayed they wouldn't be disappointed.

"This dress is going to present a problem. Let me help you take it off, and from now on we'll do your exercise before you put on your clothes."

She stripped the child down to her chemise, then poured a sweet oil and rubbed her hands together to heat the liquid before applying it to her skin. Gently, she moved the oil in a circular motion starting with her toes. Carefully but firmly, she massaged Missy's ankles, moving up to the calves of her legs. Alexandria talked the whole time she worked on her, and finally Missy relaxed while Alex rubbed the muscles of her legs.

She took each leg, bending it up to Missy's chest, and then stretching it back out. This time she didn't have her medical books to rely on; they were back home on the shelf. Counting on what she had learned in the past, Alex was thankful that she had been more than a medical doctor.

With her knowledge she was known as an exceptional healer that's why she'd chosen to be a physiatrist. This way she could be a doctor of physical medicine, and a doctor of rehabilitative medicine. It was the best among all practitioners and a very unusual field, her professor told her. There were only 1600 in the country when she started her studies, and she knew she could go to any major hospital and get a job, or at least she could have.

They worked for two hours before stopping. Alexandria could tell Melissa had grown tired, but the child had kept her promise and hadn't complained.

During the past week Alexandria had seen little of Hattie, so she ventured down to the kitchen, which was located in the back of the house. Several women stood by the hearth, talking and doing various jobs. She noticed one woman in particular with a red bandanna tied up around her head. "Excuse me, have you seen Hattie?"

The woman put down what she was doing and turned toward her. Alex couldn't help but laugh. It was Hattie!

"You look like Aunt Jemima," Alex laughed again.

Hattie frowned. "Well now, you try workin' in dis hot cuisine, cher, and we'll see how fast you tie up dose long red curls."

"I'm sorry." Alexandria tried not to laugh but failed miserably.

"How did Missy fare dis mornin'?" Hattie asked as she placed the lid back on the pot.

"She did better than I expected. With a lot of exercise, I hope one day you'll see her walking through that door." Alex moved over to the kitchen table and picked up an apple before sitting down. At least apples hadn't changed over the years.

"I do, too. Ma Petite was so different. She was an energetic little girl when her mother was alive. I t'ink mebbe she blames herself fo' her mother's death."

Alex swallowed the bite of apple before she asked, "What happened?"

"Well, dat, cher, is still a mystery. It seems Melissa and Catherine were goin' to visit someone. We do not know who. Catherine told de child it was an old friend.

"Strange." Hattie shook her head. "It wasn't like Mrs. Catherine to go out unaccompanied. I've often wondered if someone had sent word fo' her to meet dem. And if so, why didn't she tell one of us she was leavin'?"

"Perhaps she didn't want anyone to know of the meeting," Alexandria said.

"Dat could be." Hattie nodded. "De last few months, I thought her behavior had been peculiar. Her color had grown pale as if she was worried over much."

"That does sound strange." Alexandria folded her hands and leaned across the table. "You told me you were the one who found her."

"Did anything look suspicious?" Alexandria asked.

"I guarantee. You see, cher, she'd driven de road many times before. Dere be no reason fo' de carriage to have a mishap. Did you know Mrs. Catherine's neck was broken?" Hattie leaned closer and whispered, "If you ask me, cher, I saw marks around her throat. No one ever said anyt'ing about dat ... Odd, don't you t'ink?"

Hattie continued, not letting Alexandria comment. "Dere was not'ing missin' out of de coach, so robbery was ruled out. When I pulled Melissa out of de carriage I saw a bloody hand print on the outside of de rig. I guarantee de print was very large" Hattie's eyes widened. "Definitely not a woman's!"

"The diary! I--I read in the book about a bloody hand print," Alex stumbled over her words as a shiver ran up her spine. "B--but it couldn't possibly be the same. Have you seen the diary?"

"No, not since you took it with de paintin'. What did you do wit' it?"

"I had it when I fell asleep. I remember that much." Alexandria thought for a minute. "But when I awoke I was so confused, I didn't give the diary a second thought."

Hattie stood abruptly. "I'm sure you'll find it somewhere, Petite," she said and started for the door. "It's enough idle chit chat for now. I have chores to do."

Alexandria still hadn't moved. She sat with her head propped upon her hand. Strange how that book had suddenly disappeared. And whose diary could it have been? Melissa's? That was a definite possibility. And did the little book have something to do with Alex being back in this time? Could she have been brought back for more than one reason? She sighed, pushing her thoughts aside, and looking around for Hattie who had stopped by the door. "I'd like to really experience plantation life while I'm here. Can I help you do something?"

While she was here--Hattie smiled. This one was definitely hard-headed. "If you be wantin' an experience, cher, I'll see dat you get one. We'll start by gatherin' eggs."

They grabbed two baskets and left by the back door, heading toward a group of houses in the distance. Once they had reached the cabins they walked down a dirt road that ran between them.

Brown log cabins stood side by side and what Alex assumed were slave quarters, very neatly kept. As they approached, a little girl stood with her back to a pillar. She smiled and waved at Hattie, but looked down when Alexandria glanced her way. Again making Alex feel like an outsider.

The hen house sat just on the other side of the slave cabins. A row on each side of the house extended all the way to the end. She couldn't believe how many chickens Brad owned. There must have been forty hens in total.

"Where are the eggs?" she asked.

Hattie's eyebrow shot up in amazement when she looked at her. "Child, have you never been in de country before?" They stepped into the hen house and shut the door. "De eggs, cher, are under de hens."

"Of course, I've been in the country before. We used to go on picnics," Alex informed her as she shifted the basket to the crook of her arm. "But how do you get the eggs out from under the chickens?"

Hattie's mirth was plastered on her face. "You have to shoo dem ...

watch me." She waved her arms at the hens, watching as they flew off their nests.

Alex tried to imitate Hattie by swinging her arms above her head. Two brown, speckle hens flew off the nest directly at Alexandria, who screamed, dropped her basket, and ran for the door.

Hattie stood back slowly shaking her head and clicking her tongue. "Here, you hold de baskets, and I'll get de eggs. At de rate you are goin', cher, it will take all day."

After filling the baskets with brown and white eggs, they started back for the main house.

"How have I done so far?" Alexandria teased Hattie and poked her in the ribs. But the thunder of hooves interrupted Hattie's reply. They turned to see Brad effortlessly riding up from the fields.

"Good afternoon, ladies," he drawled in his lazy Southern accent.

He held the reins loosely in his right hand and leaned on the pommel. His silky shirt lay half open to the waist, displaying his bronzed, tempting skin. The golden hair on his chest just barely peeked out of his shirt, and Alexandria found her eyes lingered there much too long as an undeniable urge to unbutton the other three buttons became a real temptation.

Angry for her lustful thoughts, she forced herself to look at Brad's face. His bright blue eyes held her captive just like before. But today there was an added sparkle into their depths. Could he possibly have read her thoughts? No--that was impossible, she assured herself.

Yet she wondered.

"If you've finished your chores, Alexandria, I thought you might like to see my plantation." Brad's eyes shifted to Hattie. "You don't mind, do you, Hattie?"

"Not a bit." Hattie smiled, then ambled on to the house.

When Alex looked at Brad again, he was still smiling, and she wondered what he was up to. He was being too nice.

"You can ride, can't you?" Brad leaned forward. His easy humor caught Alexandria off guard. Was he laughing at her? She tilted her chin a fraction higher. "Of course, I can ride ... when would you like to start?"

"Right now." Brad reached down and swept Alexandria off her feet, sitting her in front of him. It was a good thing Hattie had taken her basket of eggs, because they would all have been scrambled on the ground.

"I-I thought I'd get my own horse," Alex blurted out. She couldn't believe she was sitting on a horse with Brad's arms wrapped around her ... just like in the movies. She gasped for air, realizing she'd stopped breathing the moment he slid his arms around her. She couldn't think straight when she was this close to him, and she hated herself for being so rattled, so vulnerable, so drawn to a man she couldn't have.

"I'm going to get you a mount, but I thought you might like to ride to the stables instead of walking." He shot her a glance with one dark brow arched. "However, if you prefer to walk along behind my horse, you're welcome to do so." Brad made a move as if he was going to put her down.

"No!" Alexandria squealed. She could hear the rumble of laughter in his chest.

"I hate you."

"I know." He chuckled.

The damn man! She would hit him if she could let go long enough to swing.

"I thought you might see things my way. Obedience ... that's what I like in a woman ... obedience." Brad threw back his head and laughed.

Chapter Nine

"This is the saddle." Brad looked at Alexandria, wondering if she was crazy. What did she expect a saddle to look like?

"I need one like yours. This thing—" She pointed to the sidesaddle on her horse. "--is not what I'm accustomed to!"

"That, Madame, is a sidesaddle, and all women use them," he said as he finished tightening the cinch. "I thought you told me you could ride."

"I--I can ride sort of. But I've never ridden with a side- saddle."

"I find that strange. How did you manage your skirts, may I be so bold to ask?"

"I wore jeans."

"You wore what?" His eyebrow shot up in disbelief.

"Jeans, you know--men's pants."

"Lady, you sure do puzzle me." Brad stood much too close; his breath a mere whisper on her face. "You're different from anyone I've ever met, and you talk funny. Jeans?" he questioned with a puzzled look in his eyes.

Alex just stared at him. How was she going to explain jeans or her other way of life? She wasn't. It would be next to impossible.

Brad turned her to face the mount, then place his hands around her waist. "Ladies ride side-saddle." He shoved her up and positioned her foot in the stirrup.

—)—

Alexandria sat on her horse watching a group of slaves hoed cotton. Some of the women wore brightly colored kerchiefs, tied on their heads in the same style Hattie wore, while others wore straw hats.

The years gone by--a forgotten age. Alexandria felt like she was watching a documentary on television instead of sitting on a horse actually overlooking a cotton field.

She was having some difficulty sitting astride her filly. But she'd not let Brad know, especially since he had chuckled at her when she asked about the saddle. She smiled, remembering his expression in the stables, then she refocused on the field in front of her.

The white buds of the cotton plant had yet to peek out, but the plants appeared to be healthy and green. Brad had explained that cotton seed was planted in March and April. Then the field was hoed again and again until August when the picking season began. Each slave was then given a sack, with a strap that hung from his neck.

"How much cotton can they pick?"

"An ordinary day's work is about two hundred pounds."

"I've heard of slaves being whipped." Alexandria looked at Brad. "You don't do that, do you?"

"Of course not." He frowned, gathering his reins. "I've an overseer who takes care of these slaves, but there are no beatings at River Bends. Not even the animals."

They rode for hours over the plantation grounds, which stretched as far as the eye could see in all directions. Alexandria was impressed with the pecan groves, and she told Brad so. She was also impressed with the man. He had so much responsibility yet he handled everything with such ease that it amazed her. She bet he'd never even heard the word *stress*.

They spent the remainder of the day together. Brad's mood was light, almost cordial, as he proudly showed her his home. Not once did they get into an argument. Maybe he did have a good side.

Or maybe the sun was too hot and she was delirious.

When they returned to the stables, Alex stayed put while Brad dismounted. She figured a stable boy would come running any minute to help them, because she wasn't sure of any graceful way she could get down without falling flat on her face.

Brad tied his horse, then turned and stared at her. "You going to get down?"

"I'm thinking about my options," she murmured, but she damn sure didn't know how she was going to accomplish the task of dismounting. Her feet were in an awkward position because of the damn side-saddle, and she had yards of material everywhere. Besides, every muscle in her body ached from riding.

She glanced back at Sir Galahad, who just stood there staring at her. Well, she wasn't going to ask for help. She could do it. After all, she was a woman of the '80's'.

She pried her right leg from the upper stirrup, and soon discovered her mistake. Her right foot went down before she could removed her left foot, and the big skirt caught on the saddle, pitching her sideways ... straight into the arms of Mr. Wentworth.

"Thank goodness you're fast on your feet," she said feeling a little uncomfortable in his arms.

"Easy, sweetheart. I've seen people dismount for years, but, I must say, never the way you just did," he said in a teasing manner while he clutched her in his arms. "I thought you told me you could ride?"

"I can, but not with that contraption." She pointed to the dainty saddle.

Brad chuckled as he slowly released her legs so she could stand. But the minute her feet touched the firm ground she let out a moan.

"Oh, oh, oh!" Alex half-laughed and half-cried. She stumbled and wobbled over to a mound of fresh hay, then fell in it, still whining, "Oh, oh,--look."

"What's wrong? What did I do?" Brad moved over to her, completely dumbfounded by her actions. "Tell me, what's wrong?" he said, and he even sounded concerned before he added, "What are you doing?"

Alex was pulling up her skirt as fast as she could and she sure hoped Brad didn't pass out from seeing so much flesh. But she was in pain!

"Cramp!" Alex pointed to the calf of her right leg. "There--There." She took Brad's fingers and placed them where her muscles twisted in a knot. "Rub."

"You're not serious?" He jerked his hand back as if he'd been burned.

"I'm damn serious. Rub!"

Slowly Brad's fingers began moving in a circular motion. "Damn, it is tight," he commented as he applied just the right amount of pressure.

Alex started laughing at his comment, her mind definitely in the gutter as she lie on the straw. She became aware of unaccustomed warmth seeping through her. She felt a lot like a horse being shod. The only trouble was she liked the way he rubbed her leg, the way he touched her, and that bothered her. A lot.

"I'm not doing it right?" he asked.

"Oh, you're doing it just right," she breathed. His fingers were becoming more sensual now that the pain had eased. The mere touch of his hand sent a warming shiver through her. She realized she wasn't in a very ladylike position, especially with her skirts hiked up to her thighs.

"Thank you, that's much better," she said and watched as he straightened then kneeled in the straw and stared at her in a most peculiar way. Did he feel any of the uneasiness she did?

She wished she could read his mind, but he merely smiled at her and said, "Your welcome."

Then he turned and walked away.

A month had gone by and Missy slowly began to show progress. Every morning Alexandria would work with her, repeating the same exercises over and over again. Missy could move her legs on her own, but Alexandria decided it was still too early for her to try to stand.

They worked constantly. She gave Melissa hot baths to increase the circulation in her legs. Then Alex would massage each leg with warm oil to stimulate the muscles.

Once in a while Melissa would complain, but Alexandria would remind her of their goal and Missy would try just that much harder.

Alexandria worked long hours with her patient, pushing her more than some of the patients she'd had in the past because she wasn't sure when she'd be returned to the future, and she wanted Melissa well. She was different from the other patients Alex had known, and such a sweet girl that she found herself growing fond of her. She had given up on asking Hattie when they would return home. Hattie always gave her some double-talk about how they would know when the time came. When Hattie decided this adventure was over, Alex knew she'd miss Missy very much.

Alex liked the way the child's eyes lit up when Brad came in to visit her. She smiled, thinking about the day Hattie had commented on how *her eyes* lit up when Brad came into a room. The woman must have been in the cooking sherry. That idea was absurd!

She was surprised that Brad took as much time with his sister as he did. A couple of times he took Melissa out for a ride so she could get fresh air. At those times, Alex would find other things to do, giving them time alone. Besides, Brad never invited her--and of course--she really didn't care.

But why was it getting so hard not to care?

Today was such a beautiful day that Alexandria decided to take her prized student for a picnic. She ordered a buggy and Hattie helped situate Missy comfortably in the carriage.

Alexandria hadn't bothered to tell Brad where she was going. She'd not seen him, except in passing, since he'd taken her riding. Sometimes she felt he was avoiding her, or maybe he was just afraid of upsetting his precious Julia. Thank goodness they hadn't been blessed with *her* company lately.

The warm sunshine felt good as they rode past the cotton fields. Cotton bolls dotted the land with their white flax pointing up toward the blue sky. Evidently it was getting closer to picking time because there were twice as many slaves in the fields as before.

A man on a brown bay rode up from the field and stopped in front of their buggy, causing Alexandria to pull to a stop.

"Good morning, Miss Melissa," the man greeted them. A large, heavy man with a sharp expression, he was tall and his arms were a mixture of muscle and fat. His shaggy appearance in both hair and clothes made Alex wonder when he had last washed his garments, because there were tobacco juice stains down the front of his shirtfront. He smiled, but somehow it never reached his cold, empty eyes.

He nudged his horse over to Alex's side of the carriage. "I don't think I've had the pleasure, ma'am." He grinned, showing his tobacco-stained teeth.

"I'm sorry, Mr. Rivers. I thought Brad had introduced you," Missy apologized.

"Alexandria Dumont, this is Mr. John Rivers, Brad's overseer."

"It's nice to meet you, Mr. Rivers." Alexandria greeted the man with a nod. Her eyes traveled to his saddle, where she spotted a brown leather whip tied. She looked up again into his eyes, and he grinned as if he dared her to say anything.

"What do you use the bullwhip for, Mr. Rivers?"

"Just for protection, ma'am."

She sensed something evil about the man. Brad had told her he didn't whip his slaves, but this man looked like he wouldn't hesitate to use the whip. There was just something about him ....

Anxious to be away from him, she bid Rivers good day. Alex shivered in apprehension, thinking it was a strange reaction to someone she'd just met.

They rode out into the country until they found a grassy knoll near a small creek. It was perfect. She spread out a blanket for their picnic and assisted Missy into her wheelchair. When they got to the blanket,

Alexandria helped Missy out of the chair. And for just a minute before Missy sat down, she supported herself on her own two legs.

"Did you see that, Alex! I stood on my own!" Missy's bright eyes shined with happiness.

"Yes, I did, young lady! I think we're making progress."

Melissa was in the best of moods and very proud of her small accomplishment. When she finally calmed down, they enjoyed the lunch Hattie had packed for them--a feast of crispy fried chicken and fixings. They finished off their meal with molasses and biscuits.

"This is lots of fun. I haven't been on a picnic since Mother died."

Alex folded the napkins and placed them in the basket. Maybe this would be a good time to find out something about Missy's mother. "You miss your mother, don't you?"

"She was so much fun." Melissa handed Alex an empty plate. "The only time I ever remember seeing her angry was when Brad told her he was going to marry Julia."

"Really?" Alexandria looked up, surprised, thinking it was strange that Brad had waited all these years and was just now asking the witch to marry him. "Why didn't she approve?"

Missy wrapped the last piece of chicken in a cloth. "Because she knew Brad didn't love Julia."

"Then why is he going to marry her?" To Alexandria that made no sense whatsoever. Love was the only reason she would marry.

"My brother, to be so smart, at times can be quite dumb." Melissa laughed. "But Brad is a Wentworth. And my father made a deal with Julia's father--land in exchange for Brad's hand in marriage. The deal was made when he was a baby. Now Brad says he is just being practical." She lay on her side, propping up on her elbow. "Julia's land, you see, is right in the middle of ours. She is also from a well-bred family. And now he thinks I need somebody to look after me."

"It sounds like he's breeding cows, not choosing a wife," Alexandria commented sarcastically.

Missy started laughing. "That's what Mother said. But Brad argued that people don't marry for love, only for practical reasons."

"I'd say his attitude stinks!" Alexandria stated emphatically. "Has he ever loved anyone?" She absolutely hated herself for asking, but her curiosity got the best of her.

"I don't think so. Brad always seems bored to me when he's around women."

Alex snapped a white daisy from the grass and twirled it between her fingers. "Did your mother ever accept Julia?"

"No, Mother told me that Julia was evil. Julia just put up a good front for Brad."

"I don't understand." Alexandria frowned as she pulled off the white petals one by one. "Julia is rich. Why does she want Brad? Do you suppose she loves him?"

"Well, he is considered a catch. And, of course, there are the Wentworth jewels. That's probably what has caught Julia's eyes."

Alexandria considered what the child had just told her. "When I saw her, she had plenty of jewelry. It just doesn't make any sense to me."

Melissa pushed herself back to a sitting position. "It would make sense if you saw the Wentworth jewels. They're quite expensive, and will be a wedding gift to Brad's wife. I once heard Mother say Julia would get the jewels over her dead body."

Alex raised her brow. "It would seem that Brad, knowing how your mother felt, would not be planning to marry Julia."

"I don't think he would have if Mother was still alive. She only suggested to Brad not to marry Julia, but she never really told him how she felt. The only reason I know is that I overheard Mother talking to Hattie. At first I didn't think he'd continue seeing Julia after mother died, but he did. I guess he has always been attracted to her." Melissa sighed, then changed the subject.

Alex wanted to ask some more questions, but Missy seemed tired, so Alex would wait until another time. It was time to get Missy home.

Brad sat behind his desk going over the figures in his ledger. He had been staring at the same page for the last hour, and hated to admit the reason for his lack of concentration. But a redheaded she-devil kept dancing across the page. These past two months he had made certain to keep his distance from her. The fact that she entered his thoughts now irritated him.

He should be thinking about the engagement party that Julia had planned for October. Come to think about it, he'd done a good job of avoiding her, too. Avoiding Julia--Brad frowned, that was no way to think of his future wife. He tried to picture Julia, but at this very moment he couldn't even envision her face. He had always thought this marriage made good sense, but now he wasn't sure how he felt. And worse, he didn't know why he was so confused.

Damn, his mood was getting blacker. Maybe he would go to New Orleans. Getting up, Brad walked to the window. "Alexandria," he whispered as he stood looking out the window. She was such a puzzle to him. Something about her seemed different. She had spirit. She was defiant. And she had a great deal of pride. Brad Wentworth, the rake, the master of seduction. What a laugh! When it came to Alexandria, she wasn't the least bit intimidated by him the way most women were. And evidently, she wasn't the least bit impressed. Hadn't she made it very plain that she didn't want anything to do with him?

So, why had he avoided her? He frowned. Hell, this was his house! And he felt trapped. Suddenly, he turned and went to the door of his study in search of Hattie.

Brad stuck his head out the door and called, "Hattie!" He was going to find Miss Dumont, and from this day forward he was going to get to know her. Hell, he wasn't afraid of a female. Even one as aloof as his present houseguest. When he presented his charming side, this woman would be mere putty in his hands--like all the rest.

"Hattie!" Brad called again.

"You hollerin', Master Brad, or just tryin' to wake de dead?" Hattie stood in the hall with her hands on her hips.

"You could at least show a little respect." Brad smiled at the sassy servant as he turned and went back to his desk.

"I answered you, didn't I?" Hattie mumbled when she entered the room.

Brad started laughing at Hattie's sassy tone. "Where is Alexandria?"

"Well now – dat's a question. Since when do you want to know where Alex is?"

"I want to ... wait a minute ... I'm the employer here, or have you forgotten?" Brad's eyebrow shot up. "I don't answer your questions. You answer mine!"

"*Oui*, I just t'ink it's strange." Hattie shook her head. "Remember you're engaged."

"I'm not engaged yet," Brad grumbled.

"But, what are your intentions toward Alex?" Hattie persisted.

"Her name is Alexandria." Brad walked around to the front of his desk. Leaning against the edge, he said, "And what do you mean, my 'intentions'? Maybe you've forgotten, Alexandria works for me. She takes care of my sister. It seems perfectly natural that I might like to talk to her."

"Are you sure dat is all dere is to it?"

"Yes!" Brad nearly shouted. "Hell, the lady doesn't even like me!"

"I wouldn't be too sure o' dat." Hattie smiled.

"Oh, is there something you want to tell me?" He folded his arms across his chest and waited for her reply.

"Nope, dis one you'll have to figure out for yourself."

"Hattie, damn it, what do you mean?" Brad gritted his teeth. "I hate it when you talk in riddles."

Ignoring him, she raised her eyebrows. "I believe you asked me where Alex was?"

"So now you're going to tell me?"

"If you'll quit shouting, I will."

Brad walked down the front steps of River Bends with the intention of getting his horse, when a buggy coming up the driveway caught his attention. "Damn." It was Julia.

The carriage pulled to a stop and the door swung open. The driver was quick to help Julia out of the carriage. She walked over to Brad, swaying her hips with clear exaggeration.

"What are you doing here, Julia?"

"Why, I've come to see you, of course." She put her arms around his neck, giving him a kiss that spoke of their intimate relationship. Out of habit, Brad wrapped his arms around her waist. But somehow Julia didn't feel the same in his arms.

Alexandria and Missy had thoroughly enjoyed the outing and had taken their time coming home. As they drew closer to the house, Alex jerked back on the reins to slow the horse. There stood Brad and Julia in a passionate embrace. It took all her willpower to keep the buggy steady.

The tightening in her chest startled her, and for just a moment she had the strangest urge to cry. *Get a grip*, she told herself. She shouldn't be the least bit interested. After all, the couple would soon be married.

Alexandria pulled the buggy to a complete stop right behind them, and smiled when they jumped. She ignored the lovers as she climbed down and pulled out Melissa's wheelchair, rolling it to the side of the carriage.

"Let me help you," Brad said behind her.

Alex ignored him and pulled Melissa out of the carriage. "Oh, don't let me bother you," she said over her shoulder, trying to sound nonchalant. "I can take care of Missy."

She heard Julia gasp in the background. *Maybe she'll faint*, Alex thought, knowing she was being catty, but unable to control herself.

"Well, I never!" Julia pulled on Brad's arm. "Your servants should be taught better manners!"

Melissa giggled in Alex's arms as she whispered, "That's one for you, Alex."

Brad moved around Alex while she settled Missy into her chair. "I said I would help you," he stated flatly, reaching out to assist them.

"I didn't want to interrupt you." Alex looked up at him and saw by his expression that her remark had struck a nerve.

He glared at her. "It was just a kiss and none of your business, Miss Dumont."

Brad's stinging words would have been her undoing if he hadn't added, "Why were you out by yourself? You should have better sense."

She felt her temper rise, and she didn't stop to examine why. "I have perfect sense!" *Most of the time*, she added to herself. "I'm perfectly capable of taking an outing. I'm not one of your little milksops that can't do a damn thing for themselves. I'll have you know I've been taking care of myself for a long time, and I don't need any help from you or anyone!"

She noted his set face, his clamped mouth and fixed eyes before he spoke. "That was a stupid thing to do! And try watching your language around my sister!" Brad's shouting surpassed hers.

"Why?" She glared at him. "It was just a picnic. Where I come from, we have them all the time. So, what did it hurt?" She lowered her voice when she realized Julia, who stood at the top of the stairs, was enjoying their arguing way too much.

"You could have been hurt. It's not safe for a woman to go out unchaperoned. Someone should have taught you that. But, believe me, you won't go out again unless it's with me!" Brad grabbed Alexandria's arms and pulled her up in front of him, forcing her to stand on her toes. He wanted to ensure she understood every word he said. He could see by the angry sparks in the depths of her emerald eyes that she did.

"Yes, Master," she flung at him. "I'd let go of my arms if I were you, before your fiancée becomes jealous and starts to think you care for me." She spoke the words softly through gritted teeth.

"I do care," Brad said quietly as he looked into her green eyes. Despite himself, he wanted to taste the fire they offered, but knew that he couldn't.

He watched her mouth fall open in a very unladylike manner, and knew she wanted to say something, but she seemed too stunned to do so.

For once in her life, Alexandria was totally confused as she stared into the ice-blue eyes of Satan himself. At this moment, Brad had cast a spell on her. And she would have been helplessly lost if not for the horse and rider that rode up behind them.

The spell was broken ...

Chapter Ten

"Hello, Brad, am I interrupting something?" Edmund asked his cousin.

They both turned to face Edmund.

From horseback, Edmund smiled down at them. The pleased look on Julia's face told him he'd broken up a fight. "Well, aren't you going to welcome me?"

"Edmund! What a surprise," Brad greeted. "Funny you should show up today. I was just thinking about visiting you."

"Good to hear it!" Edmund's delighted grin broadened at Brad's welcome. True, he had come to see Brad, but topmost in his mind was a certain redhead. He had thought of Alexandria often, and since Brad seemed intent to go through with his marriage plans, Edmund planned to get to know the lovely Alexandria much better. He had thoroughly enjoyed her company on the trip home.

"That's one of the reasons I'm here. I thought Alexandria might be getting bored with this country life, and would like a trip into the city." Edmund winked at her. "How about it?"

Alex couldn't help but smile at Edmund. It was apparent he and Brad were cousins. Only Edmund's blond hair was much lighter than Brad's. And he had a boyish charm about him, where Brad's bolder personality made him seem mature. "I'd love to, Edmund, but my job is taking care of Missy, remember? I'll have to take a rain check."

"A what?"

Alex noticed several pairs of eyes staring at her. She realized her slip and quickly covered it. "I can't go. I need to take care of Missy."

"That's no problem. We'll bring Missy, too." He looked at Melissa. "You would like that, wouldn't you, Missy?"

"Oh, yes, Edmund," she said excitedly. "What will we do?"

"I've something special planned. The St. Charles Theater is opening in two weeks with an opera, and I've managed to obtain a box. Everybody in town is begging for tickets. Now, that you can't turn down!"

"Sounds wonderful, Edmund! I'd love to go," Missy said, grinning from ear to ear. "And Alexandria would, too."

"It will give Melissa a chance to look for a new gown for our engagement party." Julia interrupted the conversation. "And I'll come and help her pick out the perfect one," she added sweetly.

"There's no need." Melissa reached over and took hold of Alexandria's hand. "Alex can help me, and she can get a new dress, too."

"She needs it," Julia mumbled.

Alex bristled. "I don't need a dress since I'm not going to the party."

"But you have to go with me, Alex!" Missy persisted.

"You *will* be there, Madam." Brad issued the command.

"We'll see." Alexandria arched her eyebrow. The man just loved to give orders. He must have wanted to be a general when he was a small boy.

"Miss Dumont, I'd like to see you in my study!" Brad turned and started climbing the steps.

She watched the pompous ass as he moved away. He looked more than a little irritated, she thought. But then Brad always seemed irritated at her for one reason or another. She took a deep breath. He let the least little thing aggravate him. He would have ulcers before he turned thirty-five. This man definitely needed to be liberated. I wonder what he would do if I didn't move an inch?

She soon found out. In no more than a split-second, Brad spun around and headed straight for her. He didn't say a word. He just bent down, picked her up, threw her over his shoulder, and then started back up the stairs.

"Put me down!" she protested, and for a brief second the scene of Rhett Butler carrying Scarlett up the stairs flashed through her mind.

"Madam, one day you'll learn to follow instructions and make it easier on yourself," Brad said in a harsh growl. Without saying another word, Brad entered the house and went straight to his study, slamming the door behind them. He sat her down, and moved to his liquor cabinet to pour himself a bourbon.

It appeared she'd now driven him to drink.

He slugged down a liberal portion of liquor, then glared at her over the rim of his glass. She'd been a problem since the first time he'd laid eyes on her. But when Julia commented about Alexandria's clothes, he'd taken a good look at her attire. She still wore the same dress she'd worn on the boat. Her garments were no better than rags, and she wore the same thing all the time. It irritated him that he'd let it go on this long. He took another drink, then a deep breath.

"In my home, I'll not have you dressing in clothes such as these, Madam!"

Instead of fighting back as he had expected, Alexandria flinched from the cruelty in his voice. He'd not meant to hurt her, but she was so damn stubborn, and for just a moment he glimpsed an emptiness in her. And he wanted to--to what? He had no acceptable explanation.

Then as small raindrops build to a stream, and the stream erodes the dam, the tears that Alexandria had held back for so long came cascading down her cheeks. Everything that had happened hit her all at once, and the firm control she had kept on her emotions crumbled.

She was back in a time she'd always fantasized about, but she wasn't the belle of the ball. She was poor. She had no money. And worse, she couldn't do anything about her situation. She couldn't go to town and wait tables or work in a department store like she had when she'd worked her way through school. Because there were no department stores! She had no control of her life. She'd been independent all her life, yet she really didn't know how to handle this situation.

She felt ashamed for being so weak, and turned her back, not wanting Brad to see her cry.

Alex jerked when a hand touched her shoulder. Yet Brad's touch was tender on her arms when he turned her to face him. With concern in his eyes, he gently curved her body to his, wrapping his arms around her. At first she resisted and tried to pull away, but soon gave in to the comfort he offered. Suddenly she felt safe, as if she belonged here. Alex laid her head on his chest. Her tears flowed freely. Brad's arms tightened around her. He lightly rubbed her back in a soothing motion.

"I'm sorry, sweetheart, don't cry," he murmured into her hair. "You must admit you need new clothes."

"I know." She nodded in agreement.

"All I'm doing is offering to buy them for you."

Alexandria pulled back and peered into his eyes. "I can't let you do that." Her voice broke as she tried to catch her breath from her bout of crying. "I'm not your wife to clothe, and I won't take your charity."

Brad enfolded her back in his arms. "I think I understand how you feel. I'd feel the same way. But how you've gotten so independent puzzles me. You act like you've had to depend on yourself for everything. Surely, your parents took care of you."

If only you knew, she thought. "What would Julia say if you bought me clothes?" Alexandria mumbled into his shirt. It felt good to be wrapped in his strong embrace. She had to fight her feelings and keep them in perspective. After all, Brad did not care for her; he was just being nice.

"This is none of Julia's concern," Brad said in answer to her question. "Look, I have an idea. Since you work for me, I'll merely advance you the money for your clothes. Does that meet with your approval?"

Alexandria reluctantly lifted her head to look at him. "Yes, I agree to that. Surely I've earned a good sum. After all, I am a doctor."

"A few dollars, at least." Brad grinned. "Tomorrow I'll take you shopping."

Gazing up into his eyes, she returned his smile. And for just a fleeting moment she thought he would kiss her. Instead he rubbed a knuckle down the side of her face, tenderly, as if he cared. Alexandria saw sadness in his gaze that she wanted to erase, but just as she leaned toward her a loud knock sounded at the door. She jumped and moved away from Brad.

Julia swept into the study, not waiting for an invitation. Alexandria took advantage of the interruption and left at the same time.

"I hope you've got your little doctor straightened out!" Julia said as she sat down in a wing-back chair.

Brad rested on the edge of the desk with one leg casually draped across the corner. "I believe so."

When he didn't elaborate, Julia had no choice but to ask, "Well, what did you do?"

"I promised to take her shopping."

"Shopping! Surely, you jest!" Julia jumped to her feet and began to pace back and forth. "I'll not be made the laughing stock of New Orleans. How do you think it would look for *you* to take someone other than your wife shopping for clothes?" She stopped, then glared at Brad. Her speech seemed to have little effect on him; perhaps she should try a different approach. "You realize you would ruin Alexandria's reputation?"

Brad contemplated Julia's statement. He hated to admit it, but she was right. "I'll tell you what, Julia. You and I will stay here and plan the party. I'll send Missy, Alexandria and Hattie with Edmund."

Julia smiled then pressed a kiss on his cheek. "Thank you, darling. I need to unpack, so I'll leave you now."

Just before she got to the door, Brad stopped her. "Julia, never enter my study again unless you're invited." His cold voice was harsh, but he continued, "It's off limits to everyone, including you!"

She slammed the door. Julia was taken back by Brad's coolness. "Off limits to everyone but that red-headed bitch, he means!"

Her spine stiffened. Alexandria was starting to become a problem.

Edmund rode in the fancy open coach with Missy beside him and Hattie and Alexandria sitting opposite them. The small group was quiet except for Edmund and Missy, who were talking.

Alexandria marveled at the plushness of the velvet cushions. They were so soft that she could hardly feel the bumps on the road. The warmth of the morning gently reminded her that the brilliant sun would become blistering hot by midday. But for now the heat felt good on her face as they rode to New Orleans. Some of the tension had left her shoulders and she began to relax. She found herself watching Edmund. The golden rays of the sun danced in the blond streaks of his hair. He was, she had to admit, a charming rogue. He gave her the impression he never took anything seriously, and he often made her laugh. She found him quite adorable. Wouldn't her girlfriends at home be foaming at the mouth for his attention? Yet, he couldn't hold a candle to Brad. Even though Edmund's company was exhilarating, he didn't make her heart beat a little faster. Unfortunately, she couldn't say the same about Brad, perhaps Mr. Wentworth was a symptom that would one day go away.

Alex had been surprised when she'd learned Brad wouldn't be accompanying them. She didn't know if she was glad or disappointed. Her emotions were too mixed up when he came near her. Maybe now she could straighten herself out and forget Mr. Wentworth.

A fleeting smile touched Edmund's lips as he, too, sat thinking about Brad. He could still picture his cousin and Julia waving goodbye. Somehow Brad hadn't looked like the happy bridegroom, and he'd seemed very unhappy when Edmund told him he was going to try his hand with Alexandria. The conversation still rang in Edmund's ears ... .

"Well, you're not interested," Edmund had defended. He had smiled innocently at the black look he received in return. His humor had been hard to contain for he thought Brad was as enchanted with the redhead as he was; he was just too stubborn to admit the truth. That made Alexandria fair game. "I thought I'd pursue my happiness; after all, you have Julia."

"Do you think the lady is interested?" Brad had asked in a curt voice.

"Well, cousin, that's what I intend to find out." Edmund wanted to laugh at the scowl his statement produced, but he knew better.

"Be careful, cousin," Brad warned. "Alexandria is not a toy like the other ladies you keep company with. I'd hate to end up shooting you." Finished with his blunt statement, he'd turned and left.

It appeared to Edmund, if not to Brad himself, that Brad was a little more enthralled with Alexandria than he wanted to acknowledge.

The day, as Alexandria had predicted, turned hot and sultry. A few thunderclouds were scattered across the sky, offering only momentary relief when the sun passed behind each one.

Thank goodness they'd finally arrived! Alexandria thought when they reached in New Orleans. In this day and time, these people certainly wore more garments than were needed. It was hot! She wanted a sundress--a sleeveless sundress--better still, some shorts and a crop top with her middle showing. The last thought made her laugh out loud.

"I'm glad our trip is making you happy," Edmund commented, a puzzled look in his eyes.

Alexandria quickly changed the subject. "You have a beautiful city, Edmund. What do I smell?"

"That rich aroma comes from the coffee houses and bakeries," Edmund told her.

The carriage turned onto a broad double avenue. The center of the street resembled a park with beautiful watermelon-colored crepe myrtles, park benches, and black metal gas lamps. The tree-lined avenue provided plenty of shade for the travelers.

Handsome mansions of stone and brick lined both sides of the street. As they moved farther down the boulevard, each home appeared to be bigger in size than the one preceding it. Tall black wrought iron fences surrounded each house for protection.

As the carriage slowed, Alexandria heard the driver call out to the guard at the gate. Sluggishly, the carriage proceeded under the arched, lacy iron doors and moved forward, making a wide sweeping turn onto the driveway. Brad had been right. Edmund didn't live in a modest little house. He was a wealthy man himself. Slowly, the carriage pulled to a stop in front of a set of double doors.

"Welcome to *Rué Chartress*, ladies."

Edmund helped everyone out of the carriage. Then he rolled Melissa into the house. Alexandria, Hattie, and the luggage followed. Of course, most of it was Melissa's.

The house possessed a Spanish decor made of a white stucco with windows trimmed in black ironwork. Alexandria found the house light and airy, completely different from the plantation.

"Wait until you see the courtyard, Alex. It's beautiful." Melissa beamed. "Take her there first, Edmund."

A tropical garden with trees and flowers dominated the very center of the house. Alexandria walked through one of the four main archways that lead into the courtyard. Sunlight filtered through the trees and bathed the garden in color. The trickling sound of water echoed from a beautiful fountain. It was probably her imagination, but it felt cooler here. She looked down at the rosy, brick-colored floor and noticed the squares were laid in different patterns. Smelling something sweet, she turned to find great clay pots filled with pink and white blooms, and mounds of ferns around the base of each pot.

A second floor balcony surrounded three-quarters of the courtyard. "This is divine," Alexandria whispered, not wanting to disturb the tranquil setting.

"I'm glad you like it. Why don't you stay here for a little while? Hattie will help me take Melissa to her room."

"Thank you, Edmund. I think I will."

After they left, Alexandria lingered by the fountain. She wanted to enjoy a few quiet minutes in this enchanting courtyard. Sitting on the edge of the rust-colored brick fountain, she ran her fingers through the cool water and listened to the sound of the trickling spray. She had often read about the beautiful courtyards of New Orleans, but mere words in a book could never capture the real beauty of this splendid place.

Alex observed her reflection in the water, and saw how the glorious sun caught in her red hair. As she stared at the water, the sunlight brightened, until suddenly, without warning, the water turned to fire. She gasped and jerked back her hand, but she couldn't turn away from the brilliant orange and red flames. For a moment she couldn't breathe. A fine sweat covered her face. Just as she started to cry out, the water cleared and in its place was the picture she'd bought at the flea market so many months ago.

What was happening to her? She reached a trembling hand out to touch the picture, but it was not there--only the blue water of the fountain. Trying to control the shaking of her body, Alexandria clung to the bricks with her fingers. Had she only imagined what had happened, or had she gone completely crazy seeing things that were not there?

"No!" She protested. This had been too real. Perhaps it was a premonition of something to come. "Oh, God!" What if it was? What part could she possibly play? It couldn't be much ... she didn't belong in this century. She had to keep reminding herself that she didn't belong here.

Nervously, Alexandria paced around the fountain with all these questions running through her head. If only she could see her picture again, but it was back home--in the future. Could the painting have something to do with her being in the year 1835? After all, everything had started happening to her from the moment she'd touched the oils. What could she do? The diary! It had to be the answer! But first she'd have to find it. Where could it be? River Bends--somehow she knew it had to be at River Bends. If she could find the diary, she had a feeling her questions would be answered.

Trying to compose herself, Alexandria decided that when she returned to the plantation she'd just do a little snooping. But for now, there was some shopping she needed to do.

C*hapter Eleven*

They took the first week in New Orleans to relax, and Alexandria had to admit Edmund was wonderful company. He kept them entertained. If she didn't know better, she'd swear he was trying to charm her off her feet. But why *her* when he probably had dozens of girlfriends?

This morning as she sat brushing her hair, she found herself in a pensive mood.

She thought Hattie would have taken her back home. What had happened to Alex's patients? And how would she explain her disappearance when she returned? She shook her head.

She had merely stepped into the past for an enchanting visit. Sometimes that was the only thought that kept her going. This was just temporary ... only a visit, nothing more. Hattie had said she needed a rest, but how much rest did she need? When Alex brought the subject up, Hattie's only response was a shake of the head and a quirk of a smile. What the hell was that supposed to mean?

You'd think with ten years of college she could understand a simple conversation, but every discussion with Hattie left her wanting to hear more. The woman had to know black magic. Alexandria shook her head.

Alexandria laid the hair brush down and stopped day-dreaming. It was time for breakfast.

"Good morning, Alexandria." Edmund stood when she entered the room. "Missy and I were just talking about your shopping trip. The opera is at the end of next week, or have you both forgotten?" he teased, holding a chair out for her.

"Of course, we haven't forgotten, Edmund. Sometimes you can be silly," Missy bantered back.

"Good. Because I'm looking forward to escorting the two most beautiful ladies in New Orleans." He looked to Alexandria and asked, "What color dress have you decided to buy?"

"Edmund, you must call me Alex."

He placed another spoonful of scrambled eggs on his plate before he answered. "I'm like Brad, I'm afraid. Alex is a boy's name, and you, my lady, are definitely not a male!" He looked over at her and winked. "Now, what color will the dress be?"

Alex shrugged. "I don't have the slightest idea. I've really not given it much thought, but I promise the dress will definitely not be yellow." She wrinkled her nose. "I've seen enough of my yellow dress to last a lifetime." She placed a small bit of bacon in her mouth, savoring the smoked flavor. "I guess you'll just have to wait and see."

"I'm sure you have excellent taste," Edmund said as he stood up from the breakfast table. "Ladies, if you'll get ready, I'll be most happy to drive everyone into town."

When they left the dining room, Alexandria decided to forgo Missy's exercise this morning, so they could get an early start on their shopping spree. Alex went to her room to get her handbag--a bag with little money.

She wasn't sure just what she could buy. Brad had never told her how much money she'd earned, but it had to be a good sum. Didn't it?

Brad ... Alexandria had done a good job not thinking of him this past week. She placed a dab of color on her lips and cheeks, blending carefully. She wondered what he was doing. He and Julia were probably planning their party. A stab of jealousy raced through her as she pictured him holding Julia, and Alex hated herself for it. She couldn't help remembering how Brad had held her so tenderly in his study. It had felt so good, so right, and she had wanted him to kiss her. Damn!" She had to stop these thoughts.

The slight breeze felt good to Alex as they rode to the shopping district. It was such a pretty day, they decided to take a stroll about the streets. Once they reached the *Vieux Carré*, Edmund helped everyone out.

"Will several hours be enough?" Edmund asked, climbing back into the buggy.

The women nodded.

"Good." He reached down and picked up the reins. "Hattie, keep them out of trouble."

A mixture of aromas, gumbo, and freshly baked bread hung in the air as they passed the French Market. Alex glanced into the marketplace full of women with baskets, haggling over the fresh fruits and vegetables. That was one thing that hadn't changed over the years. Heads of garlic hung on braided ropes over crates of Creole tomatoes that lined the front of every stall.

Hattie pushed Melissa's wheelchair across Chartress Street. Alex walked beside her, observing the black wrought-ironwork on the balustrades, which were adorned with hanging potted plants.

Vendors up and down the street hawked their goods, and the fragrant scents changed to spices and sweets.

"Let's get some beignets," Missy suggested, sniffing the air.

"Not now, Petite." Hattie laughed. "You've just eaten breakfast, and I know you want a perfect fit for your new ball gown."

"A--All right, Hattie." Missy sighed. "You certainly are no fun!"

"Fun, Petite, what's dat?" Hattie played innocent. "Remember," she said as she gently tugged one of Missy's blonde curls, "ladies don't eat much. Dey are dainty and pick at dere food."

"Hattie, you're constantly telling us what ladies should do." Alexandria put in her two cents. "Tell me, do you have a little book hidden in that apron of yours titled *The Proper Little Ladies Dos and Don'ts*?" She heard Missy giggle, and Alex laughed, too.

"No, I don't. But I'll tell you one t'ing." Hattie pushed the wheelchair around the corner. "It's a hard job tendin' you two."

"And we couldn't do it without you," Alexandria admitted. "Right, Missy?"

"I'll say. But at least we could eat."

The sidewalks bustled with well-dressed women and men walking and strolling. Smart carriages with high-stepping horses moved by at a slow pace. The stately buildings stood two stories tall with their sun-washed stucco sidings.

Alex couldn't help but wonder if any of these people had jobs. Of course, the wealthy wouldn't work, she reminded herself. The scene before her definitely didn't mirror the hustle and bustle of the eighties. People were calm, polite, and seemed to be in no hurry. There was no stopping at the grocery store after work, then the post office to get the mail, and finally arriving at her apartment to find she'd forgotten her hair appointment. Alex sure didn't miss the fast-paced eighties. There had been times she'd wanted to shout for the world to slow down.

At last, they came to the dress shop on Royal Street. A dazzling red-and-white awning hung over the entrance way. Large clay flower pots stood on each side of the door, bursting with scarlet geraniums.

A bell jingled, announcing their arrival, as they entered a small and very elegant sitting room where Alexandria sat down on a velvet, rose-colored settee. The small shop, Le Rougé, was one of the more elegant stores in New Orleans, according to Missy. This was the boutique where all the New Orleans's society women bought their clothes.

"*Bonjour*, Mademoiselle Melissa," a smartly dressed woman said as she entered.

"*Bonjour*, Madame Marie," Melissa greeted.

The woman smiled at them. She was quite elegant with her bright red hair piled high on her head. Her complexion was creamy and smooth, and she looked to be in her late thirties.

"Madame Marie, I would like to introduce my friend, Alexandria Dumont."

"Madame Dumont, welcome to my shop." Marie smiled.

"It's Mademoiselle," Alexandria corrected. "You've a lovely shop, Madame."

"Pardon, Mademoiselle Dumont, it's just that you are so lovely. One would assume you were married." Marie blushed, trying to cover her embarrassing remark.

"We are in need of some gowns," Alexandria informed the Frenchwoman, pointedly ignoring her remark.

"Both of you?" she asked, her eyebrows raised in question.

"Yes, Madame. Brad said to charge everything to his account," Melissa said.

Once again the door jingled as a couple of richly dressed women entered. They greeted Melissa and Marie, but ignored Alexandria. Alex wanted to laugh; snobs hadn't changed over the years. There would always be those people who thought themselves a cut above the rest.

"Please be seated, ladies. I'll be with you momentarily," Madame Marie instructed before disappearing into the back.

They had barely sat down when the woman reappeared with a bright smile.

"This way please, ladies." Marie motioned for them to follow her. "You may have your maid wait here." She nodded at Hattie.

"No! " Alex said a bit louder than she intended. "She will go with us,"

At first Madame just stared, her mouth open. "This is most unusual." She seemed startled by Alexandria's protest. But after seeing that Alex was determined, Marie conceded. "Very well, step this way. I have a fitting room in the back."

Madam ushered the three of them to the back of the shop and into a large dressing room. Bolts of material were stacked in bins up to the ceiling. Every color and fabric could be found; muslins, brocades, silks, woolens, and velvets. There were also beads, ribbons, fur, lace, and other adornments. She even had batiste for chemises.

This was quite different from going into a department store with ready-made clothes and price tags. Everything had to be made for the person doing the ordering. The seamstress started by taking Missy's measurements.

Hattie and Marie gasped as Missy stood up on her own accord to be measured.

"Ah, Petite, you can stand. I'm happy for you," Madam Marie exclaimed.

"It's because Alex has been helping me make my muscles stronger," Melissa boasted. "One day, I'll be walking."

"It's hard to believe," Madam acknowledged.

"We still have much work to do," Alex cautioned, not wanting Missy to become over-confident.

"I know. But if I keep exercising--I'll walk!" Melissa said, determination showing in her eyes.

Alexandria smiled at the beautiful child. Yes, she would walk--Alex felt sure of it.

"Now it's your turn, Mademoiselle Dumont." Marie motioned with her hand for Alex to stand on the box.

Alexandria stripped down to her chemise, and Madame starting measuring. "This chemise must be the first thing we get rid of." Marie shook her head as she felt the thin material. "One this beautiful should not be dressed so shabbily. We will start with a new chemise."

Alex smiled her approval, then straightened her back and stood completely still. The skillful Frenchwoman measured her height, bust, waist and hips. Not an inch was left unmeasured.

"What a lovely figure you have, my dear. You have little need for a corset, and your complexion is also unique. I've many colors that will look nice on you."

The next several hours were spent picking out patterns and swatches of material to go with each sketch.

Alexandria liked Madam Marie and found her quite helpful on suggesting fabrics. Alex picked out many dresses, many more than she had intended. Quite often she asked Hattie for her opinion, finding her taste excellent. Alexandria even insisted that Hattie get a couple of dresses. After all, Alex was paying for this clothing with the money she'd earned. Madame looked as if she would faint at that suggestion, but she complied with Alexandria's wishes.

All the dresses had been picked out but one. The one Alex would wear to Brad's engagement party. She had looked forward to getting some new clothes, but this one dress in particular she couldn't wait to have designed.

She smiled. Brad might demand she attend the engagement party, but ... she'd do it in the style she chose.

"Madame Marie, do you have any black crepe?"

"*Oui*, I do."

"I would like for you to make me an evening gown in black crepe."

"But, Mademoiselle, black is for widows. Surely you'd prefer a bright color."

"No. I want black." Alex moved over to the long table and picked up a piece of charcoal. "I'll draw a sketch of how I want it made."

She took a pad and quickly drew a very elegant strapless gown that flowed to the floor ... not a dress for this century, but quite different. What gossip she would stir when she arrived at the party! Brad would surely regret telling her what to do. Just wait until he got a load of her!

Showing the sketch to Madame, she waited for her response.

"This is lovely. I've never seen a dress of this style, but I must confess it's most becoming. Will you not change your mind on the color?"

"No, you'll have to trust me. This will be beautiful and most appropriate."

"We will see, Mademoiselle Dumont." Marie said. "If you don't mind, I'll take Missy into the next room for a shoe fitting."

They had no more than left the room when Hattie turned to Alexandria. "What are you up to, child?"

"Who, me?" Alex pointed at herself, feigning surprise.

"*Oui*, you! Don't go playin' dumb with me, cher! What's goin' on in dat pretty head of yours?" Hattie placed her hand under Alex's chin and tilted it up.

"Well ... I just thought I'd order a special dress for the engagement party."

"Petite, you play wit' fire."

"Why? No one will care what I'm wearing. I'm not the bride--just hired help."

"And what will Brad say?"

"I don't really care. If you recall, I told him I didn't want to go. He insisted, so I'll be there, but *my* way."

"Ah, Petite, you're so headstron'." Hattie shook her head and looked heavenward. "I hope you'll be able to handle him."

"I will. Don't worry, Hattie," Alex said with more bravado than she felt. She knew she would be testing Brad's temper, but then again, he might only have eyes for his future bride and wouldn't notice her at all.

Melissa returned, and they thanked Madame Marie for her help. She promised to have their gowns delivered in time for the opera.

Dinner that night was a spicy feast of crab gumbo, hot, crusty bread, and for dessert they had beignets and *café au lait*. Missy was her usual bubbly self as she told Edmund all about their shopping trip. However, neither she nor Alexandria would tell him what their dresses looked like. They wanted them to be a surprise.

After Missy went to bed, Alexandria and Edmund strolled out to the courtyard and sat on the bench facing the fountain.

"You look lovely tonight, Alexandria."

"Even in this old dress?"

"You'd be beautiful no matter what you wore." Edmund reached up and pushed her hair off her shoulder.

Alexandria wanted to keep the conversation light. "I bet you've told that to many women."

"Well, a few," he confessed, "but I really mean it this time."

"I've heard that line before." Alex looked at Edmund's dreamy eyes and wondered why she didn't care for him. It definitely was not because he wasn't good looking. "Edmund, you're sweet." She reached up and touched his face in a tender caress, just like a mother would a child.

"'Sweet,' Alexandria? Do you suppose you might go beyond 'sweet' and care for me just a little?" He pulled her to him and kissed her. Reluctantly moving away from her soft lips, he looked deep into her eyes. "I guess not. Tell me, who's the lucky fellow?"

Alexandria laughed and turned away from him to stare at the fountain. Edmund was so nice. Why couldn't she feel something for him? She watched the trickling water slide down the stone.

"There is no lucky fellow." She sighed. "Sometimes I wonder if there will ever be anybody at all. I guess I've always been busy and never took the time to get involved."

"Sweetheart, as beautiful as you are, there will be many. Brad will have his hands full keeping them away from you."

"Brad?" She swung back to stare at Edmund. "Why would you say that? The man hates me."

Edmund reached over and took her hand. "When it comes to love, you're as innocent as a child. Remember, sweetheart, there's a thin line between love and hate."

Chapter Twelve

Just because they were at *Rué Chartress* was no reason not to exercise. They worked harder on Melissa's muscles. She could now stand for longer periods at a time. But Alexandria was strict. The child wasn't ready to walk just yet. Alex promised that she would help Missy practice walking once they returned to River Bends. And they made a pact not to tell Brad about her progress, so she could surprise him by one day walking through the door on her own.

The days seemed to drag by. The hot, sultry weather kept them inside and they hadn't ventured from the house since the day they went shopping.

Finally, the day of the opera arrived. Alexandria had tried taking a nap, but her thoughts kept drifting to Brad. Over these past few days he'd surfaced in her mind often. She stared out the window as she rested her head against the glass, wondering why he was so strong in her thoughts.

She couldn't possibly miss him--could she? Her life was peaceful without Brad--no arguments. No, she didn't miss him. He might be the best looking man she'd ever laid eyes on, but what else did he have? Wealth? ... Yes, more than anyone she had ever met. A nice home? ... Yes, he had that, too. A good disposition? ... Well, there she found a flaw. He was very hard to get along with.

Then why was she so attracted to him when it could only be a dead-end street? She rubbed her finger across the window ledge. Because there was a bond between them. A force so strong that sometimes Alexandria felt overwhelmed, and she didn't understand anything that was happening to her. But the man definitely affected her mind, because here she stood, once again having a conversation with herself. A few more months and she'd be absolutely batty.

The bedroom door squeaked behind her. "Dere you are, Petite. Have you forgotten de opera?" Hattie raised her brow in question, carrying an armful of freshly laundered linen.

"No, I've not forgotten." Alex turned from the window. "I'm getting ready to take my bath."

"It doesn't appear so. Have you rung fo' your bath water?"

"No."

Hattie shook her head. "You have a dreamy look in your eyes, cher. I wonder what has caused it?" She placed the linen on a chair. "I'll order your bath water and den be back to help you dress."

"I don't need any help."

"*Oui,* you will," Hattie said slowly. "I see we're a bit cross today, no. Dresses are a little more complicated t'an what you are used to," Hattie said calmly as she placed hairpins on the dresser for later. "You have been wearin' simple dresses without all de finery dat normally goes wit' dem."

"All right, Hattie," Alex conceded, thinking it better not to argue.

When the bathtub was filled, Alexandria wasted little time climbing into the bubbly water. The fragrance of roses surrounded her. Laying her head back on the porcelain rim, she let the warm water work its magic.

Hattie returned as promised, entering the room with an armful of crinolines, her eyes barely visible over the top of the cream-colored undergarments.

Alex finished her bath and stepped out of the warm water. Grabbing a soft, fluffy towel, she began to dry off. "Why do you have so many crinolines?"

"Fo' your dress, Petite."

"I won't need this many," Alex said as she looked at the mountain of petticoats piled high on the bed.

"Ah, cher, you're in an argumentative mood. Mebbe you miss Master Brad."

"I do not!" Alex snapped a little too quickly. "Why would you say that?" She hated when Hattie could tell what she was thinking.

"Why else would your disposition be so sour?"

"I can think of many reasons," Alex defended, then ventured down a safer path. "Has my gown come from the dressmakers? I've only seen Missy's."

"*Oui,* your gown just arrived, and I guarantee it to be dazzlin'. Start getting' dressed, and I'll be back in a moment. Den you can see fo' you'se'f."

Alexandria slipped on silky white stockings, followed by satin lace garters. "Mm, how sexy," she commented. She caught a glimpse of herself in the mirror. Her skin held a rosy glow from the warm bath.

Hattie burst into the room, her arms full of green silk. Her abrupt entrance pulled Alexandria away from the mirror. "Let me see." Alex held the dress up in front of her. "It's stunning. I don't think I've ever had a dress this lovely."

"*Oui*. But first de corset."

"I don't need that," Alexandria protested.

"Well now -- you might not need it, but it will make your dress fit perfect. Turn around," Hattie issued the command.

"You sure are bossy." However, Alex did as Hattie instructed and waited patiently while she threaded the corset. With each tightened loop, Alexandria felt her breath slowly leaving her.

"All right, hold your breath."

"Surely, you jest," Alex complained. "I don't have any breath left."

"Come, quit complainin' and take a deep breath." Hattie pulled hard on the ribbons. "You need a small waist to get into dis dress."

"How am I supposed to breathe?" Alex whispered.

"You're not, cher ..." Hattie gave one more yank. "Now, I've got it." She tied a neat bow in the back.

Alex looked in the mirror; she felt as if her stomach had been pushed all the way to her back. But look at that bustline! Unbelievable ... and so big!

Next came layers of crinolines. The top one was a beautiful beige. Alex slipped the emerald green overdress over her head. It was made of the sheerest silk organdy and fastened with pearl buttons. The very center of the skirt opened to expose many layers of flounce. Tiny seeded pearls were sewn on the edge of each ruffle. The overdress fit tightly under her bust, leaving the beige lace showing across the bustline and down the front. As a matter of fact, it appeared that if she moved the wrong way, her breasts would be exposed.

"Does this fit right, Hattie?" Alex asked, pulling the bodice up a bit higher.

Hattie slapped her hands. "*Oui*, you look lovely. Just you set you'se'f dere and let me fix your hair."

Alex couldn't believe the woman she saw in the mirror. She no longer looked like a modern woman--she'd changed. She reached up and touched her face. She appeared like any woman in 1835. Was that really her reflection? She watched Hattie brush her hair until it took on the silken sheen of rich burgundy. She swept her hair to the side and pinned it with a comb of pearls, letting the strands fall loosely over her left shoulder.

"*Oui,* you're most lovely, Petite. Dere won't be anyone who will touch your beauty tonight. Why, your eyes are de exact color of your gown. Dey sparkle like rare gems."

"Thank you." Alex realized she'd never had anyone tell her she was beautiful before. Hattie was just being kind. "Is Missy, ready?"

"Let's go and get her."

They found Melissa in her bedroom. She wore soft pink that looked very lovely with the child's complexion. She wished Missy was out of her wheelchair, but she looked enchanting just the same. And her bubbly personality never changed. Tonight her cheeks had taken on a rosy glow from her excitement..

"Alex, you're beautiful." Melissa clapped her hands together in excitement. "Madam Marie sure knew what color to pick for you. Did she also bring your dress for Brad's party?"

"I'm afraid not. It's not finished yet."

"Mine is gorgeous!"

"The gown you have on is splendid, Missy, but then you look lovely in everything."

"Oh, Alex, you're just being nice."

"I beg your pardon." Alexandria put her hands on her waist. "Have I ever told you anything that wasn't true?"

"Well, no."

"There you have it--you are lovely--and don't you ever forget it."

"I'll try." Melissa smiled. "Let's get Edmund."

A light drizzle fell as the group entered the carriage. The carriage started to move and Alex's stomach fluttered as she realized this would be her first time out at a public gathering. As the vehicle wound its way, through the narrow streets, Alexandria watched the shadows the gas lights gave off on the rain-slicked streets. She was glad for the coolness the rain had brought.

The coach stopped in front of the stone steps leading to the St. Charles

Theater. On the way over, Edmund had told them it cost $350,000 to build this little masterpiece. She smiled. In her time the building couldn't be constructed for less than a million dollars.

Alexandria and Melissa peeked out the window trying to get their first glimpse of the grand theater. They watched the coachmen take Melissa's wheelchair up the steps and into the theater. Edmund opened the door of the coach and scooped Melissa up in his arms, then carried her up the stairs and inside.

"Please help me down." Alexandria held her hand out to the driver. It was silly to wait until Edmund returned for her, when she was perfectly capable of walking herself.

"But, Madam!" The driver protested.

"Don't worry, I'll be fine." The drizzle had picked up, so Alex simply reached down and lifted her skirt and petticoats and ran up the stairs. She couldn't help thinking of Cinderella racing away from the ball.

Edmund had entered through the double doors and that's where Alex dashed, too. Of course, hers wasn't a ladylike approach to the theater, but she couldn't allow Edmund to get soaking wet because of her.

She brushed her skirt back down, trying to remove the raindrops when she felt someone staring at her. Looking up from under her lashes, Alexandria realized she had drawn quite a few stares from her hurried entrance. She heard the soft mummers and surmised she'd blown her introduction into New Orleans society.

"If you had waited, Madam, I'd have brought an umbrella for you. Then perhaps you could have made a more graceful entrance."

Alexandria stopped adjusting her skirt and froze when she heard the rich, smooth accusing voice of Mr. Wentworth.

The heat of a blush slowly covered her whole body. Brad had not bothered to keep his voice low, which only added to her embarrassment. She didn't want to draw attention to herself, but she intended to give Mr. Wentworth a piece of her mind, However now face to face with Brad, she found she didn't have a voice. She stared at him dumbfounded, as if she'd never seen him before. He looked different. He'd cut his hair and it appeared dark tonight; there were no blond highlights, and he had shaved off his mustache, which only enhanced his good looks. He was the tall, dark stranger Hattie had mentioned at the flea market. His dark sapphire-blue eyes held her completely captivated. Alexandria was dimly aware of a warm sensation spreading quickly through her body, and she cursed herself for her weakness. It was this damn corset cutting the circulation off to her brain. She felt her legs give and she reached out, grabbing his arm for support. It was all she could do to keep from screaming, *take me … I'm yours.*

He must have sensed what she was thinking. A half-smile touched his lips and a challenging look entered his eyes.

Alexandria managed to snap out of her stupor and glared at him. But before she could say a word Edmund and Melissa came over.

"I see you two found each other," Edmund said.

"You didn't tell me *he* was coming?" Alexandria's tone was accusing.

"I thought I'd surprise you." Brad answered the question meant for Edmund. "And as much as I would like to chat, I think we should take our seats before the first act." Brad motioned the group toward their box.

"Oh, Brad, I'm so glad you came." Stretching up from her chair, Melissa gave her brother an affectionate hug. "I've missed you."

"I've missed you too, puss." Brad kissed her on the cheek. "Shall we?" He motioned the way, tucking Alexandria's hand around his arm. "How about you, Alexandria? Did you miss me?"

"Don't push your luck," she snapped.

Brad laughed. "Ah, sweetheart, how I've missed your wit," he said.

"Where's Julia?

"Why? Jealous?" he whispered in her ear.

"No," she denied, trying to pull away from him, but it was no use; he had her firmly in his grip.

They stopped several times on the way to their seats. The men's' gazes glued to Alex as they talked to Brad. He said a brief hello and kept his group moving, promising he would talk more at intermission.

An usher pulled back red velvet curtains and they entered their box. There were four chairs, each covered with the same red velvet as the curtains. Brad lifted Melissa and placed her on one of the chairs. Melissa winked at Alexandria as she still pretended to be very helpless. She wasn't going to let Brad know how well she was doing until she could walk on her own.

Alexandria spotted a chair on the end next to Missy and started in that direction. Brad anticipated her move and grabbed her elbow. Firmly but gently, he escorted her to the seat next to his and handed her a program. Alex frowned at him, only to receive a smile in return.

She had never been to an opera before. Her own life had been spent working or studying and perhaps dinner or a movie every now and then. She sat on the edge of her chair, looking over the balcony. The theater looked like the ones she had seen in pictures except the people were dressed quite differently. The gowns were elegant and all the women wore the latest fashion for their day.

Glancing down at her program, she almost laughed. The thing was written in French, which would make sense because everyone who lived here spoke French. Even though she understood the language and could speak it a little, reading French was entirely a different story. Well, she could read one thing, the name of the opera, which was the Italian "Lucia di Lammermoor" by Donizetti.

She noticed the primitive gas lights. They hissed like a room full of snakes, and the way they sputtered she wouldn't be surprised if the whole place burned down. She'd be sure to keep an eye on them.

The orchestra started tuning up. Slowly the music began, softly at first, then building until the lyrics gathered in its audience.

Suddenly, the curtain went up, and she stared down at the brightly lit stage full of actors.

Alexandria enjoyed the music, movement, and color below her. Listening intently, she found she couldn't understand a word of the Italian opera. Perhaps, if she'd had practice coming to these things, she could follow this one a little closer. Tonight, she had done well to read the title, but she would never admit that to anyone.

Brad became a distraction as she tried to concentrate. His closeness was unnerving. She could actually smell the wonderful, manly fragrance radiating from him. A clean, fresh masculine scent, but not overpowering. She stole a swift glance at the dark figure who had his head turned speaking to Edmund. Well aware of his thigh pressed close to her skirts, she jumped every time he moved. Her attraction to him was useless to deny.

"Are you nervous, my dear?" Brad asked.

"Of course not," she whispered. "What makes you think that?"

"You keep fidgeting."

"Just a little warm." She fanned herself. "I could use a cool drink."

He put his arm on the back of her chair, then whispered in her ear. "I'll get you some champagne at the end of the second act."

Alexandria nodded as she gazed into Brad's vivid blue eyes. They looked as dark and stormy as the sea. It appeared he wanted to say something more when the curtain fell and the applause began.

"Brad, you really shouldn't whisper to Alexandria," Melissa scolded. "She'll miss what they're saying on stage."

"You're correct, Missy. I'll try to control myself until after intermission."

For the briefest moment, Alexandria wondered what Brad had been about to say, but the moment was lost. It probably hadn't been important, anyway.

"Let's stretch our legs and get the ladies some refreshments, Brad," Edmund suggested.

They all moved out into the lobby, where a crowd had already gathered. The room glowed with lights from numerous chandeliers.

A few young friends of Melissa's came over to talk to her, giving Alexandria a chance to look around. People stood clustered in small groups. The jewels that hung around the women's necks were extravagant, to say the least. Alex's hand brushed her neck. In her own time she wouldn't have been wearing jewels either, however there would be costume jewelry She felt a little plain in comparison.

Brad had been headed in her direction, but stopped to talk to several beautiful women. The ladies laughed and flirted over every little word Brad said. "Who are those women, Missy?" Alex couldn't help but ask.

"They're this season's debutantes. Brad is still considered the best catch by far until he marries."

Brad looked up and caught Alexandria staring at him. She wanted to look away but she was all ready caught so why pretend. He politely excused himself from the group so he could move on. "My lady, your champagne." He gave her a glass, his fingers brushing hers ever so slightly.

"Brad ... Brad," Melissa persisted until Brad finally looked her way.

"I'm old enough to drink champagne." The child frowned at the glass of punch Edmund had handed her.

"I think not," Brad lazily replied.

Melissa stuck out her bottom lip, but wisely drank the sweet beverage.

When they returned to their seats, Alexandria noticed a bottle of chilled champagne had been added in an ice bucket. Brad picked up the bottle, filling her glass. "Just in case you're thirsty through the second half." He winked at her.

She sipped the cool drink. It was very good and quickly went to her head. Champagne had never agreed with her, and usually she tried to avoid it, but tonight she was in need.

Since she didn't understand the opera itself, Alexandria listened to the relaxing music. As the aria started, she found her eyelids growing heavy. *This is so boring*, she thought. *And the balcony is so dark. I'll just shut my eyes for a minute.*

Brad's movement and the sound of applause startled Alex awake. My

God, she'd fallen asleep! She quickly jumped to her feet, clapping, thinking everyone else was standing. Now that she was awake, she found she was standing alone. Everyone else remained seated. Not to be embarrassed again, she shouted, "Bravo" and kept on clapping.

"Alexandria, I'm glad to see you enjoyed the opera," Edmund said.

"It was great!"

"And you grasped the meaning?" Brad asked, but didn't wait for her to reply. "Some people have a hard time understanding opera."

"Yes, I did," she informed him but she thought he gave her a funny smile.

In the lobby they waited for the carriage to be brought around. The rain fell harder now, but Alexandria didn't mind getting wet. She felt warm, and she didn't know if it was the champagne or Brad.

"Alexandria, will you explain one thing about the opera to me?" Melissa asked.

A stunned look was all Alexandria could produce. "I—I'll explain it in the carriage."

Brad picked Melissa up and covered her with his cloak. Edmund had already gone ahead. "Stay here," Brad told Alexandria. He smiled to himself; he couldn't wait to hear her explain the opera when he knew she didn't have the slightest idea what it was about. After all, her head had been on his shoulder.

Alexandria watched Brad place Melissa in the carriage and then run back up the stairs for her. She didn't dare dash out in the rain herself. She might not have made a graceful entrance, but she would exit like a lady if it killed her.

"Ready, sweetheart?"

Alexandria nodded and got ready to duck under Brad's cloak. Instead she was swept up in his arms and tucked under his cape. Alex's heart thumped wildly as she laid her head on his shoulder. God where had he been all her life. "I can walk, you know," came her muffled comments from under his jacket.

"And get your pretty feet wet?" Brad chuckled. "Not on your life."

"You're so gallant, sir."

"Precisely."

He ducked in the carriage and sat down with her on his lap. She scurried to climb off his lap to the seat beside him. Hearing his deep chuckle, it was all she could do not to punch him. He seemed to know how he effected her.

Huge droplets of rain ran down the windows of the carriage as it rocked over the bumpy road on the trip to Edmund's house. It had really been a nice night and she'd felt so elegant. Something she hadn't felt in a long time. Back in her own time, she'd never gone to a opera and now that she was thinking about it she really never did much of anything but work.

"That was a sad opera," Melissa said, breaking the silence.

"Yes, it was," Edmund agreed.

Great! Alexandria thought. Everyone understood that boring thing ... but me. She sure hoped Melissa forgot about asking that question. She would try not looking in her direction, but out the window instead.

"Alexandria, why did the woman go mad?"

Too late. Alex's head snapped around. "Because someone drove her over the brink." She was thinking of her own situation of course.

Melissa wrinkled her brow. "But, I wonder who?"

"Probably some man," Alexandria quipped.

"Why? I still don't understand," Melissa persisted.

"There were many reasons, but perhaps your brother can explain better than I can." Alex turned to Brad, hoping he'd take the hint.

"I wouldn't think of depriving you." He smiled, an evil gleam in his eye. "Go ahead and explain it."

"But--" A pleading look entered her eyes. "--I really have a headache from the champagne, and talking makes me a little queasy."

"Poor darling," Brad patted her hand. "Here, lay your head on my shoulder. You probably could use a good nap." He pulled Alex closer and draped his arm around her.

Damn, this was all she needed ... to be closer to *him*. And was that laughter she heard in his voice? He knew she had fallen asleep. At least she escaped making a fool of herself in front of Melissa and Edmund. Of course, Brad already thought her a fool. She laid her head on his shoulder, and listened to his deep, cultured voice.

"Well, Melissa, 'Lucia di Lammermoor' is a hot-blooded tale of passion and betrayal. It is based on Scott's Novel *The Bride of Lammermoor*. The opera is a splendid tale of skullduggery over forged letters and a false marriage contract. The heroine goes mad and sees visions of her deceased true-love. Now do you understand better?"

"Yes." Melissa sighed. "It's kind of sad."

"It's just a play, Missy," Edmund added, putting his arm around her. "Don't take these thing too seriously."

"I know, but to lose someone you love hurts a great deal." Sadness filled Melissa's voice.

They were all silent for the remainder of the trip, each lost in the meaning of the opera and their own private thoughts.

—)—

Upon reaching the house, Alexandria thanked Edmund and Brad for the evening, then went with Melissa to help her undress and get ready for bed. Once that was completed, she kissed Missy good night and then headed to her room. Exhaustion seeped through her entire body as she moved down the hallway. The champagne had relaxed her so she hope she wouldn't have any problems sleeping tonight. Entering her room, she saw a white satin gown laid out across her bed. It looked comfortable compared to the dress she had on.

Not ringing for help, she proceeded to disrobe. At least getting undressed was easier than dressing. Pulling at the corset strings was like releasing her body from a steel trap. She scratched her ribs as her circulation returned. That thing-- she looked at the corset laying on the floor--was as bad as panty hose. She slipped on her gown and sat on the bed, brushing her long, burnished curls, trying to remove all the tangles.

She heard a soft knock before Hattie entered carrying a steamy mug of coffee.

"Did you have a nice time tonight?"

"Yes, it was different."

"Here, I thought this would help you relax." Hattie handed her the cup. "I heard Master Brad accompanied you to the opera."

Alex took a sip of the warm liquid. "He was there."

Hattie looked at her for a few minutes when she didn't comment further. "Enjoy your coffee, Petite ... I'll see you in de mornin'."

"Good night, Hattie." Alexandria sighed, placed the coffee on the nightstand, then climbed into bed. She smiled as she heard the raindrops hitting the window. The weather this evening was much like the night that started her adventure. It seemed so long ago--another life--another time. That rainstorm had changed her.

She sipped her coffee and stared out the window, watching the rain drops bounce off the balcony railing. She thought about the evening. It had been both wonderful and disastrous. Why did she have to feel anything for a man she couldn't possibly have? She sighed, feeling melancholy. What's wrong with me? I never use to daydream as much as I do now. It was as if she left her drive and determination in the other century. Sitting her cup down, she slid under the covers.

She shut her eyes, but sleep was elusive. She rolled and tumbled, kicking the sheets off, then pulling them back up only to kick them off again. Finally, she sat up in frustration. "I want something, but what?" she whispered to an empty room.

A feeling of emptiness, confusion, and restlessness assaulted her all at one time. Throwing the cover off her body, she slid from the bed, her feet hit the cool floor. Just as quickly, she sat back down, giggling. Evidently, she had drunk more champagne than she'd thought because her head felt like it was someplace other than on her shoulders.

"Okay, stand up slowly." She laughed again. "Now, put one foot in front of the other."

There, now she would walk slowly down the stairs to the library. A good book was what she needed to help her sleep.

Chapter Thirteen

"Drink it," Hattie urged Brad. "It will keep your head from hurtin' in de mornin'. And, seein' as you've done in de bourbon, I think you'll be needin' it."

"Maybe I'd rather my head hurt," Brad grumbled sourly as he stared at the cup of coffee he really didn't want. He'd come to the library to be alone.

"Only a fool would utter a statement like dat. It appears you're tryin' to solve your problems wit' de bottle," Hattie shrewdly observed.

"Are you calling me a fool?"

"Well now ... dat's a question."

"Hattie, I've killed men for less."

"I'm sure you have." She wasn't the least bit intimidated. "But you know I speak de truth. Drink de coffee and believe me--it will brin' you what you need."

Irritated, Brad took a swallow of the hot brew, burning his tongue in the process. "Damn, it's hot!"

"I didn't tell you to drink it all at one time." She patted him on the back, trying hard not to laugh.

Coughing, Brad glared at Hattie with watery eyes. "Now you can call me a fool. That is the worst coffee I have ever tasted! It's bitter," Brad accused. "Are you trying to poison me?"

Hattie laughed. "Just tryin' to change your disposition. In de morning, you'll thank me."

"I wouldn't count on it. Go on, Hattie, and leave me in peace."

"Good night." Hattie turned to leave. "Remember, you won't solve your problems with liquor."

"I don't have any problems!" Brad shouted.

"If you believe dat, you really must be drunk," Hattie mumbled as she shut the door.

Brad stared at the closed door, then shook his head. He really needed to get rid of the sassy woman; at least he'd have some peace.

He sat on the couch facing the fireplace. If it had been winter, a warm fire would have been blazing, but it was the end of summer and the fireplace stood cold, black and empty--much the same way he felt at this very moment. Earlier he had cracked open the French doors, hoping for a breeze from the rain-drenched night. Now the sound of rain falling was the only thing that met his ears.

Having polished off half a bottle of bourbon an hour ago, Brad knew Hattie was right about his head hurting. But at the moment he didn't care, because he still hadn't found the numbness he sought.

The burgundy-colored liquid Brad swirled in his glass brought Alexandria's lush red hair to mind. She had been beautiful tonight, yet she seemed so unaware of it. She thought everyone was staring because of her manners, but in reality from the softly voiced comments he'd heard, they were stunned by her exquisite loveliness. How he longed to run his fingers through her hair, to hold her, caress her, and for just a few minutes forget who he was--and make Alexandria his.

The sound of the library door opening caught Brad's attention. Looking up, he blinked twice. The object of his thoughts now stood no more than ten feet away, and seemed completely unaware of his presence in the room. Had he merely imagined her?

Alexandria appeared ghostlike in her long, flowing, white satin gown. As she reached for a book, the candle highlighted the provocative transparency of her gown, revealing the curves of her body. Brad found he'd ceased breathing the moment she entered the room.

Adding to his discomfort, the moon cast a shimmering glow to Alexandria's hair, giving it the appearance of a smoldering fire. The cascade of hot coals burned down her back, begging to be touched. Her burnished red locks teased him to come closer. Would he be scorched by the burning fire?

He had to find out.

If Brad didn't know better, he would swear he'd been drugged. He ran his tongue over dry lips, thinking how desperately he needed a drink.

As he stood, his gaze never left Alexandria. He let his breath out slowly, trying not to scare away his apparition. Then, like a black panther stalking its prey, he glided across the floor.

—)—

Why did they have to put things up so high? Granted she was still a little wobbly ... well, a whole lot wobbly from the champagne, but still the book was out of reach. *I'll try one more time*, Alexandria thought.

Reaching up on tiptoes for the volume, she felt the warmth of a body behind her as an arm touched hers. She gasped, a scream hovering on her lips.

"Need some help, sweetheart?"

Alex recognized Brad's voice and relaxed, but for only a moment before a new sensation flooded her body.

"You scared me." She whispered.

"I'm sorry. Can I help you get the book?" Brad's left arm wrapped around Alexandria's waist. He reached up with his right to retrieve a volume.

"Yes, the blue one," Alex managed to choke out. Her voice shook, and her breath grew shallow when Brad murmured in her ear. His voice was a warm caress, and she sensed tenderness in his tone, making all her defenses crumble.

He retrieved the text and held it in front of her. "This one?" he questioned as his lips brushed the back of her neck.

"Yes," Alex murmured, completely wrapped in the spell he was weaving around her. She knew she needed to leave. She didn't belong in this man's life, but she'd been too lonely to deny herself the solace of his closeness.

Her senses began to whirl. A tingle went down her spine and she felt light-headed as her traitorous body started to quiver. At the mere touch of his hot breath, her flesh broke out in goose bumps.

Brad made no move to let her go. It wasn't Julia that made his blood roar or turned him into a clumsy oaf when Alexandria was near him. It was this woman. She trembled beneath his fingers--a quivering she couldn't hide from him--and he knew she felt the same things he did. Alexandria definitely had become a fever in his blood. There was a something special about her, touching a place deep in him that he couldn't deny. How could he leave her alone? In a moment of weakness he softly spoke. "Turn around, sweetheart."

The book slipped from her grasp and landed with a thud at their feet as she turned to face him.

Brad bent down and placed a feathery kiss on her forehead, the tip of her nose, and, ever so slightly, he brushed her lips. "Look at me, Alexandria."

Slowly, she opened her eyes and found herself looking into pools of blue, and what she saw startled her. The candle had burned lower, but she could still see the passion that burned in the depth of Brad's eyes. She should be scared ... but she wasn't. God help her, she liked the feel of him. Gently, his hand caressed her back, and she became lost ... helpless, drowning in the erotic feelings he produced. She felt as if her every nerve was exposed. Slowly, but deliberately, he pulled her into his sensual spell.

Alex was drowning and now had lost all control of her body. She seemed a mere puppet in Brad's hands. He awakened a part of her that had lain dormant until now. She had dated a few men, but they had never broken the protective barrier that she'd erected around herself.

He pulled her toward him until she could feel his hardness, and she knew he had succeeded where others had failed. And no matter how wrong this relationship was, she could deny him nothing.

Brad watched her intently and moved cautiously, afraid of scaring her. Lower and lower his hands moved down her back, pressing her tighter against him and liking the way she fit next to him. The results were exactly what he wanted. Alexandria's eyes had become a green liquid fire. Everything about her felt right, as if she belonged to him in some special way, and for just a moment he experienced an odd niggling--he'd waited all his life for this woman. He didn't just want this woman, he needed her like he'd never needed anyone. She ran her tongue over dry lips to moisten them. Soft and pink, they beckoned him.

He now knew his betrothal to be a fake, but he'd deal with that later. He had to get Alexandria out of his blood. She seemed to be the only one who could quench his thirst, because his thirst was for her.

Brad took her lips, expecting only to receive a meager kiss, but instead she parted her lips with a naturalness that fueled the fire building in him.

Alex kissed Brad with all the passion that burned in her soul, and heard his growl as he tightened his arms around her. The sweetness of his embrace intoxicated her. The smell of him--that masculine scent drove her crazy. His magnificent kisses were firm and demanding as he ruthlessly plundered her mouth, leaving her breathless.

He left her tingling lips for a moment to kiss the soft lobes of her ears, whispering her name over and over again. "My sweet Alexandria, send me away--tell me you don't want me." His voice was a plea for her to save them both. "This will never work."

Alex needed to touch his skin. She reached up and started unbuttoning his shirt. She had heard Brad's whispered words, and knew everything he said was true. Nothing had been right since she'd slipped back in time. She would lose her virginity to someone who didn't even exist. But at this very moment she didn't have time to think logically. For once in her life, right or wrong, she'd grasp for the moment.

She knew it would never work between them, but right now she didn't care. No one could kiss her like this and feel nothing for her. She had kissed men in the past, but never like this. She wanted more!

Brazenly, she slipped the silken gown from her shoulders, letting it crumple at her feet. She pressed her breasts against Brad's chest, placing sweet kisses on his throat.

Brad shook as he looked at Alexandria with a strong intent before wrapping his fingers in her hair, and pulling her head back. He trailed kisses down her neck to her shoulders and finally her ripe, round breasts, which enticed him way too much. He began to fondle the soft mounds with his tongue, caressing and licking each one. Finally he took one hard red peak into his mouth, and heard her satisfying soft moan as he hungrily sucked her burning flesh. Tenderly, he made her body come to life beneath his mouth and masterful hands.

Alex moaned and arched her back. Somewhere in her fog-filled mind she felt herself being picked up and carried to the couch.

Even the weather seemed a seduction as the sound of rain drifted in through the open French doors. Brad kneeled on the couch, then laid her down while he finished undressing himself.

Alex lay on the couch, watching Brad. Her eyes toured every inch of his muscular, bronzed body. His physique was perfect with wide shoulders and slim hips. He was definitely every inch a man.

Brad's manhood throbbed with the want of her. Quickly, he joined Alexandria on the couch, pulling her next to him, fitting her hips snugly against his. He decided the couch was too small, and in one swift movement rolled them both to the floor.

Alexandria never noticed. She was caught in Brad's intimate web, and heard nothing but her heart hammering in her chest. She wanted and feared him at the same time. He had branded her with a kiss that she'd remember the rest of her life. She arched her hips instinctively toward him, and he eagerly accepted the invitation.

Brad needed her now, desperately, urgently. He wanted to go slowly, but he burned with desire. Spreading her thighs with his knees, he positioned himself and readied his entrance into her warm flesh. With an awesome thrust, he pushed and at the same time increased the pressure of his mouth on hers. He barely felt the membrane tear until it was much too late.

Forcing his lips from hers, he heard Alexandria whimper. He was stunned, then overwhelmed with a primitive stirring he'd never experienced. Tenderness filled him, but the words were lost on his lips when Alexandria pulled him back down to her.

Brad started to move slowly, letting Alexandria adjust to his size. She tensed with pain, but he kept the rhythm steady and soon the discomfort eased. Left in its wake was a want for something, but she wasn't sure what. Alex's hips started to move with a rhythm all their own as she met Brad's driving body. She wrapped her legs around his waist, taking all of him inside her.

An animal growl came from Brad as the urgency increased. "Sweetheart, you're driving me crazy!" His breathing became heavy, labored, and his head spun. By God, he was coming apart!

A white heat started to build in her as jolts of pleasure made her heart beat faster. Brad's thrusts became stronger. When Alex thought she could stand no more, the sensation inside her exploded, fulfilling her body with the satisfaction she craved. She clung to Brad, pressing tighter against his hard frame never wanting this special feeling to end.

Completely exhausted, Brad collapsed on Alexandria, his head resting on her chest. He could hear the pounding of her heart beating as fast as his. He was thoroughly exhausted and ... completely satisfied. Strange, but he'd never felt like this before. With a contented sigh, he relaxed. Feeling Alexandria's fingers running through his hair, he wondered what her thoughts were at this moment.

Alex felt much the same way, floating on a cloud of contentment. She was tired now as she absentmindedly ran her fingers through Brad's hair. Their lovemaking had been wonderful, and more satisfying than she'd ever thought possible. She had always dreamed the first time would be like this--that her lover would tell her how much he loved and adored her--he would tell her how beautiful she was, and she would be his forever.

However, reality settled in and Alex remembered she had heard none of that. No promises, no declarations of love, only passionate lovemaking.

Then, like a door slamming shut on her utopia, she remembered Brad's words, 'This will never work,' deep down she knew he was right. Tonight had been wonderful, and tomorrow there would be time for regrets, but for now she would enjoy her small piece of heaven.

Brad rolled over, pulling her beside him. For just tonight she would pretend Brad loved her, pretend he needed her, and when tomorrow came, she'd deal with this problem, just like she had all her other problems.

The library door softly opened and Hattie poked her head around the corner, then smiled to herself. She had done her part. It would be interesting to see how these two would handle their--how should she say--situation. Of course, she was getting ready to throw them a curve.

Hattie scooped Alexandria up in her arms and carried her back to the bedroom. Hattie tucked her into bed then glanced down at Alexandria, noticing how contently she slept. The child needed to find happiness. She needed to release all her painful memories, because she had so much to give to the right person.

Likewise back downstairs, Hattie dressed Brad the best she could. Between the liquor and her potion, he was dead to the world. But what a smile he had on his face. She chuckled. Just wait till morning ...

Hattie's cackling could be heard all the way out the door.

Alexandria stretched like a lazy cat and rolled over in bed. She blinked several times at the bright light invading her room. She wanted to sleep some more snuggled next to Brad.

Brad? ... Alex jerked straight up in bed, glancing next to her. She was alone, but last night ... Holding her head in confusion, she leaned back against the headboard and tried to think. What exactly had happened last night? She remembered going to the opera and having champagne ... lots of champagne. She remembered coming home and going to bed ... So far so good. She hadn't been able to sleep, so she had gone downstairs to the library. Or had she? Alexandria wasn't sure now. Perhaps it had all been a dream. She looked down at her gown. Yes, she still wore it and she really didn't feel any different.

Could their lovemaking have all been a dream? If that had been a dream, it was one vivid illusion. Alex blushed, tingling at the thought of last night.

The door swung open. "Good mornin', Petite," Hattie cheerfully greeted as she entered. "Did you sleep well?"

"No!"

"Oh, did you have a bad dream?" Hattie folded back the bedspread.

"You might say that."

"You want to talk about it, cher?"

"No ... yes ... Hattie, have you ever had a dream so real it scares you?" Alex looked up at Hattie.

"I have." Hattie patted her hand. "But remember, tomorrow always comes to chase de demons away."

"I wouldn't be too sure of that," Alexandria mumbled as she slipped out of bed.

"Now, Petite, it's a bright sunny day--let's see a bright sunny face. Everyone will be waiting for you at breakfast, and I've already ordered your bath."

"Ouch!" Alexandria squeaked.

"What's wrong?"

"I feel a little sore." she rubbed her backside. "You suppose I fell out of bed?"

Hattie laughed. "That's possible, and in your condition you probably would have never known it."

Alex chuckled, too. "I guess you're right."

"Take a hot bath, cher. It will make you feel much better."

An hour later, Alex sat soaking in the tub. Her thoughts in turmoil. How could a dream seem so real? But it had to be a dream.

She would watch Brad at breakfast and see if he acted different.

Brad awoke with a stabbing pain to his right temple. "Damn, how much did I drink last night?"

He sat up and noticed his shirt was unbuttoned and his pants were on. Where was Alexandria? He grinned, thinking of their wonderful lovemaking. Looking around, he saw no trace of her. Why would she get up and leave?

Someone cleared their throat, causing Brad to turn. "Breakfast will be served soon," Hattie announced.

"Don't you ever knock?" Brad barked. "And keep your voice down."

"*Oui*, we testy dis mornin'?"

Brad looked at her through blood-shot eyes. "I thought you said I wouldn't have a headache?"

"My coffee didn't work, no?"

Brad sat on the couch, bent over, holding his head. "Does it look like it helped?"

"You look a sight dis morning. What did you do? Wrestle with somebody?"

He laughed, then stopped because it only made his head hurt worse. "I thought I did."

"Well, you better get cleaned up fo breakfast."

"Hattie, have you seen Alexandria this morning?"

"*Oui*, she's takin' her bath. Do you want me to get her fo' you?"

"No! I'll see her at breakfast. That's soon enough."

"You want me to help you upstairs?" Hattie chuckled.

"No, Hattie! Go find something to do and someone else to torment."

Brad heard the door shut, and he glanced around the room. That was no dream! But Alexandria was up in her room as if nothing happened. Could he have been so drunk that he had conjured the whole thing up? If so, he was in damn bad shape and probably needed to get married as soon as possible. But why hadn't his dream been of Julia?

He stood up and started buttoning his shirt. What was this? He saw a small drop of blood no bigger than a smear on his waist. Funny, he didn't remember cutting himself, but then again he was having trouble remembering anything. He glanced over at the bookcase. There lying on the floor was a blue book.

The hair stood up on the back of his neck. Was it possible? He walked over and replaced the book on the shelf.

"All right, was it real or merely a very vivid dream?" Brad said out loud. He would watch Alexandria at breakfast to see if she was different.

But, first, he was going to drown himself in a tub of hot water ... .

Chapter Fourteen

Alexandria stood just outside the breakfast room door, trying to build her courage to go in. She wasn't sure what she would say to Brad; that is, if her experience hadn't been a dream.

"Good morning, beautiful." Edmund leaned over her shoulder; Alexandria jumped, bumping his chin.

"Edmund, you startled me."

"I'm sorry, sweet." He rubbed his chin. "A bit jittery this morning aren't we?"

Alexandria smiled. She wouldn't touch that question if her life depended on it.

"Let's go in and have some breakfast." Edmund slipped his arm through hers, and she had no choice but to move forward.

The breakfast room smelled of bacon and ham. Melissa sat next to the doors that lead into the garden. She seemed preoccupied as she gazed out the door. Brad stood next to her, cutting a striking figure in his brown trousers and cream-colored shirt. Alex's stomach took a nose-dive straight to her feet.

He turned at the sound of the door opening. "Good morning, Alexandria." His voice came out slow and lazy. "Sleep well?"

She felt her cheeks grow warm. Did he mean anything by that remark? She searched his eyes for clues, but found none.

"Yes, I slept very well, thank you," she replied. For a moment she thought she read puzzlement deep in his eyes, but when she looked again, his expression had become totally unreadable.

"What a pretty dress, Alex," Melissa said. "I can't wait to see the one you've ordered for Brad's party. Whoops," she rushed on evidently realizing her mistake. "Let's eat ... I'm famished."

"That's a good idea, Puss," Brad agreed.

Alex took a seat and spread the napkin across her lap to cover her watered-silk dress. She wanted to look pretty today, so she had chosen a bright apple-green dress. But she wasn't getting the response from Brad she'd hoped for. Perhaps last night had all been a dream induced by champagne.

The conversation flowed around Alex, while she remained lost in her own thoughts until she heard Edmund say, "We'll take Alexandria with us."

"Take me where?" she questioned Edmund.

"To the slave auction."

"Why?"

"Why are we taking you, or why are we going to the slave auction?" Edmund laughed.

"Both."

"We're taking you because you're beautiful, and you'll be nice to look at." Edmund teased her.

"Be serious."

"Alex probably doesn't like such things, Edmund," Melissa said. "They are not the nicest place for a lady to go."

"Have you ever been to a slave auction?" Brad asked her. Alexandria looked radiant, captivating him with her sparkling eyes as she looked straight at him.

"No."

"Then perhaps it will be interesting. I have need of an additional man," Brad explained. He really hadn't planned on taking Alexandria until Edmund had issued the invitation. Brad needed some distance from her. He'd hoped for some clue to the mystery of last night, perhaps a dazzling smile this morning, to confirm he'd not been dreaming. But she sat in front of him cool and collected, eating her breakfast. Was his mind playing tricks, or was she?

"And you're planning on buying this man?" Alexandria asked.

"Yes, if there is one worth buying."

He noticed the horrified look that slipped into her eyes, and wondered if her family owned slaves.

"We are talking about people, not animals," she said. "Do you really believe that humans should be bought and sold?"

"Personally ..." Brad stared at her a long moment, thinking her statement odd. Slavery had always been a part of the South. Come to think of it, he really didn't know where she was from, but her voice wasn't that of a Yankee. The vibrant sparks in her eyes warned him a fire could easily be started. "I don't believe in buying and selling people. That's why I let slaves buy their freedom later. They earn wages for the work they do. But, Alexandria--" he reached out and took her hand, "--this is the way of the South, and we do what has to be done to survive."

"I see. But that still doesn't make it right." Alex felt like she was coming apart, because Brad still seemed no different. She'd been right. Last night had all been a dream.

The trio rode to the warehouse located down by the wharf. From the number of buggies and wagons gathered by the time they arrived, today's sale had drawn a big crowd today. The auction house was a huge gray building with tall archways on both sides. When they entered the building, it took several minutes for Alexandria's eyes to adjust to the dim light.

She followed Brad and Edmund behind a small platform. In the back there were stalls sectioned off where black men and women were chained by their ankles. Some stood while others sat on the straw in holding pens. The musty smell of body odor came at Alex from every direction. She observed the prospective buyers as they inspected the slaves.

How sickening! she thought, but she was careful not to say anything; this wasn't her century, but it made her steam nonetheless.

Each slave was made to hold up his head and walk briskly back and forth. Alex saw overseers examining the slaves' teeth; much like a person did when buying a horse.

Disgusted, she looked away, noticing a black man in a stall by himself over to one side. He wasn't chained to another slave, but was alone. With his head propped up against the wall, he stared at her with a silent plea for help. Something about him was unusual. Most slaves wouldn't dare look at her for fear of being beaten. Yet, this man refused to cast his eyes to the floor. Alex had started toward the black man, when a gentleman she'd not seen until now stopped her.

"You want to buy him, lady?"

Alex looked at him skeptically. "Who are you?"

"I own the darkey." He had his thumbs looped in his britches. "And

I'm here to tell you he'll be a good worker now that he's broken in good and proper."

"He looks sick."

"Well, he's a bit under the weather, but he'll be a good one." Still, the man stood, blocking the entrance.

Alex tried to sidestep him. He didn't budge. "I suggest you move out of my way, so I can see for myself."

"You alone, lady?"

"I don't see that that's any of your business; however, I am with friends. Shall I get them for you?"

"No, lady. T--that's all right." In a blink of an eye, he left her.

Alexandria knelt beside the black man and placed her hand on his forehead. "You're sick, aren't you?"

"Yes ma'am." He nodded. "Not feeling too well."

Right away she noticed he spoke differently from the other slaves she'd encountered. His voice was more cultured and minus the heavy Southern accent.

"What's your name?"

"You can call me whatever you like, ma'am."

His lifeless voice was void of all emotion. Alex wondered just what this man had been through. "No. What is your *real* name?"

He seemed to study her through dark and doubtful eyes. "You seem like a nice lady, but--down here in the South, you don't trust nobody."

"I understand." Alex patted his hand. "That's okay."

"My name's Abraham."

"How long have you been sick, Abraham?"

"For about two weeks, ma'am ... Can you help me?"

"I'll try ..." Alexandria broke off when his owner came back.

"Lady, you'll have to go around front." The owner stood at the gate behind her. "It's time for the auction."

"But, this man is sick!" she protested. "Look at him. He's dehydrated and needs medical attention."

"Don't really care, lady!" He moved toward her. "If you're not going to buy him, then get around front!"

Roughly, he yanked her up by the arm when she refused to move.

"Get your hands off me!" Unsuccessfully, she tried to jerk her arm away from him. "I intend to help this man!"

"Like hell you will!" He squeezed her arm painfully.

She stomped his toe.

In retaliation, he slapped her, and sent her sprawling to the floor.

As Alexandria pushed the hair from her face, she heard a grunt. The man who had hit her was now sprawled on the floor in front of her, and she was being hauled up by one arm.

Brad brushed the dirt tenderly from her cheek. "Are you all right?"

"Yes, I'm fine." Even though her head still buzzed from the blow, she wouldn't let Brad know. Alex moved her jaw, making sure it still worked, then brushed the straw from her skirt. Once again, she had caused a scene although she hadn't meant to. She only wanted to help the sick man.

"I demand satisfaction!" the man on the floor shouted out to Brad.

"And you shall receive it, after I've bought a slave," Brad told him matter-of-factly.

Brad took Alexandria by the arm, escorting her none-too-gently to the front of the stage, where the bidding would take place. "Just what were you doing back there?" Brad demanded. "I can't take you anywhere without you getting into trouble?"

"The man ..."

"The man didn't have your welfare in mind, madam." Brad didn't bother to let her explain. "Come on, the bidding has started."

With a superhuman effort, Alex bit her tongue to keep from arguing. Automatically, he had assumed everything was her fault without hearing her side. She was so angry with him, she wanted to stop dead in her tracks. And her cheek still stung, too. But she didn't want to miss the bidding on Abraham, because she intended to buy him.

Alex stood between Brad and Edmund, watching the auction. Brad put her in the middle to make sure she didn't disappear again, or so he'd said.

Edmund inquired where they had been, only to receive a scowl from both.

Almost thirty slaves had been sold. Children brought the highest price. The cries of their mothers echoed in the room when they were sold to different buyers. It was heart wrenching, yet no one seemed to care.

Finally, Abraham was brought up on the platform. He tripped on the last step and fell. The man who had hit Alexandria was quick to give him a vicious kick. Abraham stood up before he was kicked again and climbed onto the platform. Even though Abraham was underweight, it was obvious that he had once been a big, strong man.

The auctioneer pointed to Abraham. "All right, gentlemen, what do I hear for this fine specimen?"

"Fifty dollars."

"Gentlemen, gentlemen, this man has only been sick ... he's not dead. And when he's well, what a slave you'll have."

"One hundred." The bid came from a man in the front row.

"Two hundred." Was heard from the far left.

"Two hundred. Do I hear more?"

"Five hundred," Alexandria called out, much to the surprise of all the men in the room.

"Well now, it seems the little lady would like her own slave." The auctioneer laughed and several other gentlemen chuckled.

"Five hundred. Do I hear more ...?"

No response. The room fell quiet.

"Five hundred once, five hundred twice, five hundred ... sold to the little lady with the red hair."

Alexandria breathed a sigh of relief.

"Would you care to tell me what that was about?" Brad inquired, still in shock from her bidding, and even more surprised that he hadn't tried to stop her. Women didn't bid at auctions ... women didn't do any of the things this hardheaded lady did.

"You said you needed a slave."

"But I intended to pick him myself, or didn't that occur to you?"

"He's sick, Brad, and needs help. Surely, even you can understand that."

Grabbing her arm, he pulled her to within inches of his face. "Madam, I'm not heartless!"

"Good. Then you understand why I bought him."

"And just how do you intend to pay for your purchase?"

"With your money. I left my visa card at home."

"Visa?"

"Sorry, I can't even begin to explain plastic money to you."

"You spend my money even though you're not my wife. Madam, you take too many liberties," Brad told her. Actually, he wasn't angry anymore, finding himself amused at the situation. The woman standing before him was the most puzzling female he'd ever encountered. Plastic money – who'd ever heard of such a thing? He never knew what she would do next.

"Well, you can take it out of my pay."

Brad laughed. "Has it ever occurred to you that you may be in my employ forever?"

"No, it hasn't. I'll pay you back every last cent," Alex said sincerely. *If it kills me*, she added silently.

"I can think of some interesting ways you could pay me back." Brad thought of last night. In his dreams she'd been a warm giving person. One he wanted very badly. He saw her as he had that night--the moon cast a shimmering glow to Alexandria's hair, giving it the appearance of a smoldering fire. The cascade of hot coals burned down her back, begging to be touched. He wanted this woman way too much for his own good.

"Excuse me." Edmund cleared his throat. "If you two don't mind, I think it's time to collect your property."

Brad paid the auctioneer and helped Abraham to the buggy. Both Brad and Edmund could now see the man was very ill.

"Edmund, would you accompany me for a moment?" Brad asked.

Edmund did as requested and followed Brad over to a stranger who stood inside the auction house entryway.

"I believe earlier, sir, you asked for satisfaction," Brad stated bluntly.

"That's right. The name is Charles Lawson. I don't believe I know your name, sir?"

"Wentworth Brad Wentworth." He watched the flicker of recognition cross Lawson's face; other than that he showed no outward emotion.

"Mr. Wentworth, I believe the choice of weapons is yours."

"Weapons? What's this about?" Edmund demanded.

"I need you to be my second."

"Of course, but why?" Edmund asked.

"I'll explain later."

"Mr. Lawson, I will let the choice of weapons be yours. After all, it is your funeral." Brad stared at Lawson, never flinching a muscle.

Charles Lawson swallowed hard. "I've heard how deadly you are with pistols, so I'll chose swords, especially since I am a master swordsman. Rapiers at dawn."

Brad nodded in agreement.

After Lawson left, Edmund looked at Brad and calmly said, "Can you tell me why we're defending your honor with the likes of him?"

"He challenged me."

"And you did nothing to provoke him?" Edmund asked.

"No. You can thank Miss Dumont for that."

"What could she have possibly done?"

"It seems they got into an argument over a slave ..."

"Don't tell me ... the one you now own." Edmund chuckled.

"That's right." They turned and started back to the wagon. "When I went to get Alexandria, I arrived just in time to see Lawson slap her."

"I'd have killed him!" Edmund's temper flared.

"You probably would have, and then I would have to defend you for murder." Brad slapped Edmund on the back affectionately. "However, I took a milder approach and merely hit him. I was willing to let it go at that, but the young fool demanded satisfaction."

Edmund started laughing.

Brad cut his gaze to his cousin. "And what do you find so amusing?"

"I've always admired the way you handle women. But I do believe you've met someone you can't handle, and somehow I find that very amusing." Edmund continued to laugh.

"Well I'm glad I can make you so happy," Brad said sourly. "But I beg to differ. I don't have a problem in handling Alexandria."

"No?" Edmund said wryly. "Then why do you now have an expensive and, I might add, sick slave in your possession?"

"Shut up!"

—)—

When they returned to Edmund's home, Alexandria went to the carriage house with Abraham. She didn't want him around anyone else until she'd made a diagnosis.

She knelt beside him. "How long did you say you've been sick, Abraham?"

"About two weeks ma'am. On the ship they said I had smallpox."

Alexandria's hands stopped her examination. Even though she had studied the illness in textbooks, this was the first case she'd seen. Smallpox was a highly transmittable viral infection. She could see the lesions on his face, forearms and hands. All the crusts had been shed, so he wasn't contagious, thank goodness. "Tell me how you felt."

"I had terrible pains in my head and back. For three days, I couldn't see at all. I've felt better the last couple of days." He shook his head. "I'm just weak--that's all."

"I'm sure you are listless. I'm going to give you something that will make you sleep." She reached in her black bag. "Perhaps the only thing you need now is rest. It seems you've been through the worst part."

"I hope so, ma'am."

"You're not from around here, are you?"

"No, ma'am. I'm from New York."

"How did you get so far south?"

Wariness entered his eyes. "You wouldn't believe me--nobody has."

Alexandria sponged his forehead as she talked to him. "If you don't trust me, I understand."

"You've been mighty nice to me, Miz Alexandria, but I've learned not to trust anyone who's white."

"Perhaps in time you'll change your mind." She looked at him and smiled reassuringly. "If so, I'll be glad to listen."

Abraham studied Alexandria with his doubting, dark eyes, wondering at this strange lady who'd come to his aid. Why was she being so kind? He hadn't met any other white people that were nice, that is, unless they wanted something. Should he trust her, and tell her his secret? As it turned out, he didn't have to make that decision, because a stout black woman entered into the barn to stand beside Alexandria. The woman stared down at him. She was pretty, Abraham thought.

"What's wrong wit' *him*?" Hattie asked. "Why hasn't he been brought to de house? Looks mighty poorly and ragged. Doesn't Master Brad know better than to buy someone who is sick?"

"He's had smallpox," Alexandria replied.

"What! Den what's he doin' here, and what are you doin' wit' him? Don't you know you could die?

"I'm a doctor, Hattie. And I'm used to taking care of people when they are ill--or have you forgotten?"

"I don't want you to catch somethin', cher. Master Brad would have a hissy fit. I'll stay here and watch him, you hear."

"Rest your ruffled feathers, Hattie. Abraham is over the contagious stage. He has been very ill and needs some rest, that's all. Don't you think you could be a little nicer to him?"

"Hum, probably just some old black trash," Hattie mumbled to herself. "De man looks old, but I'll tend to him. And I promise to be nice," she added begrudgingly.

"Thank you. Besides, you don't have to worry about me getting sick. I've been vaccinated for smallpox."

"You've what?"

Alex smiled at Hattie, not particularly feeling the need to explain about vaccines. She was tired. Today had been trying to say the least, and last night's hangover wasn't helping either. "Never mind, Hattie. Just trust me. I can't get smallpox."

"All right," Hattie agreed as she sat down. "But tell me what happened today. Master Brad seems in a foul mood! Did I say seems? --how about is in a foul mood. He said somet'ing about fighting a *duello*, which means dere was some kind of trouble today."

Alexandria looked stunned. "Duel? But why? Brad did hit a man, but that's no reason to shoot each other."

"Ah, Petite, dat's plenty reason to demand a fight."

"I do remember the man saying something about satisfaction," Alexandria admitted.

"Do you know why Brad hit him?"

Alex avoided Hattie's inquiring eyes. "Yes."

Hattie raised her eyebrow as she scrutinized Alex's worried face. Hattie sensed Alexandria was involved. It would be the one reason Brad would fight. Hattie's silence lingered, and Alex finally had to look at her.

"The man hit me."

"In dat case, Petite, I don't blame Master Brad. But why did he strike you?" Hattie took Alex's face in her hands, examining her cheek.

"I was trying to help Abraham when the man started arguing with me. But I don't want Brad to fight him. I'll just talk him out of it."

"It's too late, Petite. They have already left and will not be back until mid-morning tomorrow."

"But this is so silly!" Alex stood up. "You don't kill people o--over something so frivolous. Where have they gone?"

"To practice der fencing. It's been a long time since Master Brad has had to handle a sword. Most of his duels have been wit pistols."

"You mean he does this all the time?"

"No. But dere have been a few other times."

"Well, I've got to stop them! Will you take me to the place in the morning?"

"I don't think dat's wise."

"Please, Hattie, I don't want Brad hurt," Alex urged. "It was nothing worth a man risking his life for."

Hattie gave her a faint smile. "*Oui,* I'll take you, but I warn you now; Brad will not like it. Now go and get some rest, and I'll sit wit' Abraham. So far he seems to have caused more trouble t'an he's worth."

Abraham had been all but forgotten. The medicine already taking effect, he was sound asleep.

Chapter Fifteen

"Where is this place?" Alex asked.

Hattie clicked her tongue and the horse started through the gates of *Rué Chartress*. "We're goin' to a place where flared tempers find dere satisfaction, Petite."

"Oh, my God! We must hurry." Alex reminded herself someone could get killed. She gripped Hattie's arm. "This whole thing is crazy! It wasn't that big of a deal. Can't they just forget yesterday?"

"Honor is not taking lightly, cher. In New Orleans, *duello* is most common, and the reasons can be many. From a breach of etiquette, a suspicion cast of unfair dealings, aspersions against de moon." Hattie moved her arms in a sweeping motion. "De night, de temperature, or almost anythin' can provoke a challenge," she finished, simply.

"What can I do to stop this cold-blooded behavior?"

"De game is deadly, cher, resultin' in death, but in dis case, Brad is defendin' your honor." Hattie shook her head. "Dere's little can be done."

At the mention of death, Alexandria felt the color drain from her face. Her stomach clenched. She had seen death in the hospital many times before, but the thought that Brad could die made her sick. What was she going to do?

The short ride only took a few minutes. Maybe she could somehow stop all the craziness. She had to do something. She could see the Dueling Oaks, their twisted branches hung thick with Spanish moss, and the two black buggies already there.

Hattie had barely stopped before Alexandria scrambled out of the buggy, scattering the fog hovering just above the ground. She ran around to the front side of Edmund's carriage and found Brad talking to Edmund. Thank goodness, she was in time.

Alexandria grabbed Brad's arm, gaining his attention. "You cannot do this!"

"What are you doing here?" Brad snapped.

"Trying to stop this nonsense. The man only struck me. I assure you I will live. But that's no a reason to risk your life!"

Brad's eyebrow shot up. "You have little faith in me, my dear. You seem to assume it will be my death."

"That's not true." She shook her head. "I do have faith in you but--"

He placed his fingers under her chin. "But, what? Are you afraid for me?"

His breath was gentle and warm, and Alex found she couldn't speak. Despite her twisting emotions, she could only stare into Brad's mysterious blue eyes, knowing she would die if he was hurt. "Please don't do this. I'll apologize if necessary."

Brad rubbed his thumb tenderly across her chin. How he would love to take her in his arms and kiss her. This crazy desire he felt for her would one day be his undoing. But hopefully not today.

Before he gave into his desire, he withdrew his hand and stepped away, turning to Hattie. "Hattie, why did you bring her out here? I'd have thought you had better sense."

"Because she told me to. Since I'm a slave, I always do as I'm told."

"You're only a slave when it suits you. Now take her home. I don't want her here!"

"I'm not going anywhere." Alex's words sounded shaky. "If you're hurt, I'll be able to take care of you."

His gaze shot to her. "Sweetheart, there is no hurt, only death ... now go home!"

"No!"

Brad saw the stubborn tilt of her chin. She was much too pale. What in the world did she expect? He didn't want her to see the ugliness of bloodshed, but she seemed determined. He stared at her for a long moment before he shrugged his shoulder and gruffly said, "Suit yourself." He turned abruptly and walked away.

Alex and Hattie climbed back into the carriage where they could observe the two men as they met in the middle of the field. The sun, just coming over the crest of the hill, caught the reflection of the razor-sharp blade of the rapier in Brad's hand. He flexed the saber, testing its weight and balance.

Lord, Alex hoped he knew how to use the thing. She found herself twisting her hands. Something she'd never done before. Even at a time like this she noted how dashing he looked. He was so much a man in every sense of the word. His dove-gray pants molded tightly to his muscular legs. He wore a white shirt with billowing sleeves and a pair of shiny black boots that came just below his knees. There was a hardness in his face. His movements precise. He definitely looked like he meant business.

Four men and a referee stood in the middle of the field, conversing. The men nodded. Alexandria assumed the referee was explaining the rules. The seconds withdrew. Everything was ready. Silence surrounded the clearing as she drew in her breath, willing Brad all her strength.

The adversaries crossed blades in a salute, and the duel began. The deadly sound of clanging rapiers echoed through the stillness of the morning, sending chills down Alex's spine.

Charles Lawson launched his attack on Brad, showing unexpected dexterity as Lawson thrust his rapier at him, catching Brad's shirtsleeve. Taken by surprise at Lawson's skill, Brad moved slowly. He barely stepped aside in time, just missing Lawson's blade as it sliced again through the sleeve of his shirt.

Alex jumped up. She almost fell off the carriage, but Hattie steadied her and cautioned her to be quiet, so as not to distract Brad.

It seemed like forever while the two swordsmen fought. Brad gained control, and appeared to be wearing his opponent down. He was powerful and quick and now attacked Lawson with a series of lunges.

"I hadn't thought you to be so skillful," Charles grated out.

The cold steel tip of Brad's sword entered Lawson's body. Charles gasped and grabbed his wounded shoulder, then smiled at Brad in a mock salute. "Go ahead, sir, and finish the deed." But Charles' legs gave way and he collapsed on the ground.

Brad stepped back, withdrawing his blade. The doctor, who had been standing with Edmund, examined Lawson, then announced he would live to see another day.

"Such a waste," Brad said, turning and walking toward the carriage and Alexandria.

Stunned, Alexandria couldn't believe what she'd just witnessed. She had read about duels and watched fights on television, but nothing had prepared her for this. The books made it sound romantic, but in fact …

it was murder or be murdered. This time Brad chose to let his opponent live. She knew fighting was the way things were done in this lifetime, but still...

Brad stood in front of her, his eyes unreadable as he stared. A muscle twitched in his cheek and his eyes reflected cold blue steel. Alexandria trembled under his scrutiny and found she couldn't speak. What could she say to a man who could have lost his life over her? She sense Brad could be very dangerous. She realized that in this time period, the strongest survived and the weak perished.

"Senseless killing has never sat well with me," he stated, still staring at her. "Madam, I have now killed a man and wounded another for you!" Brad's strained voice carried a hint of anger. "Hattie, take her Rué Chartress and get ready to return to River Bends."

Finally, they were home. And yes, River Bends did feel like home, Alexandria thought as they rode up the drive. She had been quiet for the duration of the trip. Brad's words kept running through her mind. One person had lost his life and another could have, all because of her. Perhaps, she was more trouble than she was worth. Of course, she hadn't told Brad to defend her, and she couldn't understand why he was so angry. She had been taking care of herself for years, and she could do so now without his help.

The carriage and the wagon carrying Abraham stopped. Brad had chosen to ride his horse, leaving the ladies to the carriage. She thought the idea splendid, especially since she didn't want to talk to him. If she admitted the truth, she was embarrassed by Brad's sharp words from this morning. Yes, some of the situation had been her fault. However, she'd needed to rescue Abraham. He might be just one slave, but at least she could do some good while she was here.

She watched Brad dismount and walk over to open the carriage door, still clothed in the same garments he'd worn this morning--the blood stains a small reminder of what he'd done for her. She wished she didn't experience this giddy feeling every time she looked at him. She used to keep better control of herself, but lately--

Alexandria noticed the square jaw that proclaimed his stubbornness, but his sensual lips, as always, were compelling, and she found herself thinking of her dream against her will. If her dream had been real, Brad would be everything she'd ever wanted. Even though they clashed at every given moment, she knew she'd always want a strong man.

"Alexandria," Brad said as he held his hand out. She placed her hand in his and moved to the carriage door. His strong muscular fingers encircled her waist as he lifted her down to the ground. Her body brushed against his, and she felt as if she'd been jolted, so much so that she stepped quickly away. Why did he affect her like this? She cursed her traitorous body. She wasn't some silly schoolgirl.

Brad picked up Melissa, and took her into the house, where he sat her down in the wheelchair. Alexandria, having followed him, leaned over and helped straighten the child's clothing.

"Brad, darling, you're home."

Alex flinched. There was no mistaking that screeching female voice.

"I thought you were going home?" Brad accepted Julia's kiss on the cheek, which was his duty.

"What happened to your arm?"

"I had a small mishap. Don't worry, it's not my blood."

"But--"

"I had to fight a duel on Miss Dumont's behalf."

"Why, I never! *She* is trouble, darling. That's twice you've been hurt because of *her*."

Brad almost laughed at that statement. Miss Alexandria Dumont was definitely trouble in more ways than one. He wasn't quite sure how he was going to handle her in the future, but the woman needed to learn to obey him. "I repeat, I thought you were going home."

"I decided to wait, darling, so you could take me home. Besides, I need to get the feel of my new domain. And now that you're here, I'll get to spend some time with my future sister-in-law."

Alexandria watched Missy frown and stick out her tongue; thankfully, the child was blocked from Julia's view.

As Alex straightened and turned, she took a deep breath, putting on her most dazzling smile. "Julia, what a surprise. Did you miss us?"

Julia's face turned beet red. A sneer twisted her lips as she spoke. "Of course, I missed my family, but I had plenty to do trying to get this house in shape. You have a very stubborn staff, Brad."

The front door slammed shut and everybody turned at the sound.

Hattie had ridden in the wagon with Abraham, and had just entered the house. "And what's wrong wit' my house?"

"Your staff is quite disagreeable, Hattie! I'd have thought you'd have them better trained!" Julia lifted her nose just a little higher. "You should have something done with them. Why, they didn't obey a single command."

"Hum ... strange ... I don't have any trouble," Hattie told her. She looked at Julia as if Julia was completely stupid.

"Well, it must be, because you're one of them." Julia stressed the word *them*. "Changes will have to be made after we're married, Brad."

"I might be colored like all de other servants, but I assure you, we speak and understand English." Hattie stated each word very plainly. "I've been runnin' dis here house fo' a good many years without any problems. De staff probably didn't follow any of your commands because you're not de Mistress of River Bends!" Hattie said the last a little louder. "You are only a temporary guest who can be evicted at anytime." Hattie's eyes glowed embers of red as she stared at Julia.

Julia took a step closer to Brad.

Alex stood behind Melissa, enjoying every minute of this exchange. She had never seen Hattie so angry. Trying to keep a straight face was getting harder by the minute. Her money was on Hattie. *That-a-girl, get her.*

"Brad!" Julia clutched his arm. "Are you going to let her talk to me like that?"

"She's only telling the truth, Julia. The servants take orders from Hattie or myself."

"But what happens when we've married?"

"You and Hattie will have to work that out. And I wish you all the luck in the world." Brad frowned at Hattie for giving Julia a hard time. "I really need to talk to you, Julia. Meet me in my office I'll be there in a minute." But when he turned his back, Brad smiled and secretly would have loved to hug Hattie's neck. He resisted the urge and thought this was a good time to take his leave. There were other things to be done. It was time to get Abraham settled in. After all, a slave with the man's price tag deserved a nice home.

When Brad went to his study, Julia sat in a chair opposite his desk tapping her foot on the floor. He leaned against the corner of his desk, folding his arms across his chest.

"Julia, I know my father made a promise to yours, and I fully intend to carry through that agreement. However, I will not tolerate you pushing me into anything. Hattie has run this household since I was a child, and she does a darn good job." he took a deep breath, then ran a hand through his hair "I don't ever remember you complaining as much as you have lately. Maybe I really don't know you at all."

Julia came over to him. "I'm just anxious, darling." She wrapped her arms around his neck. "You know that I've had offers to buy the land, but I would never dream of destroying River Bends."

Brad took a deep breath. How his father had been so stupid as to make such an agreement, he didn't know. Half of River Bends had belonged to Julia's father, David Tucker, many years ago. Brad's father had ran into bad times and agreed to lease the land from David with the promise that their firstborn children would be married. If Brad refused to marry, Julia, the land then went back to David--and, since David was dead on to his daughter, Julia.

Brad had never had any doubts about this marriage, until lately. If he lost that land, he would lose the water rights and the brickyard, which help support the plantation when crops were bad. River Bends might survive, but it would be rough. He just couldn't let everything his family had worked and died for be destroyed. But he wouldn't let Julia push him, either. She couldn't sell until he said no.

"Julia, don't push me. Plan your party, but do get along with Hattie." He saw her smile and accepted her kiss, realizing he felt very dead inside.

Julia spent the rest of the day with Melissa and Alexandria. Julia watched as Missy went through her exercises. "I don't see why you insist on this silly routine. Seems such a waste of time. Everyone knows Melissa will never be able to walk again."

"If you can't say something positive." Alex looked at Julia, "you should leave."

"You forget your place, Miss Dumont!"

Alex gritted her teeth. *Her place.* How was she ever going to put up with this woman? She decided for the moment she'd ignore her, pretend Julia wasn't there, but it was hard. Every time Julia opened her mouth, something negative came out. Oh, how Alex would love to stuff a rag in the woman's mouth.

Missy started to say something, but Alex squeezed her arm. Julia wasn't worth wasting her breath on.

When dinner was announced, Alexandria pleaded a headache and stayed in her room. Let the others suffer Julia's company. Alex had had enough.

She waited until everyone had retired to their rooms before going down to the kitchen. "Hattie."

The black woman turned and asked, "Why weren't you at dinner?"

"I had a headache." Alex picked up a piece of bread.

"Are you sure you're not lettin' Miss Julia scare you off?"

Alex swallowed the dry bread and washed it down with a sip of tea before answering. "Of course not! I just didn't feel like hearing her mouth."

"Ah, you disappoint me, cher. I t'ought you had more gumption."

"I don't want to argue. I *do* have a headache and you're not helping it in the least." She said, accentuating the annoyance she felt with herself. "I came down here to ask where they put Abraham. Thought I'd look in on him."

"He's in de first cabin on de right." Hattie removed her apron. "Come on, I'll show you."

"I can find it."

"Maybe so, but you don't need to be out alone."

—)—

When they opened the cabin door, the soft glow of the lantern gave ample light to the neat, clean room. Abraham was propped up on some pillows, reading a book.

"I see you're feeling better," Alexandria said.

"Yes, ma'am. Still a little weak though, but with meals like tonight I'll have my strength back soon." Abraham smiled.

"What are you reading?" Alexandria asked.

"Poetry."

She cocked her head sideways to see the name of the book. "Where did you get a volume of Emily Bronte?"

"It's the one thing I've managed to keep hidden since I left home."

"Why are you readin' poetry?" Hattie frowned. "Such a frivolous pastime."

Abraham's gaze cut to Hattie. "Because I like it, old woman."

"Who you calling, old?"

"You." Abraham watched Hattie. "You're the crankiest thing I've ever encountered, old woman."

"Look Boy, you call me old one more time, and you're goin' to be sicker t'an you was." Hattie put her hands on her hips. "Perhaps it's de likes of you dat makes me cranky, you hear."

Abraham started to laugh, a deep laugh that was infectious. Alex began laughing, too.

Hattie attempted to keep a straight face, but couldn't.

"Come sit down and let me read you some of my poems." Abraham smiled at the reluctant Hattie. "You might find you like them ... just a little."

"You sure are a pushy scoundrel." However, Hattie sat down beside the bed and Abraham started reading.

> *Love is like the wild rose-briar,*
> *Friendship like the holly-tree--*
> *The holly is dark when the rose-briar blooms*
> *But which will bloom most constantly?*

Alexandria recognized the poem, titled *Love and Friendship*, and if she was right it just might apply to these two.

Abraham read smoothly and without hesitation. Once again Alexandria thought how different he was from the other slaves, and wondered where he came from.

After he finished the first poem, he glanced up as Alex waved goodbye and quietly shut the door. Just before the door closed, she heard Hattie ask Abraham to read her another poem. Alex smiled. They did make a very unusual couple.

Alexandria entered the house by the kitchen door. She stopped by the library and picked up a medical book called *Modern Medicine*. She smiled. This book would be an antique next to her medical books at home, but at least it was something to read. She left the library and climbed the stairs, thinking now lucky she'd been not to run into anyone. She really didn't feel like talking.

Her candle went out halfway up the stairs, and she stopped, laying her book on a step while she relit the wick. If they had electricity this wouldn't have happened. It was definitely an amenity she missed. Picking up her textbook, she tucked it under her arm, then she cupped her free hand around the flame, so it wouldn't go out again.

Upon reaching her room, Alex stretched to turn the doorknob when a noise down the hall drew her attention. She peered into the darkness. At the end of the hall another candle glowed, this one held by Julia dressed in a pink nightgown and looking very lovely. She turned her head and smiled at Alexandria as she twisted the handle on Brad's door and entered his room.

A pain stabbed through Alex's chest. With some effort, she remained calm. She twisted her own doorknob and forced her feet to move as she sought the safety of her room. Her hand trembled as she set the candle down, spilling hot wax on her hand.

"Damn." She gently removed the wax from her fingers, then put the injured spot to her mouth to stop the burning sensation. Hot tears ran down her cheeks. How silly to be crying over a burn, she thought. However, deep down she knew she cried for another reason. Here she was in the wrong century and in love with a man who would soon marry another. Alex had no right to feel any of the things she felt for this man. Brad had never made her any promises. He had only kissed her. Even in her dream, he hadn't promised her anything, nor spoken of love. Wiping away her tears, she started undressing.

She pulled back the covers and slid under the sheet, wondering if Brad was the tall dark stranger Hattie had referred to. If he was, Hattie's crystal ball had a short circuit, for it was Julia who had the tall, dark stranger ... not Alex. And, though she hated to admit, she was jealous. She had never been jealous before, and she didn't like the feeling.

She punched her goose down pillow in frustration. "He's probably returning the kiss, too! Damn him. Damn him to hell!" She quit assaulting her pillow, blew out the candle, and willed herself to sleep.

As she drifted off, she couldn't help wondering why she had dreamed of Brad in her own time. Had she secretly longed for this man so hard she'd been whisked back here? She'd been brought back for a reason. She knew Missy was one of the reasons, but Alex still felt there was something else. And, for the hundredth time, again she asked herself if she would ever return home.

Now she found she had another question--did she want to?

Brad wasn't in his room.

He lay on the couch in his locked study, thinking. It wasn't the first time in the last few days he'd asked himself if he was doing the right thing. Several months ago his life had been simple, everything planned out, and now second thoughts haunted him. Could he throw family honor out the door? Did he want to? Not having any ready answer, Brad shut his eyes.

He wondered if he would have the same dream again... .

Chapter Sixteen

Harvest time arrived with a flurry of activity at the plantation. Everyone pitched in except Melissa, but Alexandria kept her busy with their workouts. It was now time to put Missy's legs to the test. Alexandria hadn't forgotten the promise made in New Orleans. She fully intended to have the child walking but it would take some very hard work on both their parts.

Missy insisted her progress be kept a secret so that she could surprise her brother by one day walking up to him. Alex needed to have a set of parallel bars constructed without Brad's knowledge. But she couldn't make them, by herself. So now what could she do?

She thought about the question as she entered Abraham's small cabin. He had completely recovered, and his appearance had changed, too. He was taller than Alex had first thought, standing six feet one inch, and his shoulders were broad, but he'd lost too much weight. Those pounds would take time to recover.

"How are you feeling today, Abraham?"

"Just fine, Miz Alex." He stopped straightening up his cabin when she entered, and smiled at her. "Isn't it about time for me to be doing some work?"

"Sure. What kind of work did you do before?"

"I've done many things, Miz Alex, but my real trade is that of a carpenter."

Her eyes widened. Had she heard him right? "Did you say carpenter?"

"Yes, ma'am."

"Abraham, you couldn't have said anything I wanted to hear more. If I draw a picture, do you suppose you could make me something?"

"I'd sure try, Miz Alex."

"Look at this." She sat at the wooden table and sketched out the parallel bars she needed. "Here." She shoved the paper over to him. "What do you think?"

He studied the drawing. "This shouldn't be too hard atall. It's a mighty funny looking thing ... is it a hitching post?"

Alexandria laughed. "It does look like one, but it's an exercise bar for Melissa to practice her walking. We don't want them any taller than Missy's waist. Oh, one more thing, we must keep this a secret from Mr. Wentworth."

Abraham frowned. "I don't know, Miz Alex." He shook his head. "I sure don't want Master Wentworth angry with me. He might want me out in the fields where I belong."

"Nonsense." Alex started for the door. "I'll tell Brad I need a few things done around the house and since you're a carpenter...it will be the perfect solution."

Alex had been correct. When she asked Brad, he was so busy, he merely nodded his approval.

It was easy to get the work done without Brad finding out, because he worked in the fields from sun up to sun down. Melissa didn't even know what Alexandria was planning. She would wait for everything to be completed and then surprise her.

There was a room at the end of a hall, which really wasn't a room, but a small area in the eave of the house, located on the second floor of the sleeping wing. Missy said the space was what her mother had called 'her little sewing room.' Alex loved the chamber the minute she saw the cozy place with a large window that provided plenty of light. A rocking chair and a small table with a kerosene lamp stood by the window. In a corner, a quilting rack draped with a white sheet. Beside a small sewing table that held threads and yarn, there were three trunks that had belonged to Melissa's mother. It would take some cleaning and dusting, but Alex was determined to make it into a perfect exercise room.

Missy said Brad hadn't entered the chamber since their mother had died, so it was the ideal place for their secret exercises.

On one particularly bright sunny morning Alexandria decided

everything was in place, and it was time to surprise Melissa. They began their routine as usual.

"Alex, I can feel everything you do to my legs now. That's a good sign, isn't it?"

"Yes, ma'am, and I believe it's time to put these limbs to the test."

Missy's eyes widened. "What do you mean?"

"We're going to practice walking. Come on, I'll help you get in your chair."

"Chair ... but you said walk!" Melissa said.

"Be patient, young lady."

At the end of the hallway, she opened the door and pushed Melissa into the room, rolling the chair up to the parallel bars.

"Where did this come from? What is it?" Melissa asked.

"I had this," Alex swept her hand around, "set up just for your exercise. These bars are where you're going to practice walking."

"Now?"

"That's right. Here, I'll help you stand." Alex placed her hands under Melissa's arms and pulled her up, positioning her fingers on the bars. "Now slowly put your weight on your legs."

"Like this?" Melissa's voice trembled halfway between fear and excitement.

"That's right. Remember the bars are here to keep you from falling," Alexandria reminded her. "Can you feel your legs?"

"Yes, they're burning a little. It kind of feels like pins are sticking in them."

"That will go away. Just remember the pain is a good sign. Now, I want you to look down at your right foot."

Eagerly, Melissa followed the instructions.

"Wiggle your toes."

They stared at Melissa's feet. She could move her big toes only slightly. "I'm going to pick up your right foot and help you take a step," Alexandria told her as she squatted by her patient's feet. "Remember, concentrate hard, and tell yourself... I'm moving my right foot ... I'm taking a step. You have to convince your brain that you can walk."

"Why can't I make my foot move by myself?"

"Your brain has simply forgotten how to communicate with your feet, so we're going to retrain it. Now, we'll move your left foot just like we did your right, so concentrate."

Over and over again, Alexandria patiently moved Melissa's feet, constantly offering encouragement. After ten minutes went by, Melissa's legs developed cramps, and she had to sit down. Alex's nimble fingers massaged the cramps out of her legs.

"I'm so dizzy and tired, Alex. Can I go back to my room?"

"Of course you can. I think we've done enough for today."

After getting Missy settled in her room, Alex wondered what she was going to do. Hattie had gone with Brad this morning, so she couldn't visit her.

At loose ends, she paid little attention where she was going, walking right past her bedroom to the exercise chamber. The comfortable room invited her with its flooding sunlight.

"I meant to go to my room," she swung around, but on second thought decided to stay. She could see why Brad's mother liked it here. It had such a serene feeling. As she looked around the walls, she spotted the trunks. Earlier, she hadn't paid much attention to them, but now her curiosity got the best of her.

"Why not?" Alexandria decided. "I'll just do a little exploring." Maybe something in the trunk would tell her more about Brad's mother, after all, she had the afternoon to kill.

She sat down in front of the chests. The old brown trunk, trimmed with brass on all the edges, looked expensive. Made of sturdy oak, there was no heavy lock to bar the entrance, only a single gold catch with the initials 'CAW' engraved in the latch.

Funny, she didn't even know Brad and Melissa's mother, but somehow she felt close to the woman. Perhaps it was because they both disliked Julia.

The hinges creaked and groaned in protest as Alex opened the lid and propped it up against the wall. A layer of tissue paper protected the trunk's contents. She removed the tissue and the first thing she saw was a tiny beige dress. "This must be Missy's," she said to the empty room. It was a cute little gown, and just the thing a mother would save.

There were all kinds of trinkets. Among them Alexandria discovered a silver comb and brush that were wrapped neatly and laid in one corner. Laying in the middle on a red piece of silk was a picture turned upside down, she flipped it over. It must be Brad's mother because the name under the picture was Catherine Ann Wentworth. Catherine had been a very pretty woman with a radiant smile. Alex could see Melissa favored her mother, especially the blonde hair. Even though the picture was in black and white, she could picture her vivid blue eyes.

Alexandria sat for an hour looking at all the childhood trinkets. She was getting ready to put the picture back with all the clothes when her fingers brushed against a leather book. Grasping the book, she pulled it out of the trunk. Her breath caught in her throat. She'd done this very thing once before in a different century. Was this the journal that she'd bought with the painting? Turning it over, Alex saw she did, in fact, hold a diary, but not the one she was looking for ... this was Catherine's diary.

This journal probably has a lot of personal information, she reasoned with herself. She really shouldn't read it, but ... just maybe, she would find some answers to the many questions plaguing her. Alex carefully packed everything back into the trunk, all except the leather-bound book, which she put in her dress pocket.

Finding there was still plenty of daylight, she sat down on the rocking chair and began to read.

> *What a beautiful little girl I have. She has blond hair and beautiful blue eyes. Her smile reminds me of Brad when he was a baby. I hope she and Brad will grow up close. There is such an age difference between them. I worry about this.*
>
> *My little Melissa will grow up to be a special child, and I will always guard her secret.*

"Secret? What secret?" Alexandria laughed because as usual she was talking to herself. She wanted answers from this book, not more questions.

She turned several more pages. Some were faded and hard to read. Moisture had evidently gotten to the papers, causing the ink to run. She thumbed through the beginning, picking up words here and there, but stopped when Julia's name appeared on an entry.

> *Julia is a strange child. I've watched her grow up and yet still do not care for her. I had hoped she would one day take on the gentle nature of her father. Maybe, if her mother had lived she would have been different, but she is a schemer and not to be trusted!*

"I could have told you that, Catherine," Alexandria mumbled as she flipped through several more pages.

I regret that Brad ever made such a crazy agreement. People should marry for love. Brad seems attracted to Julia, even though, he has not said he loves her. Of course, I've always known she has eyes for Brad and my jewels. Sometimes I find her staring at them with such envy in her eyes. Do you suppose she would cut off my head just to get them?

I feel sad today. David died after a sudden illness. Julia said her father was delirious the last two days. She did stay by his side, and I truly believe she is saddened by his death. I have lost a very good friend.

Alexandria sighed as she looked up, and glanced out the window. It was getting late. She wanted to read more, but it would just have to wait. She placed the diary back in the trunk. It would have been nice to have known Catherine, Alex thought as she shut the door.

Back in her own room, she ordered a bath. The steam rose around her as she settled in the hot water. The weather was cooler now, and the bath helped take the chill out of her bones. The diary was still very much on Alexandria's mind. She had hurriedly scanned the book today, but she would go back and read again. She felt like she was getting to know Catherine, but it also brought up other questions.

What was the secret concerning Missy? Alex couldn't imagine. She did find the background on Julia very interesting. But she had been right. Julia was a true bitch, and it was hard to believe Brad was going to make her his wife. Just what kind of hold did she have on him? His mother had mentioned an agreement. That must have been the marriage agreement Missy had mentioned.

Alexandria dressed for dinner in a gown of deep-purple velvet cut fashionably to show off her slender figure. She brushed her hair back and let it hang loosely around her shoulders. Looking into the mirror, she pinched her cheeks, thinking of the tons of cosmetics on her bathroom counter. That life was beginning to fade with every passing day. Her cheeks took on a rosy glow.

It was quite as she walked down the staircase. She entered the dining room, and found Brad and Melissa already there.

"Good evening, Alexandria," Brad greeted as he rose from his chair.

"I'm sorry I'm late. The time just slipped by this afternoon." She took her place.

"What did you do?" Melissa asked.

"Do?" Alex felt herself blush. She couldn't tell them she'd been snooping. "I--I read a book."

"It must have been an interesting volume to make you forget about food," Brad's voice held an amused tone.

"Yes, it was." She wanted to steer them in a different direction. "Shall we eat?"

"Brad said they finished picking cotton today," Melissa cheerfully told her. Then she proceeded to fill her in on their previous conversation.

"I know you're glad. It seems like you've been in the fields for two weeks," Alex remarked.

"We have been." Brad said as he refilled his wineglass. "We're a little late harvesting this year, but we do have a bumper crop," he boasted.

Alex noticed how tired he looked. Of course, he always looked good, but the dark circles under his eyes spoke of the many long hours he'd put in the fields. Apparently they were starting to take their toll. She wondered if other plantation owners took such a personal hand in the crops. She was beginning to realize how much River Bends meant to Brad. When she came to this time, she'd thought of most plantation owners of being wealthy and spoiled. But a lot of hard work went into making a successful plantation and she admired these people more and more everyday.

When they finished dinner, Brad indulged in a glass of brandy, and Alex chose white wine. And, of course, Melissa had tea. As they sat talking, Alex's thoughts returned to the diary.

She thought about the bits and pieces she'd read in the book, then remembered Catherine mentioning her jewels a couple of times and Julia's greed for them. Alex wondered.

"Missy," Alex said. "You once mentioned how beautiful the jewels were that your mother wore. Can I see them?"

Brad's eyebrow shot up. "I have never seen you wear jewelry. "Do you like gems, Alexandria?"

"Of course I do. What woman wouldn't. Missy has raved about the jewels so much I must say my curiosity is up."

"You don't mind, do you, Brad?" Melissa butted in. "I know... I know you said not to brag, but it was just Alex," she explained in her childish way.

Brad frowned at his sister, "Come with me and I'll show them to you." He pushed Missy's chair and Alexandria followed behind them to his study.

Once inside, Brad went the wall behind his desk, and tapped a panel which popped open to reveal a safe. In a few minutes he had the safe door open. Then he pulled out a black velvet pouch and laid the bag on his desk.

"I've not seen Mother's jewels in ages," Melissa giggled. "It does look like my brother would let me wear them once in a while."

"You're too young, Puss," Brad reminded her as he opened the velvet wrapper, revealing two necklaces, a ring and several pairs of earrings.

Alexandria could do nothing but stare. To say she was looking at a small fortune would be an understatement. The priceless necklaces were beautiful, but one in particular stood out. A heavy gold necklace took her breath away, dazzling her with every precious stone one could imagine. A glorious marquise-cut diamond, a ruby, an emerald, a sapphire, a garnet, and an opal adorned the necklace. Each gem was surrounded by smaller diamonds. Suspended from the middle was an intriguing pear-shaped diamond that had to be at least four carats.

Alexandria reached out and touched the necklace. She had never seen anything so rare.

"Would you like to try it on?" Brad asked.

"No." Alexandria shook her head and jerked her hand away. She couldn't imagine wearing anything this priceless. "It's exquisite. I bet your mother was stunning wearing them."

"Mother was always beautiful," Brad admitted. "I think she'd have liked you."

Alex's stomach fluttered at the odd expression in his eyes as he looked at her. Could he possibly care just a little, and if he did--.

"There's a picture of Mother in the sitting room," Melissa interrupted. "Come on, I'll show you." They left Brad behind.

The house had so many rooms, it was not surprising Alex hadn't been in this particular sitting room before. When they opened the door it was dark, so she lit a candle before they entered the room, then proceeded to light several more.

"I've not been in here for a long time," Melissa told her. "Isn't Mother beautiful?"

Alex straightened after she lit the last candle, then turned toward Melissa. Her eyes traveled to what held the child's attention ... Catherine's portrait.

Alexandria gasped and momentarily forgot to breathe as she stared at the painting on the wall. She stumbled, then caught herself, grasping the back of a chair.

Slowly, she moved toward the painting.

"What's wrong, Alex? A--Are you all right?" Melissa's worried voice called to her, but Alex was too absorbed to answer.

She stood in front of the painting. Her lungs felt as if they would burst. She gasped for air. Reaching out, she touched the oils making sure the picture was real. At first glance Alexandria thought this was the painting she had purchased, but it was different.

"Alex, what's wrong? You look ill! Should I get Brad?" Melissa asked fretfully.

"No, Missy, I'm fine. Just give me a moment." Alexandria's words sounded weak. She felt again the foreboding, and it left her shaken.

It was uncanny. The picture could almost be a twin of the one at home. It had the same house, the same lake ... only the dark water held no reflection. The house had not been burned. It was completely untouched. And Catherine stood beside the lake, but there was no hat hiding her appearance. The dress... the dress was exactly the same.

How could two pictures look so much alike yet be completely different?

She now realized the painting ... the one she had at home, was of River Bends. She had suspected the painting could have something to do with her time-travel, but now actually seeing the painting confirmed that she had something to do with this house. She remembered how much at home she'd felt when she had first come here. But why was there no reflection in the painting?

The sad woman in her picture back home was still unknown. When Alex had first seen her picture she'd felt a strangeness, she assumed the dwelling had been through the Civil War. And that was why the woman has been so sad. But living her mystery, she knew it was too early for the Civil War. Alex frowned. How had she gotten involved in all this? The diary. It all started with the child's diary. River Bends ... a child. Alexandria's head started to spin and her face turned pale. Not a child's diary ... but Melissa's diary! Oh, my God! It was the diary all along. What part did she play in this? And why had she really been brought back to this house?

"Alex, you don't look well." Melissa sounded worried. "Brad! Brad!" she screamed.

He ran into the room. "What's wrong!"

"It's ... it's Alex, she's sick!"

Automatically, he noticed Alexandria's pale appearance and in three strides was across the room, catching her as she keeled forward.

"What's wrong?" Tears streamed down his sister's face. "I'd die if anything happened to her."

"Calm down, Missy. She's just fainted." Brad supported Alexandria as he bent her down from the waist slowly lowering her head until she came to and started to move.

"You're all right, sweetheart stop struggling."

"I'm sorry. I've--I've never fainted before," she said weakly.

Brad dried her face with his silk handkerchief. "You're not in a family way, are you?"

Her face turned a lovely shade of red before she spoke, "And who would the father be?" she asked.

Brad laughed. If his dream had been real he could be the father. Funny, it wasn't a thought that displeased him, but he had been teasing her. "Do you feel better?"

"Yes, but I'm so sluggish." She clung to his sleeve. "And I'm hot."

"What's wrong, Alex? Are you getting sick?" He watched Melissa wipe the tears from her eyes. She really loved the woman in his arms.

"If you have caught something from that slave you bought, he's gone from here!" Brad was serious this time.

"I'm fine. Perhaps, I got a little too warm. I'm not sick, nor pregnant, so you both can relieve your minds. If you don't mind, I think I'll get some fresh air." She tried to stand on her own swayed and reached for him.

"I'll go with you." Brad's held firm to her elbow. "Missy, would you like to go outside?"

"No, I'm going to bed." She rubbed her eyes. "Are you sure you're fine?"

"Yes, sweetheart. Don't worry about me." She bent down and kissed Missy on the cheek. "I'll see you in the morning."

Brad called a servant to help Melissa, then he and Alexandria strolled outside. A cool breeze stirred the night air.

Autumn's crisp air was approaching, and it felt wonderful after the hot humid weather of summer. There was a faint sound drifting in the air. Was it music?

"What's that?" Alexandria inquired.

"The slaves are celebrating the finish of the cotton season. Would you like to see? It can be quite festive."

"Yes, I would." Alex felt better now that they were outside. She wasn't even going to think of the painting or all the questions she needed explanations on. She had the feeling she'd find all her answers in time, and when she found her answer would she be returned to the present?

They walked down a shrub-lined path toward the slave quarters, listening as the music grew louder with a rhythmic sound of different drums. Brad still held her arm. She shivered ever so slightly.

"You are cold?"

"Just a little." Her voice trembled as she admitted the truth.

He stopped, pulled off his jacket, and draped it around her shoulders.

She smiled at his thoughtfulness. The warmth was welcome, but she felt guilty. "Thank you, but now you'll be cold."

"Not when I'm this close to you, sweetheart."

Chapter Seventeen

Flames of yellow and orange danced high in the air as a warm inviting bonfire flared in the middle of the compound. The small houses, once cloaked in darkness, came alive as the fires bathed the earth with an orange glow. As Alexandria and Brad drew near the festivities, it appeared that everyone from the plantation had turned out for the party. Women and children sat on blankets spread on the ground, the bright flames illuminating their round faces. To look at their smiles, one would never know they were slaves.

A table located on a side porch of one cabin displayed an assortment of meats and vegetables. From the appearance of the empty plates and satisfied smiles, everyone had already eaten and now enjoyed the merriment.

Tonight the slave's clothes were festive, not the drab everyday garments they usually wore. The women added color to the crowd by wearing brightly dyed scarves and ribbons tied around their waist.

Alex spotted an empty blanket and sat down. Brad took a seat behind her, so she could lean against his knees.

In no time, Alex became intrigued with everything going on around her. The older women chatted with each other while carefully keeping an eye on excited children running back and fourth. Their giggles had such a pretty sound as they played their children's games. These simple people had a joyous spirit, and Alex immediately felt a sense of family. No matter how poor they were, she saw they found happiness in the simple things.

The brisk music was different from anything she'd ever heard before. Of course, she was used to rock-n-roll, but this unusual beat came from hollowed-out logs and empty barrels with tight animal skins drawn across them. The sound reminded her of the Tarzan movies she'd seen as a child. The contagious, vibrant rhythm affected everyone, and she soon found herself swaying to the music.

Both men and women, young and old, danced--not together but separately. Bare feet stomped the ground and callused hands clapped a unique rhythm in time with the drums. Everyone seemed caught in the exotic drumbeats as they twirled around the fire. One woman, in the middle of the group, caught Alex's eye. Dressed in an orange skirt and a bright yellow blouse, she wore scarves in a mixture of both colors tied around her head. Her expressive movements were fascinating. Layers of skirts swirled around her ankles as she moved closer and closer. The flames enhanced her dark golden skin, giving it the appearance of pure bronze. Alex strained to see the woman's face before the dancer turned in her direction. Hattie! Tonight she looked so much younger than her years.

Hattie came to a standstill when she spotted Alex. A slow smile appeared on her lips, then Hattie began dancing once again, moving closer until she could reach her hand out to Alexandria.

Alex shook her head, refusing the invitation. She'd never been much of a dancer in the past, and when it came to rhythm she'd definitely missed the boat.

"Come, Petite, let your soul free."

Alexandria stared into Hattie's yellow-green eyes, mesmerized and once again under her spell ... She stood slowly. Her cheeks flushed hot and she was no longer in control of her body. Hattie pulled Alex's skirt up, tying it to the side, exposing her long, shapely legs. Hattie moved her out toward the glowing fire.

"Watch my eyes, cher. Let de rhythm enter your body."

Alex observed Hattie's movements. Hesitant at first, Alex began swaying her hips just as Hattie had done. Alexandria closed her eyes and let her head roll slowly around to the pulsating sound of the drums. Feeling the vibrations of the instruments enter her body, she became lost in the music as she danced and whirled. The chill in the air was all but forgotten, even the diary had been forgotten. There was nothing but the music.

"Open your eyes, Petite."

Soot black lashes fluttered open searching the crowd until Alexandria met the ice-blue eyes of her enemy ... her friend... her love. Her shyness vanished. Brad's thoughts were unreadable as she danced before him moving in a slow, sensual rhythm. The liquid green fire deep in her eyes couldn't be smothered by the clear blue gaze that now held her captive.

Intrigued, Brad watched the flirting enchantress who enticed him as she circled the fire. Her auburn hair took on the colors of the fire as she swirled, and for a minute she appeared part of the flames. He felt his arousal as her dreamy gaze locked with his. Was she dancing for him? Seeing her outstretched hands, he knew he couldn't refuse her.

Standing to his full height, he left his jacket on the blanket and moved toward her. Teasingly, she drew close to his body, lightly touching his arms, his chest, and lingering only a moment before she backed away again. Brad heard the slaves clapping in the background, giving their approval of the two white dancers. The heat of the fire grew intense, or at least he thought it was the fire that caused the sheen of perspiration to form on his brow.

She twirled in front of him again, leaving the air full of her fragrance. It was everywhere. And it was a scent he now knew all too well. She rolled her shoulders, revealing the creamy mounds of her breasts. Damn, he wanted her.

"Kiss her ... kiss her," the slaves chanted.

Brad needed no encouragement. He pulled Alexandria to him, crushing her against his hard chest, and captured her soft mouth in a smoldering kiss. His hot kiss became demanding as he pushed his tongue past her lips to the velvety smoothness of her mouth. Her lips tasted as sweet as honey, a true nectar from the gods. He, too, was caught in the primitive beat of the music, and found he wanted to tear off her clothes and view the magnificent body he imagined lay hidden beneath.

Lost somewhere between heaven and hell, Alex yearned for the things this man could do to her body. And she was in hell knowing that shortly he would belong to Julia, and Alex would have to leave River Bends. But right now nothing mattered. Her senses pounded. How could he kiss her like this when he had plans to marry another? Did he feel nothing but lust? It was thrilling, the sensual desires Brad produced in her body. She wanted to shove him away and pull him closer all at the same time. One thing was certain, she couldn't think straight when he was near her.

Faintly, Alexandria heard Hattie clear her throat. Placing her hands on Brad's chest she pushed hard to put some distance between them. She dared to meet his gaze. There was something in the depths of his eyes-- tenderness--pity--she couldn't be sure. But it was quickly replaced with a heartwarming smile. Anxious to shatter the awkwardness, Alex was relieved to hear Hattie clear her throat again.

"I believe dat was a good luck kiss fo' your up-and-comin' marriage," Hattie said.

Alex stood dazed and not quite in command of all her faculties. A few moments passed before she realized Hattie was trying to help her out of an embarrassing situation. She saw Brad frown at Hattie's remark.

"Exactly," Alexandria said. Her voice sounded a little shaky. "And I wish you all the luck in the future. I'm sure you'll need it," she mumbled under her breath.

Brad gave her a lopsided grin. "I like the way you wish me luck."

"Would you care fo' some food and refreshments?" Hattie asked, steering Brad away from the previous subject.

"No, we have already eaten."

"In dat case, you're just in time," Hattie announced.

Alexandria looked puzzled. "In time for what?"

"A weddin'. Liz and John have decided to get married, and we need Master Brad fo' de ceremony."

"Wouldn't it be better to have a priest?" Alexandria couldn't see what Brad would have to do with a marriage ceremony.

"You forget, cher, we're slaves. Most slaves are never allowed to marry at all, but Master Brad has given his permission, and dat's all we need."

Brad bent down and whispered so only Alexandria could hear. "Lord and master, don't forget that."

"Give me a break!"

"What?" Brad asked, puzzled.

"Never mind. You wouldn't understand." She looked around. "Where's Abraham?"

"I tried to get him to come to de gatherin', Petite." Hattie frowned. "But he refused. Why don't you try and convince him he should join us? I t'ink he's in his cabin."

"I'll go find him."

Alex left the group in search of Abraham. She didn't understand why he wasn't outside with the others. Reaching the cabin door, she knocked and heard his call to enter.

Not giving Abraham a chance to say hello, she got straight to the point. "Why aren't you outside?"

"Because I haven't been working with the other slaves. I don't seem to fit in."

"Oh, I never realized." She frowned. "I'm sorry, Abraham. I just thought keeping you around the house would make it easier on you, not harder."

"I know, Miz Alex, and I appreciate it. You're the nicest lady I've met." His eyes glistened with sincerity. "You've done a lot for me."

"There is something about you that's different, Abraham. I can't put my finger on it, but you're not like the others."

"Suppose I do owe you an explanation."

"No, Abraham, you don't owe me anything."

"Come sit down, Miz Alex." His gaze followed her as she took a seat. She thought he looked hesitant.

"You see, I'm not a slave, or at least I wasn't until about a year ago. I was born and raised in Massachusetts. I was a carpenter there."

"You're from the--"

Abraham held his hand up. "Let me finish." He folded his hands back on the table. "One day a friend of mine told me about a card game down by the river. It sounded good to me, so I went with him. It turned out to be the last I ever saw of home." Abraham sighed. "After we got there, we were hit over the head and knocked completely out. I awoke bound and gagged and on my way to Mississippi."

"That's terrible!"

"Miz Alexandria, you don't know the half of it. Can you imagine having your freedom taken away? Can you imagine never having anyone listen to what you have to say, and being treated no better than an animal, and sometimes worse? You're white... you'll never know," he said in all sincerity.

Alex looked at his downcast eyes. He was correct; she couldn't possibly know how he felt. "I guess you're right, Abraham. Have you told anyone you're free?"

"I tried at first, only to be beaten senseless. After a while you kind of give up and just try to survive day to day."

"Brad's not like the other slave owners." Alexandria laid her hand on Abraham's arm. "I'll talk to him, and ... " she never finished her statement because a girl's piercing scream came from behind the cabin.

Jumping to her feet, Alex flew out the door and ran around to the back of the cabin, Abraham at her heels. The overseer, John Rivers, stood over a slim black girl. He held a brown whip loosely in his right hand. Before they could stop him, he brought the lash down on the girl's back. Screaming and crying, she begged him to stop. But Rivers only laughed. Once again he raised his hand.

"Don't touch her!" Alex screamed.

Abraham grabbed Rivers' arm from behind. Rivers struggled, trying to break the hold, but Abraham was too strong.

Alexandria ran to the girl and picked her up, brushing the dirt from her clothing. Quickly she steered the girl away from the two tussling men.

Abraham wrapped his arms around Rivers' leg and pushed him over backwards. Immediately seizing the advantage, Abraham put his foot on Rivers' neck and he was left powerless.

"How would you like to feel the bite of this whip?" Abraham snatched the lash from Rivers' hand and threw it to the ground. Alex could see hatred pouring out of him, and she realized the beatings he'd probably endured.

Rivers fought with all his strength, but he couldn't break Abraham's hold. "You'll not live another day!" Rivers swore.

Brad, Hattie and several slaves came running.

"What's going on here?" Brad roared, pulling Abraham off Rivers.

"I'll tell you what's going on," Alex said. "Your overseer was whipping this girl." She pointed at the woman who clutched her torn blouse. "I thought you told me you didn't beat slaves."

Brad noticed the crowd that had already gathered, and he glared at Alexandria for being so direct in public, which did little for his disposition. Didn't she know her place? She was after all, a woman.

At the moment, however, he had other problems. He turned his attention to Rivers and Abraham. He saw the whip lying ten feet away. Once before Brad had suspected that Rivers used a whip, but when he'd confronted him, Rivers had firmly denied the accusation. That time Brad had believed him, but now the lash was in full view. Besides, Alexandria wouldn't lie to him.

Before Brad could speak, John Rivers scrambled to his feet. "You black son-of-a-bitch, I'll kill you for touching a white man." He slapped Abraham hard, sending him to the ground.

"I think not." Brad's voice had a deadly calm about it. "Is that your strap?"

"Sure is."

"I told you a long time ago, Rivers, I don't believe in whips. If you cannot control a man other than beating him, then in my eyes you are not much of a man. And you, sir, are no longer in my employ!"

"But, Mr. Wentworth, I can't believe you'd take a slave's side over mine. This man attacked me! I knew he'd be trouble the minute I saw him." Rivers spit at Abraham. "He's too uppity for his own good."

"Go pack your things, Rivers. I expect you to be off my plantation by sunrise."

"You've not heard the last of me, and you ..." Rivers pointed to Alexandria. "You're the cause of this, and I promise you'll pay!"

Brad grabbed Rivers by the shirtfront. "Don't threaten the lady if you wish to live beyond tonight." He shoved the man away, sending him sprawling to the ground.

Getting up, Rivers brushed off his clothes and glared one last time at Alexandria before stomping off.

Alex shivered at the hatred she saw in the man's eyes. That man was mean. She was glad Brad had fired him.

When everyone had left, Brad turned to Abraham. "I want to thank you for stepping in and taking up for Ruby, but in the future perhaps you'd better get me first. If you had been anywhere else, it could have gone hard on you for hitting a white man. Now go on and forget about tonight." Brad reached over and slapped Abraham on the back.

"Wait, Brad," Alexandria interrupted. "I want to tell you something." She told Brad everything Abraham had said to her.

Brad listened patiently. "Is this true, Abraham?"

"Yes, sir."

He looked at Abraham intently, rubbing his chin. "I'm sorry, Abraham. Tomorrow I'll draw up the papers and arrange for your passage home. From this moment on, consider yourself a free man once again."

"Thank you, Master Wentworth." Tears glistened in Abraham's eyes. "I know you paid a lot of money for me I'd like the chance to work off my debt."

"That's not necessary, Abraham."

"Yes, sir, it is."

Brad smiled. "I like your grit. Can you read and write?"

"Yes, sir."

"Do you think you could handle the job of overseer?"

"Yes, sir, Master Wentworth."

"Then you have a job."

Abraham smiled and shook his hand. "Thank you. You won't be sorry."

"Call me Brad."

"Good night, Master Brad." Turning to Alexandria, he said, "Thanks, Miz Alex." Abraham shuffled off into the dark, heading back for his cabin.

Tears trickled from Alexandria's eyes. She was happy for Abraham and proud of Brad.

Brad stood and watched the tears slide down her cheeks. His brow shot up. "Didn't you want me to offer him a job?"

She nodded her head yes, sending the rest of her tears tumbling down her face.

"Then why are you crying?"

Alex could only stare at him. At this very moment she could swear there was a halo over his head. She ran to him and threw her arms around his neck. "You're wonderful," she mumbled into his chest. She heard the deep rumble of laughter, a rich, enduring sound that she liked very much.

"Sweetheart, it's about time you realized that fact." He bent down and kissed the top of her head, hugging her close to him. "It's probably best I'm leaving in the morning."

Chapter Eighteen

Two weeks had passed since Brad had taken the cotton to New Orleans to sell, but before he left he'd made good his promise to Abraham who now held the role of overseer for River Bends.

Abraham was doing a good job, too. The other slaves appeared to like working for a member of their own race. They worked twice as hard, and, to show his appreciation, Abraham pitched in by helping them make repairs on their houses. He also kept a watch on the big house while Brad was gone, so Alexandria got to see him often. She wondered if there were other reasons Abraham liked to visit the big house.

It was late when Alexandria went down to the kitchen to see Hattie. Alex opened the door and smiled when she found Hattie in a brightly colored dress.

"What's that smell, Hattie? Are you making a cake?" she asked. "Something sure smells awful sweet."

"What smell?" The sassy woman looked at her like she was absolutely crazy. Then looked around the counters to see if she could see anything.

"I can't put my finger on it, but it smells ... like vanilla to me."

Hattie frowned. "Why, dat's me you smell. I use vanilla fo' fragrance," she explained. "Don't you like it?"

"Yes, I do, and I bet the person you're going to see will, too." Alexandria gave her a knowing smile. She knew Hattie wasn't dressed up for nothing.

"Who said I was goin' to see somebody?" Hattie snapped.

"Well, you have on a pretty dress and your hair is fixed special. I'd say you have a hot date."

Hattie blushed profusely. "Can't I get gussied up without someone makin' a fuss? You'd think it was a crime to look nice once in a while." She opened the door, still mumbling to herself. "Good night, Petite."

"Good night, Hattie. Tell Abraham hello."

"Hum." She shrugged her shoulders. "I will if I see him." Walking down the path, Hattie was still mumbling. "Nosey child, she's just guessin'--dat's all."

Alexandria kept herself busy while Brad was gone. Melissa still needed the rails for walking, but by the time of the party she would be strolling on her own.

Until now, Alexandria hadn't had a chance to pick up Catherine's diary, but tonight she had purposely retired early. She propped her pillows up behind her and opened the book to the place she'd marked.

> *Melissa is such a joy to me. She is sweet and affectionate, like her father. I love to watch her with Brad. Her eyes tell me how much she adores him. I think he will always be an idol to her.*

Alexandria smiled. Catherine would be proud of the way her children had turned out.

> *Bradley has been dead three and a half years now. How I miss him, but I can see him every day in Brad. Brad is strong, just like his father.*

Alexandria often wondered what had happened to Brad's father. She couldn't remember anyone mentioning him. "This family has seen much tragedy," she said quietly, adjusting her pillows.

> *Melissa is three years old today. Brad bought her a pony.*

Alexandria thumbed through more pages that talked about Melissa growing up, and then she spotted Julia's name again. *Good, more gossip.*

> *Julia returned from her trip abroad. I don't even think Brad missed her while she was gone. She seemed nice enough while she was here ... Wonder when her real personality will surface again?*

Brad is so stubborn. Sometimes there is more to life than honor. Why can't he see he'll never be happy with Julia? She is nothing but trouble!

Alexandria had heard all this before. In search of something new, she flipped to the last few pages and began to read, but her eyelids grew heavy in protest. The book slipped from her finger as sleep claimed her.

When Alexandria opened her eyes, she discovered morning had arrived. Darn, she had fallen asleep without completing the diary. She seemed so tired lately. Maybe she needed some vitamins.

She heard voices in the hallway and put the small book in its hiding place, promising herself she would read more later. So far, the journal hadn't revealed any new information, but she would continue reading in hopes of learning more about this family she'd been brought to.

Rolling over, Alexandria felt her stomach roll again. Damn! She tried to lay perfectly still, willing the queasiness to go away. For a week, she'd felt this way every morning when she first woke. Her stomach churned again. This time her feet hit the floor and she ran for the chamber pot.

"Good mornin', Petite." Hattie swung into the room.

Alexandria grabbed a damp towel and wiped her face. "You think so, huh?"

"Aren't you feelin' well?"

"No. And I don't know what's wrong. I don't have a fever, but in the mornings I'm so nauseated. I must have some kind of flu bug."

"Flu?"

"It's something we have in my time."

"How long have you felt this way?"

"About a week."

Hattie raised her brow. "I thought you were a doctor."

"I am a doctor, Hattie, but we don't know everything."

Hattie laughed, "You're pregnant, Petite."

Alex felt herself blush scarlet. "I am not!" she protested. "I do believe I remember that chapter. I'd have to have sex in order to be pregnant, and I can assure you I've not done that!"

Hattie sat down on the edge of the bed. "Haven't you?"

"No, I have not." Alex was quite indignant at Hattie's suggestion.

"Should I remind you of de opera?"

"What about it?"

"Just what happened after you came home?"

"I went to bed, of course."

"And?"

"I-I'm not sure." Alexandria felt her mouth go dry, and she quickly pressed the wet towel to her lips. It was a dream she told herself ... nothing but a dream.

"You're not sure?" Hattie's look told Alex she didn't believe that.

"No. It's kind of fuzzy," she admitted.

"Well, what do you remember?"

"I couldn't sleep that night, so I decided to go downstairs and get a book, or at least I think I did. I'd had too much to drink, so everything was fuzzy. Brad was in the library and... and ..." Alexandria just couldn't tell Hattie exactly what happened, "and ... I fell asleep in the library. But when I woke up I was in my bed, and I didn't have a book." She screwed her face up in thought. "I probably dreamed up the whole thing."

"Sit down, cher."

"I don't want to sit down." Alex didn't like the tone of Hattie's voice. It reminded her of the first morning she'd started this so-called adventure. When Hattie had told her they were poor. Somehow, she didn't think she wanted to hear what Hattie was about to say. However, it was clear from Hattie's express that she wasn't going to speak until Alex sat down, so she reluctantly obeyed.

"It wasn't a dream."

Alex's eyelids snapped up. "How do you know?"

"To start with ..." Hattie paused. "It's true you can't get pregnant from a dream, but, cher, you are pregnant. Just look at that tummy. It's not flat like it once was."

"It is, too!" Alexandria jumped up and looked into the mirror. How long was it since they'd been to New Orleans ... two or was it three months? It was hard to keep up with time here since there were no calendars on the walls. She tried to hold her stomach in, but sure enough, there was a slight bulge. But she still wasn't convinced.

"How do you explain my waking up in bed the next morning? And wouldn't I know if I were not a virgin? I am a doctor, after all. In my own time I never felt strong enough for the men I dated to have sex--not that I dated that much. I was too busy with my career, but that morning was kind of hazy."

Hattie chuckled, watching Alexandria pace. "You were up in your bed because I put you there."

Alex froze. "What! ... Why?"

"You didn't want me to leave you dere to do a lot of explainin' de next mornin', did you? Besides, you two needed to know each other better before becomin' involved. You didn't like Brad then."

"Well, Miss Fix-it." Alexandria stared at Hattie in disbelief. "Did it ever occur to you for just one minute that I might get pregnant? Now the father of my child doesn't even have the slightest idea that we, ah--had a wonderful experience, much less conceived a child. Hattie, I ought to give you a fat lip." Alex threw up her hands in disgust. "At least *I'd* feel better."

Alex began to pace. "First you bring me on this trip without even bothering to ask me. I do agree I needed a vacation, but I could have gone to the beach." She stopped and glared at Hattie. "Normal people go to the beach, Hattie, not another century! And then you introduce me to this impossible man. And now you tell me he's the father of my child. Hattie, this is my life. What am I supposed to do now?"

"Now, cher, you're getting' hysterical. Jus' you set you'se'f dere, and if you don't want de whole house to know what's going on, you should keep your voice down." Hattie took Alexandria by the arm and led her back to the bed. As usual, just the smooth sound of Hattie's voice calmed Alex. "Was it wonderful, Petite?"

Alexandria thought back to that night. She'd tried hard to put that experience behind her, but now as she thought back a dreamy-eyed expression came to her eyes. "Yes, Hattie it was. It was everything I expected it to be, except there was no love between us."

"But you made love, no?"

"Yes, but there were no love words spoken. Come to think about it, it was probably just lust."

Hattie patted her hand. "So you don't love him?"

"No."

"You spoke mighty quick," Hattie observed. "How do you know you don't love Brad? Perhaps your love and lust are confused."

"I'll grant you that point." Alex nodded. "I'm confused."

"Well now ... we'll just have to tell Master Brad. Trust me, he'll be thrilled."

"No! We'll not tell him anything!" Alexandria protested. "Hell, he still thinks it was a dream the same as I did." She sighed. "It's better this way."

"Oh, but I think you're wrong." Hattie shook her head.

"It won't be the first time, Hattie." Alexandria started laughing. This was absurd. She was going to be an unwed mother. Even in her time, unwed mothers carried a stigma, but in 1835, unwed mothers were scorned and thought to be harlots. Oh, God, she would be stoned--no, tarred and feathered--and Julia would be leading the pack.

"You've found something amusing?" Hattie asked.

"Could you picture Julia if I told her congratulations on your marriage. You have him ... and I have his baby." Alex looked at Hattie and then burst into tears.

Hattie hugged her and gently patted her back.

Alexandria let her head rest on Hattie's soft bosom. "Hattie, what am I going to do?" she asked between sobs.

"We'll think of somethin', cher."

"Hattie."

"*Oui?*"

"I want to go home."

—)—

Alexandria sat staring out the window of her bedroom. There wasn't a cloud in the sky, just beautiful blue as far as the eye could see. She had been sitting here ever since Hattie had left. She really didn't know what she'd do if she hadn't had Hattie's shoulder to cry on. But she was through crying now. She would have to decide what to do and be strong no matter what decision she came to. And how could she be pregnant in a century she didn't belong to?

"Unwed mother." She frowned. It made her sound like a terrible person. Alexandria wasn't sure she was ready to be a mother. She knew absolutely nothing about children, except what experience she'd had in the hospital. But how hard could it be.

After all, people had children every day.

Of course, they usually got married first.

She definitely didn't intend to tell Brad. That was one thing she was sure of. It would be different if they loved each other, but they didn't. They just lusted after each other. She couldn't stand the thought of Brad feeling sorry for her. It was better for him to continue with his plans, no matter how ridiculous they were.

This pregnancy sure complicated things. Maybe she wasn't going to return to her own time like she'd first thought. Even though she had grumbled to Hattie about interfering, the fact remained Alex was beginning to like it here. And what did she have waiting for her back home? An empty apartment and, of course, Carol. But Carol would meet a man, and then Alex probably wouldn't see her again.

Her condition wouldn't show for a few months. That should give her time. Time for what? She sighed. That was the big question. She knew she couldn't stay at River Bends, but exactly what she would do was yet to be seen. Alex stood up, stretching her back muscles. Maybe she would have Hattie look in her crystal ball for the answers.

Moping wasn't Alex's style. Yesterday she had promised to take Melissa out for a ride, so she finished dressing, thankful the nausea had passed. She grabbed her coat and hurried downstairs.

When she reached the front entryway, Melissa rested in her wheelchair, reading a book.

"Good morning, Missy. Did you bring a jacket?"

"Hi, Alex. My coat's over on the rack."

Alex helped Melissa with her coat. "We're going to leave this chair behind today."

"You aren't serious? What if Brad comes home?"

"He's not coming home this early, so quit worrying. Let's put your legs to use. Stand up and put your arm around my waist."

Melissa stood. They pushed the wheelchair aside. "It feels strange to leave the house without my chair," she admitted.

"The day is coming, Missy, when you'll never have to see that thing again." Alex opened the door. The steps were the first obstacle to tackle. "We're going to take this slowly, one step at a time."

Carefully they moved down each step. Upon reaching the landing, Alexandria smiled. Missy squeezed her waistline so tight that Alex knew she'd have a bruise there. "How do you feel?"

The child let her breath out. "Wonderful! My knees are a little sore, but that's all."

"Missy, you don't have to hold your breath with each step. Remember, air is important, too." Alex couldn't help but laugh.

Melissa started giggling. "Did I do that?"

"I wouldn't believe it if I hadn't seen it with my own eyes!" Hattie stood in the doorway, hands on hips. "*Oui*, I don't believe dat child's walkin'," she said.

Alex helped Melissa up in the buggy. "You mean you doubted my abilities, Hattie?" Alexandria said, trying to sound offended. "Shame on you."

"Of course I never doubted. But I never dreamed it would happen so soon."

"Hattie, you mustn't say anything to Brad. I want to surprise him," Melissa cautioned.

"Don't worry, Petite, I won't." Hattie smiled. "You two have a good time. And, Alexandria, please be careful."

Alexandria blushed at Hattie's remark and gave her a scalding *you'd-better-keep-your-mouth-shut* look.

"What's wrong, Alex?" Melissa asked.

"Nothing, sweetheart. Hattie just wants us to drive carefully."

The trees wore their autumn colors of orange and yellow. One tree in particular, Melissa pointed out, was green in the middle, but the edges of the leaves were a bright fiery orange. She told Alex it reminded her of Alex's red hair.

When they came upon a grassy meadow not too far from the house, Alexandria pulled back on the horses' reins . She tied them off so the horses wouldn't move. "This is the place."

"The place for what?"

"To practice walking." She helped Missy out of the carriage and helped her stand where she could hang on to the side of the carriage for support. Then Alex walked out in front of her about fifteen feet. She turned and held out her arms to the young girl.

"Walk to me," Alexandria instructed, feeling a lot like a mother teaching her child to walk.

"I didn't know we were going to do this today. I thought we were just going for a ride ... I'm not ready. I--I don't think I can." Melissa's voice shook.

"Yes, you can!" Alex held her hands out to her. "Let go. Take a step."

Melissa squeezed her eyes tightly. "I'm scared. I can't do this, not yet." But when she opened her eyes she looked at Alex's outstretched hands. Reluctantly, Missy let go of the wagon and took a step and then another. But on the third she fell down, hitting the ground none-too-gently.

"Get up, Missy. Do it again!" Alexandria said in a stern voice. Deep down she wanted to go to the child and help her up, but she knew Missy must rely on herself. She'd been relying on others for too long.

"I can't," Melissa cried.

"Do you want to spend the rest of your life in a wheelchair?" Alexandria shouted.

"No!"

"Then get up and walk to me!" Alex could see the fire in her eyes. Good! That was what she wanted.

Melissa struggled, pulling her knees up under her. Then, very slowly, she rose up until she finally stood straight. No smile lit her face, just sheer determination. Carefully, she put one foot out, and then the other. Alex knew Missy's feet would feel like lead, but she could do this ... she had to. Missy threw her hands out to keep her balance, and this time she didn't fall. She kept taking steps, moving ever so slowly, intently watching her feet, and concentrating very hard on what she was doing.

Alexandria smiled and backed up a few more feet. The child was doing it--she was walking on her own. Tears of happiness filled Alex's eyes.

Melissa looked up to see how much further she had to go, and found she had reached Alexandria. "I made it!" She jumped in Alex's arms and began to cry.

The look in Missy's eyes said it all. They both hugged and cried, each filled with happiness.

"Thank you for helping me." Missy wrapped her small arms around Alex's neck, then leaned back and kissed her on the cheek. "I love you, Alex. Please don't ever leave me."

Chapter Nineteen

Nothing had gone as planned.

By the time Brad arrived to sell his cotton, his buyer had departed a week earlier. Sellers had left a message saying their quota for cotton had been filled. Brad knew he was late this year, but he hadn't worried about selling his cotton since he supposedly had a prearranged deal.

It took several weeks before he found a buyer, willing to pay his price. Standing in front of the cotton exchange, his business complete, Brad breathed a sigh of relief. He decided to relax a little and sought Edmund's company.

Brad was damn tired when he arrived at Edmund's. He had been driving himself hard, and the dark circles under his eyes were proof. It wasn't that he didn't have people to do the work for him ... he did. But Brad liked the backbreaking work because he didn't have to think. And thinking was beginning to be a nasty habit of his. More often than he would like to admit, Alexandria popped into his thoughts.

"You look like hell, cousin," Edmund said as Brad entered the house.

"Thank you, Edmund, for your encouraging observation."

"Don't mention it. How about we go out and kick up our heels?" Edmund suggested. Brad readily agreed.

They made their rounds of all the taverns. By two in the morning, neither Brad nor Edmund felt any pain as they sat at a corner table.

"Well, Brad, you've mentioned everyone except Alexandria, so I guess I'll have to ask. How is she?"

"Fine. Why?" His eyebrow shot up suspiciously. "You still interested?"

"I would be if the lady saw things my way." Edmund sighed, replacing his mug on the table. "But in answer to your question, no. I've given up on her. She said she wasn't interested in getting married."

"You mean you asked her?" Brad's jaw tensed as he realized his cousin had been serious about Alexandria.

"No, just hinted strongly. I must say, though, she is one fine kisser."

Brad sat up straight and leaned toward Edmund. "You kissed her?"

"Sure did." Edmund grinned.

Brad's expression grew dark as he slugged down his drink and called the barmaid for another.

The well-endowed barmaid moved over to the table. Her low cut blouse hung off her shoulders in a blatant display of her attributes. Grinning from ear to ear, she set the beer on the table and purposely rubbed her breast against Brad's shoulder. Brad laughed at her flirtatious manner, and laid his hand on her butt. Seeing her lusty smile told him she was more than willing to satisfy his needs. But this woman wasn't who he wanted. He was beginning to realize he really didn't know what he wanted.

"I get off in a half hour, honey. How about buying me a drink?" Her smile held a promise of more to come.

"I'll be right here, sweetheart." Brad gave her his most devilish smile, then pulled her down in his lap and kissed her. Not a mere peck, but a sultry kiss that left the barmaid quite breathless.

When she had left, Brad looked at Edmund. "Is that the way you kissed her?"

"Kissed who?" Edmund appeared confused.

"Alexandria."

"Yes, you could say it was just about like that." Edmund laughed at Brad's scowl. It was hot enough to burn. "I do believe you're jealous, cousin."

"I am not!" Brad quickly denied. "Just mildly curious at the way you treat my hired help."

"Oh, I see." Edmund didn't believe a word of it. "By the way, isn't your party next week?"

"Yes. And don't try to change the subject. What does that have to do with anything?"

Edmund rested back in his chair. "What are you going to do with Alexandria?"

"I'm not going to do anything with her." Brad looked surprised at the question. "She can continue helping with Melissa. Besides, Missy likes her."

"I imagine Julia will have something to say about that."

Brad's jaw tightened. "You know as well as I do that Julia and I were promised to each other. Half of River Bends came from that agreement, and I could never go back on that promise. Until recently, Julia has always been pleasant and I've enjoyed her company."

Edmund started to laugh. "Julia is only putting on a show for you. If she displayed her true personality, you'd run for the hills."

"Oh, really?" Brad said skeptically.

"Why do you think your sister has little to do with her?"

"Melissa is just a child, for Christ-sake. I do admit Julia hasn't been herself since Alexandria came to River Bends, but where Alexandria is concerned, Julia has no say-so." Abruptly Brad changed the subject. "Are you coming to the party?"

"I wouldn't miss it."

Brad frustration grew at the way Edmund grinned his know-it-all smile. He looked like the cat who had just swallowed the canary. "Well, I'm glad I can provide you with your amusement. Would you like to tell me what you're smiling at?"

"Have you told her you love her?"

"No. Julia knows this is more a marriage of convenience than love."

"It wasn't Julia I meant," Edmund corrected. "Have you told Alexandria that you love her?"

Brad looked at his cousin, completely dumbfounded. But he never had the chance to answer Edmund, because the barmaid was back in his lap, smothering him with kisses and doing an effective job of blocking out any further thoughts. And tonight Brad intended to completely lose himself in her charms.

Brad winced as the steaming cup of morning coffee burned all the way down his throat. His good intentions last night had hit a snag as soon as his head had touched the pillow. He had passed out and awaken early this morning to return to *Rué Chartress*. His head felt three sizes too big. To look at Edmund, sitting across from him, paper in hand, it appeared he felt much the same way. Brad wondered if there was any liquor left in the bar; surely they had drunk every last drop.

"Damn," Edmund swore. "This is a direct challenge. And damn if Leathers won't take him up on it."

"Must you shout!" Brad said irritably.

"Sorry, Cousin." Edmund chuckled. "Which wore you out, the liquor or the wench?"

"If my head didn't hurt so much, I'd get up and give you a fat lip," Brad swore. "Why are you shouting? What did you read in the paper?"

"The article by Anthony Boggs. He's bragging that his boat, *The Dogwood Blossom,*--what a name for a boat--can deliver passengers and cargo faster than any boat on the Mississippi. Leathers told me he has bumped heads with Boggs on more than one occasion. I think it's time to shut him up."

"What are you planning?"

"Well, it just so happens, *The Dogwood* is leaving on the twentieth of next month, and I do believe the *Magnolia* will sail at the same time."

"Sounds like there is going to be a race." Still trying to ease the pain in his head, Brad swallowed more hot coffee.

"You can count on it. Would you like to make a friendly wager?"

"Sure. I'll take any fool's money who thinks he can beat Captain Leathers. Why, he's been on the river since Noah built the ark." Brad laughed, then grabbed his head at the pain it produced. However, he didn't miss Edmund's smile.

"Well, you might be exaggerating just a little, but I agree he's an immortal on the river. It looks like I'm going to be a busy man for awhile, getting the boat in tiptop shape."

"I think you're right." Brad nodded, taking the paper from him.

"Would you like to help?"

"I'll go with you to the docks today, but then I need to be heading home."

Edmund stood up. "We'll leave in half an hour."

The long-awaited week was here.

Brad's engagement party was Saturday. He would have to come home now. That is, unless he changed his mind, which Alexandria seriously doubted. She wondered why Brad had been gone so much longer than expected. She found it harder to put him from her mind now that she knew his child grew inside her.

Besides a slight bulge of her tummy, Alexandria couldn't see any other sign of pregnancy. Her morning sickness had slacked off, and she hadn't been sick for the past two mornings. Hattie had been sympathetic but at times had a hard time controlling her laughter.

Melissa was walking. They had increased her exercises since the day she had first walked in the field. Everyday she and Missy would take walks to strengthen her legs. Melissa positively glowed with happiness.

Alex supposed she should help Hattie with the party. But Alex was trying her best to forget the whole thing. Instead, she decided this morning would be perfect to take a ride. Entering the foyer, she approached Hattie and a young black girl she hadn't seen before.

"Petite, I need for you to go and look at the children," Hattie told her. "They have sores all over their bodies."

"Where are the children?" Alexandria asked.

"Ann will take you to them."

Alexandria retrieved her bag, and started back to the foyer. She saw Ann, the young black girl, standing by the front door, waiting to take her to the children. Just before they left the porch, a rider and carriage caught Alex's attention.

Alex put her hand over her eyes, shading them from the morning sun's bright glare. The rider was Brad. She would recognize those broad shoulders anywhere. He sat tall on his horse, and the sun picked up the blond streaks in his hair. Butterflies churned in her stomach at the sight of him. She admitted, if only to herself, she was delighted he'd come home. She paid little notice to the carriage as she said, "Welcome home. Did things go well?"

Brad smiled, and she thought him the most captivating creature she'd ever met. Why, he could turn the pyramids to crushed stone with one of his smiles.

"I did have a little trouble finding a buyer for the cotton, but the trip was very successful," Brad explained. He had ridden ahead of the carriage, but the buggy now pulled up behind him.

"It's good to be home." Brad's eyes held hers captive with unsaid meaning.

The carriage came to a complete stop. "I agree, darling. We've a lot to do before the party," Julia said.

The smile faded instantly from Alex's face. She jerked her eyes away from Brad to see Julia sitting in the carriage. Why hadn't she noticed her before? She knew why, because that blue-eyed devil had held her captivated with his eyes and innocent smile. It was now quite apparent what had taken him so long. Business, hell! While she'd been sitting here missing him, he'd evidently been having a wonderful time. Alex couldn't control the green-eyed monster that seemed to rule her. She cursed herself inwardly, and of course cursed Brad to hell.

"Darling, please help me down," Julia purred.

Brad had seen the instant change in Alexandria and knew she'd jumped to the wrong conclusion. He had been on his way home when he happened to bump into Julia heading down the road to River Bends.

He assisted Julia from the carriage. "Oh, Brad, we've had such a wonderful talk. I'm looking forward to Saturday."

Brad knew Julia was purposely misleading Alexandria, but what could he say? He couldn't call his future bride a liar. His future wife? Lately, he was having a hard time with that idea.

"Hello, Alexandria. Are you playing doctor again?" Slipping her arm through Brad's, Julia smiled.

"I don't have to play, Julia." Alex refused to get into a verbal debate with the woman. "Excuse me, we have some children to look after." She started down the steps, pulling the black girl behind her.

"What's wrong with the children?" Brad called after her.

"They're sick!" Alex didn't bother to explain. She didn't even bother to stop.

"At least you could stop walking when I'm speaking. Do you need some help?"

"No!" Alexandria called over her shoulder as she continued toward the slave quarters. The damn man should have stayed in New Orleans! And she shouldn't have let herself think of him in any other way--he was her employer.

Ann led Alexandria to the first cabin. She opened the door and found the room dark and stuffy. When her eyes adjusted, she discovered the room was a nursery. Beds lined both sides of the walls. At first glance there appeared to be about ten children in all.

"Let's get some light in here." She went around and opened the curtains to let in the morning sun. Then she raised both windows to get some fresh air circulating. A potbelly stove stood in the corner of the small room.

Walking over to the first bed, Alex bent down and felt the child's forehead. She had a fever and her eyes were dull. Alexandria took a thermometer out of her bag. "Put this under your tongue and close your mouth."

Alex unbuttoned the child's shirt. She'd already seen some sores on the face, and her chest was covered, too. The lesions were small, clear blisters, about the size of a match head. They would soon break and quickly form itchy crusts or scabs on the spots. There were several sores starting to pop out. She took out the thermometer and read it: 103 degrees.

"Am I going to live?"

"I think so." Alexandria smiled. "Have you been itching a lot?"

The little girl nodded.

"You have chicken pox, young lady. You must not scratch the bumps or they will leave ugly scars. Do you understand?"

"Yes, ma'am."

Alex turned to the woman whom she knew by the name of Kate. She was in charge, even though she was pretty young herself.

"Kate, the children have chicken pox and probably will be sick for about a week. We need to get some gloves made for their hands to remind them not to scratch. Can you find somebody to make them?"

"Yes, ma'am."

"Good. I'm going to the house to get some oatmeal from Hattie. We will give the children oatmeal baths to help with the itching and reduce their fever. And you'd better put some water on to heat. I'll be right back."

After she gave Alexandria the oatmeal, Hattie insisted on helping.

"Chicken pox are highly contagious, Hattie. If you come with me, we might be there several days." Alex was thankful she'd had the disease as a child.

"You're going to need help, cher. Besides, I've had chicken pox, though I didn't know what it was at the time," Hattie explained. Hattie promised to mix an herbal tea that would also help.

Over the next four days, Alexandria didn't leave the children's cabin. Besides taking care of the youngsters, she kept them entertained by playing games and telling stories she had heard when she was a child. She also made up stories about automobiles and planes which produced much laughter among the children.

Finally, the last child fell asleep. The new moon provided very little light as Alexandria stepped out the door and sat down on the top step. She rested her back against the door and looked at her hands. She'd had them in so much water bathing the children they were rough and sore to the touch.

"My hands look like an old woman's."

"Shh. What you say, cher? Dose are workin' hands. They have de ability to heal people."

Hattie stood beside a big black, iron pot suspended by a chain in the middle of three legs. The fire had burned down and in its place glowed red hot coals, which provided the only light. Hattie looked like a witch stirring her bubbly brew. Who knows... she probably was a sorceress, but what a delicious smell came from her steaming black pot.

Mmm, crab gumbo. Alex licked her lips thinking of the mixture of tender crab meat, potatoes and okra in a tomato 'rue. Alexandria had learned to like gumbo and now considered it one of her favorite meals. The Shrimp Boil and other seasonings Hattie had mixed in the gumbo gave the most heavenly smell. The aroma made her mouth water.

Alexandria stretched, trying to relax the muscles in her back. She dropped her head forward and rolled it around before looking up at Hattie.

"Tired, Petite?"

"A little. It feels good to be out in the fresh air." Alex brushed her hair over her shoulder. "How are things at the house?"

"Hectic. We're finally through with de cleanin'."

"How is Melissa?"

Hattie chuckled. "Trying to avoid Julia."

"I don't blame her." Alex rubbed her neck. "Julia hasn't been mean to her, has she?"

"No." Hattie lifted the big spoon and sipped her brew. "Julia is tryin' to be nice to Missy. After all, she doesn't have de ring on her finger yet. But to everyone else," Hattie shook her head, "you'd think she is mistress of de house de way she is issuin' commands."

"You're taking orders from her?"

"Of course not. She just issues orders, and everyone ignores her."

Leaning back against the door, Alex said, "You won't be able to do that after they're married."

"Dat house ain't big enough fo' de two of us." Hattie brought a spoonful of broth for Alex to sample. "I could just slip a little rat poison in her tea."

"Hattie!"

"Just kidding, cher."

Alex tasted the gumbo and nodded her approval. "Have you seen, Brad?" She asked as she watched Hattie walk back to the fire.

"Oui, I have. After all, he lives here."

"I know that. I was just wondering if he had been helping with the arrangements for the party."

"No, Petite. He is staying as far away as possible and has pretty much left everythin' up to me. Somethin' seems to be botherin' him. He's much too quiet, lately."

Alex was dying to know if he had asked about her, but she couldn't ask Hattie, so she continued beating around the bush with her questions.

"Have you talked to him?"

Hattie smiled as she stirred the gumbo. "He asked how de children were doin'."

"That's all?" Alex pulled an old quilt around her arms.

"*Oui,* dat was about de extent of de conversation." Hattie removed the ladle from the broth. "How about some gumbo?"

Something moved across the yard.

"That would be good, Hattie." Brad called to her as he walked out of the dark shadows surrounding the buildings. "I'm starved."

Alex watched his long powerful strides. Brad had something draped over his arm, but she couldn't make out what it was until he came closer. Just how long had he been standing there? Even as he neared, she couldn't hear his footsteps.

"Master Brad, what's wrong? Aren't dey feedin' you good enough at de house?" Hattie smiled.

"The food is never as good as when you're there, Hattie. Must be those magical spices you put on everything."

Hattie chuckled and asked, "What's that you're holding?"

"I brought you both shawls. I figured with the cooler nights you'd need them."

"You got dat right," Hattie admitted. "I'll take mine right now, and I'm sure Alexandria would prefer hers over dat quilt she's been usin'."

Brad turned and walked toward Alex. "Let me put this around you."

She leaned forward and pushed the quilt down. He wrapped the shawl about her. "You look tired."

"I am, a little." Alex glanced up at him. Was that tenderness she saw in the depths of his eyes? It was hard not to stare at him when he looked at her that way. Even though he often acted high-handed, he possessed a gentleness that drew her. "You shouldn't be here. The children are contagious until tomorrow."

He put his finger under her chin. "You're here, aren't you?"

"But I'm their doctor," she said, her voice no more than a whisper. She felt like she was melting at his mere touch.

Hattie cleared her throat. "I thought you said you were hungry. Come get this gumbo while it's hot."

Brad handed Alex a bowl, and the three of them sat down on the steps of the cabin and ate their fill.

Brad told them about Edmund's up-and-coming boat race.

"Sounds wonderful. Will we be able to go?" Alexandria asked.

"Of course, both of you can come down. Edmund will like that."

"Julia won't mind?" Alexandria would have to take her into consideration now.

"Who?"

"Your future bride."

"I doubt it. She probably won't care anything about the race."

Alex thought Brad very nonchalant about his future wife. Most husbands would want their brides with them as much as possible. Could it perhaps be true ... he didn't love Julia? Alex couldn't help but wonder. She sighed. What would Brad have been like in her time?

They continued talking. Brad filled them in on the trouble he'd had selling his cotton.

The snap of twigs caught Alex's attention. She wondered if Julia was getting ready to join them ... on second thought, Alex couldn't picture Julia anywhere near the slave quarters. The woman would think it beneath her.

"Something sure smells good," Abraham said as he ambled into the light.

"Smells good and is good." Brad laughed.

"Master Brad! I'm surprised seeing you," Abraham admitted. "Thought you'd be helping Miz Julia."

"No, Abraham, I'm trying to stay out of her way as much as possible."

"I know what you mean, sir." Abraham shook his head slowly as a slight smile touched his lips. "Women can be a might touchy at times."

"Who you callin' touchy, old man?" Hattie stood, hands on her hips evidently she was highly insulted at Abraham's remark.

"Now, don't go getting your feathers ruffled. Some women can be touchy, but not my sweet Hattie."

"Dat's more like it." Hattie laughed. "How are you goin' to get some gumbo without a pot?"

"You got a good point, old woman. How about walkin' back to

my cabin with me? I'm going to bring back a big pot for that delicious brew."

Hattie walked off with Abraham, but not before Alex and Brad heard Hattie say, "You call me old woman again and you won't be needing a pot ... cause you won't have any teeth left." Abraham just laughed and put his arm around the feisty woman.

The dying embers gave off a dusky orange glow. Brad turned to Alexandria and watched her for several minutes. "I love the way the fire plays tricks with your hair." He reached up and took the end of one curl, rubbing it back and forth between his fingertips. "You're very beautiful."

"Thank you." She stared at her hands folded in her lap.

Brad sighed. "It's probably time for me to go back to the house."

"Brad --"

He felt her touch his arm as he rose to go. "Yes?" He turned back toward her.

"I've been wanting to talk to you."

Brad pulled Alexandria to her feet, so he could see her face clearly. "Now is as good a time as any."

Alex didn't know how to say this, but she had to tell him before she changed her mind. "It won't be long before Melissa won't need me." Alex tried looking at his chin, but her eyes drifted up to his.

"I agree she is making progress, and for that I thank you. But she is a long way from recovery."

If only he knew Melissa was better, Alexandria thought, this conversation would be easier. "When you announce your engagement Saturday, I think it would be wise if I moved in with Hattie."

"No!" He pulled her up on her toes. "My being engaged to Julia has nothing to do with you."

Alexandria bit her lower lip. What did this man want from her? Did he know it was sheer torture resisting the urge to fall in his arms at his mere touch? She gazed deep in his eyes, trying to communicate her emotions. If only he wouldn't look at her with such tenderness, she could forget about him. Just what did he feel for her?

"I think it's best," Alexandria finally murmured.

"No! I won't let you go." Brad pulled her into his embrace.

She pushed hard against his chest, but knew her efforts were feeble, because as she pushed she automatically tilted her face up to receive his kiss. What the hell, she thought. He wasn't engaged yet.

Brad took her lips in a passionate kiss that was much hotter than any of the embers in the fire behind them. His hands moved slowly down her back until they reached the soft curve of her hips where he tightened his hold, pulling her toward him until she could feel his hardness pressed against her. His lips parted hers with a hunger that was not gentle but demanding. The urgency of his caress suddenly awoke a tormented longing that lay deep in Alexandria's breast. She wanted to rip the clothes from both their bodies, so they could share their heat. She wanted to feel Brad in her again. Yet, the realization of the last time they made love persuaded Alex to push him away.

It took Alex a few minutes to catch her breath as she stared at his smoldering eyes.

"What's wrong, sweetheart?"

Brad's comment was like throwing ice water in her face. "What's wrong? What's wrong?" Alex exploded. "I'll tell you what's wrong. I'm not your sweetheart, and I am not your plaything," she informed him, then rushed on, "Do you get your amusement out of coming down here and tempting me with your passionate kisses, when in two days you're to announce your engagement to the woman who's in your house right now?"

She reached out and grabbed his shoulders as the tears streamed down her face. "I am not a toy! I have feelings! Do you understand?" she screamed. "And for that reason, I will be moving in with Hattie." Alex turned and ran up the stairs into the children's room, slamming the door. Sinking to the floor, she pulled her knees up and sobbed into her skirt, trying not to awaken the children. "Damn man, I hope he rots in hell!"

Brad stood completely dumbfounded, staring at the closed door. What had started out as a moment of pleasure now twisted in his gut like a knife. Alexandria was right. He had been treating her like his personal plaything. He would remember in the future. She was a forbidden toy. And if he didn't want to pay the price, then Alexandria was off limits.

"Damn woman," Brad swore. His cheeks started to twitch, and he cursed himself for his weakness as he stomped off in the darkness toward the main house.

"Just what's with those two?" Abraham asked Hattie.

They had stood back in the darkness, observing the whole scene.

"They're both crazy." Hattie slowly shook her head. "If you ask me, they can't see what's right before their eyes. I've never met two more stubborn people in all my days.

Come on ... let's get the gumbo."

Chapter Twenty

It was a perfect autumn day. The warm sun rode high in the sky and the cool, nippy air held a promise of the approaching cold weather.

Alex had checked the children for the last time. Now their parents were allowed to fetch them, and she could go back to the main house. She had developed a nagging backache, which she attributed to sleeping in a chair.

Having managed with a few birdbaths, her hair was dirty, shaggy and extremely irritating, causing her to constantly push it over her shoulders. Now as she neared the main house, the thought of a hot bath and a soft bed was all she longed for.

She entered the house through the kitchen door and asked for hot water to be sent to her room. She then continued on through the dining room and down the hall past Brad's study. Her footsteps thudded against the floor as if her feet were made of iron. She breathed a sigh of relief that she hadn't bumped into Brad or anyone else so far. She'd started up the stairs when her luck ran out.

"My, my, look what the dogs dragged up. You look and smell terrible." Julia crinkled her nose in disgust.

Alex was too tired to do battle. She moved around Julia and kept climbing the stairs, but at the last minute Alex couldn't resist saying, "Go to hell."

"What! Why, I never! You won't get away with your little ol' remarks once I'm mistress here!"

Alex glanced over her shoulder. Julia stood with her hands on her hips, shouting up at her. "Your days are numbered. Do you hear me? Your days are numbered!"

Alexandria would liked to have thrown her medical bag at the yelling shrew, but decided Julia really wasn't worth the effort. Opening the door, Alex placed her bag on the dresser. She glanced at her image in the mirror and shook her head. Julia was right about one thing--she did look as if the dogs had dragged her up.

The maids entered the room right behind her with buckets of hot water and began filling the tub. Alex looked in the wardrobe and pulled down the white box she had brought from New Orleans. She lay the box on the bed, then removed the top, pulled out the black crepe dress, and shook out the wrinkles. It really was a beautiful dress, Alex thought as she hung the gown up so it would be ready for tonight.

The tub had been filled, and she wasted little time stripping off her clothes and slipping into the warm, inviting hot water. A small sigh escaped her lips as the heavenly water caressed her body. She was damn tired. Ever since her last argument with Brad, she hadn't seemed to have much energy. She'd come to the conclusion that she was clinically depressed. Perhaps a good nap would make her feel better, but she doubted it.

"Hi, Alex," Melissa called from the door. "Can I come in?"

"Sure."

Melissa wheeled herself into the room. Once inside, she got out of her chair, and shut the door. She couldn't help giggling at her well-kept secret.

"Just think, after tonight I won't have to use that thing again." Melissa's bubbly mood showed as she neared the tub and sat on a stool.

Alexandria submerged under the water to wet her hair. Coming up she said, "That's right. Tonight you'll walk into that ballroom like a queen." She wiped the water from her eyes and grabbed the soap. "How have you been this past week? I've missed you."

"Here, let me do that." Melissa took the soap and lathered Alexandria's hair. "I've missed you, too. It has definitely been a *long* week. Every time I've left my room, Julia has been my companion. And for the past two days Brad has been crabby and very hard to live with." Missy frowned. "Mostly, I've been staying in my room. It's safer that way." She poured fresh water over Alexandria's hair to rinse off the soap.

"What has put Brad in such a foul mood?" Alex couldn't help asking, even though she swore she didn't care.

"I don't know. He's too grumpy to ask," Missy said, handing her a towel.

Alex slipped on her robe, and sat down in front of the fireplace. Melissa helped towel dry her hair, rubbing peach oil on every strand to bring out the shine. They spent the next hour talking and enjoying each other's company.

Sadness filled Alex. She would miss Missy when she returned to her own time. At least she would have the satisfaction that she'd helped one child.

"I'm tired, Missy. I think I'll take a nap." Alexandria moaned when she stood. "Gosh, I'm exhausted and stiff," she complained as she crawled into bed. "It's been a long week."

"Take off your robe and lay on your stomach," Melissa instructed.

"Why?"

"I'm going to pay you back for all those massages you gave me." Melissa took the bottle of oil off the nightstand and poured a small amount in her hand. She rubbed the oil between her palms for warmth, just like she'd seen Alexandria do. Missy gave her a rubdown and before she was through Alex was fast asleep.

Smiling, Melissa pulled the covers over Alexandria and quietly left the room.

Brad looked up from his ledger and once again found himself staring out the window, unable to keep his mind on the figures in front of him.

He had done the right thing. He was sure of it.

A knock on the door intruded on his thoughts. "Hell!" He really didn't want to see anybody, but the persistent knock sounded again.

"Come in," he growled.

Hattie sauntered into the room, shutting the door behind her. "Well, today's de day."

Brad slammed his pen down. "Did you interrupt me to tell me something I already know?"

"Ooo-eee. Tell you de trut', you're still in a fine mood."

"And just what's wrong with my mood?"

"Well now dat you asked. You've been bitin' everybody's head off fo' two days. Even de house servants draw straws, and de loser is de one dat serves you dinner."

Brad's eyebrow shot up at that tidbit of information.

"And Julia has been whinin' around de house dat you're not payin' her any attention, no" Hattie informed him. "Now I ask you, is dat any way to treat your future bride?"

"When have you ever had Julia's welfare in mind?"

"Since I'm de one who has to listen to her infernal whining."

Hattie sat down in the chair facing his desk. Brad got up and walked over to the bar. "It sounds like you could use a drink, Hattie. How about a bourbon?"

"Ooo-eee - make mine a double," she insisted.

Brad smiled when he handed Hattie her drink. It was the first time he remembered smiling in days.

Hattie sipped the golden liquid. Her eyes grew wide from warmth of the liquor before she coughed. "Y-You're goin' through wit' it, are you not?"

"If you mean my engagement, the answer is yes." He took his drink and moved back to his chair. "You've known what my plans have been all along."

"What about Alexandria?"

He flinched at the sound of her name, recalling his last conversation with Alexandria. "What about her?"

"Do you deny you have feelin's fo' her?"

Brad stared at Hattie without a ready answer. He took a sip of bourbon. He had thought a lot about Alexandria. He hadn't meant to, but she kept popping up in his thoughts. He had never met a woman who intruded into his mind like this one did.

"Well?"

He cut his eyes and fixed a hard stare on Hattie. "Yes, I feel something for Alexandria. Are you satisfied?"

"But you won't change your mind?"

"No. Why should I?"

"It's as plain as de nose on your face!" Hattie knew she was really pressing her luck, but she was angry.

"What did you say?"

Hattie didn't miss his sharp tone. "Nothin'." She decided not to repeat her last statement. Instead she hit him with another. "What if I told you Alexandria was pregnant?"

"What!" Brad stood up so fast his chair fell over backwards. "Who's the bastard that did ... who got her pregnant? He'll pay dearly. I promise you that."

"You really are dense, aren't you?"

Brad gripped the edge of his desk so hard his knuckles had turned white. "Come on Hattie, I'm waiting on the name. Who is he?"

"You sure you want to know?"

"Yes, damn it, who?"

"Well now -- I believe his name is Brad Wentworth."

"The bastard will definitely ... wait a minute, that's me!"

"Precisely."

He looked stunned by her words as he moved closer to her. "Hattie, this isn't a very funny joke."

"I'm not jokin'." She watched him lean back against the front of the desk. "Just think back to de night of de opera."

"This isn't the time for reminiscing."

Hattie ignored him. "What happened after de opera?"

"I came home and went to bed," Brad snapped at her ridiculous question.

"If I recall, you didn't go to bed. You went to de library," Hattie reminded him.

"That's right. I couldn't sleep and I went to the ... library ..." It all came flooding back, and Brad grew extremely quiet for a few minutes as he relived everything that had happened that night.

He remembered watching <u>her</u> intently as he moved cautiously, afraid of scaring her. Lower and lower his hands moved down her back, pressing her tighter against him and liking the way she curved into his body. The results were exactly what he wanted. Alexandria's eyes had become a green liquid fire. Everything about her felt right as if she belonged to him in some special way, and for just a moment he experienced an odd niggling that he'd waited all his life for this woman. He didn't just want this woman, he needed her like he'd never needed anyone before.

Brad blinked. "And I thought it was all a dream because when I awoke, she wasn't there." He looked at Hattie suspiciously. "Why hasn't she said anything?"

"Because she thought it was a dream, too. I put her back in her bed while she was still sleepin'."

"So the spot of blood I found was hers?" he whispered.

"*Oui*. She was a virgin until you seduced her."

"I did not," he quickly defended. "If I recall correctly, she was a very willing partner." Brad smiled, remembering Alexandria's response. Yes, she was very willing. "A virgin, huh?" Somehow he liked that idea.

"What you be doin' about de baby?" Hattie persisted.

He picked up his glass. "Why hasn't she told me herself?"

"She doesn't want you to know. She said she wouldn't marry you if you were de last man on earth."

"She said that?"

Hattie nodded.

Brad let out his breath slowly. "Alexandria can be very stubborn."

"And you're not?" Hattie laughed. "Dat's like de pot callin' de kettle black."

"Of course, I'm not stubborn." Brad looked offended.

"So what are you goin' to do?"

"I don't know, Hattie. For the moment I'm going to think about it." He looked at Hattie, frowning. "Don't you have some cooking to do?"

After Hattie had left the room, Brad stared down at the amber liquid in his glass, realizing his earlier decision was definitely the right one.

Melissa couldn't sit still as Hattie arranged her long blond hair on top of her head. Missy's hair felt like silk beneath Hattie's fingers as she arranged the curls, leaving them hanging over Missy's left shoulder.

"Hattie, I'm so nervous."

"I know you are, but it will go away after you make your *entrée*," Hattie assured her. "I bet you'll be de belle of de ball."

"Do you really think so?" Melissa's eyes sparkled with excitement.

"*Oui*, I do. Come over here, and let's slip on your crinolines."

Melissa stood so Hattie could help her step into the big hooped skirt. She pulled it up and tied the ribbon in the back. "It seems so strange to see you walkin', cher. Your brother is goin' to be very happy, you hear."

"I know." She giggled. "I can't wait to surprise him."

Hattie let out a long sigh. "I hope his mood has changed."

"Me, too. He's been a real bear lately." Missy turned to face Hattie. "Do you know why, Hattie?"

"Guilty conscience, I guarantee," Hattie mumbled.

"What?" Melissa asked, tilting her head to the side in puzzlement.

Hattie smiled at the innocent child standing in front of her. She had a pretty good idea why Brad was in such a foul mood. "Probably pre-wedding jitters."

"I guess you're right. I wonder when they will marry?"

"If we're lucky, Petite, it will be ten years from now."

Melissa giggled. "I know what you mean."

Hattie helped her into a turquoise dress. The rich satin skirt shimmered and depending on the light, appeared green or blue. The silver netting, covering the skirt, had silver sequins scattered like stars with the modest top that just barely slipped off her shoulders. Hattie found a few sequins that had fallen off the skirt and threw them into Melissa's hair for added accent. Now the sparkles in her hair matched her twinkling blue eyes.

"You're exquisite, cher. Your brother will have to fight off de young men."

"You're teasing me." Melissa blushed, then added, "Do you really think they will like me?"

"Unless dey are blind, cher." Hattie winked at her.

"I can't wait." Melissa spun around in front of the mirror. "Have you seen Alexandria?"

"No. I've not seen her all afternoon," Hattie admitted.

"Then, I'll go by and check on her. Have Brad and Julia gone downstairs?"

"*Oui,* I saw dem goin' down when I came in here. The guests should be arrivin' any minute, so you'd better get down dose stairs, too," Hattie said as she picked up Melissa's robe and placed it on the bed.

"I will, I will." Missy rushed to the door. "But first, I'm going by Alex's room. I thought we could go down together."

"Dat's good, but it's late and Alexandria could already be downstairs. I've been busy in de kitchen so I could have missed her, which reminds me, I should be getting' back now."

Hattie mumbled to herself all the way to the kitchen. She'd been occupied preparing food all day. One of the kitchen girls had taken sick, and Hattie had had to take up her slack. She hadn't even had a chance to help Alexandria dress, and she felt bad about that. Hattie was also worried about Brad. As far as she knew, he hadn't said anything to Alex. Hattie couldn't believe he was going to let that child have a baby by herself. She was extremely disappointed in him. Oh, he probably would make sure Alexandria was financially taken care of, but that wasn't what she needed.

Absorbed in her thoughts upon entering the kitchen, Hattie ran headfirst into Brad, sending her a few steps backwards.

He reached out and steadied her before she fell. "Is everything under control in here?"

"Isn't it always?" Hattie snapped. "Is everythin' under control wit' you?"

"Hattie, I must say I've never been happier." Brad grinned at her devilishly. "I'm really looking forward to tonight."

Hattie shook her head making a clicking sound with her tongue. "You should be ashamed of you'se'f!" Hattie's face registered her disgust. What in the hell was he so happy about?

Brad kissed her on the forehead. "You're a true gem, Hattie." Then he turned and walked out the door.

Flabbergasted, Hattie couldn't think of a thing to say.

Missy ran to Alexandria's room, where she stopped and slipped on her shoes, feeling very elegant in her high-heeled slippers. Even though she was only thirteen, she felt much older tonight.

She peeked into Alexandria's room and found it completely dark. Alex must be downstairs, Missy thought. A little disappointed, she shut the door. Why hadn't Alex waited for her? Perhaps she was waiting at the bottom of the stairs.

Melissa peeked down at Brad and Julia greeting the arriving guests. Missy started to take the first step, but hesitated. All of a sudden the stairs seemed a mile long. She wasn't sure she could do this. Panic overtook her. She wouldn't cry, she just wouldn't. It would ruin everything.

"Be strong," Missy told herself. Taking a deep breath, she repeated, "You can do it. Just open your eyes and take the first step." Somehow, Alex's words came flooding back, giving her the strength she needed.

Missy grabbed the handrail and, with her right hand, lifted her skirt slightly. After the first two steps she gained her confidence and with her head held high descended to the bottom.

Brad looked up just as she reached the bottom part of the stairs. His stunned look absolutely pleased Melissa. Why, he had lost all the color in his face.

"Hi, Brad. Do you like my dress?" Melissa smiled, beaming from ear to ear.

"You can walk!" Brad shouted. He ran to her and hugged her tightly. "I don't believe it! How long have you been doing this?" He held Missy away from him. "I've never seen you look so lovely."

Pleasure filled Melissa at her brother's response. His eyes appeared watery, and if she didn't know better she'd swear he was about to cry. But Brad was strong. He never cried. Perhaps he just had a little something in his eye.

"I've been walking for about two weeks now. Isn't it wonderful?"

Brad stood back so he could see her better. His Missy... she was her old self again. "Why haven't you told me before now, puss?"

"Alex and I wanted to surprise you." Melissa looked beyond her brother, trying to find Alex. "Have you seen her?"

"Brad, you're neglecting our guests," Julia snapped behind him.

Brad barely glanced at Julia. "I'm sure you can handle them, Julia. Why don't you go ahead? I want to talk to my sister."

"I'd rather you went with me." Julia hadn't even acknowledged that Melissa was standing, and not in her chair.

"Don't push your luck, Julia!" Brad bit out.

Her eyebrow raised, but she wisely didn't say a word as she left and went into the ballroom.

"Where is Alex?" Melissa asked again.

"I've not seen her, Puss," Brad said.

"She's not downstairs?"

"I could have missed her. Maybe she's in the ballroom." Then Brad thought how reluctant Alexandria had been about coming to the party. As a matter of fact, they had had an argument about it. "She is coming, isn't she?"

"I hope so. She bought a special dress for the occasion, but she wouldn't let me see it."

Brad relaxed just a little. He would have been damn mad if Alexandria was deliberately defying him. Yet, she had done what she said she could do. Alex had been the life saver for his sister, and for that he'd always be eternally grateful. He glanced down at the frown on Missy's face.

"I'll tell you what I'll do. We'll go into the ballroom, and if I don't see her, I will go upstairs and find out what's keeping Alexandria. Does that make you happy?"

Melissa smiled and bobbed her head.

"Come on, I want to escort the most beautiful young woman here tonight into the ballroom." He draped her hand across his arm. "Later on I have a surprise for you."

She looked up at her brother with adoring eyes. "A surprise, Brad. What is it?"

"You'll see shortly."

When they made their entrance, it was hard to tell who was smiling the most, Brad or Melissa. No sooner had they entered the ballroom than everyone immediately noticed Melissa was walking. Loud whispers raced through the crowd, and soon well wishers gathered around her to offer their congratulations.

Brad was so proud of his sister as he stepped back, letting her become the center of attention. He scanned the room, hoping to locate Alexandria among his lavishly dressed guests. But she was nowhere to be found.

When he turned to leave, he bumped into Julia. "Excuse me."

"Where are you going, darling?" Julia asked.

"I'll be back in a few minutes." Brad quickly left before she could ask any more questions.

Julia watched the crowd gather around Melissa. *Well, well, the little chit was walking.* That was the best news she'd had lately. This meant Alexandria's days were numbered. Tonight was going to be her night. Julia would have Brad officially committed to her, and she would be rid of Alexandria. Julia smiled. Yes, it was going to be a grand night.

Chapter Twenty-One

Before Brad went to get Alexandria, he stopped by his study to pick up something very important. He slipped a pouch into his pocket and left.

Taking the stairs two at the time, his long strides carried him down the corridor. In no time he arrived at Alexandria's room. He knocked calling her name, "Alexandria ... Alexandria." Silence answered him. Where could she be?

The doorknob turned easily beneath his fingers. When he pushed the door open he found nothing but darkness. Maybe she had packed her bags and left. Hadn't she threatened to do just that the other night? The very thought quickened Brad's steps as he went to his room to retrieve an oil lamp.

With the lantern now lighting his way, he immediately returned to Alexandria's room. The flame cast a soft glow upon the room's contents. In the middle of the bed, snuggled beneath the covers Alexandria lay fast asleep. He paused to light several candles, then set his lamp on the table beside the bed. Strange, Alexandria hadn't moved an inch. Was she ill?

Her long auburn curls, strewn in disarray, completely covered her face. Reaching down, he brushed the soft hair back away from her eyes, and gently touched her cheek, checking for a temperature. No, she didn't have a fever; she was just blissfully sleeping.

"Alexandria." He shook her arm. "It's time to get up."

"Go away," she muttered a sleepy protest. "I want to sleep."

"And let you miss my celebration? Not on your life." He tried nudging her again, with no results. Alexandria!" His booming voice roared in the quiet room.

Startled, she bolted straight up in the bed. The covers slid to her waist.

"Oh, God," Brad said hoarsely as he stared at her gleaming white breasts. His eyes fixed on the firm mounds that were so perfect ... so inviting. "Oh, my God."

What time was it anyway? Alex thought. The rude awakening had left her a little foggy. Where was she ... in the children's room? No. They were well. Her eyes began focusing more clearly now on the person in front of her. Brad! She gasped. What was he doing here? Then she noticed he wasn't looking at her face. Glancing down, she realized why. She was stark naked. Quickly, she snatched up the covers and tucked the blankets under her chin, feeling herself blushing all the way to her toes.

"What are you doing in here?"

"Have you forgotten?" Lazy mockery lit his eyes. "I've come to escort you down to the party."

"Yes ... I mean no, I've not forgotten." Alex yawned, thinking she had all the time in the world. Did the man want her to stand in the receiving line next to Julia and welcome the guests? Wouldn't that be a hoot. He couldn't possibly be that crazy. So why was he acting so impatient? She would really rather sleep than go to his soiree, anyway. "What time is it?"

"Seven o'clock," Brad informed her.

"Seven o'clock. Damn ... I must have been tired." Alex yawned. "How about I go back to sleep, and you can tell me about the festivities tomorrow?"

"Alexandria," Brad said in a rather impatient voice. "Either you get up and get dressed, or I'll dress you myself."

"You wouldn't dare."

"Oh, wouldn't I?"

Seeing the look in his eyes, she had no doubt he would carry out his threat. "All right, all right," she said irritably. "You've made your point. But I still don't see why I have to go."

"Because it will please me, and that's all that should concern you." Brad stared at her intently, as if he dared her to object. "I'll go back down to the dance. I trust you can find your way downstairs?"

"I think I can manage." The man would never quit amazing her. *Because it would please him!* Where was women's lib when she needed it?

"By the way," Brad said just before leaving the room. "Thank you for helping Melissa. I never thought she'd walk again." His voice once again softened. "I've left a present for you on the dresser as a token of my thanks. Please promise me you'll wear it tonight."

"All right, if it will get you to leave," Alex said, not even bothering to ask about the gift.

As the door closed behind him, she realized she hadn't thanked him for the present, nor asked how Melissa was doing. "Well, what did he expect after waking me up so rudely?"

Alex rubbed her eyes. She felt much better after getting some rest. Casting aside the covers, she climbed out of bed and stretched like a lazy cat just up from a nap. She retrieved her robe and stumbled across the floor to the washbasin. There she splashed cool water on her face and rubbed it briskly with a towel, trying to wake herself up.

When she sat down in front of the large mirror, her eyes seemed plain in her oval face. Picking up a kohl pencil, she lined each eye then smudged the line, which enhanced her eyes. Her thick, dark lashes could use a bit of mascara, but there was little hope of finding any. Thank goodness, she did have some powder Hattie had mixed up especially for her. Hattie had told her to save it until tonight.

Opening the container, surprise curled through her. The bronze powder sparkled. She took the puff and dusted her face and shoulders.

She peered into the mirror amazed at the results. Perfect. Her black eyelashes sparkled with gold and accented her emerald eyes beautifully, and her face had taken on a healthy glow. But what to do with her hair? It had always presented a problem, and with no hair spray her tresses definitely had a mind of their own. Bending her head over, she back-brushed her hair to add body.

Standing up straight, Alexandria shook her head, and the burnished-red curls went everywhere. There was absolutely no controlling her red mane. Taking her hands, she pushed the hair away from her face.

Deciding there was simply nothing more she could do, she gave up and let it hang in curls around her shoulders, then walked over and took her dress off the hanger. The seamstress had done an excellent job. She had put stays under the bust line to help shape the gown. The black crepe dress felt like silk as it slid across Alex's body. She struggled with the twenty black pearl buttons that marched down the back of the dress. Twisting and turning, Alexandria made sure she hadn't missed a single button. Where was Hattie when she needed her?

Alexandria smiled at her reflection. The strapless gown fit tight in the bust and then fell in folds to the floor. How elegant, she thought as she slipped on charcoal-colored opera gloves and wondered at the stir she would create. True, her gown was elegant for the 1980's, but there had never been anything like it in this time period. And black! In 1835, black would have been strictly for mourning ... that is, until now.

Well, it was now or never ... she preferred never. But she knew Brad would come back and get her. She slipped on her ebony kid pumps and started for the door. "I'll teach him to demand my appearance!" She said with bravado.

"Brad!" She had forgotten the gift. She went back to the dresser and found a small, velvet pouch on the corner. No, it couldn't be, she thought as she remembered the black pouches she'd seen earlier. She pulled open the drawstrings and spilled the contents onto her hand.

Alex gasped. "The necklace!" Brad must have mistakenly picked up the wrong pouch. He would never give anything this valuable to a stranger. True, he was thankful that Missy could walk, but this was too much. Alex laid the necklace back on the dresser. She just couldn't accept it.

As she stared at the lovely piece of jewelry, a nagging little demon entered her head, and told her, *You'd really irritate Julia by wearing that necklace. She doesn't have to know that Brad gave it to you by mistake.* A small, devilish smile touched Alex's lips ... why not? She picked up the necklace and fastened it around her neck.

She felt like a queen. Each stone glittered with magnificent highlights, and the emerald in the middle exactly matched the color of her eyes. "Eat your heart out, Julia," Alex said as she shut the door.

Feeling like Cinderella descending the stairs, she wondered if her Fairy Godmother lurked nearby. As a matter of fact, there was no one in the foyer so much for a grand enterence.

Her dress floated around her feet with each step, and though she didn't realize it, the crepe material clung to every inch of her body, revealing her luscious curves.

Soft music floated through the air from the main doors of the ballroom. Alex hesitated. All her previous confidence suddenly vanished. Here she was getting ready to walk into a crowd of people who she didn't know, and in a dress that was sure to draw attention. Why hadn't she worn a gown like everyone else's, so she would blend into the crowd? If Brad hadn't made her mad, she wouldn't be in this situation now. He was always the reason for any trouble she got herself into.

Opening the doors slightly, she peeked into the grand ballroom, but she could only see the backs of the guests' heads as they watched the dancers.

While no one was looking she ducked behind the latticed wall located in the rear. Now she could check everyone out without being noticed herself. What had happened to the brave woman she'd been upstairs? Somehow that person had disappeared.

Enormous crystal chandeliers bathed the room with bright lights, illuminating at least twenty dancing couples. A variety of flowers and greenery were scattered around the room, adding colorful embellishments. The musicians stationed on a raised platform performed just the right music . . . no hard rock or electric guitars--thank goodness.

All the fashions were exquisite. Gowns of every bright color imaginable twirled around the ballroom floor--every color except black. Laces and silks adorned the gowns, and the more affluent women flaunted their finery with much pride.

Scanning the room to locate Melissa, Alex spotted her straight across the room. What an angel she appeared tonight with her blond curls piled high on her head. Her blue eyes were the same turquoise color as her dress. She was an adorable young lady tonight, and Alexandria was proud of her. At least she'd made a difference in someone's life.

Several boys vying for her attention gathered around Missy, who batted her eyelashes flirtatiously. It became apparent she had picked up that trick very quickly. The child absolutely glowed with the attention she was receiving.

Excitement seemed to fill the air as people chattered in different groups all around Alex. One group in particular caught her attention when she heard them say, "Look at Brad and Julia, don't they make a lovely couple?"

Alexandria looked sharply to her right. She stood very still, trying to hear what the women were saying.

"Yes, they are lovely, dear, but to tell you the truth I thought they would never announce their engagement."

Alexandria followed their eyes and, though she couldn't see well through the latticework, she could make out Brad's figure on the dance floor. Stepping out from her hiding place, she could now see him dancing with Julia.

Brad cut an extremely dashing character tonight. Earlier, when he'd awakened her, she hadn't paid the least bit of attention to what he'd been wearing. Now she was awake and could see he wore a jacket not of emerald, but of a dark forest green. So dark it gave the appearance of being black, and his fawn-colored trousers fit snugly to his thighs. She couldn't see the rest of him, because his back was to her as he waltzed. A twinge of jealously fluttered through her as she noticed Julia laughing at some comment he'd made.

Alexandria hated to admit it, but Julia looked very pretty tonight in a light green ball gown. The dress was not modest by any means, but cut extremely low. Even her dark brown hair pulled up into a chignon added to her allure.

Once again Julia's laughter rang out. Brad joined with his own deep baritone laughter. A lump formed in Alex's throat. She felt the tears she wanted to cry, but fought her emotions, swearing to herself that she didn't care. She'd heard expecting mothers were very emotional, and apparently in her case it was true.

"So, you've taken to hiding in corners," Edmund said from behind her."

A startled cry escaped her lips as Edmund tapped her on the shoulder. She'd been contemplating so hard; she hadn't heard him approach. She had also gained the attention of the gossiping women. They both turned and looked at her.

"You scared me," Alex whispered.

"Edmund, come here and bring your friend, dear," one of the ladies called to him.

Alexandria stood like a frightened jackrabbit ready to flee. But Edmund ended any idea of escape by grabbing her elbow and escorting her over to Susan Rathchild and Lucy Simmons, two of the biggest gossips around. He greeted the two women.

"Edmund, why don't you introduce us to your lady friend?" Susan asked.

"Of course." He nodded his head to the ladies. "May I introduce Alexandria Dumont. Alexandria, this is Susan Rathchild and her long time friend, Lucy Simmons."

Alexandria murmured an appropriate response.

"My, you're a mighty pretty thing," Lucy commented. "I'm sorry for your loss, my dear. It must be terrible for one so young."

"My loss?" Alexandria didn't know exactly what to say.

"Was it your husband, dear?"

"No, I've never been married."

"Your mother, then?" Susan added.

"No ... I haven't lost anyone."

Both ladies' eyebrows shot up. "We're sorry, but since you're wearing black ... We assumed ..." Lucy stammered, her face turning a deep red. "No one wears black, unless someone is dead," she finished blurting out.

Alexandria laughed nervously. This was it ... she better make her story a good one. "I can understand your confusion, ladies," she said, trying to put them at ease. The woman named Lucy looked like she was going to faint at any moment. "But you see, black is the latest rage in Paris and will soon be seen everywhere in the United States."

"Black? I for one can't imagine it catching on here." Susan's snooty voice sounded doubting.

"I don't know about that, Susan," Lucy said. "You must admit the dress she has on is simply stunning."

Alexandria glanced around, certain now that she was drawing more attention than she wanted. As the music began again, she was just about to ask Edmund to dance and get her out of the conversation, but he beat her to the punch.

"Would you care to dance?" Edmund didn't give her a chance to reply as he led her on the floor.

Alexandria heard Lucy ask Susan, "Aren't those the Wentworth jewels around her neck?"

The crowd had grown quiet ... too quiet. Alex felt as if every eye was fastened to her as Edmund whirled her around the dance floor. She kept her eyes on him. Her courage left her; perhaps this hadn't been such a good idea. "I hope I'm not embarrassing you, Edmund."

"Are you kidding?" He laughed. "You're definitely going to make this a party to remember. And you're the only woman here who would dare wear black. All those old biddies are just jealous. I do believe a few are grabbing their smelling salts."

"So you like my black dress?"

"Yes, I do. Just what are you up to, Alexandria Dumont?" But he went on before she could answer, "I'd say you are definitely making a statement."

"I'm not that obvious, am I?"

"Probably only Brad will catch your meaning." Edmund smiled at her. "The other two women are some of the biggest gossips we have. In no time, they will have your Paris story spread around the entire room."

Alexandria couldn't help the laughter that bubbled forth.

At the sound of her laughter, several men sighed at the enchanting creature moving by them. They commented on her flaming red hair. Another talked of her emerald green eyes. And the third turned to ask Brad, "Isn't that your mother's necklace she's wearing?"

Brad nodded as his gaze, too, was glued to Alexandria. Humor danced in his ice-blue eyes. Black! He had figured she would defy him in one way or another, but he'd never dreamed she'd go this far by wearing such a gown, the likes of which he'd never seen. His little hellcat had found yet another way to surprise him. But tonight he'd have the last laugh.

Edmund led Alex from the dance floor over to Melissa, who came running up to hug her.

"Alex, you look stunning, but ..." Missy made her bend down so she could whisper in Alex's ear. "You are not supposed to wear black. It's for mourning."

Alexandria smiled and in turn whispered to Melissa, "I'm mourning the loss of your brother's sanity."

Melissa started snickering, and they both enjoyed a good laugh.

"I'm glad to see you two are enjoying my party." Brad's gaze traveled over Alexandria.

His evaluation of her did not go unnoticed, but she couldn't read his thoughts. His eyes appeared distant. Did he approve or disapprove? She couldn't be sure.

"Oh, Brad, it's perfect. I'm having such a good time," Missy said.

"I've noticed you've been talking to several young men," Brad teased. "Perhaps I should be chaperoning?"

"No, Brad! You'd scare them all off," Melissa replied too quickly, a panicked look on her face.

"Who, me?" He looked shocked. "I'm just a mere pussycat."

Alexandria almost choked on the iced champagne she was sipping.

Brad arched an eyebrow in her direction, but he had yet to say anything to her. Instead, he asked, "Melissa, how about dancing with me?"

"I can't dance, Brad," the child confessed. "I just learned how to walk."

"And you didn't think you could do that, either," Alex reminded her. "Go ahead and try. Just follow your brother's lead."

Alexandria grimaced when she saw Missy step on Brad's foot. However, he never missed a step. In no time, Melissa looked like she had been dancing for years.

Edmund had gone to get Alexandria another glass of champagne, and for the moment she stood alone. It was amazing how thirsty she became when Brad was near.

"What are you doing with that necklace on?" Julia's eyes glittered with fury.

"I beg your pardon?" Alex hadn't realized the Wicked Witch of the East was anywhere around. "It was a gift from Brad," she said smoothly. "It's lovely, don't you think?"

"Are you sure you didn't steal it?" Julia accused. "It's to be handed down to Brad's wife. And that's me," Julia held her hand out.

Alex stared at the outstretched hand. The stupid woman thought she was going to take off the necklace and give it to her ... not in this lifetime. Then she remembered what she'd read in the diary. Catherine had mentioned how Julia had greedily stared at her jewels. Alex now knew what Catherine had meant, for she could see the greed in Julia's eyes.

"Julia, you can stand there until you're blue in the face, but Brad put this necklace on me, and only he can take it off." Now, that was a good lie, and she could see it hit the mark by the redness in Julia's face.

Julia drew back to slap Alexandria, but Edmund caught her arm, and at the same time smoothly handed Alexandria a glass of champagne.

"Now Julia, you wouldn't want to cause a scene and let Brad see your true personality, would you?"

"Stay out of this, Edmund! She has my necklace!"

"Funny, I thought those were the Wentworth jewels, and I don't believe you are a Wentworth."

"Shut up, Edmund," Julia snarled.

"Did you say dance? Why I'd love to, Julia."

Even with her protesting, Edmund escorted Julia to the dance floor. She immediately straightened and smiled at him.

Alex looked around to find that once again, she was drawing more attention than she wanted. Why not go back to her original spot behind the lattice wall? Brad and Melissa were coming her way, so that idea was shot.

"You did very well, Missy." Alexandria praised her.

"It's all thanks to you." The child hugged her. "Why don't you two dance? I want to go over and talk to my friends."

Alex grew uneasy under Brad's intense scrutiny. "You don't have to dance with me," she blurted out.

"Did someone die, Alexandria?" Brad's eyes danced with merriment.

She was determined he wasn't going to bait her; after all she'd just put up with Julia. "I told you, you don't have to dance with me."

He grinned. And Alexandria couldn't help the weak feeling that washed over her every time he gave her a devilish smile. He was so good-looking in his crisp cut jacket, and snowy-white cravat, which only enhanced his dark complexion. He took her hand, slowly leading her onto the center floor.

The band began playing a soft waltz as Brad took her into his arms, drawing her forward. He held her much too close. When she looked up to tell him so, she found his eyes had turned a deep, passionate blue. Neither said a word. They just danced, yet neither looked away. She searched for some deep meaning, some small feeling she might discover that would tell her what he was thinking, or how he felt. Now Alex wasn't sure if she'd seen passion earlier, for his eyes were well guarded. Perhaps she should face the truth ... he felt no emotional attachment for her. It was just her imagination. The announcement would be made tonight, and it would finally put an end to this crazy crush she had on him.

Strong arms urged her body closer to his, and she felt the warm, tingling sensations spread through every inch of her. *Please save me,* Alexandria thought. For she definitely, no matter how much she denied the fact, had feelings for this man. Even if she wasn't quite sure what those feelings were.

She ceased to think. Brad was such a smooth and skillful dancer that she felt as if she were dancing on air. Giving up her earlier struggles, she closed her eyes and let her body relax against his. For one last time, she'd enjoy his arms around her and the feel of his masculine body.

Much too soon the dance ended. Quickly, Julia claimed Brad and moved him to the other side of the room. Alexandria thought it strange they had danced the entire waltz without either of them having said a word.

Perhaps Brad had thought it was his duty to dance with her, and that had been the reason he hadn't spoken. If that were the case, he could have saved himself the trouble.

Alex managed to spark anger in herself again--exactly what she needed to get through this night. Her anger, she was learning, became a shield to protect herself.

The next hour or so became a whirl to Alexandria. The guests readily accepted her, and the women began asking where she had purchased such a lovely dress. It seemed they heard it was all the rage in Paris.

She had danced with so many men she'd lost count. Despite her inner turmoil, she was having a good time, and she couldn't help noticing Edmund had kept her supplied with punch. Hot from the last dance, she stood in the corner, fanning herself. Across the room, she observed Brad and Edmund deep in conversation, their heads together as if sharing a secret. Suddenly Edmund chuckled and patted Brad on the back. She wondered what they could be talking about.

"I see you like corners, too." The voice came from beside her. "If you're hot, I'll be glad to get you something to drink."

Alex turned to thank what she assumed would be one of her dance partners, but it wasn't any of them. The man was a priest. "Thank you, Father, but I'll be fine."

"Are you sure?"

"Yes," she assured him. "I don't believe we've met, Father. I'm Alexandria Dumont."

"I'm Father Barrett. It's nice to make your acquaintance, Alexandria. That's a pretty name. Did you know it means defender of mankind?"

"No, I didn't. I'm a doctor, so I guess the name fits." She smiled.

"It is rather stuffy in here. I guess I'm not used to such affairs," Father Barrett confessed.

"I'm not, either." Alex fiddled with the fan that dangled from her wrist. "I can truly say this is my first ball."

"How long have you been grieving, my child?" Father Barrett looked sympathetic.

Alexandria couldn't help but laugh, which in turn produced a surprised look on the man's face. She had been asked that question a dozen times now. "Father, I'm not in mourning. This is a new style. Can't you tell by the way it's made?"

"Now that you mention it, your dress is very elegant, and, I might add, looks very nice on you."

"Thank you. You said you normally do not come to these affairs. If you don't mind me asking, what made you decide to come to this one?"

"Mr. Wentworth requested that I perform his wedding ceremony tonight."

"You mean engagement, Father. He's supposed to announce his engagement," Alex informed him.

"No child." He flushed with embarrassment. "I hope I've not said too much, but Brad decided to surprise his bride. He said he has waited long enough, and is going to skip the engagement and get married instead. It's rather unorthodox, but he certainly was insistent." The priest looked at her. "Are you sure I can't get you some water? You look mighty pale, child."

Alex thought she was going to be sick. The room seemed to be closing in on her.

Married ... Married ... tonight?

Brad was getting married. She tried to let it sink in. *Why are you so upset?* She scolded herself. An engagement would have just been the last step before marriage ... so what was the difference? *The difference is he'll be married ... and to that witch.* She felt the tears form in her eyes, and knew the priest was waiting for her to say something. He looked so sympathetic.

"I--If you could get me a glass of water," she said brokenly. Her voice sounded strange, even to her.

She watched Brad and Julia. She felt a tear slip and roll down her cheek. Swiftly, she wiped it away before anyone noticed. Alexandria wished she could leave without drawing any attention, but just then the melody faded and Brad looked her way. All she wanted to do was ask why. She sensed tenderness in his eyes. Or pity? That had always been the problem ... she never knew now he felt.

She never thought Brad's getting married would affect her so. After all, he'd been already promised to Julia when Alex had first met him. But now, as she searched her soul, she knew she secretly hoped he'd change his mind before getting engaged. Now there seemed little hope. However, she wouldn't run and hide like she had previously wanted to do. She would stay and wish them well.

"Here is your water, Alexandria." Father Barrett handed her a glass.

Her hands shook slightly as she held the glass to her lips.

"Are you all right, my child?"

"Yes, Father. I'll be fine."

Chapter Twenty-Two

The music seemed to hold a strange haunting melody just for Alexandria. Brad and Julia had finished their waltz and were heading her way. Her instincts told her to run as the couple drew near to where she and Father Barrett stood, but her pride demanded she stay.

"Father Barrett, I'm glad you could come tonight on such short notice." Brad reached out and shook his hand. "Are you having a good time?"

"Yes, this lovely lady--" he put his hand on Alexandria's arm-- "has been keeping me company. However, I don't believe she's feeling well."

"Are you sick, Alexandria?" Brad's voice expressed his concern as his eyes took in every little detail. She appeared pale and there was a haunting look in her eyes, but other than that, she seemed fine.

"She does look bad. Perhaps she should go lie down," Julia added.

Brad chose to ignore Julia's comment. "Are you all right?" As he repeated his question, he placed his hand on Alexandria's arm. For some strange reason, he wanted to touch her, just to make sure for himself that she was indeed all right.

She finally shook her head. "Just a little hot."

Still, he stared a moment longer, before turning to the priest. "Father Barrett are you ready?"

"Yes, Mr. Wentworth."

"Ready for what?" Julia wanted to know.

Alexandria knew, but she couldn't say anything for fear of crying. She could only regard the couple in front of her.

"You'll see in a minute, Julia." Brad walked with Father Barrett to the bandstand, talking in a soft whisper. Julia followed close behind, trying to hear what they were saying, but it appeared she was unsuccessful. Brad stopped just before reaching the platform and said something to his sister.

Melissa shook her head in answer to Brad's request, then made her way to Alexandria. "Well, Alex it looks as if Brad's going to make his announcement."

"Yes, Missy, it appears you will be getting a new sister-in-law shortly."

"It's only an engagement, Alex. He'll change his mind," Melissa said.

"Ladies and Gentlemen, may I have your attention?" Brad raised his voice and shortly the crowd grew quiet.

"I want to thank all of you for coming tonight. This ball has turned out to be a celebration in a couple of ways. First, as I'm sure you've all noticed, my sister has recovered and is now able to walk again." The audience applauded and several cheered.

"This achievement would not have been possible without the help of Dr. Alexandria Dumont. I would like for everyone to meet her now." Brad held his hand out in the direction of Melissa and Alexandria. "Missy, will you bring Alexandria up here?"

Alex groaned. She didn't want to be a part of this. Couldn't he just let her leave *now*? She could start packing right this minute and be out of his life forever. Then again, where would she go?

Melissa took Alexandria's elbow, and when Alex hesitated Missy looked at Edmund for help.

Never missing a cue, Edmund took Alexandria's left arm, and they escorted her to the platform.

Why did she feel like a lamb going to slaughter?

Brad helped her up on the platform, then turned to face the audience while he held her elbow in a firm grip. "Ladies and Gentlemen, Alexandria Dumont, a lady to whom I'll be eternally grateful." He smiled at her, and the crowd applauded their approval.

A forced smile remained frozen on Alex's face. She was just doing her job. She really didn't expect all this fuss. And, after Father Barrett's earlier announcement, her joy had evaporated. She merely wanted to get the hell out of here.

"My second surprise," Brad said, and Alex tensed. "Instead of announcing my engagement tonight, I've thought long and hard, and thus have decided to give up my bachelorhood instead of waiting ..."

A hush fell over the crowd.

"Father Barrett has agreed to perform my wedding ceremony tonight, and all of you are to be my witnesses."

Everyone began to whisper all at once about Brad's surprise announcement. Alex just stood there, perfectly still, as if someone had turned her to stone. If he thinks I'm going to stand here and witness this ... he's crazy.

Brad faced the priest, dropping Alexandria's arm. "Father Barrett, if you will begin."

Now was her chance. She started to leave, but Brad's hand shot out and seized her wrist before she could take another step.

He looked down at her. "I need you to stand right here."

"Why?"

"Because I said so." He regarded her in an odd sort of way. "Damn it, Alexandria, must you question everything?" Brad angrily whispered to her, before he turned to make sure Julia and Missy were on his other side.

Father Barrett started, "Dearly Beloved, we are gathered here ..."

Was the man going to make her stay and be a witness? Alex felt strange. She stood on Brad's left and Julia stood on the right. Wasn't she standing in the wrong place?

"Do you, Alexandria Dumont, take Brad Wentworth to be your lawful wedded husband?"

"Huh?" Alex wasn't sure she'd heard him correctly. Surely he meant to say Julia. Alex peeked around Brad to look at Julia. She appeared red in the face. Wasn't she going to say anything?

"She does," Brad answered for Alex, just as he heard Julia screech on the other side. A collective gasp rose from the crowd. In the confusion, Edmund easily waylaid Julia and moved her out the side door.

"And do you, Brad Wentworth, take Alexandria Dumont to be your lawful wedded wife?"

"I do," Brad's voice was firm and steady.

He didn't sound insane, Alex thought. Maybe she was the one who was insane. Yes, she was sure of it ... none of this could be happening.

"If anyone here can show just cause why ... "

Alexandria was getting ready to object, but Brad seemed to anticipate her move. He took her in his arms, kissing her before she could utter a word. Her small hands pushed on his chest in protest. He just deepened his kiss until finally her arms went around his neck.

Father Barrett cleared his throat. When he saw it did no good, he finished, "I now pronounce you man and wife."

Alexandria's heart pounded to a new beat. Could someone tell her what had just happened? Everything had taken place so quickly. Did she hear 'man and wife?'... *Wife* ... Was that her? She slowly opened her eyes to gaze into Brad's laughing eyes.

"Hello, Mrs. Wentworth." Brad wanted to laugh at the confusion he saw on her face.

"I can't be Mrs. Wentworth. I didn't get to say anything."

"You didn't have to ... I answered for you."

"I don't recall you asking me to marry you?"

"And what would you have said."

"No."

Her blunt answer made him laugh. "I rest my case. I just saved us both a lot of aggravation."

Soon they were besieged by people wishing them well and expressing surprise at their well-kept secret. Alexandria was as amazed as they were, but she did a good job of hiding it. She was surprised at the happiness she saw on everyone's face. She had expected they would be angry and upset.

"I'm so happy," Melissa all but shouted when she threw herself in Alexandria's arms. "Now we can be sisters, forever."

"We sure can." Alex smiled fondly at the child.

"Why didn't you tell me you were going to get married?" Missy looked at Alexandria and then Brad.

"I was as surprised as you were, Missy," Alexandria admitted.

"It's a good surprise. However, if Brad would have let you know earlier, you could have worn white." Melissa giggled. "I bet you're the only bride ever to be married in black. You should be ashamed of herself, Brad."

"Well, Missy, if I had told her she might have gotten cold feet and run away. Then you wouldn't have a new sister-in-law."

"She wouldn't have run away, Brad. Alex loves you." The innocent child stared up at her brother as if he were crazy.

"Oh?" Brad arched an eyebrow at Alexandria, a questioning look in his eyes. "She forgot to mention that small fact."

What could she say in front of Melissa? That she didn't love him?... No ... that wasn't the truth. As she stared at Brad, the truth became clear. She did love him, even if he didn't love her. Now she would have to be very careful. He had the ability to break her heart.

"And you love her," Melissa broke into Alexandria's thoughts. "That's all that matters."

Brad looked at his bubbly little sister. "Now that you have solved all our problems, don't you have something to do? Alexandria and I need to say good night to all our guests."

Alexandria was tired of smiling as they bid farewell to the last couple. She rubbed the back of her neck. "Did Edmund leave? I don't remember seeing him."

Brad started chuckling. "I haven't seen Edmund since he waylaid Julia. Damn, I hope he survived." Brad quit laughing and took Alexandria by the hand. "Come on, we really do have to talk to Julia." As he pulled her along behind him he said, "I guess she does need an explanation."

Alexandria followed and, for a change, she kept her mouth shut. But she couldn't wait to hear this explanation.

She opened the door of Brad's study. Julia sat in a green, wing-backed chair, and Edmund was propped against the mantel.

When they entered the room, Julia immediately jumped up and walked over to Brad.

"You bastard!" Julia slapped Brad hard across the face. "How dare you humiliate me like this!" She drew back to hit him again. This time Brad caught her wrist.

"I wouldn't do that if I were you," he warned. "Edmund, will you take Alexandria out, so I can have a word with Julia?"

Though Alex would really rather stay and hear his explanation, she did feel a wee bit guilty. She supposed she did owe Julia this much.

"Why, Brad?" Julia asked when the door had shut. "You know we had planned to be married for years."

"Julia, our marriage would have been one of convenience. There was never any love. Mother had tried to tell me that before her accident, but I wouldn't listen."

"That's not true ... I've always loved you. Why do you think I've waited all this time? I've given up so much for you." Her voice broke and tears trickled down her cheeks. "What about your precious River Bends? You can't have the land unless you're married to me."

"I've thought about that, Julia. The merging of our plantations would have made River Bends the largest plantation in New Orleans. Since that can't happen, I'm willing to buy the portion of River Bends that your father had a deed to."

"Never," she spat. "I'll never sell to you!"

"In that case, River Bends will experience a set back, but somehow we'll survive."

"Oh, Brad, won't you reconsider?"

"It's too late, Julia. I'm married." Strange, he wasn't affected by her crying. Looking at her, he knew the tears were for his benefit. His mother had been right; Julia was after his wealth. He knew that the minute the bills started pouring in. She had run up quite a tab as his future wife. He did feel bad about not holding to the agreement his father had made, but he had the strongest feeling his mother wouldn't have been happy with his original plans. It was as if she were here with him.

"You love her ... don't you?" Julia said with resignation.

This was the second time tonight someone had told him he loved Alexandria. Brad wasn't sure how to respond to that question. He did feel something for Alexandria. She made him angry, she made him laugh, she made him want her ... In the worst way, but were any of these things love? Then there was the baby, his baby, that grew within her. And he was proud, damn proud. With that thought on his mind he said, "Alexandria is pregnant with my child."

"What! You two-timing ...!" Julia started beating on his chest. "You've been sleeping with her the whole time. Of course, she pulled the oldest trick in the world, and you fell for it. I'm warning you now, both of you will pay dearly. Do you hear me?" she shouted. "I'll destroy River Bends before I'm through."

"I don't care what you do to me, Julia, but leave Alexandria out of this." He grabbed Julia's wrist and shoved her away from him.

"Like hell I will!" she said as she slammed the door to his study.

Edmund and Alexandria walked outside. The chill in the air made Alex wrap the shawl closer around her, but the coolness felt good on her flushed face. Maybe she could clear her jumbled thoughts out here.

"It was better for you not to stay inside with Brad and Julia," Edmund said. "I'm sure she is pitching a fit by now."

"I know." Alex shrugged her shoulders. The nagging in the back of her mind refused to be stilled. "But I would like to have heard the explanation he gave Julia for marrying me."

"That's easy. He loves you. It's the reason I bowed out." Edmund gave her a mock bow.

Alexandria started laughing. "How much have you had to drink?"

"Probably twice as much as you have, but I'm serious." Edmund stared at her. "Hasn't he told you?"

"No, he hasn't."

"You'll just have to give him time. After all, he did wise up and marry you and not Julia."

"I'm not sure that was wise of him, Edmund." She bit her lip and looked away. "You know how we fight."

"I think you have wedding jitters. Come on." He put his arm around her. "Let's go back in. After all, it's your wedding night."

"Don't remind me."

They were getting ready to walk up the front steps when Julia ran around the corner of the house.

"There you are, you little bitch," Julia snarled.

Edmund quickly stepped in front of Alexandria before Julia could reach her. "All right, Julia, let's not get violent."

She ignored Edmund as he held onto her arm. "I hate you," she stormed at Alexandria. "I never had any problems until *you* showed up!" Julia looked directly at her with glassy eyes. It was as if she stared right through her. Alex shivered.

"He'll never love you!" Julia shouted. "He just feels sorry for you, that's all." She sneered insultingly, then laughed. "He'll come back to me after you have that brat of yours ... You'll never be able to possess his love, so you'll end up with nothing."

Alex gasped, feeling uncomfortable with the fact that Julia had spoken the truth. How did she know about the baby? Alex would find out later, but for now she couldn't stand and take her insults any longer. "I have his name, Julia, and the jewels," Alexandria fingered the necklace around her neck. "And, for whatever reason ... Brad *did* choose me." Julia looked so miserable standing in front of her, Alex did feel sorry for her in a way. "I'm sorry you were hurt."

"Don't pity me! In the end, I'll get what I want." Julia's eyes darted to the necklace hanging around Alexandria's neck, Alex could see the greed building in Julia. "You'll regret the day you put those precious stones around your neck." Julia's face turned into an ugly sneer and her crazed look erased the last vestige of her beauty.

"Come on, Julia." Edmund tugged on her arm. "I'm taking you home. For you, the party is over."

Alex didn't wait to see if Edmund had to struggle with Julia. She wanted to go to her room. As she entered the house and climbed the stairs, she thought, *this had been one hell of a night.* So many emotions filtered through her mind. She had always wanted a big wedding, and to be able to wear a beautiful white dress. But most of all she had imagined seeing her future husband standing there waiting for her to come down the aisle with love in his eyes.

Reaching her room, Alex opened the door and went in. The candles had burned down low, but there was still enough light to get undressed. A champagne-colored satin nightgown laid across the end of the bed. She sat on the edge of the bed to remove her slippers and sighed. Tonight had proven to be most unusual. It definitely hadn't been a normal wedding.

"Married," she whispered to the empty room.

Had Brad only married her because he felt sorry for her? She felt her chest tighten. When Missy had commented that Brad loved her, he hadn't confirmed if his sister had spoken the truth. He hadn't said anything at all. Only that they needed to say good night to their guests. Julia was right. She had nothing but his name. She didn't have his love. And his pity was something she'd never accept. Just how did he find out about the baby? There was only one answer. Alexandria snatched at the buttons in the back of her dress. Her patience had worn thin, making the hooks all the more difficult to undo.

A knock sounded on the door, causing her to jump. Surely, Brad wasn't here already. She held her dress up in the front as she opened the door.

"*Bonjour,* Petite." Hattie entered and shut the door. "I wanted to make sure you are not overly upset over Brad's engagement. He is bound to come to his senses before he actually marries Julia." Hattie came closer. "Need some help wit' your gown?"

"You might say that. I can't reach these damn buttons," Alexandria said, exasperated.

"Did you have a good time?"

"Hattie, where have you been?"

"Well now ... after de party started, I went to visit Abraham. And I've just returned, cher." Hattie turned her around and started unbuttoning the gown. "Julia damn near run me over comin' out of Brad's study." Hattie chuckled. "Funny, I'd have thought she'd be happy after her engagement, but she looked quite upset."

"I guess she did." Alexandria had finally lost the rest of her composure and swung around to face Hattie. "I can't believe you were nowhere around while my life was falling apart."

Hattie frowned, placing her hands on Alex's arms. "Ah, cher, if I had known you were havin' a crisis ... I'd have been dere." Hattie placed a hand under Alex's chin. "I didn't t'ink you would get dis upset over de engagement. Don't worry. I guarantee, he'll not marry her."

"I guess he won't!" Alex pulled away. "He just married me!"

"To be sure?"

"Yes, I'm serious. We were married at the end of the party by Father Barrett."

"*Oui,* dat's wonderful. I knew he'd do de right thin'." Hattie's mirth was obvious in her bright eyes.

"You had a hand in this didn't you?"

"What do you mean, Petite?" She tried to look innocent of any wrongdoings.

"You told him about the baby." Alex threw the shoe she held in her hand. "You promised not to say anything."

"He had a right to know, cher. I didn't want to see him throw his life away."

"Hattie, you had no right! How do you think I feel, knowing he *had* to marry me?"

"Let me finish unbuttonin' your dress." Hattie began unfastening the tiny, black pearls. "You see dat necklace hangin' around your neck?"

Alexandria nodded.

"If Brad didn't care fo you, he'd never have given you somethin' so priceless. Dat necklace meant de world to his mother." Hattie helped Alex out of her gown. "You love him, and I believe he loves you, Petite ... Give it time. Use dat brain you have up dere."

"I didn't say I loved him."

"You didn't have to." Hattie grinned, then moved to the door. "Good night. Sweet dreams."

Slipping on the satin gown, Alexandria couldn't recall seeing this garment before, but then she had bought so many gowns this was probably packed in the back. Funny, it looked just like something a bride would wear.

"Well, Mrs. Wentworth, look how far you've come," she said, looking at herself in the mirror. Alex unfastened the jewels and lovingly put them in the black pouch. She never dreamed she would have anything this lovely. She never thought she'd have a husband, either. And, she most definitely had one of those.

So big and strong, Brad at times appeared like a mountain to her. The blond streaks in his brown hair accented his cobalt-blue eyes ... eyes that could turn her to mere putty with just one look. What in the world was she going to do with him?

"Madam, you are in the wrong room." Brad stood in the doorway casually leaning against the door. His shirt was unbuttoned and the hair on his chest peeked through and appeared most inviting.

Well, it was now or never, Alex thought as she turned to face ... the enemy?

Lord, she hoped not.

*C*hapter Twenty-Three

"Wrong room?" Alex echoed, hearing the nervous quiver in her own voice.

"I believe you should be in the suite at the end of the hall," Brad informed her.

"But that's *your* room."

"Precisely. And *you* are my wife."

Her annoyance increased when she found that her hands were shaking. Why couldn't he be loving and gentle? Instead of issuing commands and expecting them followed. It would make everything so much easier. She didn't even know the exact reason Brad had married her, but pity wasn't something she wanted. "I might be your wife, but I'm not your possession to be ordered about."

"My dear, there you are mistaken. I give the orders around here, and it would be wise for you to remember that small fact."

She wanted to laugh at his superior attitude. He'd have a difficult time in the twentieth century.

"I'll try to make a mental note," she said with much sarcasm.

In a split second, Brad came away from the door and crossed the room to stand before her. She took a step back, finding he made her extremely nervous. "If you married me because you felt s--sorry for me, then ... then this will be a marriage in name only!" she blurted out.

Brad reached out and grabbed her wrist. "I don't think so." He felt her tremble when he ran his hand up her arm. "Are you afraid?"

"No, of course not."

"Good. I wouldn't want you to be afraid." He leaned down and swept her up into his arms, then turned around and left the room, heading down the hallway to his room.

"W--what are you doing? You can't do this to me," she protested.

"I'm taking you where you belong. I figured it would be easier to carry you rather than drag you. Tomorrow you can move your clothes in here," he said, shutting the door behind him with a nudge of his foot.

"You'll regret this," she informed him. "I'll not be easy to live with."

Brad chuckled. "Regret is a fool's emotion, and I assure you, my love, I'm no fool." He gazed down and looked into her searching emerald eyes. "And sweetheart, I hate to tell you this, but you haven't been easy to live with since the moment I first laid eyes on you."

He didn't bother to release her, but instead thought back to the first time he had tangled with this little hellcat. Then, too, she had sparks flying from her expressive eyes and had completely captivated him. He couldn't believe he'd married the girl. He certainly hadn't intended to. Now what was he going to do with her? A smile started slowly at the corner of his mouth and spread into a wicked grin. Right now, he knew exactly what he was going to do with the headstrong Alexandria. And he intended to enjoy every minute.

As he held her captive with his eyes, he released her legs, letting her body slide slowly down the length of his. Still, he kept his arms around her waist, molding her body into his.

God, she felt good, he thought as he lowered his mouth ever so slowly, capturing the soft pink lips she offered him. He felt her body tense as she pushed on his chest, but he would not be put off. His blood surged through his veins in a rush while his senses filled with her fragrance. Brad found himself thirsting for this tempting creature with the emerald eyes. He had dreamed of her a thousand times before, always wondering how he could have conjured such a vivid dream in the library. Now he knew it had been real, and his dream-lover stood in front of him anticipating his next move. Would it be as good as before?

Alex felt every inch on this muscular body, but wasn't sure what to do or what to say. She didn't have much experience in the sex department. Of course she'd had hours of sex education and courses in anatomy, but knowing *what* goes *where* didn't bring her a bit of comfort at the moment. Her mind told her to resist him, and she tried to, that is, until his mouth lowered to hers and her traitorous body overruled her common sense. Her breath caught in her throat when Brad's lips touched hers. They were firm and hot as he placed light kisses on her face. She felt like she'd been branded as she slipped into a sea of erotic feelings. A moan from deep within her sounded faint as she began to tremble. Once again smoldering lips captured hers, and she ceased to think logically. Her defenses shattered, and no longer provided a shield from this man who held her so protectively in his arms. She wanted to tell him she loved him, that she'd waited all her life for this special moment. But it was impossible ... she knew that.

His words were unintelligible against her ear and his kiss blistering hot. Strong arms like tempered steel held her, but strangely enough they didn't hurt her. Instead she felt shielded as his kiss deepened, and she clung to him, wanting with her very soul all he could give.

Sweeping her up in his arms, Brad carried Alexandria and placed her on the satin cover of his bed. Her auburn hair fanned out across the pillows, and her mouth parted every so slightly. He wanted her so badly that every moment it took him to undress seemed like an eternity. His desires were so strong they surprised him. He felt like a young man, and longed to surrender to the urges that soared through his loins. But he needed to go slow, so he wouldn't frighten her. This would be like the first time they made love. At least this time they were both sober.

He knelt on the bed, and in one quick motion pulled the gown over her head. "Magnificent," he murmured, short of breath.

Alex's fingertips brushed his cheek and strong jaw; then slowly she traced his lips. She felt Brad nibble the ends of her fingers. His splendid body appeared like a bronzed god's. None of this seemed real. He was supposed to marry someone else. But when Brad pulled her back into his arms, she knew he was sincere.

His tongue parted her lips and plunged inside. A heady sensation started in Alexandria's head and spread like wildfire though her body. Slowly, she became intoxicated with his manly scent and his powerful body. Her body burned for the pleasure he could provide. She wanted more.

Tender lips brushed the side of her throat before his head moved lower. She gasped for air as his mouth covered her hard nipple, and his tongue began to move in a rhythm of its own. She couldn't believe the warmth that quickly spread through her body. When she thought she couldn't stand the torture any longer, Brad's mouth once again descended, crossing her belly, touching every tender little spot with his fiery lips. He knew exactly where to touch, and how to stroke. She felt helpless as her fingers entwined in his hair. Lower and lower his lips moved until he parted her thighs.

He could feel her wetness and knew she was ready. He wanted her badly, so badly he almost stopped his sweet torture. But the warmth and the taste of her was like a drug and he wanted more.

A desire like she had never known before grew in her belly. She raised her hips, and felt his tongue tease her as it probed everywhere. *God, it was hot in here!* She needed relief of some kind ... somehow ... "Please," she moaned and whimpered at the things he was doing to her. And finally, when she thought she could take no more, Brad entered her warmth and she cried out his name.

No longer shy, Alex wrapped her long, silky legs around Brad's waist. He leaned down to kiss her, rubbing against her taut nipples, just one more thing to drive her absolutely wild. She met his thrusts and felt all of him inside her.

Brad now knew the meaning of sheer ecstasy, because he was surely in its grips. He tried to hold back, tried to make it last, but the wild creature beneath him stirred a blazing fire in his loins. When she raised her hips to take all of him inside, he lost what little control he had left. A fine sheen of perspiration covered both their bodies as Brad penetrated her again and again. Finally, the release they both sought came in one powerful shudder.

As they both floated back down to earth, the room was quiet except for their labored breathing. Brad rolled over so his weight would not crush Alexandria. As he did so, he pulled her by his side, keeping her folded in his arms.

"Alexandria," Brad said in a ragged voice.

"Yes."

"I just wanted to make sure this wasn't a dream."

"If it was ... I don't ever want to wake up," she admitted, softly.

Alexandria awoke the next morning feeling extremely contented, but when she rolled over to tell Brad good morning, she found herself alone.

She frowned and her new found contentment completely disappeared. Last night had been so wonderful; more than she had ever dreamed it could be. They had made love once more, and in the early morning hours had fallen asleep in each other's arms. There had been little conversation last night, and this morning she was looking forward to talking. Evidently, Brad had different ideas.

What kind of marriage was this going to be? Unusual was the only word she could think of. How was she supposed to act? After all, they were not a lovey-dovey pair. They simply desired each other. Since she lacked answers to her problems, she would simply try not to think about them.

Getting up, she dressed in a dark blue morning dress. She was starved and it only took her a moment to descend the stairs and head for the breakfast room. She found Melissa already there.

"Hi, Sis." Melissa giggled.

"Good morning, Missy. What's for breakfast? I'm famished." These last few days Alexandria had noticed she was always hungry.

"I'm having some sweet rolls and hot chocolate. Would you care for some?"

"Mmm, that sounds good," Alex said and went to the carved oak buffet to serve her plate.

"What are you going to do today?"

"I have been instructed ..." Alexandria smiled to herself. Ordered would have been a better word. "...to move my things into your brother's room. Would you like to help?"

Melissa snickered. "I think it's great you two got married. Just think, I could be sitting here with Julia." Melissa made a terrible face, showing her dislike. "You know, Alex, she was always mean to me."

"Was she?" Alex frowned as she came back to the table. "What did she do?"

"She'd pinch me all the time, especially if I said something she didn't like. One time, she shoved my wheelchair toward the top of the stairs. I just knew I was going to go flying down the steps, but, thank goodness, she stopped me before I got there. I was so scared!"

"Why didn't you tell somebody?"

"Julia said if I told--the next time she wouldn't stop my chair. Now that I can walk, I won't have to worry about being helpless any longer. Hopefully, we'll never see her again."

"I wouldn't count on it."

"Why?"

"I just don't think we've seen the last of Julia." Alex sipped her hot chocolate. "Remember, she blames me for everything that's happened. And in a way she's right. If I'd never come here, she and Brad probably would have married."

Missy lowered the roll she was about to put in her mouth. "Do you think she will try to hurt you?"

"No, nothing like that, so don't worry." Alexandria wasn't quite sure what Julia would do, but she didn't want Melissa afraid. "Missy, if Julia threatens you again, you're to tell us. You don't have to be afraid of her."

After breakfast, it didn't take long to move the few things Alexandria had accumulated. She'd worked half a lifetime and these few belongings were all she had. Then she smiled because she realized she now had something she'd always longed for--a family.

She picked up her medical bag she kept by the nightstand and, remembering Catherine's diary, slipped it into the bag.

Brad's masculine room was much like the master himself. Lord, she'd begun thinking like these people.

The room's decor was a dark forest green with deep cherry furniture. A fireplace stood on the far wall and a cozy fire had been built, since the days had turned cool. Beautifully crafted chairs of burgundy leather stood on both sides of the fireplace. Several forest green throw rugs lay scattered about the hardwood floors, and in the middle of the room, a high, four-poster bed appeared larger than most beds. Brad had probably had it made especially for himself.

Melissa hung up the last dress in the wardrobe. "That's it, Alex."

"Good." She finished opening the drapes, so the sunlight could invade the room. "Have you done your exercise lately?"

"No, I don't need it anymore."

"Well, that's not exactly true. You still need a little exercise to keep your muscles strong. Jogging each day would help."

"Jogging?" Melissa looked at her quizzically.

"Never mind. Come on, and I'll show you some new moves."

Abraham had just left Brad's study. They'd decided to build another barn to keep hay in during the off season.

Brad liked the sketch that Abraham had shown him. He had a good head for numbers, Brad thought, as he glanced down at the figures the man had presented for the supplies he'd need.

Pleased with Abraham's work, Brad smiled. Alexandria had definitely known what she was doing the day she'd bought him. She'd also been correct about his sister walking, too. Yes, his wife had turned into a rare gem.

Alexandria ... his bride. What had made him marry her? The little hellcat didn't love him, and if he had asked her properly she surely would have turned him down. It was true they desired each other. Hadn't she become pure butter in his arms? He smiled at the thought. The fact remained, his child needed a name, and now it would have one. But how did he feel about Alexandria?

"How about some coffee?" Hattie entered the study with a steaming mug in her hand. Of course, she hadn't knocked like everyone else did. Hattie rarely did what everyone else did.

He raised an eyebrow, wondering what tricks she had up her sleeve. "Thank you, Hattie. You haven't slipped something into my coffee, have you?"

She frowned then brightened. "Congratulations."

"I guess I'm in your good graces again?" He smiled at her affectionately.

"I never said you were not." She set the cup down on his desk. "You were, how should I say, bull-headed, but I knew you'd come to your senses." Her gentle laughter rippled through the air.

"So you approve of my choice?" he called to her as she walked away from him.

"You couldn't have made a better one." Hattie smiled then shut the door, leaving Brad to his work.

Missy had gone to take a nap, so Alex retired to her new room. She poked at the embers in the fireplace until the flames rekindled, then sat down in one of the large wing back chairs. Taking a sip of hot chocolate, she pulled out the diary. She decided to go back and read the pages she had skipped earlier. She wanted to get the true feeling of how Catherine thought, because everyday Alex felt more drawn to the women.

> *I went to see David today. He has such a gentle character. It has always been easy for me to talk to him. Our meeting seemed awkward at first, until I brought up the subject we were both trying to avoid.*
>
> *We agree now it was a mistake, and we both will be careful to guard the secret.*

I miss Bradley so much. If he hadn't died I wouldn't be in the predicament I'm in. I'm not sure how I'm going to deal with this in the future. It seems to be a dark cloud hanging over my head.

What secret? What happened? Surely the answers were in here someplace. Alexandria read a few things about Missy she had read before, then she came to some new pages previously skipped over.

David's upset with Julia. He says the child is going to spend every dime he has. He has put a stipulation in his will, but will not tell me what that stipulation is.

David looked at me with the saddest eyes. I know with his mild disposition he has had a hard time with Julia. He told me she reminded him of a buzzard just waiting and watching for him to die. I just laughed. He is not sick and should live to be a hundred.

Today Melissa is eight years old. We had a party for her, and I invited David. Melissa took to him right away. She climbed right up in his lap, her bouncy golden curls looking like a halo in the sun. She placed a kiss on his cheek before hopping down. Missy saw her brother and couldn't wait to run to him. I think I saw tears in David's eyes. I smiled to let him know everything would be all right.

Had to have a talk with Brad today. I caught him and Julia kissing in the summer house. She had her bodice pulled down to her waist. It wouldn't surprise me if she tried to get pregnant in order to hurry Brad into marriage. Brad told me not to be too concerned. He has enough sense to practice control so he would never have to marry anyone.

Alexandria's face turned bright red. Where was that control when she'd become pregnant? And she certainly didn't like the idea of him and Julia fooling around.

Until today, it has been six months since I've seen David. He looked strange ... not well. His face appeared shallow and drawn.

He told me he was going to change his will. He would leave Julia something, but not his entire fortune. I just hope he knows what he is doing.

Alexandria then discovered a page she had read before. She reread it again; it seemed important in this mystery.

I feel sad today. David died after a sudden illness. Julia said he was delirious the last two days. She did stay by his side, and I truly believe she is saddened by his death. I have lost a good friend.

Alexandria found the next page stuck. Carefully she pried the corner loose, holding her breath, hoping she'd not tear the page.

I talked to Julia ... asked her if there was anything I could do. She smiled at me ... a strange smile and told me not yet ... I had done enough. What an eerie feeling I had. I have no idea what she meant. I'm probably wasting my time being nice to her, but David was my friend. I owe him.

The next page had a date on it. Funny, most entries didn't have a date.

April, 1831 - I was at the lawyer's today for the reading of the will. They told me it was David's request that I be present.

Julia arrived late. She informed all of us she wanted the reading of the will postponed until her return. I wonder, now that I'm home, exactly what she is up to. She has taken a trip, but why not read the will first and settle her affairs?

I wonder ... did David change his will? And why do I have to be present?

Alexandria looked up. The sun had started to set. She had been reading for the past two hours, but this time she was determined to finish. There was some message in this book ... she was sure of it. She skipped the section of Julia's return since she had read that before.

May, 1 - We had the reading of the will today. Everything but the house was put in a trust fund for the next five years. At that time, a special envelope that the attorney held up would be opened and the heir named. Julia didn't look surprised, but when she looked at me the hate was unmistakable in her eyes.

Brad and I had another argument about Julia. Since the reading of the will, she's been his constant companion. Brad again told me not to worry. He says he can handle Julia.

May 15 - I received a note from Julia today. She wants to meet me tomorrow to talk. She knows the truth ... the whole ugly truth. I don't know what I'm going to do ...

There were no more entries, just blank pages, silent pages that would never speak the thoughts of the owner. "Oh Catherine, if only you could tell me what happened," Alexandria said to the empty room. She shivered. What was the secret that Julia had on Catherine?

Somehow Alex had to find out.

Chapter Twenty-Four

The hissing fire crackled and popped and the logs burned brightly in the hearth. Alexandria and Melissa were already seated at the long formal dining table when Brad finally made his appearance. It was the first Alex had seen of him all day.

He took his seat at the head of the table and apologized for being late, explaining he had been busy and had simply forgotten the time. Alexandria was beginning to think he might be avoiding her, but he sounded sincere. Perhaps he really had been busy. At least she'd like to think so.

Between the three of them, they managed to keep the conversation flowing. Alex fought with her awkward emotions. She knew she was being silly, but she couldn't help this strange feeling. She really was lost between two worlds. Hadn't she sat here many a night talking to Brad, just as they were doing tonight? So why should she feel any different now? Alexandria frowned; maybe all brides felt this way.

After dinner, Alexandria retired early. Surprise rippled through her when Brad gave up his bourbon and followed her.

She sat brushing her hair at her dressing table, determined she would talk to him tonight. Bolstering her courage, she said, "I hope you don't mind my dressing table, but since you insisted, I had the servants move it for me."

"That's fine, Alexandria." He sounded totally bored as he sat on the bed slipping a boot in the bootjack to remove it. "You can redo the whole room, if you like."

Well, she surely hadn't expected that response. Did he sound indifferent or was it just her nervous imagination? What was wrong with her? She didn't like this unsure feeling churning in her stomach.

Alex observed him in the mirror as he removed his shirt. The curly hair on his chest did nothing to calm her nerves. They needed to have some kind of conversation, but she wasn't quite ready to talk about their--their--situation just yet, so she proceeded down another path.

"Brad, I saw some of your mother's things in the spare room. Tell me a little about her."

"What would you like to know?" He finished undressing and slipped on a royal blue robe. As always, Alex marveled at the fine specimen of a man.

"Did she have a bad temper like you?" Damn, there she went again. It didn't seem like she could say anything right. Maybe deep down she truly liked fighting with this man.

This time Brad's eyebrow shot up, but he smiled tolerantly and let the remark slide. "No, she was fairly even-tempered about most things."

"She didn't like Julia, did she?"

"No, she didn't," Brad admitted. "She was definitely against us getting married."

"Why?"

"Mother thought Julia was money hungry. Of course, she was right."

"Yet, you were still going to marry her?"

"I was in no hurry to marry, but Julia would have been my choice. I never saw the evil in her; Mother did. She was always pleasant enough company, and we'd been promised since birth by our fathers." Brad sounded tired.

"But promises can be broken?"

"At a price."

"I don't understand."

"You see, when I married you, I broke my father's word. A man's word is his bond, but I also lost some of River Bends."

Alex's eyes widened as she swung around to look at him. "How?"

"Julia's father owned a portion of land between our plantations. We have always considered it ours until yesterday."

Alexandria's face turned red. She had not missed 'Julia would have been his choice.' He couldn't realize how those words hurt. And worse, she now realized she'd cost him his pride along with River Bends, but why had he given up so much?

"If Julia was your choice, why did you marry me?" Alex stood, tossing her hair down her back.

Brad just stared. He seemed to be lost in his own thoughts. "What did you say?"

That was the last straw. Her guilt at what she cost him made her feel terrible. She had tried to be patient. She'd tried to have a decent conversation, but what was the use? He hadn't heard a word she'd said. Her temper exploded.

"Why did you marry me if Julia was your choice? You've lost so much. I should just leave, and you can pretend you've never met me."

"Julia was my choice, but things change. And I simply changed my mind," Brad told her. "Why are you so upset? After all, I married you instead of Julia."

"Oh, pardon me. I forgot I'm supposed to be grateful. It was because of the baby, wasn't it?"

Brad reached over and took Alexandria by the arm. Pulling her close, he looked deep into her eyes. "Since you have brought up the subject, I want some answers. Why didn't you tell me, Alexandria?"

"Would it have made a difference?" She sighed, feeling rejected from his earlier comment. Her voice was no more than a whisper when she spoke again. "Would you have cared?"

"Of course the baby makes a difference. It's my son you carry, and my responsibility."

"Oh, I see." Alexandria eyes narrowed. Brad had done well until he'd added the word *responsibility*. "Everything in your life has a little slot," she commented in a clipped tone as her anger simmered. "One little slot for each responsibility. Everything packaged nice and neat, so it fits in the spot it was designed for. And just what slot do you have for me? Mother of your child ... servant ... doctor?" Her voice grew louder, and she knew she was losing her composure. All the years she had spent hiding her emotions, never wanting anyone to see how she felt, were going down the drain quickly. Somehow she couldn't mask her emotions with this man. But what she didn't realize was a single tear had slipped down her cheek. "I'll tell you right now, Mr. Wentworth ..." She stared into his eyes. "I'll not fit into any slot! Life is not that easy. You need to feel ... to love ... to experience life's ups and downs ..." She choked on her last word.

With his index finger Brad lifted the tear from her cheek. "And will you be the one to show me these experiences?" he asked, his voice husky with desire.

"Only if you'll let me," she whispered. The fight had left her body. What more could she expect? Brad had married her for the baby, not because he loved her. Hadn't he just told her she was a responsibility? A burden. But he *had* married her, and she'd just have to build on that fact. She would be very careful not to let Brad know how she felt about him. With that knowledge he could destroy her.

"Oh, Brad, I'm so sorry I ever came here."

"Do not ever say that again!" His hands slipped around the back of her neck. "Give me time, Alexandria. Show me." Brad's voice was full of tenderness as his mouth slowly claimed hers, not in a tender kiss, but a demanding one that tore at her mouth and her heart. And, as always, once he touched her she became mere putty in his hands. A little voice somewhere deep inside spoke to her. *Even though he doesn't love you now, perhaps one day he will.* With that comforting thought she surrendered to her desires.

The next few months were heaven for Alex. She and Brad seemed to have reached a truce of sorts. They hadn't had any arguments and had settled into a family routine. She saw little of him in the daytime, except for breakfast, which they always shared together. Their nights were spent in heaven, and Alexandria didn't know when she had been so happy. She no longer thought of home, because she was building a family here.

One day, Brad took time to take her on a picnic. The weather was cooler, but this particular day the sun shown brightly and the day was perfect. They finished their picnic making love on a blanket under a tree. Anyone could have come up on them, but they didn't care.

A change seemed to be occurring in Brad. Was it possible he was beginning to care for her? Once or twice she thought she saw tenderness in his eyes before he could mask his feelings. And last night he asked if their frequent lovemaking would hurt the baby. Of course, she had assured him it wouldn't. Brad might not love her yet, but she hoped he'd change. He did desire her. There was definitely no question about that.

Alex was busy learning what was expected of the Mistress of River Bends. Of course, she intended to let Hattie run the house just like she always had. Hattie did an excellent job, and Alexandria knew she couldn't change Hattie even if she wanted to.

Alex had thickened in the middle, and now when she looked in the mirror there was no denying she had a slight bulge. Deciding to let out some of her dresses instead of buying new ones, she went to the little sewing room where she spotted her favorite rocking chair sitting in the warm sunshine waiting for her. She could very easily have servants do her sewing, but she needed something to do.

As she sewed, her mind wandered. It seemed odd, she hadn't thought about home in a long time. Now that life seemed like an illusion, she had thought about telling Brad she came from another century, but he probably wouldn't believe her. For that fact, she still found it hard to believe herself. Of course, she missed the electricity and fast foods, but at this very moment she wouldn't trade anything for what she had now. She truly felt she had a family, perhaps not the perfect family, but what relatives didn't have problems? Glad to be here, she didn't ever want to go back. This was home, she admitted as her eyelids flickered shut. The warm sun had worked its magic, and lulled her to sleep.

The nap, however, was not peaceful.

In her sleep, Alex dreamed she was near a lake. She glanced down at her reflection and saw how the glorious sun caught in her red hair--like the day at Edmund's fountain. Again the water turned to fire, and all she could see were brilliant orange and red flames. The fire raged. Flames shot higher in the sky. Where were they coming from? She had to get there, but where? Then, just as before, the water cleared. In its place was the picture she had bought at the flea market many months ago.

Dirty and drenched in sweat, she felt as if she had a fever. Glancing down at her clothes, she saw they were stained with blood, and the scalpel clutched in her hand fell to the ground. With trembling, bloody fingers, she reached out to touch the picture, but it wasn't there--only the blue water of the fountain.

"No!" Her whimpering cry woke her. She gasped. Her heart beat like a drum as she looked frantically around her. Where was she?

Several minutes passed before her breathing slowed down.

She peered out the window. She was still on the plantation.

'It was a dream," she sighed. "What a relief!" But it was the same dream she'd had once before. Could it mean something? She couldn't think what and why was the dream about fire? She hadn't been near a fire.

She rested her head on the back of the rocker. Perhaps it was just her active imagination.

—)—

Brad left River Bends to help Edmund prepare for his upcoming boat race. He told Alexandria and Missy he'd be back in two weeks. He seemed in a hurry to be away as he gave Alexandria a quick kiss before leaving. She frowned, wanting more than a hurried kiss.

Alex decided she would not sit idle while he was gone. The first thing she was going to do was set up a clinic for the slaves and their children. She might as well put her talents to use by hanging out her shingle. It might not be the kind of practiced she'd imagined, but it was a challenge she looked forward to.

Abraham was always near if she needed him. He had been helpful in fixing up the small makeshift office consisting of a table and two chairs.

Time for a complete physical to make sure everyone was well was the first thing on her agenda. She made a point to take care of everyone.

It had been a long five days, Alexandria thought after seeing her last patient. Let's see, at one hundred dollars a head, for the hundred and fifty people she had seen, added up to a nifty little sum. She would have to remember to present Brad with the bill. Not bad for her first practice ... she laughed.

Of course, Hattie, always the stubborn one had insisted she'd never been sick a day in her life and didn't need a doctor.

Tomorrow, Alex decided, she would take the day off. A do-nothing day with plenty of relaxation. Maybe she would take Melissa riding. As she walked to the stables, she looked forward to feeling the wind in her face and the exhilaration that came with riding. She walked down to the stables to check the horses out.

As she neared the barn, she spotted Abraham's broad shoulders as he leaned against a pitchfork, staring out across the paddock.

"Abraham!" she called out to him, gaining his attention. "Missy and I would like to go riding tomorrow. Can you find us two good horses? Better make them gentle."

Abraham jumped a foot and Alex laughed.

"I didn't mean to scare you."

"That's fine, Miz Alex. If I hadn't been standing here day-dreaming, I'd have seen you coming."

"Well everybody needs time to daydream once in awhile."

"I guess you're right. You know, Miz Alex, I've worked off my indebtedness to Master Brad," Abraham informed her. "I'm a free man now."

"That's great, Abraham. But I don't think it's made you very happy. You look like you've lost your best friend."

"Yes, ma'am, I have," his voice sounded sad. "I've lost my whole family."

Alex figured he must have been thinking of home. "You've not lost them. They'll be waiting for your return. How big is your family?"

"I have five brothers and three sisters," he paused. "I was supposed to be married."

"I see." She raised her eyebrow. Now she knew the problem. "Hattie?"

"Yes, ma'am. I feel kinda bad ... you know ... guilty."

"You've just lost touch with your family." Alex grew quiet as she thought for a moment. "Do you like it here?"

"Sure do."

"Good. Let's go to the house." Alexandria took his arm. "You can write your folks a letter so they will not worry about you, and I'll make sure it is mailed properly. You also can ask about your girl back home. You never know, she might have married someone else." Alex brightened. "At least your conscience will be relieved."

"That's a good idea, Miz Alex." Abraham's grin spread from ear to ear. "Now why didn't I think about that?"

That night after dinner, Alex had just undressed when Melissa breezed into her room.

She heard Melissa gasp. "Hattie said you're going to have a baby?"

Alex smiled at the child, then slipped the gown over her head. "It shows, huh?"

Melissa face lit up. "Not much, but why didn't you tell me?"

"We were going to tell you at the right time, and I guess this is it." Alexandria patted her stomach. "Missy, you're going to be an aunt."

She ran and wrapped her arms around Alex. "That's wonderful." Missy's excitement bubbled forth, and she began talking exceedingly fast. "I bet Brad's pleased, and I think he'll make a splendid father, too."

Alexandria smiled. "And you'll make a fine aunt. We will call you Aunt Missy."

"I like the sound of that."

"Would you like to go riding tomorrow?" Alex asked.

"Can you ride with the baby?" Melissa blushed.

"I'm only pregnant, Missy, not disabled. We'll be taking an easy ride." Alex hugged Melissa to her. "Would you like to sleep in here with me tonight? I'll tell you some wonderful stories."

"I'd like that. Let me go get my nightgown. I'll be back in two minutes."

Pride welled up in her as she watched the youngster run out the door. A year ago, Missy couldn't even take a step.

That night she and Missy had their own pajama party. Alex told her stories of planes and rockets and men on the moon. Melissa giggled. "You're crazy. Men can't fly much less go to the moon ... how unbelievable!"

If she only knew, Alexandria thought before she finally fell asleep.

The next morning Alexandria beamed with the enjoyment she felt from riding. The wind whipped her hair, tearing it from its pins, and blew it free in the breeze. Even the cool crisp air felt good as she breathed in its freshness.

She and Melissa raced through the meadow, jumping a small stone wall before they proceeded to the paths that cut through the forest. Melissa didn't have any trouble handling her mount. Alex had found out she used to do quite a bit of riding before her accident.

They had been traveling for an hour when a shot sounded. Immediately, Alexandria pulled up her brown bay. "Someone must be hunting. Perhaps we should head back."

"But who?" Melissa asked. "Our nearest neighbor is Julia."

"Well, it has to be a hunter," Alexandria insisted. "It's the only thing that makes sense."

Another shot rang out, slamming into Alex's left arm. She jerked forward, landing on her horse's neck. Searing, hot pain ran though her arm, and she almost dropped the reins. Her horse reared. Somewhere behind her, Melissa screamed. Struggling to keep her horse under control, Alex paid little heed to her arm. "Head for home, Melissa!"

"But your arm--"

"Go home!" Alex commanded, realizing they needed to get out of the woods. Evidently, someone thought they were the game to be hunted. She kicked her horse in the sides, and they bolted forward.

Racing through the woods, they dodged the low-hanging branches that could knock them from their horses. Alex thought she heard the sound of hooves pounding right behind her. She laid her face against her horse's mane and urged him faster. Soon they cleared the forest, and she felt a little safer until an another shot flew past her head ... too close for comfort. Both became a blur as they urged their horses across the meadow, not taking the chance to stop again.

It seemed like forever before they reached the front steps of River Bends and Alex could breathe easily again. They were dismounting when Hattie came running out.

"I guarantee you both are tryin' to break your fool necks gallopin' in here like de devil's on your tail." Hattie stood on the steps with her disapproving stare.

"S--Someone was chasing us!" Melissa gasped, still excited from her ordeal.

"Funny, I don't see nobody," Hattie said. "And you should know better, especially now that you are with child."

After what Alex had been through, she didn't need this lecture, especially since her knees felt like jello and were just barely supporting her weight. Her arm forgotten for the moment, she came around the horse to argue with Hattie. "Hattie, I know how to ride. I am also a doctor ... I think I know what is best for my condition."

"You don't act like it, you hear." Hattie grumbled, shaking her head. "If Master Brad knew you had climbed on dat dere horse, he'd tan your hide fo' sure." Hattie's eyes widened. "What's wrong wit' your arm?"

"Nothing. It's a scratch." Alex glanced down at the bright red stain.

"She's been shot, Hattie!" Melissa said, moving closer to Hattie. "Someone shot at us in the woods."

"It just grazed my arm."

"Shot!" Hattie shouted, causing Alex to jump. "Someone was shootin' at you?"

"Three times," Missy informed her.

Alexandria wished Melissa would be quiet; she was just making matters worse.

"*Oui,* you know how to take care of yourself, huh?" Hattie scolded. "Not only do you go bouncin' around on a horse, but you evidently provided a target fo' someone." Hattie took her right arm. "Come on, let's go in de house and fix dat arm. Wonder why someone was shootin' at you?"

"I didn't stop and ask them, Hattie." Alex winced at the throbbing in her arm.

"You might be flippant now, but you'll change your tune." Hattie opened the front door and shooed her in.

"Oh, Hattie, unruffle your feathers. I think it was hunters and they mistook us for animals."

"What you goin' to tell Master Brad tomorrow?" Hattie asked.

Alex bit her lip. "Is he coming home tomorrow?"

"Not exactly, Petite. He sent word he's still busy helping Edmund, so we're going to ride into New Orleans to meet him," Hattie explained.

"Really." Alex was surprised. But what was she going to tell Brad? She definitely didn't want him angry, not after they had been doing so well. "I want you both to promise me you won't tell Brad any of this. After all, it was just an accident," Alex repeated.

"But, Alex--" Missy frowned before she said, "I promise." Missy turned and went to her own room.

"So just what are you going to tell him?" Hattie's eyebrow shot up.

"I don't know." Alex shook her head. "I'm sure I'll think of something," she replied with more confidence than she felt.

"What do you mean ... you missed her? Are you losing your touch, Rivers?"

"Hell, no, I ain't losing my touch!" Rivers informed her. "The groom I bribed gave me perfect information about where she'd ride. Had her in my sights, but my damned horse nudged me, causin' my aim to be off. I winged her though--I'm sure of it." A sly grin showed his tobacco-stained teeth.

Julia looked away. The sight of the man made her sick. She didn't know why she put up with Rivers. Yes, she did. She knew exactly why. He liked money as much as she did, and would go to any length to obtain it. After all, he'd helped her in the past. But this time Rivers had a stronger desire than money. Revenge. She'd had no problem talking him into helping her. They both had the same goal: get rid of Alexandria Dumont!

"Well, if you did wound her that might present problems," Julia reminded him.

"Why?"

"Now she'll have her guard up and perhaps be more careful."

"I don't think so. I heard her tell the brat she thought it was hunters."

"Good. Maybe she's dumber than I thought." Julia smiled. "Since that plan failed, I've developed another. I don't think you'll have any trouble pulling this one off."

"Yeah, what is it?"

"There is to be a big riverboat race tomorrow. I know for a fact that Brad and Edmund are working on the *Magnolia,*" Julia explained.

"What's that got to do with her?"

"If you'll shut up a minute, I'll tell you," she snapped.

"You better watch how you talk to me, Julia," Rivers warned. "Don't forget you need me ... just like you needed me in the past. You might dress in those fancy clothes, but underneath you're just like me, whether you admit it or not."

"I'm nothing like you!" Julia shouted, then looked at him with disgust. But she chose to say no more; she knew he was right. She needed his help to pull off her scheme. "Let's just remember this is a business deal."

"So what's the plan?" Rivers ask.

"You know how touchy those boilers can be?" A wicked smile spread across Julia's face.

"Yeah, I know they can blow sky-high."

"Exactly!"

"You're crazy!" Rivers took a step back. "That will kill a bunch of people."

Julia laughed, a haunting sound that made the hair stand up on the back of River's neck. "Why do you care?"

"You're one crazy bitch. Aren't you the least bit worried that your high and mighty Mr. Wentworth might be killed too?"

"You leave Brad to me," Julia snapped as she continued setting her plan in motion.

Chapter Twenty-Five

Brad and Edmund sat on the dock staring down at the gleaming white *Magnolia* as she sat waiting to take on the mighty Mississippi River yet another time.

"Thanks, cousin. Couldn't have done it without you." Edmund slapped Brad on the back.

"Sure you could. You have a dozen men helping you."

"A dozen men waiting on my instructions; I can't be everywhere at once."

"You could have fooled me." Brad chuckled. "The day before yesterday I ran into you so many times, I thought you had multiplied. I'm surprised you're even letting Leathers navigate the boat."

"Very funny." Edmund smiled. "When are Alexandria and Missy coming?"

"They'll be here this afternoon." Brad closed his eyes as he thought of his new bride, and he felt the first stirring of his arousal. He could almost picture her flaming red hair and snapping green eyes. Yes, he'd missed her, and that surprised him. With most women, Brad had always been glad to be away from them, and how many times had he heard his friends complain about how their wives showed them nothing but mild affection? With Alexandria it was different. She was vivacious and added a spark to his life he didn't know he missed, and she responded to his every touch. He admitted he enjoyed her company. She was neither pretentious nor calculating. Instead, Alexandria said exactly what she thought. Perhaps she was a tad hardheaded, but he'd work on that slight flaw.

"How has married life been so far?" Edmund asked.

Brad weighed the question, then smiled. "I've no complaints. As a matter of fact, it's quite enjoyable." He couldn't help being pleased with himself. "You should try it, cousin."

"Well, not all of us are as lucky as you are, my friend. I'm afraid I'll just have to keep looking."

"I'm sure you'll find someone to meet your fancy," Brad commented.

"I did, but she had eyes only for you," Edmund reminded him. "Have you told Alexandria that you love her?"

"No," Brad confessed. "I'm not sure she loves me."

Edmund fell back on the dock. He laughed so hard he held his side.

"What's so damned funny?" Brad didn't find anything amusing at all.

"All these years I've looked up to you, thinking how smart you are. But you can't see what's right before your eyes." Edmund slapped him on the shoulder. "The lady is crazy about you. Tell her you love her before it's too late."

Daylight was fast slipping away when the carriage pulled up in front of *Rué Chartress*. Alexandria was glad to arrive finally. She was tired, and her arm ached. The trip had taken longer than expected, because a carriage wheel had broken, and Abraham had had a hard time making the repair.

Alex gently shook Melissa. "We're here sweetheart--wake up."

"Thank goodness. I'm hungry," Melissa mumbled sleepily.

They left the carriage and walked up the steps to the front door. Hattie rapped on the door, but no one came to greet them.

When Hattie turned the knob the door opened easily. "Isn't this a fine hello?" she grumbled. "We've been cooped up in that carriage all day, and now the house is deserted. Anybody home?" she called as they all stepped in the foyer.

The butler appeared. "You're here?" Surprise showed clearly on his face.

"Shouldn't we be?" Alex wondered why he acted so stunned.

"Yes, of course you should. But you were so late, Mr. Lucas and Mr. Wentworth went looking for you," he explained. "Didn't you see them?"

"No, we took a shortcut Hattie knew about. Have they been gone long?" Alex asked.

"About an hour, ma'am. Would you care to have dinner now?"

She nodded. "Yes, that will be fine."

Alexandria and Melissa went to the dining room, and Hattie said she would see about Abraham. It wasn't long before hot savory plates of red beans and rice appeared before them. They couldn't decide if the meal was absolutely delicious, or they were just starved. As they took their last bites, they heard a clamor in the foyer.

"I wonder who dropped something," Alexandria commented to Melissa, thinking one of the servants had been careless.

The front door flew open with a bang. Brad's mood was anything but pleasant and had grown worse when they had found no trace of Alexandria. He couldn't help but think of all the dangerous things that could have happened to them.

"There is a logical explanation," Edmund told Brad as they walked past the dining room to his study. "We'll simply get some more men and go back out and look ..." Edmund didn't finish his sentence. When he glanced around, he found Brad had stopped at the dining room door.

"Who's in the dining room?" Brad asked Edmund as he opened the door to find his wife and Melissa gaily laughing and talking.

"Just where have you been?" Brad demanded, staring angrily at Alexandria. He had been worried sick and here she sat eating dinner like nothing had happened.

Alex stared in disbelief at her husband. He stood in the doorway shouting at her like she needed to account for every little minute. This wasn't the greeting she had expected! Wouldn't a hug have been a better greeting? But not from her husband. There he stood full of righteous anger. She didn't stop to think he could be worried. No she could only see she had once again inconvenienced him with her late arrival.

She was tired. And her temper had just reached its limit. "Just where in hell do you think I've been? I've been in a broken down carriage for the better part of the day. If I had known you were so anxious to see me, I'd have walked. Would that have pleased you?"

"Why are you shouting?" Melissa looked back and forth, obviously confused by the two people she loved.

Edmund laughed. "I think it's their way of saying they missed each other."

Brad took a deep breath. What was it about this woman that made him shout? He wanted to kick himself for the way he'd greeted them. It was definitely not what he had originally planned. "I'm sorry for shouting, Puss, but I thought something had happened to both of you." Brad leaned over and kissed Melissa on the cheek.

He moved in his wife's direction, watching her intently as she stood up to greet him. God, how he'd missed the fire in her eyes. And, from her previous outburst, there definitely was a blaze in them now. He wrapped his arms around Alexandria in a big bear hug.

"Ouch," Alexandria cried as pain shot through her arm.

Brad immediately held her away from him. "What's wrong?"

Alex wasn't sure how to tell him about her injury. She didn't want to trigger his temper again, but she couldn't think of any pleasant way to say she had been shot. Biting her bottom lip, she replied, "I had an accident."

"An accident!" His gaze moved over her body. "What kind of accident?"

"You don't have to shout!" Alex snapped. "There's nothing wrong with my hearing. Melissa and I went horseback riding..."

"You *what*? I thought you had a brain in that head of yours. You are with child, or had you forgotten?"

Alex's anger soared to new heights. Since Edmund and Melissa were intently watching them, she decided not to entertain her audience any longer. Evidently, dinner was over.

Turning back to Brad, she said, "I will see you upstairs!" Briskly she left the dining room. *Just let him try and stop me*, she swore to herself.

At the top of the stairs, Alex went into the first bedroom. Plopping down on the bed, she waited. Her foot tapped the floor impatiently.

In less than a minute, Brad's muscular form filled the doorway. His anger had faded when Alexandria flounced from the dining room demanding he meet her upstairs. *He'd like nothing better.* "Is this the room of your choosing or had you rather go to our room?" Humor danced in the depths of his eyes ... "it appears you're in the wrong room again."

"If you don't change your sour disposition, this could be my room permanently." Alexandria jumped up and brushed past him, her head held high. "Just where in hell is *our* room?"

"Try two doors down on the right. Sweetheart, you really should watch your language." He smiled as his little hellcat stomped down the hall. God, she was beautiful when she was angry.

When Alexandria reached their room she turned on him. "Don't ever talk to me like that in front of an audience again. I assure you, I do remember I'm pregnant. As I told Hattie, I'm also a doctor, and I just might know a little bit more than you do about being pregnant. Of course, I know you find that hard to believe," she added sarcastically. "Since you don't think I have a brain in my head.

"For your information, I was perfectly fine riding. I didn't fall from the horse ... I was shot!" Whoops! She hadn't meant to tell him that, but he had her so agitated she'd slipped. Well, it was too late now. She could see the storm clouds building in his cobalt blue eyes.

"Shot?"

Alexandria felt the walls vibrate with his roar.

"Who?"

"I will not answer you if you insist on shouting." Alex stood beside a chair, gripping its back for support.

Brad lowered his voice. "Who?"

"I--I don't know," she stammered. "I think it was hunters. Melissa and I were out riding in the woods when we heard gunshots. We never saw anyone." Taking a deep, unsteady breath, she stepped back. "I think they mistook us for animals."

"They were trespassing and shouldn't have been there. Strange, I've never had this problem before." A tired look passed over his features, and she heard the strain in his voice as he continued, "I'll be sure to check this out when we return home."

She could see Brad struggling with his rage. Maybe he did care ... just maybe. She reached out and touched his arm. "It was just a flesh wound," she said softly. "I'm a little sore, but I'll be fine. And the baby's fine, too."

Brad melted at her touch, and the fury within him died. This time he pulled her gently into his arms. But murder still raged within him, because he wanted to kill the person who had tried to hurt her. He felt urgency in the moment and was swept away with overwhelming desire. Swinging Alexandria up, he carried her to their bed, where he gently placed her down. His body taut with desire, urged him on, and he wasted little time joining her on the bed. Pulling her firmly against his chest, he took her lips, savoring her sweet taste with a tenderness he didn't know he possessed.

"Where did you learn to kiss like that?" Brad whispered with a mixture of tenderness and desire.

"Does it matter?"

"No ... not at all." Brad burned with the need to touch her skin. Expertly, he unlatched the buttons on her dress while he kissed her. He winced when he saw the bandage. "I'm hurting you."

"No," Alexandria whispered.

When the dress slipped to the floor, he wasted little time trailing kisses down her creamy white throat.

He captured a soft white breast in his hand and began slowly and sensuously rubbing his thumb back and forth across her nipple until he felt it harden at his touch.

Swept away by Brad's gentleness, Alex welcomed his candy kisses, and one was just not enough. Opening her lips, she boldly offered her tongue. Hearing his groan of desire, she had the satisfaction of knowing she'd just set his body on fire.

He whispered seductive promises as his breath fanned her ear and made her shudder. Her body grew hotter with desire. "Don't you have on too many clothes?"

"I believe you're right," Brad agreed, and quickly disposed of the problem while she finished removing her dress and stockings.

He looked magnificent standing before her. Without any shyness she reached out and touched him, letting her fingers glide lightly over his body. She soon found she could give him as much pleasure as he gave her. Taking him firmly in her hand, she massaged with a slow, rhythmic motion.

Brad could stand no more. His body threatened to explode. He pulled her hand away and sank to his knees in front of her, resting his head on her chest as he hugged her to him, trying to control his breathing.

"What's wrong?" she whispered. "Did I do something wrong?"

"No, sweetheart, you were doing everything exactly right. If you'd kept that up, I would have lost all control," he explained in a strained voice while he looked deep into her eyes. "I want to give you pleasure, too."

Alex watched his head moved to her taut nipples. His tongue outlined the tips of her breasts as he played with each nipple. She wrapped her fingers in his hair, pulling him against her breast. His hand slid along her thigh until he reached the triangle of hair. Instinctively, she opened her legs so Brad could reach what he sought. His fingers burned into her tingling skin, moving in and out of her warmth, while his mouth continued its assault as he nipped the rosebuds of her breasts. She didn't know agony could be so sweet.

Alexandria became hot with tantalizing desire. A tremor raced along her spine. She felt drugged. Her body grew limp as passion burned deep in her belly, causing her skin to tingle with delight. Suddenly her desire exploded with a thousand tiny lights dancing before her eyes. "Brad ... please ..."

Hearing her cry, Brad pushed her father back on the bed and spread her legs wide. He couldn't wait any longer. His shaft entered her wetness and he felt the velvet smoothness surround him. He thrust deeper and deeper until he, too, found the heavenly release he sought.

The traditional starting point for the race was Canal Street. A multitude of onlookers milled about the streets and levees. The majority of men wore varnished boots, high hats, and ruffled, white shirts. Vendors selling pastries and candies filled the air with the fragrance of a carnival. As the Lucas carriage neared the gangplank, Alexandria could see the boat full of passengers preparing to leave. Everyone appeared happy as they gathered to see the race. Evidently, race time was near.

The coach finally made its way to the walkway, leading to the *Magnolia*. Edmund and Melissa stepped out first, then Brad lifted Alexandria out of the carriage, holding her for just a minute longer than necessary. Wide-eyed, Alex gasped as she looked up at him.

Brad smiled, remembering last night and the love he had for his little wildcat. Evidently, she had read his thoughts because her cheeks had turned a deep shade of red. Resultantly he let her go and they joined everyone else.

They passed a man on the wharf taking wagers. "Place your bets right here," the young gent said as he stood on a box collecting money. "See the *Magnolia* beat the *Dogwood Blossom*."

Brad and Edmund couldn't resist taking the man up on his bet.

"You must see the improvements we've made in the boiler room," Edmund said while taking Alex's elbow. "The boilers can be dangerous," he warned. "But we have taken special precautions.

"I had to hire a new man off the street," Edmund told her. "I really don't like to, but this man seemed knowledgeable, and I needed help." He glanced back over his shoulder. "Did you meet him, Brad?"

"No, never got the chance. You kept me busy elsewhere."

As soon as she boarded the *Magnolia*, Alex saw Captain Leathers, who barked out commands like a general. Everyone on board jumped to obey his orders. When the captain spotted her, he waved.

"Well, I do believe you've grown even lovelier, Miss Du-- I mean Mrs. Wentworth." Captain Leathers nodded, then laughed.

She blushed again--a nasty habit she didn't like. Alex wasn't used to her title or her new husband. "Thank you, Captain Leathers."

"Tom."

"Thank you, Tom. It's good to see you again."

"I was glad to hear you two decided to marry instead of killing each other." Tom's chuckle rumbled in his chest. "Yes, sir, that trip down river was an exciting journey."

"Brad ... Edmund." A voice sound from behind them.

The group turned at the sound of a woman's voice. Julia walked across the deck, looking fresh and beautiful in a dress of fuchsia and white, with her hair piled high.

"I insist you show me your enchanting boat. After all, I have a large sum of money bet on you, Tom Leathers." Julia smiled sweetly.

Tom grinned at the praise Julia bestowed on him. He looked like a peacock spreading his tail feathers. "I'll be glad to show you, Miss Julia."

She kissed Brad on the cheek. "Hello, darling. You look like you've lost some weight. Isn't your little bride taking care of you?"

"Hello, Julia," Brad said, showing little emotion.

Damned man! Alex swore inwardly. At least he could have taken up for her. She could think of more to say than hello, but she was going to be nice if it killed her. With much restraint Alex chose to ignore Julia's remark, reminding herself that she had what Julia actually wanted.

The group moved down the stairs to the boiler deck with Julia clinging to Brad's arm, forcing Edmund to help Alexandria descend the stairs. Melissa had stayed on the dock to talk to some of her friends.

The engineers ran about excitedly, checking on last minute details. "We have installed eight boilers filled with water supplied from the river by this main pump." Leathers pointed to a red pump with a spinning wheel. "The water pours directly into two cylindrical heater tanks attached to the engines. These tanks take heat from the steam that's already hissing hot, and travels through pipes in the hold to the boilers."

After Captain Leathers finished explaining the system, he started to move the group back to the main deck. Just then an engineer announced it was time to start the engines. Alexandria lingered a moment to watch the black fireman hurl fuel into the bulge under the battery of eight big boilers. This definitely wasn't a place where she wanted to spend much time.

Edmund urged her up the steps so they could join the group who now stood on top deck to await the starting of the hissing boilers. The hum of the engines began as a faint sound, then grew louder until, little by little, sooty clouds started trickling out of the tall smokestacks.

"Brad, darling, I've something for you in my carriage. You simply must come with me," Julia insisted.

"It can wait, Julia."

"No, darling, it can't. I'll be leaving shortly and be gone for awhile. You must come with me now!" Julia pulled on his arm.

Brad turned and looked at Alex. His eyes flashed in a display of impatience. "I will be back in a moment."

Alex watched as they left the gangplank and started down the wharf. She felt her chest tighten with jealousy and she wondered what Julia was up to this time.

"It's about race time. Are you ready to go to shore?" Edmund asked.

"I suppose so." She smiled at the captain. "Good luck, Tom."

They stepped up on the gangplank and had taken no more than three steps when suddenly the clang of the great engines roared behind them.

"Something doesn't sound right," Edmund said, looking back over his shoulder.

"What's that hissing?" Captain Leathers shouted, turning back to the boat. "Something's wrong!"

Just then the vessel trembled, causing Alexandria to grab Edmund's arm.

"That doesn't sound good." Edmund steadied her.

"Better take Mrs. Wentworth off the boat," Captain Leathers shouted, then started back up the plank. "I'll go below and see what's wrong. That's all we need ... problems before the race."

Below, the engineers worked feverishly, having found a break in the lines. A sleeve joint jarred loose, then apart with a violent shudder. Steam sprayed everywhere, burning anyone who came near.

The boat shuddered.

Alex and Edmund started to run. They had barely reached the dock when a rumble began in the lower structure of the boat. It shook and buckled. The boat exploded with a deadly sound that blocked out everything else. Alex found herself being propelled forward with Edmund right beside her.

"Keep your head down," Edmund warned as he tried to cushion her fall.

"What's happening?" she screamed.

"The boilers have exploded!"

One eruption triggered another as debris flew through the air. She peeked from under Edmund's arm to see big pieces from the boiler flying through the air. One metal plate hit a mule, slicing the animal in half.

Then as quickly as the chaos had started, everything became still. Only a few hisses and the sounds of people screaming could be heard.

Brad felt as if his life had just flashed before him. First the explosion, then the flash of Edmund and Alexandria going through the air.

Shoving Julia away from him, he started to run. "Alexandria! Edmund!" Brad shouted. *Please let her be safe,* he prayed.

He took her arm and hauled her to her feet. "Are you hurt?" Brad asked as his eyes quickly ran a check over Alexandria's body to make sure she wasn't injured. Finally she recognized it was him and she laid her head on his chest.

She felt good within the confines of his arms, and her warm breath on his neck told him his life was complete. Alexandria was what he had wanted all the time. No, he hadn't married her because of the baby. His decision had been made before Hattie had told him about the baby. He hadn't realized it at the time, but he knew now it was because he loved her.

"I love you." Brad's soft lips brushed her forehead. "I was so afraid you were hurt," he whispered, his voice choked with emotion.

She leaned back to look at him. A momentary look of confusion crossed her face. "You love me?"

"Yes, sweetheart." He kissed the end of her nose. "I love you--I guess I always have."

The radiant smile she bestowed upon him made his heart soar.

His words seared into her brain. How long had Alex waited to hear him say those three little words? She felt dizzy with happiness, because Brad's love meant the world to her. She wanted to tell him that she loved him, too, but something held her back. He needed to know the whole story of how she came here--and what if something happened to take her away? When they were back home she would tell him all about herself and hope he didn't think she was absolutely crazy. She heard Edmund groan, bringing her back to the catastrophe that had just taken place.

"I'll be fine, too, Cousin. Just in case you're interested."

—❩—

Alex twisted free of Brad's embrace and turned to where the ship had been. "My God," she gasped as she surveyed the damage. The acrid smell of smoke burned her nose and she covered her mouth.

The destruction she saw around her reminded her of a bomb exploding. The *Magnolia* wasn't there anymore. Just a partially burned hull protruded out of the water. Splinters of wood floated in the murky Mississippi, and worse, bodies were floating in the water and strewn along the waterfront.

Edmund groaned when he saw his boat was no more than a floating heap of rubble.

"Your shoulder, Edmund." Alexandria tore open his shirt. "He has a nasty cut that needs tending, but it can wait." She tore off the bottom of her slip and made a compress to stop the flow of blood. Then she took small strips and tied the bandage to his shoulder.

"Where is Tom?" Brad asked.

"He was on the boat," Edmund choked, the pain evident in his voice.

"My God! What could have caused this?" Brad said what they were all thinking. The three of them stood staring at the smoky water.

"I wish I knew." Edmund rubbed his eyes as if to erase the sight of all the destruction.

"Alex, Alex, come quickly." Melissa ran up, pulling on Alex's arm.

Good heavens, in all the excitement they had forgotten all about Melissa. Alex looked at her soiled and torn dress and grabbed her arms. "Are you hurt, Missy?"

"I'm fine, but my friend, John's not. I think he's broken his leg. It looks terrible! It's bent in an odd shape ... come quick!"

The trio of them ran, following Melissa to where her friend lay. Two of Melissa's friends sat on the ground beside the boy. They had cuts, too.

"Get my bag, Brad." Alexandria's physician's instincts took over and she was glad she insisted, taking her bag everywhere she went.

John's leg was definitely broken, and Alexandria would have to set it with the help of Brad and Edmund.

—)—

Standing off in the distance, Julia sneered at the scene in front of her. It made her sick to her stomach the way Brad had jumped to help that bitch.

She had seen how he'd run to her. It almost appeared as though he loved her, but Julia knew better.

"Brad loves me! He always has. He's just infatuated with Alexandria. But he'll forget her once she's gone." And she would be gone! Next time there would be no mistakes. It was time for a one-on-one meeting with Miss Alexandria Dumont ...

That woman would never be a Wentworth as long as there was breath left in Julia's body.

Chapter Twenty-Six

Alex had worked feverishly tending the wounded. For a moment, she felt like she was back in the emergency room, except she desperately needed the modern supplies.

A few men wouldn't let her help them because she was a woman and they wanted a 'real doctor'. She didn't bother to argue since another doctor had arrived. Instead she moved on to the next person.

She had just finished binding the last wound when she glanced over her shoulder just in time to see Brad and Edmund pulling a body clad in white out of the water.

Alex jumped to her feet and ran to them. Captain Leathers couldn't be dead. He just couldn't!

When she got to the dock's edge she could see Brad's shoulders shaking as if he were crying. She placed her hand on his back. "I'm so sorry," she said, trying to console him. Then she heard the oddest sound ... he wasn't crying at all.

"I can't believe you're laughing at a time like this," Alex stated indignantly. She moved around him so that she could see. Beneath a pair of soaked, red eyebrows a pair of pale gray eyes looked up at her. "You're alive!"

"Just barely, ma'am." Captain Leathers chuckled. "Takes more than a big bang to stop Tom Leathers."

Alex half-laughed and half-cried as she stooped down to check the captain. He had a small cut on his cheek. His arms were all right.

Edmund punched Leathers playfully in the arm. "Damn lucky. That's what you are. Looks like we'll have to forfeit the race, Tom."

"Tarnation, boy!" Leathers grabbed Edmund's arm. "If I can swim the Mississippi with this bum leg, then you can find us another boat. Forfeit, hell! Tell him he'll get his race."

"I'll help Edmund finance your new boat." Brad looked at Edmund, then back to Leathers. "As long as you promise to take care of yourself."

"Your leg is broken, Tom." Alex ran her hands down his leg. "I'm afraid it will take awhile to mend."

"Ah, hell, little lady. The leg might slow old Tom up, but I can navigate that river with my eyes shut."

"Somehow, I don't doubt that a bit." She looked at Brad. "Can you both find me something to make a splint, so that we can set this leg?"

After they had mended Leathers' leg and put him in the carriage. Alex found Melissa and they all got into the carriage bound for Edmund's. Alex was so tired, she put her head on Brad's shoulder.

"I think you have done a little too much considering your condition," Brad whispered. "When we get home you shall rest, sweetheart."

Alex didn't correct him, because at the moment rest sounded great. But she wouldn't be the helpless invalid while she was pregnant.

Drizzly rain clouded the windows on this cold, dreary morning just as it had for the past two days. And she was tired of resting.

Alexandria snuggled further under the covers, feeling the weight of Brad's arm securely around her. As she lay in bed looking out the window, she wondered what she could do cooped inside for yet another day. She loathed the main pastime for women ... sewing! And Melissa didn't even need her anymore for exercise.

Alex was still thrilled with the love Brad had showered on her in the past two weeks, but the boredom of nothing to do grated on her active mind.

Perhaps this afternoon she could go down to her clinic. She smiled, remembering her argument with Brad over the clinic.

He had told her, in no uncertain terms, that he did not want his wife working. But she'd informed him, just as firmly, she wouldn't sit around and do nothing. After much fussing Brad gave in to her.

She sighed. The mind was a terrible thing to waste. However, she definitely didn't miss the hustle and bustle of the eighties.

"What's wrong, sweetheart?" Brad asked, his voice raspy from sleep.

Alex turned to face her husband. She still couldn't bring herself to tell him about her past. However, she'd never get tired of seeing his face in the morning. She smiled a greeting. "Good morning, I thought you were sleeping."

"I was, but your sighing woke me. What's going on in that pretty head of yours this early in the morning?"

"It's raining outside ... again! And I don't know what I'm going to do today. I'm sick of mending and tatting. And I've read almost everything in the library." She sighed again. "I'm bored out of my mind." She paused a moment thinking. "Perhaps I could help you with your ledgers. Surely you could use a good bookkeeper."

"I assume by the word bookkeeper that you mean someone who keeps my ledgers and books?" Brad arched an eyebrow, as Alexandria nodded, confirming his statement. "That's man's work, sweetheart. You shouldn't worry your pretty self with such things."

"And just why do you consider that task man's work?" Alex sat up indignantly. "Do you think I cannot add up a simple column of figures? Why, I'll have you know I was at the top of my class in algebra, and trigonometry. Where I come from men hate to do such jobs."

"Class?... Algebra? You are speaking an American language?"

"Yes."

"You know, Alexandria, I don't know very much about your background. Just where do you come from that life is so different? I must admit you're not like the other females I've known." Brad propped his pillows up behind him and waited for her answer.

Alexandria could only stare at him, wishing she hadn't brought up this subject. Damn, she had a big mouth. She'd decided last week she wouldn't tell Brad she had come from another century. He would never believe such a wild story. Hell, she didn't even believe what had happened to her. She'd be sure not to tell him she wasn't born yet, and would not be until many years down the road. Perhaps beating around the bush would be the best answer.

"I came from North Carolina, where I worked very hard for my doctor's degree. You see, I didn't have a lot of money, so I had to study very hard to make good grades. Even there, men have funny notions that women can do very little, except clean, cook, and look pretty."

"You actually cleaned and cooked?" Brad gave her a quizzical look. "Didn't you have servants?"

"Well, yes," Alexandria lied, knowing he'd never believe she lived in her own apartment alone, drove her own car, shopped at a grocery store. "I was just using that as a figure of speech. Women have to work twice as hard as men to prove themselves."

Brad thought a moment. "I guess you're right, but in my opinion, women should be pampered and cared for."

"That's nice Brad, and I'm not complaining. But I want to be appreciated for my mind, too." After all, she'd never been much on woman's lib. She liked men opening the door for her and paying her way on dates.

"I do appreciate every part of you," he teased. A devilish smile touched his lips. "I can think of some parts I could really appreciate right now." He pulled her back down and folded her in his arms.

"Oh, Brad, be serious."

"All right, you can help me with my ledgers, but I've a better suggestion?"

"What's that?"

"Hattie has recommended we use Melissa's cradle for our child. However, it's been in the attic so long, I'm sure the cradle will have to be cleaned and washed. I know it's still a little while before the baby arrives, but since it's raining, maybe you would like to start fixing up the nursery."

"That does sound like fun, although I don't remember seeing a cradle."

"You've been in the attic?" Brad wondered aloud. What could she have been doing up there?

"Isn't the attic your mother's sewing room?"

"No. It's on the back side of the house. Melissa can show you later this morning."

"If you think I'm going to forget about helping with your books, then you have another thought coming." She giggled before adding, "I like your suggestion. I feel like going on a treasure hunt."

"How about I give you the first clue?" Brad rolled over on top of Alexandria, and smothered her with kisses. "It starts right here."

After breakfast, Alexandria pulled her hair back with a ribbon. Melissa had told her the attic would be dirty, so she should wear something old. She also confessed it had been a long time since she'd been to the attic.

With oil lamps in hand, they went to the far end of the hall where a door that Alexandria had always thought led to a closet opened to a narrow hall about ten feet long. At the end of the hallway stood yet another door. Melissa pushed it open to reveal a steep staircase that wound to the left. By the time they reached the attic, Alexandria felt like she had been through a maze.

She set her oil lamp down on a small table, and turned up the wick. A soft glow bathed the dusty contents of the room. And as she had told Brad, this room was a treasure chest of relics from the past.

The upper room stretched across the top floor of the house. There were two windows at each end, but the day was so cloudy with the rain that not much light came in through the glass. There were pieces of furniture, pictures, and boxes everywhere.

"Look," Melissa called as she held up a doll. "I used to play with her when I was younger."

"And you're old now?" Alex laughed.

"Well, you know what I mean. I'm not a baby anymore," Melissa announced. "You want to know a secret?" A grin illuminated her face.

"Sure, what is it?" Alex moved around a stack of crates.

"I think John likes me."

"John?" Alex thought for a moment. "The boy whose leg I set?"

Melissa nodded, her eyes shining brightly.

"That's great, sweetheart." Alexandria smiled fondly at her sister-in-law. "He seems like a nice boy."

"He's wonderful," Melissa gushed.

"Maybe you can ask him over sometime, but right now I need to find a cradle."

Alex began her search again. She opened several boxes and found a carton containing baby blankets and a few clothes. She moved the box over to the top of the stairs so they wouldn't forget it when they left.

"I found the cradle," Melissa called out.

Alexandria climbed over numerous crates and squeezed between a couch and a chair to reach Melissa. With the edge of her apron she dusted off the cradle. The lovely piece of furniture was made of the finest oak wood. In the headboard there was a carving of two babies: one crying and one laughing. Melissa carried the cradle to the stairs, and Alexandria went to retrieve her oil lamp. Just before she collected the lamp, she saw something tall standing next to the window. The shape reminded her of a statue.

Her curiosity got the better of her, and she moved closer. Picking up the corner of the sheet, she quickly pulled it off. Then froze. There stood a dress mannequin clothed in a well-preserved ball gown.

Not just any ball gown ... one of peach-colored satin and lace.

Alex gasped. Somewhere behind her Melissa screamed. It was the dress in the picture. Catherine's dress!

Startled by Melissa's screams, Alex quickly turned to her. "What's wrong? Are you all right?" Alex knew why she trembled, but she didn't understand Missy's reaction.

Missy appeared terrified as she stared at the dress with tears streaming down her cheeks.

"Are you all right?" Alarmed, Alex moved toward her. Still no response. Melissa stood as if in a trance. She didn't move at all. She just stood there, seemingly unaware of her surroundings. Alex grasped the child by the shoulders and shook her.

Melissa blinked several times before her eyes began to focus, and she realized she was in the attic. She grabbed for Alexandria, and wrapped her arms around her, unable to hold back the tears.

"I thought I had forgotten ... It was awful, Alex," Melissa whispered between sobs. "Visions of that day kept flashing through my mind."

She sobbed as if her heart would break and Alex's heart went out to her. "I don't understand, Missy. This is the dress your mother wore in the picture. Why would that make you sad?"

"This--this is also the gown Mother died in. I--I thought Brad had burned it. Look closer, and you'll see a tear and a bloodstain on the left-hand shoulder," she whispered brokenly.

It was true. The tear and bloodstains were exactly where Melissa said they would be.

"Come sit with me, Missy. I think it will do you good to talk about this. Perhaps the dress will help you recall what happened." Alex's hands shook, but she wouldn't admit how shaken she was herself by seeing the gown in person. A gown she'd thought beautiful in the picture, but one she never imagined she would see in person.

"Tell me, what do you remember?" Alexandria prompted.

"That's just it. I could never recall anything. But just now when you pulled the sheet off, flashes of that day appeared before my eyes. It was like I was back at the accident again."

"What did you see?" Alexandria prodded gently, anxious to hear the truth.

"A man."

"Could you tell who the he was?"

"No. He had his back to me, and ... and he was behind the carriage. Mother told me to stay in the rig, so I never saw his face."

"Was your mother talking to the man?"

"No, she was speaking to someone else, but she wasn't talking, she was arguing." Missy's blue eyes filled with tears that began to race down her cheeks. "It--it sounded like a lady. I remember hearing my name a couple of times."

"What happened then?"

"Mother came back to the buggy. She was angry. I'd never seen her so upset. Mother shouted at the person that she was going to put an end to this. Before she could gather the reins, the man hit the horse and it bolted with the carriage." Melissa stopped, wiping the tears from her eyes as she recalled the rest.

Alexandria forced herself to keep quiet. She knew it was good for the child to cry and release her pain. She felt the tears in her own eyes and blinked several times to hold them back.

"I remember the carriage tumbling over the rocky cliff. I can't remember anything else, except Mother reaching out to me and then ... then ..."

"Then what?"

"A weird kind of laughter ... not normal ... scary and high-pitched. I'm sorry, I'm not much help am I?" Melissa started crying again.

"Sure, you are." Alexandria hugged the child to her as agony surged through her heart. "Just look at what you've remembered today. And perhaps one day you can put names to those faces."

"I wish Mother were here," Melissa whispered before she buried her face in Alexandria's shoulder. All the years of hurt came pouring out, all her childish fears, the ones she hadn't been able to share with anyone until now.

"I do too, Missy ... I do, too."

Still shaken, Alex was careful not to show her emotions as she sat rocking Missy, letting her sob. When Missy finally raised her head, she looked emotionally drained and wanted to go to bed.

Alex took an oil lamp and they went downstairs where Alex tucked Missy in. Then Alex returned to the attic for the cradle. She deposited it in the nursery and went to her room.

She knew Brad had ridden out early this morning and wouldn't return until supper, so Alex pulled out the diary. She couldn't shake the scary feeling she had inside, almost as if it were a forewarning. With the diary clutched tightly, Alexandria went downstairs to the room where she'd seen the painting of Catherine. Quietly, she shut the door behind her. The day had turned a dusky shade of gray, and the rain slapped against the windows in the sitting room. It did nothing to ease her feeling of dread. Everything felt damp as she reached over to light a couple of candles.

Sitting in the high wing back chair facing the portrait, Alex pulled her shawl tighter around her shoulders as she tried to get comfortable. It was funny; this room seemed so much colder than the other rooms.

Was this her painting? The one she'd bought at the flea market? It had to be. Yet, there was no reflection in the lake, and Alex could plainly see the woman was Catherine because there was no hat hiding her identity.

Alex felt as if she knew the woman in the painting. Why did she feel such closeness to Catherine? Was it because they both loved Brad? Or was Catherine trying to tell her something?

Alexandria felt obsessed with finding the truth. She opened the diary and started to read again. What connection did David have with Catherine other than they were friends? The diary said he was going to change his will. Perhaps, he was going to leave everything to Catherine because of their friendship. Alex looked up at the picture. Could Julia have found out and killed her own father? For some reason Alex didn't believe Julia would do that. Or would she?

So many questions and all unanswered. The solution had to be here somewhere. She just wasn't seeing it.

Flipping to the page dated May 1st, Alex began to read.

> *May, 1 - We had the reading of the will today. Everything but the house was put in a trust fund for the next five years. At that time, a special envelope that the attorney held up will be opened and the heir named.*

> *Julia didn't look surprised, but when she stared at me the hate was unmistakable in her eyes.*

Alexandria turned the next two pages scanning for clues, and finally she read the page dated May 15th.

Brad and I had another argument about Julia. Since the reading of the will, she has been his constant companion. Brad again told me not to worry. He says he can handle Julia.

May 15 - I received a note from Julia today. She wants to meet me tomorrow to talk. She knows the truth ... the whole ugly truth. I don't know what I'm going to do ...

Alexandria closed the small, brown book. There were no more entries, no more clues. Just empty pages that would never be filled.

With her unexpected marriage, she had forgotten her vow to find out what had happened. She had also forgotten this last entry. Gazing at the picture, she stared deep into Catherine's eyes. Again, Alex felt drawn. For a moment there seemed to be a flicker of light in Catherine's eyes ... a plea from her to avenge her death. Cold chill bumps ran up Alexandria's arms, and she shivered. The chilly air in the room smelled of magnolias.

"Speak to me, Catherine ... Make me understand." Alex shut her eyes and a scene flashed before her of Catherine.

Catherine tried desperately to grab for the leather straps as they slipped farther and farther from her reach. How foolish she'd been to meet *her* here. "Hold tight, Melissa!" Catherine called to her daughter, who'd been asleep on the seat.

A sob rose from deep in her throat. "Oh, God!" They were not going to make the deadly curve just ahead. Grabbing Melissa, she held her tight to her breast.

The buggy hit a rock, jolted, teetered on two wheels, then plummeted down the hill. Over and over the carriage flipped until it came to rest by a big oak tree.

Then, as if a silent message reached out from the past to the present, enveloping Alexandria, she thought of what Missy had just told her. Catherine had been arguing with someone, and the voice sounded like a woman's.

The diary.

The meeting.

Julia! There could be no other answer. After receiving the note, Catherine had taken Melissa to the meeting Julia had demanded. They had argued over something. But what? ... Brad? ... The will? When Catherine had gotten back into her buggy, a man, whose identity was unknown, had purposely caused the carriage to wreck. But the accident hadn't killed Catherine, because Melissa remembered her mother reaching out and taking her hand.

So Catherine had been murdered! Tears ran unchecked down Alexandria's face. She could feel Catherine's pain of leaving her children. And the hopelessness Catherine felt when she knew she wouldn't be there to keep watch over them.

The door hinges squeaked behind Alex. She jumped.

"Why you sittin' in here by yourself, cher?" Hattie asked from the doorway.

Alexandria's head jerked up in response to the sudden sound. With the back of her hand, she wiped away her tears. She didn't even bother to turn toward Hattie, but instead stared at the portrait.

"That's my picture, Hattie."

"No, Petite." Hattie shook her head slowly. "If you'll remember your paintin', dere's a difference. Dis one is similar, however it's not de same. One day, cher, you'll understand."

"Understand what?" Alexandria turned to face Hattie, but she wasn't there. How could that woman disappear so fast? She had been there-- hadn't she?

Alex went upstairs to Catherine's sewing room. There she placed the journal back where she'd first discovered it. She didn't need the diary anymore. For the rest of her answers, she could no longer rely on the little book. Tomorrow when the weather cleared, Alex would send a note to Julia, requesting a meeting.

Chapter Twenty-Seven

Alex wrote a short note to Julia, requesting a meeting with her in two days. Before she could find a message boy, she heard a knock at the front door. Not seeing any servants around, she answered the door herself. A small, black boy stood on the other side. Alex didn't recognize him as being from their plantation.

"Good morning," she said. What can I do for you?"

"I'm looking for Miz Alexandria Dumont."

"You mean Mrs. Wentworth?" she corrected.

"Ma'am?" The boy looked confused.

"I used to be Alexandria Dumont until I married Brad Wentworth. Now I'm Alexandria Dumont Wentworth."

"Are yo' sure?"

She couldn't help but laugh. "Yes, I'm positive."

"Hows come yo' answered the door then?" the boy inquired.

"Because I was the closest one to it."

Cocking his head to one side, he thought for a moment. "Well, Miz Julia would never answer no door. Said it ain't proper."

"So Julia sent you?"

"Yes, ma'am." He dug down into his pocket and pulled out a crumpled piece of paper. "I got a letter for yo'." He handed it to her.

Alexandria thought about sending her message back with the boy, but decided she'd wait until after she saw the contents of this note.

After giving the child some cookies, she sent him on his way. Then she went to the library to read Julia's letter, wondering what the woman could possibly have to say. Maybe it was a note of congratulations. Alexandria chuckled ... probably not, since it was addressed to <u>Miss</u> Dumont.

> *Miss Dumont,*
> *I would like to see you tomorrow morning at 10:00. I know Brad has a meeting at the Ashworth plantation. And if you are wondering how I know that, then you're a fool. I told you he would always be mine. You'd be wise to keep this meeting. There are a few things we need to get straightened out. If you dare stand me up, I'll make life real miserable for that brat, Melissa. I have the power--believe me! Meet me on the back road that cuts between the plantations. The one where you were shot. Surely you can't forget that.*
> *Julia*

Alexandria laid the letter down in her lap. Jealously twisted her insides. Julia was bluffing. She had to be. Brad had been so loving, he couldn't possibly be seeing that woman. But how did Julia know Brad was going to the Ashworth Plantation? Alex reread the note. What could Julia possibly do to make Melissa's life miserable? And how did Julia find out about Alex's wound? Had Brad told her? Well, the witch didn't have to worry about being stood up. Alex wanted to see Julia just as bad as Julia wanted to see her.

Folding the note, Alex slipped it in her pocket, then tore hers up. It wasn't needed now.

I've given this a lot of thought, she told herself as she climbed the stairs to the attic. If Julia did have a hand in killing Catherine, Alex intended to find out. She could no longer sit around and wonder. She had to have some answers.

In the attic, Alex pulled the sheet from the mannequin. She was going to wear the same dress Catherine had worn the day she was killed. Alex was sure it would fit. Her stomach only had a slight bulge, and Catherine had been just a little larger. There should be no problems.

The dress of peach-colored satin and lace hung limp without the hoopskirt underneath. She felt the material and was surprised to find it still strong and not dry-rotted. She shook out the wrinkles, and the dust flew everywhere, provoking a bout of sneezes. As she grabbed for a handkerchief, she felt something hit her foot. She looked down. A hat lay at her feet. Alex stared at the floppy white hat with tiny peach and white flowers around the brim. She was certain it was the one in the painting back home. Shutting her eyes, Alex remembered the hat was worn down on the right side, but there was no hat in the portrait downstairs. She couldn't figure out why the pictures were so similar, yet different.

Stooping to picked up the hat, she hoped her plan would work. If, in fact, Julia had something to do with Catherine's death, maybe, for just a moment, Julia would be shocked into thinking she was meeting with Catherine.

It was definitely worth a try. Alexandria planned to tuck her red hair up under the hat so Julia wouldn't be able to distinguish the color.

After bundling up the dress, Alex took the back stairs in the rear of the house. Now wasn't the time to be bumping into Hattie, and having to explain why she had Catherine's dress. She took the path though the garden and headed to the small white washhouse down by the river. A young black girl worked there, and Alex counted on her being too young to recognize the dress.

She was thankful for the cooler weather, because her cloak made it easier to hide Catherine's dress. Entering the laundry room, Alex breathed a sigh of relief. Faye was by herself, humming and scrubbing on a washboard.

"Good morning, Faye." Alexandria pulled the gown from beneath her cape.

"Mornin', ma'am. You didn't have to bring your pretty dress down here. Someone would have gotten it for you."

"I know. But this is a special garment that I want cleaned. And Faye, I'd appreciate you not letting Hattie see this gown."

The girl's eyebrows raised ever so slightly in question. "I know this seems like a strange request," Alex went on to explain. "But I'd like to surprise her. It wouldn't be much of a surprise if she saw the dress before I could wear it. Do you think you could clean it, and get it back to me by tomorrow?"

"Sure, Miz Alex. I'll take special care that no one knows."

"Good. See you tomorrow." Alexandria had just opened the door when she heard Faye call to her.

"Oh, Miz Alex." Faye waited for her to turn around. "Do you want me to fix this tear?"

"No, that won't be necessary."

Faye shook her head as and Alex heard her mumble, "White people sure are crazy sometime!"

—)—

After dinner Brad and Alexandria went to the sitting room where a cozy fire snapped and glowed. Brad indulged in his brandy. He draped his arm across her shoulders as she sat curled up next to him, sipping her hot chocolate. Melissa had retired early, leaving them alone.

They relaxed by the crackling fire and talked of various things, but Alex couldn't get Julia's note off her mind. She kept pushing it to the back of her mind and tried hard to pay attention to what Brad was saying, but the green-eyed demon surfaced most unexpectedly.

"Have you seen Julia?" Alex blurted out. She hadn't meant to bring the subject up in this abrupt manner. She'd wanted to approach it more subtly. Well, so much for being subtle.

Brad arched a brow at her sudden question. The tone of her voice sounded almost accusing. Since her head rested on his shoulder, he couldn't see her expression. However, she seemed very casual as she stared into the fire. "Why do you ask?"

"I was just wondering."

"Just out of the blue, you were wondering?"

Alexandria hated the way he answered every question with a question. She had no intention of telling him about her intended meeting, because he might stop her. But she was evidently going to have to tell him something.

"I received a note from Julia today. It strongly suggested that you had paid her a visit."

Brad set his glass on the table, then removed the cup from Alexandria's hand. Turning her around to face him, he looked deep into her eyes. "Did you believe her?"

"No." She realized she'd replied a little too fast.

Brad stared at her with a bland half smile, and Alex knew he didn't believe her.

She watched intently, trying to judge his mood. Was that anger she saw? Her heart skipped a beat and she started again. "No, I didn't believe her. But you were going to marry her once, so you must have felt something." She paused, taking another deep breath, then, with a long, exhausted sigh, she went on. Her voice was as soft as a whisper when she spoke. "Besides, you only married me because I am pregnant."

Brad showed his irritation with a scowl, which made it perfectly clear to Alex that he didn't care for her talking about Julia.

Closing his eyes, he took a deep breath, letting his temper simmer down. He was tired of this! It was time to do what he should have done before!

He placed both hands on Alexandria's shoulders. "I do *not* love Julia, nor did I ever love her. I've never cared for anyone until I bumped into you. Alexandria, I wasn't looking for anyone! Marrying Julia was an easy way to have a family with very little attachment. Do you understand?" He watched as Alexandria nodded slowly.

"Would you have been happy living that way?"

"No ... I realize that now." Brad smiled at her. "But I didn't know that then. Mother tried to talk me out of marrying Julia, but I knew I could handle her. I never saw the devious side of her that Mother did."

"Perhaps she was putting on a show for you."

"Maybe," Brad admitted. "Now, in answer to your original question, no, I've not seen Julia, and I don't have any desire to." His expression grew warm and tender. "Alexandria, I married you because I love you. I was not aware of it at the time. I only knew I wanted you, and not because you were with child. For your information, I'd already decided to make you my wife before Hattie came into my study to tell me you were expecting.

"That's right." Brad chuckled at her astonished expression. "Though I would never admit that to Hattie. You are my life, sweetheart. You make me happy!" His hand came up to brush the hair from her face.

Brad's admission stunned her. All this time Alex had believed he had been forced into marrying her. Alex threw her arms around him. "I love you, Brad Wentworth. I've waited all my life to hear those words." She pulled back just slightly, so she could see his chiseled features now softened by love. His eyes had turned a crystal blue as devotion danced in their depths, and she would never tire of seeing his gorgeous eyes.

"I love you, too." Brad bent his head to her lips. He kissed her slowly, savoring all the manly feelings that ran through his body.

The glow of the fire bathed the two lovers in its soft orange glow, and once again they were transported back to a night very similar to this one. But this time all the love words were spoken as they both opened their hearts to each other.

Alex found she was nervous on the morning of the meeting. Brad had left early for the Ashworth plantation to go fox hunting. It was perfect, she thought. Now she would have the chance to get out of the house without anyone noticing her attire.

She struggled with the corset and hoopskirt. They were hard to maneuver without help, but she finally won the battle with her persistence. Alex carefully slipped the dress over her head. The peach-colored satin and lace fell in soft, ruffled layers from her waist to the floor. After adjusting the bodice, which fit just off the shoulders, she turned to look in the mirror. A small squeal escaped her before she could stop it. The dress fit perfectly, almost as if it had been made for her. She examined the slight tear in the top, but other than that the dress was perfect.

Alexandria twisted her long auburn hair, and secured it with hairpins. Then she covered her tresses with the white hat. As she stared at her image in the mirror, she shivered; for it was not her face she saw, but Catherine's. Catherine's smile was radiant, as if she were pleased with what she saw. Shaking her head to chase the ghost away, Alex once again observed her own features.

She sat down, wondering what had just happened. Was she hallucinating, or had the ghost of Catherine entered her body? Maybe Catherine was with her, pushing her in the right direction.

Could it be possible Catherine was the real reason Alex had been brought back to this time?

Before leaving the room, Alexandria placed the note she'd prepared the night before in the book on the nightstand. Brad read the volume every night, and if something unexpected should happen, he would be sure to find her note. It would tell him of her meeting with Julia and the location of his mother's diary. Alex slipped into her cloak and picked up the medical bag as she always did. Then, quickly before she changed her mind, she left.

By the time Abraham had harnessed the horse and hitched it to the buggy, the sun was just coming up. Alex plodded along at a slow pace, not wanting to arrive before Julia. Alex's mind swirled with many thoughts, and before she realized it the time had flown quickly and her destination lay ahead. She could now see a mounted horse lingering under a tree.

She pulled her mare to a stop. A nagging voice kept telling her this hadn't been a good idea.

Something terrible was going to happen.

But she had never been a coward, and she wouldn't start now. However, a little precaution wouldn't hurt. Reaching into her medical bag, she pulled out a scalpel and tucked it into her waistband. Taking a deep breath, she flicked the reins, and once again began moving forward--moving toward the unknown.

Julia saw the horse and buggy. A slow smile spread across her face. So, the stupid fool actually had the nerve to come. How foolish! Julia had her mount beside a huge oak tree and a large rock--all the better for her plan.

When the carriage pulled to a stop, Julia caught her first glimpse of the familiar white hat she had given Catherine for her birthday. Julia gasped and clutched her throat. Catherine! She had come back. But she couldn't have. Catherine was dead.

Seeing the startled look on Julia's face, Alexandria pushed the cloak from her shoulders, hoping to gain the advantage before Julia figured out she wasn't Catherine. She left the carriage her skirt billowed out as her foot touched the ground. Purposely she had tilted the hat to one side to block her face.

"Surprised, Julia?" When Julia didn't brother to respond, Alex continued speaking. She felt Catherine's presence within her body. "Why did you try to kill me?" Catherine's voice had replaced her own voice.

Julia looked lost in time as she dismounted her horse. Doubt flickered in her eyes, and she hesitated slightly before answering. "I did kill you. And I'll do it again if I have to!"

A tremor of shock ran through Alex and she forgot all about her masquerade. Her head snapped up. She had full control of her body again as Catherine's spirit left her.

"So you did kill her!" Alex shouted, outraged that Julia had gotten away with murder.

"Why, you little bitch!" Julia snapped. Her eyes blazed with fury. She swung, out to hit Alex, but Alex quickly sidestepped the blow.

"Julia, you really are the scum of the earth. Were you really that desperate to have a man?" Alex taunted. "I want to know why you killed Catherine!"

Alex's words sliced through Julia like a warm knife through butter. It was a fact that she was desperate. Her father had been disgusted with her when he'd found her in the stable making love to the stable boy, and had been quick to cut off all her funds. He'd told her he'd provide her with clothes and food only.

Julia shrugged, "Why should I tell you anything? You're the one who intruded on our lives. You don't belong here!" Her cat-eyes seemed to glow. "Don't talk about me being desperate for a man when you were so quick to spread your legs and trap Brad into marriage."

"Brad loves me, Julia. He never loved you."

Unreasonable hatred took hold of Julia. She lunged at Alexandria, catching her long red hair with her fingers. Alex fought back, holding her own until Julia called out. "John, help me!"

Alex felt herself being pulled off Julia and her arm twisted up behind her back. Who was this person who had her?

He held his victim firmly with one arm swung across her breast. Julia slapped Alex hard across the mouth, splitting her lip. "Now you'll show me some respect," Julia spat. "Just maybe I'll keep you around for my own personal slave."

Julia's eerie laugh seemed to echo in the hills around them. "Meet my partner, John Rivers. I think you'll remember him."

Alex shuddered at the mention of his name, but outwardly she remained calm. She couldn't let either of them think she was the least bit afraid. "What are your intentions, Julia? Will you kill me just like you did Catherine and your father?" Common sense told Alexandria to keep quiet, but she found that task all but impossible. There were too many unanswered questions. "Do you enjoy murdering innocent people?"

Julia's eyes narrowed to tiny slits. "What do you know about my father?"

"I found Catherine's diary. She mentioned David and how he suddenly became sick. You were the only one with him those last two days. Just how did you kill him?"

Julia's glassy pupils fixated, and for a moment Alexandria didn't think Julia would respond.

"Father was being very unreasonable." Julia laughed. "Just because of a little misunderstanding. He had the nerve to cut off all my money!" she shouted. "Do you know what it's like not to have any money? I decided to teach him a lesson!

"Every night I'd slip a small amount of rat poison into his dinner ... not enough to kill him, mind you, just enough to make him sick." She paced back and forth as though she had gone back to that particular day. "I don't know what happened, but suddenly he became delirious. I tried to tell him I loved him, and that I was sorry," Julia choked a moment with emotion, "but he shoved me away. He said I was evil. As he got worse, he kept calling for Catherine, saying he was sorry for taking advantage of their friendship, but at least they had a beautiful baby girl. My father announced he was proud to have Melissa for a daughter ... and ashamed of me." Julia pointed to herself. "The bastard! I smothered him with a pillow." She stopped and stared at Alexandria with an anguished expression. "I loved him. Couldn't he see that?"

Alex had gasped at Melissa's name. Why hadn't she put everything together before now?

Recovering from her confession, Julia smiled wickedly. "That's right. Your darling Catherine slept with my father."

"So you blackmailed her."

"Of course, I did."

"But your father's will--"

Julia cut her off with a wave of her hand. "Yes, my father's will. I can't help but laugh. He was smart there. I didn't know he'd rewritten his bequest until it was too late. But Father left me a personal note that no one else knew of. He said he was so disappointed in me that he was leaving everything to Melissa." Her lips thinned with anger. "And I was his first daughter first!" she screamed before adding, "He was decent enough to give me five years to find a husband."

The wild look in Julia's features terrified Alex. "Don't you see. Time was running out. And then *you*—"

Julia pointed her finger, "--you interfered. But everything will be all right now, and I'll soon be wearing that beautiful necklace. I'll be a Wentworth. I'll have it all!" She glanced to Rivers, who had been extremely quiet.

"Come on, let's get her to the cabin," Rivers complained. "I'm tired of fighting with the girl and listening to your ranting and raving."

To the left of the road, a path cut through the woods to a brown log cabin settled by a small creek. Alex struggled with Rivers, but to no avail. When she stumbled, he dragged her. When she tried to kick him, he simply jerked her arm higher.

"This is where we're going to keep you until I figure out what I want done with you," Julia informed her.

Alex wasn't as afraid as she probably should be. Maybe it was because she'd been through so much, but she did realize she had to keep Julia talking as they walked to the cabin. Alex had to find out just what Julia had done, and what she was capable of doing. "Why didn't you kill Melissa the day of your meeting?"

"My, my, you are persistent." Julia sneered. "Well, seeing that you'll never see any of them again, I guess it won't hurt to satisfy your curiosity. You see, Catherine didn't like me very much. She didn't think I was good enough for her son. And her constant interference became bothersome.

"I had just about convinced Brad to marry me when she started to protest strongly. The bitch! Why couldn't she just leave things alone? All I wanted were the jewels and Brad.

"Of course, what woman wouldn't want him? He's such a superb lover. But then I guess you know that, don't you?" Julia looked over her shoulder accusingly at Alexandria.

"If Catherine had just left everything alone, she and that little brat could have had a nice life." Julia sounded more and more deranged.

Alex now realized the woman was crazy. A cold trepidation seeped through her veins.

"Catherine demanded a meeting with me." Julia laughed insanely. "And she was stupid enough to come alone ... just like you have. Maybe you both are just alike." She cackled again before continuing, "Catherine threatened me! Said she was going to tell Brad the truth. She promised she'd put an end to my blackmailing her and also my plans to marry Brad. I argued it would ruin her. But she didn't care, said it was worth it to be rid of me. Catherine wanted to protect her precious son. Well, I couldn't let her do that, so John here gave her horse a little nudge. Unfortunately, it didn't kill her, and John had to help her along.

"We thought Melissa was dead. Then I heard she'd survived, but was paralyzed. I thought that was even better. When she inherited my father's money, I would gain control by being her guardian ... her loving aunt," Julia inserted sarcastically. "Do you get the picture? Melissa has always been afraid of me. And by the time I'd gotten through with her she'd do whatever I wanted."

"You really are twisted! You make me sick. I'll kill you if you ever touch Melissa," Alex said just as they reached the cabin.

"You really think you're in a position to threaten me?" Julia jerked her hand at Rivers. "Get her inside."

As soon as they entered the building, musty smells assaulted Alexandria's nose, indicating the cabin had been empty for a long time. There was one bed and a small table within the four dingy walls.

Rivers shoved her toward the bed. "Don't give me any trouble, bitch, or I'll tie you."

Alex got up and sat on the bed. She must be teetering on the brink of insanity because it was hard to believe any of this was happening to her. She watched as the enemy put their heads together in conversation. Her mind raced wildly. Blood surged to her head, giving her a splitting headache.

She had made a definite mistake, and it would take a small miracle to get her out of this situation.

"I'll see you later," Julia said as she turned to leave.

Alex knew she must keep the woman talking. Julia was crazy and Alex wasn't sure what Rivers would do to her once they were alone. "You'll never get away with this, Julia."

"Oh, yes, I will." She turned back to Alexandria. "Brad will conveniently forget about you when I've told him you've left with another man." Julia smiled when Alex gasped in surprise. "You see, I even have a witness who will swear he caught you in a secret rendezvous with Edmund. The baby your carrying is his ... not Brad's!"

"He'll never believe you." Alex clenched her hands in a tight fists. "Edmund will deny everything!"

"He would if he were here, darling, but, you see, he's not." Julia chuckled. "He left his morning for the Carolinas, and it's reported you left with him. Wasn't that clever of me?"

"But he'll be back," Alex screamed, losing her composure as she sprang to her feet. She couldn't let the woman control her destiny. She couldn't lose Brad. Her mind raced frantically to stop Julia. But how?

"I'm afraid not." Julia laughed--a spine-tingling sound. "Edmund will have ... shall we say ... an accident," she informed her. "Needless to say, he won't be returning. I never liked him anyway."

Absent-mindedly, Julia slapped her riding crop against her boot, but Alexandria still wasn't intimidated. Hadn't her long lost friend, Carol, told her a bunch of times that Alex didn't know when to be afraid? Julia thought she had her little scheme all planned out, but Alex was getting ready to put a kink in Julia's scheme. She eased her hand to her waistband. Feeling the cold steel of her scalpel, her confidence renewed.

"Well, Julia, your plan won't work. You see, I left Brad a note before I left, explaining where to find his mother's diary. I also told him I was paying you a little visit." Alexandria now found it was her turn to laugh.

"The note can easily be destroyed," Julia said with confidence, slapping the crop against her skirt. "If I'm not mistaken, Brad left early this morning."

"But you'll have to find the note and the jewels."

"What did you do with that necklace?" Julia screamed wildly. Her eyes glowed as she moved closer to Alex.

"I've hidden them where you'll never find them. I'm the only one who knows of their whereabouts. And I'll damn sure not tell you where they're located!"

Julia's brows came together and her eyes narrowed to slits. "I've waited too long for that necklace, and now ... now--" She drew back her riding crop and swung, hitting Alexandria across the abdomen. "You bitch! You'll tell me before this day is over! That is, if you want to live."

Alex screamed and grabbed her stomach. Bending over, she gasped. Her legs wobbled, then gave way and she slumped to the floor.

Julia stared at her laying crumpled on the floor. "That's a good place for you ... at my feet," she ridiculed. "John, I'm going to River Bends. I don't think Miss Dumont will be giving you any more trouble. From the looks of her, I'd say she's well into losing that brat she's carrying."

"I thought you said I could have a little fun with her." Rivers complained.

"You can still have all the pleasure you want, and probably have more fun. She's going to be too weak to fight you." Julia put her arm around his shoulder. "Think how your hard shaft's going to feel in that warm, soft woman."

"Yeah." He licked his lips.

"When you're through, be sure to kill her, but not before she tells you where the jewels are hidden."

"Where you going?"

Julia pulled the door open. "To take my rightful place as Mrs. Wentworth."

"And what if *he* don't want you?"

"Then I'll simply kill him, too. I love Brad, but he won't stand in the way of my wealth. All I need is the brat ... my lovely half-sister."

Alex held her abdomen as another pain shot through her. Her body was fast aborting the baby. Still in the early months, she knew her miscarriage would not be as bad as if she were seven months along.

A sadness settled upon her. She'd never know the pleasure of holding Brad's baby. To have the beautiful child they had created. And it would have been a beautiful baby. But that was all gone now. Another cramp took her breath.

Through the haze of pain, Alex heard Julia and Rivers talking as they stood by the door. She would have to summon strength from somewhere to fight off Rivers. The filthy man would never touch her.

Never! She'd die first.

The door slammed shut. She felt herself being picked up and carried over to the small bed where Rivers tossed her none-to-gently to the mattress. She moaned and drew her knees up as her stomach cramped again.

She had been foolish to come here alone.

What was she going to do?

Catherine, I need your help ...

Chapter Twenty-Eight

"Appears like you're not so high and mighty now, Mrs. Wentworth. How'd you like for me to make you forget about that pain you're havin'?" Rivers laughed. "Hell, I might even plant my own seed deep in you, so you can carry my brat 'round."

"Go to hell," Alexandria warned. "Don't even think about touching me!" She knew contempt showed in her glaring eyes.

"Still feisty, huh? Well, my monster here will take some of that fight out of you." He grabbed his crotch to emphasize his meaning, then started unbuttoning his pants. He pulled out his penis, holding it in his hand as he proudly displayed its size to her.

Bile rose in Alex's throat as she watched beneath half-closed lids. Rivers slid his pants down. God, he made her sick! She'd rather die than let this man touch her.

Slowly her fingers inched their way down to her waistband. Pretending to have another pain, she carefully reached for the scalpel and slid it out. With the weapon now concealed in the palm of her hand, she waited, all the while keeping her eyes on him.

Rivers was so absorbed in playing with himself that he wasn't paying any attention to her. His eyes grew wild and his breathing heavy as he became more excited. He moved over to her, shoved up her skirt and reached down, grabbing between her legs. A filthy smile crossed his face when she didn't protest. He snatched off her undergarments. It took all her willpower not to react.

"That's the way, honey. Just relax and let me show you a good time. I want to fill you up."

Alex's body turned to ice. Yet, she waited. Her slow and shallow breathing helped with the pain in her abdomen. She must stay in control.

She must wait.

She must endure.

Right now she felt numb and void of all other feelings as cold fear seeped through her.

Rivers knelt on the end of the cot, straddling her. He positioned himself ready to enter her.

Very slowly, she let her right arm fall off the cot where she gripped the scalpel with dexterous fingers.

"Ready, honey?" Rivers hollered as he plunged into her warmth, falling forward. "Let me taste those lush red lips of yours."

A little too late did he see the flash of silver as it sliced through the air and across his throat.

Rivers grabbed the gaping hole in his neck. His eyes grew big as saucers. Blood flew everywhere. Small gurgling sounds were all he could make as he gasped for air. His windpipe and jugular vein had been sliced in two. River's eyes were frantic. He rolled to the floor, incapable of any speech. He sounded like a drowning man as he took his last breath.

For a moment, Alex was too stunned to react. She felt no remorse for taking the man's life, even though she'd taken an oath to save lives; but this day her heart had turned cold. She loathed everything he'd been.

Wiping the blood off her scalpel, Alex realized her arm and hands were covered in blood. She slipped the knife back into her sash. Her stomach cramped again with abdominal pain. This one more intense, but in her stage of pregnancy the baby was very small. The first signs of her own blood felt sticky on her thighs. The miscarriage wouldn't be as bad as it could have been. Now infection would be her major concern. It could kill her, so she'd have to be careful.

Alexandria pushed on her abdomen, hoping to dislodge the *cast*. She bit her bottom lip, trying not to scream. Perspiration soaked her hair as she grabbed her stomach and pulled her knees up in the fetal position. With the next intense pain she passed out.

In her delirious state, Alexandria tossed and turned, calling out, "Catherine, I've killed a man." Then as if a movie projector had been turned, on Alex could see and hear the whole scene ...

—)—

"You'll never get away with this!"

A masculine, brown hand reached out and slapped the horse viciously on the rump. Bolting forward, the bay jerked the reins from Catherine's slim fingers, sending the carriage bouncing down the road out of control.

Catherine tried desperately to grab for the leather straps as they slipped farther and farther from her reach. How foolish she'd been to meet *her* here. "Hold tight, Melissa!" Catherine called to her daughter, who'd been asleep on the seat.

A sob rose from deep in her throat. "Oh, God!" They were not going to make the deadly curve just ahead. Grabbing Melissa, she held her tight to her breast.

The buggy hit a rock, jolted, teetered on two wheels, then plummeted down the hill. Over and over the carriage flipped until it came to rest by a big oak tree.

A few minutes passed before Catherine realized she'd survived. Dust blanketed the air and choked her as she breathed in the fine particles. She had underestimated how insane her opponent had become. Every bone in Catherine's body felt as if they had been broken. Struggling to lift her head, she searched frantically for her child. Melissa lay like a limp rag doll with her legs twisted in an awkward position ... she wasn't moving.

"Melissa," Catherine called, but received no response. Slowly, she reached her trembling hand toward her precious daughter, but Melissa was too far away. Pushing with her elbows, Catherine twisted her body and inched her way until she felt the smooth cotton beneath her fingertips. She tugged on Melissa's sleeve. A faint moan escaped the child's tiny lips, and Catherine silently prayed, "Please, help my baby live."

A man and woman stood at the top of the hill, looking down at the wreckage below.

"I think I just got rid of my problem." The woman smiled victoriously, but the smile faded when she heard a faint moan from below. "What's that?"

"Sounds like your problem still lives," her partner commented.

"Then you'd better finish the job!"

Catherine heard tiny pebbles hitting the carriage, and knew someone was coming ... but not to help. The skin on her neck prickled. Silent tears formed in her eyes at the thought she'd never see her son again. She wouldn't be there to warn him. And what would happen to Melissa?

Again gravel hit the overturned vehicle as the sliding footsteps drew closer. Perhaps, she could convince her assailant she was already dead. Quickly, Catherine laid her head back down. Her chest ached and her heart pounded wildly. She was trapped! A large thump of dirt hit the carriage. The vulture drew near.

Fighting a wave of dizziness, she shut her eyes and lay motionless. Catherine felt the sinister presence and smelled the foul odor of his sweaty body. Her breathing grew shallow as she played the game of possum. But her enemy wasn't easily fooled. Large fingers gripped her torn shoulder and viciously jerked her toward him. She couldn't suppress the scream that tore from her throat.

She heard his ugly laugh as his brawny, working hands closed around her neck as his calloused fingers tightening as if he were gripping a branch off a tree. She coughed and sputtered, gasping for air as her strength quickly left her body. Summoning her last bit of life, Catherine glared at her attacker and whispered.

"One day I will get my revenge ... One day."

"I'm so sorry, Catherine." Alex murmured to the empty room.

"*Don't cry my child*," Catherine's voice came from far away. "*Today you've settled my score and you've protected my children. I can rest now.*"

Alex was too weak to reach out to Catherine, but she could feel her spirit as it left her body.

"It's so hot in here." Alex tossed and turned as dreams turned to nightmares. Again she could see brilliant orange flames, shooting high in the sky, consuming everything in sight. Something was burning, but she couldn't get to it. She felt so helpless. *Won't somebody please help me?*

As the fire cleared, Hattie stood beside her, holding her hand. "Hattie, you've always been here when I needed you," Alex murmured. "I'm losing the baby!"

"I know, cher." Hattie gently held her hand. "I've come to help."

"But you can't save the baby?" Her voice caught in her throat. Tears slowly found their way down her cheek.

"No. But I can make you well, so you can have more children."

"Brad will be so angry with me."

"Not as long as he has you." Hattie wiped Alex's face. "Hush now. Let me work."

"Hattie, the fetus is no bigger than a rosebud. It will look like a small capsule."

"I'll take care of you, Petite."

"Hattie-- Julia killed Catherine."

"I know, Petite. I know." Tears welled in Hattie's eyes. "You must believe--" Hattie choked on her words. "--I've always had your best interest at heart. I've taken care of you just like I did my Catherine. I only let her down once ... when she went to see Julia. I tried to get to her, but by de time I arrived it was too late." Hattie shook her head. "Catherine was dead and Missy left crippled. Somehow I knew dere would come a day when I could revenge her death and make dem pay.

"You were the one, cher." Hattie reached over and kissed Alex on the forehead. "You were de one dat made all our lives complete."

—)—

When Alexandria awoke, she shivered from the cold, and automatically searched for Hattie, but no one was in the dirty cabin. Alex was alone. Perhaps it had only been a dream, and Hattie had never been here.

Alex had to get up. Somewhere the strength must come. She stood slowly on shaky legs sticky with blood. But they held, and she knew she needed to cleanse herself.

Her foot hit Rivers. She screamed. God, how could she have forgotten? His body would be better outside, but it would take what little strength she had left to move him, and she couldn't waste that precious commodity.

The fire that had been built earlier had died down to a bed of hot coals. She needed to rebuild it. Fading sunlight meant it was late, too late to go back home, so she would have to spend the night here. She swung open the creaky brown door and stumbled outside. Her head began to spin, and she grabbed the side of the cabin, feeling the course splinters under her fingertips. She waited a few minutes for the dizziness to subside. She couldn't give up now. It was too cool to go without warmth. Luckily, she found plenty of small branches on the north side of the cabin to carry her through the night.

She had to force herself not to give in to the weakness she felt. Finally, when she had enough wood, she moved with heavy footsteps back to the cabin.

Alex stoked the fire until it rekindled. Seeing a small black iron pot on the table, she filled it from a bucket of water by the hearth. Evidently someone had put the water in here earlier, she thought as she dipped the ladle into the bucket. She swung the pot full of liquid over the fire. It would take no time before she'd have hot water. Next she tore strips from her petticoats.

When the water was warm she began cleansing herself. Even though the pain had lessened, she was drained from her ordeal.

After putting another log on the fire, she went to lie down on the small bed, but found it covered in blood. Instead she grabbed the two pillows. It seemed strange to step over a body before climbing into bed, but this had been a strange day. She tossed the pillows in front of the fireplace and curled up to sleep. Tomorrow she would worry about everything. But right now she needed rest.

Sleep, once again, was not serene. Julia's hideous laughter plagued her dreams. The evil, demented woman wouldn't let her rest. Just what would she do next?

—)—

"Miz Alex. Wake up, Miz Alex."

Alexandria felt someone shaking her, but she was weary and wanted to sleep. However, the persistent shaking finally woke her, and she opened her eyes to find someone leaning over her. "Abraham?"

"Yes, Ma'am. It's me."

"Thank Goodness." Alex pushed herself into a sitting position. "How did you find me?"

"Saw the smoke this mornin'. Thought it was kind of strange when you didn't come home. Didn't believe that story none Miz Julia was spreading around." He shook his head in disbelief. "Never did trust the woman."

"Julia's at River Bends?"

Abraham nodded as he bent down to roll over the body on the floor. "Rivers. What got hold of him?"

"It's a long story, Abraham." Alexandria sighed. "He tried to attack me."

"And you did this?" Abraham turned back to her. "That must have been a pretty sharp knife," he said, showing his surprise. "The man's throat was slashed deep. That explains the blood on your dress."

"I lost the baby."

"I'm sorry, Miz Alex." Abraham's soft brown eyes showed his sympathy. "Are you going to be all right?"

"Yes, but we must go back to River Bends. There's no telling what Julia has told Brad or what she'll do." Alex struggled to her feet.

"I don't think Master Brad believed a word of what she told him." Abraham grabbed Alex's elbow to help her up.

"I hope he didn't. Did he throw her out?"

"No, ma'am." Abraham opened the door. "It was late when he returned home. Guess that's why Miz Julia spent the night."

Abraham assisted Alexandria into the carriage and wrapped her cloak around her. Her dress was torn and stained with blood, yet, she didn't complain. Abraham smiled gently at her. "Once I get you home, my Hattie will make you well."

They saw the smoke rising above the trees long before they reached River Bends.

"My God! It's a fire!" Alex shouted.

"Doesn't look good, Miz Alex. Just look how high those black clouds of smoke are rising!"

"Abraham, you can go so much faster on horseback." She grabbed his arm. "Ride ahead. They will probably need you."

He pulled back on the reins. "Are you sure you'll be all right?"

"Yes. Now hurry!" She watched as he mounted his horse and galloped off.

By the time she reached River Bends the entire upper floor was consumed with fire. She stared in horror at the brilliant orange flames.

Her dream had come true.

Formed into several bucket lines, the slaves passed the water. But the blaze flamed so large their efforts didn't doing much good.

Alex saw Abraham duck out the front door, carrying someone. He laid the woman down on the lawn, coughing from the smoke he'd inhaled.

Snatching up her black bag, Alex started running toward them, but the cramps in her stomach quickly slowed her to a walk. She scanned the crowd for Brad and Melissa. But they weren't there. And where was Hattie?

Alex recognized the black girl Abraham had rescued as Mary, one of the kitchen staff. Her badly burnt arm needed immediate attention.

"Where are Hattie, Brad and Melissa?" she asked Abraham as she laid strips of wet bandages on Mary's arm.

"Haven't seen them yet, Miz Alex." He stood back up. "I'd better get back in there. Don't worry none, we'll find them."

She grew uncomfortable by the minute. What if they were still in the house? She swallowed the lump in her throat and forced her eyes away from the house and back to her patient.

"Is that better, Mary?"

"Yes, Ma'am. But it still burns."

"Mary, did you see Brad?"

A strange look appeared in Mary's eyes and uncertainty marred her features. Her face clouded with uneasiness as if she was frightened to say anything.

"Mary, I know Julia was here. Don't be afraid. Tell me what happened."

"I--I don't know much. A--All's I know is Master Brad and Miz Julia was hollering at each other early this morning." Mary looked down at her lap.

"What did they say?"

"I heard Master Brad accuse Miz Julia of puttin' laudanum in his drink. He had a hold of her arm as they walked out of his study door. And Master Brad, he wasn't too steady. He shouted at Miz Julia to get out of his house before he killed her."

"Did she leave?"

"No, ma'am." Mary shook her head. "She jerked away and run upstairs with Master Brad right behind her." Mary looked at Alex with guilt in her eyes. "I know I wasn't suppose to, but I eased up the steps to hear what was going on. Miz Julia screamed she'd never leave. And the next thing I know, Miz Julia must have thrown an oil lamp, 'cause fire was everywhere.

"Then--then I heard the funniest laughter, but it died in a choking sound that sounded even stranger."

Alex's heart pounded in her chest. "Did you see Brad come down the stairs?"

"No ma'am. I was so scared by the fire, I turned to run down the stairs, but I tripped and didn't wake up until Abraham done carry me through that door." She pointed to the front of the house.

Alexandria stood, her eyes fastened on the doorway. Where could they be? Brad was so strong. He could survive anything. But Mary said he'd been staggering. Could he have been drunk or possibly drugged? What if Brad had passed out? Oh, God no! She had to help him.

She had already started for the house when she heard the first rumble. The brick walls began crumbling just as Abraham ran out the front door to safety, clutching someone in his arms. The whole first floor and walls fell inward. The flames shot higher.

Melissa's sooty blond hair hung limply over Abraham's arm. He took her to a grassy spot and laid her on the ground. She didn't move. Alexandria wondered why Abraham hadn't brought Melissa to her, so she could make her better. When Alex tried to go to her, she was stopped short by Abraham.

"You don't want to see her like that, Miz Alex."

"But I can help her," she protested. She clenched her hands until her nails cut her skin. Tears streamed down her face.

"No one can help her, Miz Alex ... Melissa's dead."

Alex gave up her struggle and laid her head on Abraham's chest. Her body trembled and she clutched his shirt. "Did you see Brad?"

"Yes, Miz Alex. I--I'm sorry," he said in a soulful voice.

"Tell me, I have to know," she cried hoarsely. "Where was he?"

"On the second floor in your room. I don't understand why he didn't get out. Apparently, he had some kind of struggle with Julia. There's no doubt he killed her." Abraham shook his head. "His hands were still around her neck, but I just don't understand why he didn't get out himself."

"Mary told me." Alex blew her nose and wiped her eyes before continuing. "Julia put something in his drink this morning. He was probably drugged or poisoned."

"I went back for Master Brad, but I must have gotten confused 'cause I couldn't find him nowhere." Abraham scratched his head. His brows drew together in puzzlement.

Alex pulled herself together, then spent the next three hours tending to the wounded. She looked up to see Abraham walking slowly toward her.

"It's time to bury the dead," he said.

"Where's Melissa body?"

"Don't know. There's been so much confusion--" Abraham shook his head. "I went to bury her myself, but her body's gone ... suppose someone else got to her first."

Alex struggled to regain her strength. "I'll help you."

"You don't have to."

"Yes, I do, Abraham. They were my family."

In the distance, lightning streaked across a sky of dusty purple hue just as the breeze blew wisps of hair about Alexandria's smudged face. Even her tears had not managed to wash away the soot. Her gown was torn and tattered where she had ripped material for bandages.

It was gone ... all gone. She had been too late.

Standing by the lake, she gazed at the smoldering ruins of River Bends. Everything she loved was gone--dead--destroyed. If only she had been in time to warn them of Julia's insanity.

Julia had gotten her revenge. Somehow, she had sneaked laudanum into the drinks of the family and household staff. Brad must have realized he'd been drugged too late. The house had already been set on fire. However, Brad had made sure Julia didn't escape.

They never had a chance. And it was strange they hadn't found his body. Perhaps Abraham had been confused and had gone back to the wrong room.

Thunder rumbled all around them.

"Looks like a storm." Abraham walked over to her. "You all right, Miz Alex?" His weak voice sounded dull.

"Yes, Abraham." She turned pain-filled eyes to him. "Have you found Hattie?"

"No." He choked as a tear rolled down his cheek. "I've searched everywhere for my beloved Hattie, and I even burned my hands going through the hot ashes." He held his palm up to show her. "We've found everyone except Hattie. Her body's nowhere to be found."

"I'm so sorry." Alex brushed her face with the back of her hand. "I loved Hattie, too. She is as mysterious in death as she was in life. You know, she was the only family I've ever known. Funny, it never mattered that our skin was a different color. I loved her as I would have loved a mother. I don't know what I'm going to do without her. I just don't know what I will do." Her raspy voice sounded desperate and strained as she whispered, "I'm alone again."

"I found this in Miz Melissa's hand," Abraham said. "I thought maybe you'd like to have it."

When Alexandria didn't answer, he put it in her hand and left with his head hung low. His footsteps dragged as he walked back toward what used to be a house ... a home ... a family.

Alex stood staring at the charred remains when a bolt of lightning cracked the sky, bringing her out of her stupor. She blinked, then glanced at what Abraham had given her. With the edge of her dress she wiped the soot off the brown leather cover. Panic like she'd never know welded in her throat. Her hands began to tremble. She laughed hysterically.

For so long she had searched for this thing ... this thing that had transported her back in time. And now when she no longer needed or wanted it ... here it was held tightly between her fingers. The diary. *Melissa's diary.*

Alex started to cry. "Don't leave me, Brad. Take me with you." No longer could she look at what used to be her home, so she turned to the lake. The wind had died down and the water was as smooth as glass, making it a perfect mirror.

She glanced into the lake and froze at the horror she saw before her. The dark waters of the pool reflected the charred remains of a home that was no more. The reflection showed her once beautiful gown now torn and tattered, hanging in rags from her shoulders. A single tear lingered on the bottom of her cheek as *her* face was clearly reflected in the dark waters.

"Oh, my God," Alexandria screamed to the heavens. She had been the girl in the painting. The answer had been in the portrait all along. It had foretold her future. Or was it her past? She wasn't sure where she belonged any more. She was torn between two worlds.

Hattie had been right. There were two paintings, and hers had been the second. It was the one that had spoken of the tragedy of this day. Alex's picture told of the horror produced by someone gone completely mad over money. Greed had caused all this destruction and tragedy.

Alexandria sobbed. "Hattie I need you! What am I going to do? Where am I going to go?" She couldn't take any more pain today. She clasp the diary to her chest just as a streak of lightning struck with a blinding light. Her knees gave way, and she fell to the ground in blissful unconsciousness.

She had finally reached her breaking point ...

Chapter Twenty-Nine

Beep ... Beep ... Beep.

What was that irritating sound? Alex thought somewhere in the depths of her unconsciousness.

She peeked from underneath heavy eyelids, giving her eyes a moment to adjust. The darkened room had just a hint of light filtering in through the window.

Strange, nothing looked familiar ... where was she?

The beep again penetrated her thoughts, and she turned to find the red glow of a heart monitor. So that was the source of the irritating racket. She was in a hospital room.

Wait ... Heart Monitor? They didn't have such things in 1835, she thought in her hazy state. Alexandria moaned as she tried unsuccessfully to sit up. It was too much of an effort just now and the darkness was much more inviting. Giving up, she shut her heavy lids and succumbed to sleep.

Confusing images danced before her eyes as painful memories went round and round in her mind. Her family was gone and she felt alone. She really didn't want to wake up. Why should she? This dream world was much more peaceful and reality was just too painful, but someone kept shaking her. Alex was unaware of the tears that slid down her cheeks.

Slowly her eyelids fluttered open, but she promptly shut them again when the bright sunshine hit her eyes. "Turn off that light," she grumbled. A shadow passed over her face and she could tell the light was not as bright. Perhaps the sun had gone behind the clouds. She attempted again to pry her lids open this time with success, but she had to wait a minute before her pupils adjusted. Just how long had she been sleeping? It seemed like a hundred years.

Someone tugged on her arm again and she heard a faint female voice, but it was vague. Her mind clouded with confusion.

She wasn't outside anymore. Abraham must have put her in here. Wait ... her room had been burned.

Where was she?

Then she remembered the heart monitor. Her breath caught in her throat...

She was back home.

Alex tried to sit up, but found herself too weak. Hearing the woman's voice again, she turned toward the sound.

"Welcome back!" Carol said cheerfully, holding her hand. "I was beginning to think I'd never see those green eyes again."

"Carol?"

"Yes, it's me."

Back in the present. Alex couldn't believe it. But what did it matter? What did she have to look forward to? "Carol, what are you doing here?"

"Visiting you, of course. Now that you're not contagious, they have let me sit with you the last few days."

"Few days? Contagious?" Alex frowned. Carol wasn't making any sense whatsoever.

"You've been a very sick human and gave us quite a scare when you stopped breathing. I guess you'll be able to tell your grandchildren you actually died for a few minutes." Carol smiled. "You don't remember anything ... do you?"

"I've had a miscarriage, but I don't remember--"

"Miscarriage!" Carol all but shouted. "Believe me, you didn't have a miscarriage. You've had Typhoid Fever."

"No. I've been on a trip."

"You've not been anywhere, Alex. Believe me, I know. I've been here checking on you the whole time. The doctor said you'd be confused when you woke up," Carol told her.

"What doctor?"

"Dr. Stewart. He's the one who had you admitted when he brought you to the hospital."

"Brought me to the hospital from where?"

"Don't go getting excited. Here, put this ice in your mouth and I'll start from the beginning." Carol helped her sit up and propped a fluffy pillow behind her back. "Let me see, I don't know where to start. Do you remember the Sunday we went to the flea market?" she asked.

Alexandria nodded.

"The next day you went to take your final inboard exam. You apparently had a high fever. And how you ever made it there is beyond me, but you did. You even finished your test. Dr. Stewart said you collapsed when you stood up to turn in your paper." Carol shook her head. "They brought you to the emergency room. The doctors couldn't figure out what had caused your temperature, so they ran all kinds of tests. As soon as they diagnosed your illness as Typhoid, you were whisked away to isolation. The doctors managed to control the fever with antibiotics and avoided the intestinal bleeding, thank God. You've been in the hospital, let me see--" Carol counted on her fingers. " --Five weeks."

"Five weeks?" This whole thing sounded as absurd as what had actually happened to her. "How did I get Typhoid Fever?"

"We're not sure. I think it was that trip you and I took to Mexico? Maybe that little kid who sold you a hot dog was infected with the virus and gave it to you."

"That could be possible," Alex mumbled, determined not to panic. "You said I've been here five weeks?"

"That's right. Excuse me, Alex." Carol stood and squeezed her hand. "I want to tell the nurse you're awake."

There was a flurry of activity with nurses coming in to check on Alexandria, welcoming her back. They all knew her from working at the hospital. Finally the room cleared out just before the doctor came in. "I'm glad to see you've joined the living again." Dr. Stewart smiled as he entered the room. "I've heard I give knock-out exams before, but I must admit I've never actually picked a student up off the floor. You're the first."

Alex smiled at him. He had always been her favorite professor, and now that she looked at him, he reminded her a lot of Edmund. Dr. Stewart was the one who'd told her she had a special gift with children. "I'm sorry, Dr. Stewart. I don't seem to remember being in the classroom at all."

"I can understand why. When we got you to the hospital your temperature was 104 degrees and climbing. Since you listed Carol as your next of kin, we contacted her right away. We were puzzled by your symptoms and asked Carol if you'd been acting strange."

"I told them you always acted strange," Carol butted in. "Then I remembered Hattie had given you some tea for the headache you had, so I went to your apartment and got the tea."

"Was anything wrong with it?" Alex asked. She knew Hattie would never hurt her.

"We don't know." Dr. Stewart rubbed his head. "To be truthful, the labs can't tell us what's in that tea. All the ingredients were foreign to them."

Alex smiled. Somehow that didn't surprise her. "What did you do then?"

"We asked Carol if you'd been anyplace different, and she told us about your trip to Mexico. Don't you know you have to be careful about food and drink from sidewalk vendors?"

"Yes, I know. But the little kid was so persistent and adorable. I just couldn't resist."

"Well, young lady, you've paid a high price for your weakness. You didn't have to eat the dammed food."

"It's not the first stupid thing I've done, doctor." She frowned at him. "I've not infected anyone else, have I?"

"No." He picked up her chart. "We're safe on that account."

"When can I go home?"

"Let's keep you here a couple more days just to make sure there's no relapse. You also need to regain your strength."

Alexandria nodded. She watched as Dr. Stewart and Carol left. Alex saw the doctor slip his arm around Carol's waist; evidently they had become good friends during her illness.

Everything Dr. Stewart said made sense, but Alex knew she hadn't been here. They might have had her body, but, her spirit had been at River Bends. Everything was so confusing. She felt absolutely dizzy. The logical part of her brain told her there was no such thing as time-travel. But maybe for just those few minutes when she had died she was able to slip into another century.

A week passed before Alexandria was ready to go home. She had been in bed so long she had to practically learn how to stand on her feet without getting dizzy. The day finally arrived and Carol came to pick her up.

"Carol, you wouldn't believe what happened to me!" Alex said once they were in the car.

"You're probably right." Carol started the car. "But I do know you've been crying a lot. Have you been in pain?"

"Yes. The worst kind of pain ... pain of the heart."

"You're having a heart attack!" Carol completely misunderstood, and slammed on the brakes right in the middle of the parking lot.

"No, Carol. I meant a broken heart."

She breathed a sigh of relief. "Don't scare me like that." Carol looked completely confused as she shifted the car into drive. "I think you'd better explain."

As they drove home, Alex told her everything that had happened. Carol was quiet and seemed to hang on every word. She nodded her head but remained quiet.

"That would make a wonderful book. Are you sure you've not read the story somewhere before?" Carol looked at her and smiled.

"No. It actually happened! I know it sounds crazy. I had a hard time believing it myself. I argued with Hattie that she couldn't do this."

"Hattie?"

"Yes. She was the one who gave me the diary and the painting. You remember. You were there that day. I was the woman in the picture."

"Give me a break. How could you be the woman in the painting when you'd never seen the picture until Hattie gave it to you?"

"I know it sounds crazy, but I actually lived back then." Alex glanced at Carol and saw sympathy in her eyes.

"You've just had a very vivid dream. I've had dreams like that myself." Carol tried to make her feel better.

"It wasn't a dream, Carol!" Alex stated emphatically.

"Alex, you've been here the whole damn time. You're just baffled. Don't think about it now." Carol patted her hand as a mother would a child's.

Alex didn't feel like arguing any further. It was evident her friend didn't believe her. She would have thought if anyone would have understood it would have been her best friend. But she supposed she had been delirious.

There was her apartment: 325 E. With no heavy suitcases to carry, Alex eased herself out of the car, thinking this had been the second unplanned trip she'd made without packing any clothes. She slipped the key in the lock and turned the doorknob. It was late in the day, so she flipped on the light. The glow bathed the hodgepodge of furniture she'd accumulated over the last several years.

Nothing had changed.

Yet, she felt strange standing in her own living room. The air was musty and stifling, the direct result of the house being shut up; other than that everything looked the same. Somehow this room didn't feel like home anymore.

Carol dropped her purse on the couch. "How about I fix you some dinner before I go home?"

"You've done so much already, Carol."

"Nonsense. Go take a nice hot shower and I'll whip us up something."

Alex admitted she was a little hungry. As she entered her lemon-yellow bedroom, the first thing she spotted was the painting propped against her old, oak chest. She was weak and had to lean onto the walls for support, but she resisted the urge to stop and stare at the painting. There would be time for that after Carol was gone. Slowly she made her way to the bathroom. Turning on the light, she smiled. How long had it been since she had turned on a simple light switch? According to Carol, a few weeks.

But Carol was wrong.

Alex glanced at the counter top and found her makeup scattered about, just like she'd left it. She slipped off her clothes and stepped into the hot shower. The invigorating water did make her feel a little better, but Alex felt as if she was moving in a daze. Her perceptions were foggy. Everything was familiar, yet nothing seemed real.

After drying herself with a fluffy pink towel, she dusted her body with the heavenly scent of bath powder. Slipping on her silk robe, she peeked at herself in the mirror and shook her head. A pathetic waif stared back at her. She had lost weight, and her eyes were not only swollen but dull. There was no life in the person who stared back at her from the mirror ... only sadness.

The spaghetti dinner Carol prepared was delicious. It had been a long time since she'd had her favorite meal.

Alex knew Carol was trying hard to cheer her up, but found the task more difficult than she'd imagined. Carol kissed Alex on the cheek before leaving, promising she would call tomorrow. "Perhaps you just need time."

Alex turned off the living room lights and walked into her bedroom. Lying on the comforter, face down, was the diary. The little book that had changed her life.

She climbed into bed and picked up the leather journal. It had been opened to the last page. Alex frowned. Before, she had only read the beginning, so why was it on the last page? Maybe someone had moved the book while she'd been in the hospital. No matter, tonight she would start at the beginning and read the diary to the end.

It was four a.m. when Alex turned to the last page of the book.

> *Dear Diary,*
> *Something strange is going on. Julia told Brad that Alexandria will not be coming back. She said that Alex had left with Edmund. She's lying, diary. Alex would never leave me. Brad said we would look for her tomorrow. He let Julia spend the night, I guess because it was so late.*
>
> *This morning, Julia brought me a glass of milk. She said she wanted to be friends and we must forget the past. I thought it was strange, diary, but I was thirsty and accepted the milk. I want to finish this entry, diary; however, I'm so sleepy.*
> *Wait ... I hear Brad and Julia hollering. Did he yell he was going to kill her?*
> *I want to go to the door but I'm so ...*

Alex knew why the diary ended so abruptly. Melissa had been drugged. The whole account had been in the diary . . . everything that had happened to *her* but from Melissa's viewpoint. Could she have read the story and dreamed the rest?

Perhaps she really was crazy. Maybe none of it had ever happened. Alex sighed as she turned off the light for the night.

It was a long night ... so many thoughts ... so many memories ... so many emotions.

—)—

Two months crept by.

Physically, Alexandria had recovered. She was eating well and her strength had returned. Emotionally, she still lived on the edge of the past and present.

"I've had enough, Alex!" Carol finally lost patience with her. "I've been patient, but it's no use! You're determined to wallow in self-pity. And what's worse, it's all in your imagination. It was a dream ... do you hear me, a dream.... A figment of your imagination!"

"It hurts, Carol! Don't you understand, *I hurt!*" Alex screamed with all the anguish she felt.

Carol looked at Alex, shaking her head. "A part of me wants to shake some sense into you. The other part wants to comfort you." Carol picked up her purse. "I'm leaving. When you've decided you want to join the living again ... let me know."

The hell with Carol, Alex thought, as she watched her shut the door. However, deep down she knew her friend was right. She had to go back to work.

And tomorrow she would take the first step.

Alexandria threw herself into her work at the hospital, and on the weekends she volunteered for the emergency room. She did not see Carol, but stayed mostly to herself. Alex's days were routine; she worked and went home to sleep, then returned to work again. She functioned one day at a time.

But that was all ... just functioning. No sorrow. No pain. No happiness. And most of all no emotions.

She had helped save many lives, but on one rain-drenched night she lost one. Alex tried to be professional when she broke the news to the man's wife, but in the end she wept with the widow. For Alexandria knew how it felt to lose a husband.

That night she could barely remember driving home. The rain slicked roads added to the stress she felt. She felt numb as she opened her apartment door. Her black bag slipped from her fingers and hit the floor with a thud. Next her coat dropped to the floor. She didn't even bother to eat, but instead went straight to her bedroom.

Sleep was not to come for Alex; her only thoughts were of Brad. She sat in the granny rocker thinking back to a place called River Bends as she stared at the painting.

How she would love to see Brad's tawny brown hair with the gentle streaks of blond that highlighted the front. And his hard-chiseled face ... she could never forget it. To look once more into his vivid ice-blue eyes would be pure heaven.

She thought back to their turbulent meeting when Brad had accused her of being a thief. She could smile about that now. Hattie had been right; there *was* a thin line between love and hate.

Alex had never really hated Brad at all. She'd loved him from the moment he had taken the bullet meant for her. She would give anything to be held in his arms just once more, and know the strength of his protection. She was weary of being strong.

Lord, how she needed someone to lean on.

The morning sun rose in the sky.

She had sat in the chair all night. Her cramped muscles ached, and her eyes were once again swollen from crying. She was tired ... damn tired.

Slowly, she got up and went to the medicine cabinet. Opening the door, Alex took out a prescription bottle of sleeping pills.

She got a glass of water. Twisting the cap opened, she poured out a handful of pills. Twenty blue pills danced in her hand.

Twenty tiny pills that promised no more pain.

She walked back to her bed and put the glass on the nightstand. Opening her hand, she stared at the small but powerful blue pills. Anguish swept over her.

"Please!" she screamed to the empty room.

Then Alex did something she had done very little of in her life. She got down on her knees and prayed. Not just a prayer you might say every night before going to bed, but she actually talked to God.

"Please, God, help me," she cried. "I don't know what to do, and I have reached the end of my rope ... please, help me," she begged. "I've nowhere to turn, and I need your help. I've done everything I know how, and I'm turning it over to you," she sobbed. "I'm putting everything in your hands ... I need you so much," she kept repeating to herself in desperation. "Please, God, show me what to do ... Help me!" Alexandria pleaded, laying her head on the bed in total submission.

She wasn't sure just how long she lay there crying, but finally her tears dried. Still on her knees, she lifted her head and looked up. She opened her hand that still held the pills--such powerful little demons that beckoned her.

Alex drew her hand up slowly to her mouth. The first blue pill touched her lip, saying, *Take me take me I'll make it better.*

She stopped.

Looking up toward the heavens, she closed her fist and threw the pills, sending them scattering in all directions. Then she did something she thought she'd forgotten how to do. She laughed for the first time in months.

God had touched her. He had listened and reached out his hand when she needed it the most and given her strength. A feeling of contentment spread through her body and she felt peaceful.

Standing up, she knew everything would be all right. Pulling back the covers, she climbed into bed and slept. It was the first restful sleep she'd had in a long, long time.

Chapter Thirty

Alex slept all day Saturday and Saturday night. Sunday morning her beeper finally woke her. She fumbled for the phone, then dialed the number.

Nurse Liles answered the phone. "Dr. Dumont, we need you here STAT."

"I'm on my way. What's happened?"

"It's bad. There's been a fiery wreck on Interstate Forty. The casualties are just now starting to come in. And if this is any indication of what's to come, we're going to need every available hand."

"I'll be there right away."

Alex leaped out of bed and ran to the shower. In no time, she had on her clothes. After pulling her hair back with a ribbon and pinching her cheeks for color, she was ready. She could remember when she wouldn't have stepped a foot out the door without makeup. Taking another quick look at herself, she smiled. Somehow, she looked different. Her eyes sparkled once again with life.

The emergency room had been a madhouse when she'd arrived three hours ago. Rubbing her aching neck, Alex walked out of the examining room. She poured herself a cup of black coffee and walked over to the window. Where had the day gone? It was now late into the afternoon. The accident had involved many cars and brought in all sorts of injuries.

There were many broken bones to be fixed and cuts to sew up. The arrivals were starting to slacken up. She had two more patients to see and one still due to arrive. Massaging the back of her neck, Alex made her way into the next room. Her auburn hair had escaped its ponytail, and she felt just a little frazzled.

Picking up the chart on the door, she walked around to the right hand side of the bed as she read about the patient. All the vital signs appeared normal, which was good, she noted as she scanned the chart further.

"Are you experiencing any pain?" Alex asked as she jotted her name on the bottom of the patient's record.

"*Oui,* just a little."

Alex's pen fell from her hand and her head snapped up in complete surprise. "Hattie! You're here!" Alex screamed and hugged her.

"It's good to see you, cher."

"I knew you wouldn't leave me! I've missed you so much." Tears streamed down Alex's face as she squeezed her old friend again. "Why did you give me such happiness only to take it from me?"

"Ouch." Hattie flinched. "My shoulder hurts just a little, cher."

"Sorry. I didn't mean to squeeze you so hard." Alexandria, once again the doctor, glanced down at the chart. "It appears you've dislocated your shoulder. I don't see much of a problem in fixing it. I'll get you something for pain. But answer my question."

"Cher, still you've not learned to trust me." Hattie shook her head. "I love you, Alexandria, and I'd never cause you any unhappiness."

"But--"

Just then the door flew open, and a child came running in the room. Her blonde curls bounced about her shoulders. "Hattie, are you all right?"

"Melissa?" Alex gasped. "I can't believe it's you. But--I thought you were dead."

"Goodness gracious, I hope not. I just had a small cut. The doctor down the hall fixed that with what he called a butterfly." Melissa smiled at her.

Alex hugged the child to her. "Boy, have I missed you, too."

Melissa stared at her with wide blue eyes. "You're very nice, but do I know you?"

Alex never even heard Melissa's question because she once again stared at Hattie, holding her breath with anticipation to her next question. "Brad?"

"Dey're bringin' him in. He's not yet arrived," Hattie told her.

Alex had already turned and was heading for the door when Hattie called out, "What about my arm?"

"I'll get you in a minute," Alex called over her shoulder. She had to see Brad. It had been too long.

"Good thin' I'm not dyin', you hear," Hattie grumbled.

"You'll be fine, Hattie."

"Dumont! STAT!" The announcement rang over the intercom.

Alex ran down the long corridor to the rear doors of the emergency room. The ambulance door swung open and two medics appeared pulling a stretcher out of the back. Brad was on the gurney. He wasn't moving. Alex picked up his wrist and groped for a pulse. The medics filled her in on Brad's statistics as they rolled him down the long hallway.

He didn't look good. And if she was going to help him she'd have to put her personal feelings aside. "Take him to operating room one."

One of the other physicians walked up beside her. "You look beat, Alex. Let me take this one."

"Thanks, David. I'll be fine. He's one of my patients."

"Are you sure?"

"Yes, I'm sure. There is a woman down the hall with a dislocated shoulder. I'd appreciate it if you could handle that case." She smiled her thanks. If he could handle Hattie, then he was a better doctor than she.

Brad had a broken leg, but that could be set later. Right now it was the least of his problems. He had lost too much blood. Preparing him for surgery, Alex said a small prayer as her scalpel touched his skin. Luck was on her side; she found the artery that had been slashed. Her dexterous fingers worked as a seamstress would, carefully stitching the walls. She held her breath as she slowly removed the clamp. Mopping the blood from the wound, she watched. Good ... no leaks. Alex let her breath out slowly and glanced at Brad. His coloring still wasn't the best.

"Please God, help me." She felt Brad slipping away from her. "Oh, God! There's no pulse! Get the fibrillator over here!"

No sooner said than done, Alex began rubbing jelly on the pads. "Stand clear."

She shot a charge to Brad. His body bounced up, and his heartbeat thumped once but stopped.

"Let's do it again. Stand clear!" She repeated the procedure.

"Brad, damn you, don't leave me now!" There it was. A beat. Then another one. "Come on, you can do it ..."

A cheer went up as the steady rhythm began to establish itself. This time the heartbeat grew steady.

"I love you, Brad," Alex whispered and she breathed a sigh of relief.

She knew he might not be able to hear her, but he'd hear the same thing when he woke up.

Alex's medical assistants stared at her. "Would you like for us to finish, Dr. Dumont?"

"No, I'm going to stay with this patient. This patient is special. He's a friend," she stammered.

She did leave Brad, but only long enough to check on Hattie and Melissa. She assured them that Brad would recover. Melissa and Hattie looked beat. "Look, there's a small room where the doctors usually sleep when we're on duty. Make yourselves comfortable and get some rest."

Alex spent the remainder of the night beside Brad's bed. Holding his hand, she willed his strength to return. The hours slowly passed by, and she recalled another time she had sat beside his bed. She also remembered her remedy for Brad's fever, but this time she was going to try to restrain herself.

Tears choked her as she murmured, "I love you. I didn't know what happiness was until I met you." She lifted his hand, placing a kiss on it. "Please don't leave me."

Her head felt heavy and the thought of laying it on the soft bed was overwhelming. If only she could shut her eyes for just a minute. Sleep ... peaceful ... sleep ...

"Why doesn't somebody get a damn doctor?" Brad swore.

Startled, Alex jumped to her feet. His big, blue eyes stared at her. He was awake! She leaned over him and smiled. "You have a doctor right here."

A look of dismay crossed his brow. "Have I died and gone to heaven?"

"No. You've not died." Alexandria laughed.

Brad turned his head as though he were searching for someone. "My family, how are they?"

"They're both in better shape than you are."

"It was pretty bad, huh?"

"You might say that." She watched Brad's eyes as he studied her. His brows drew together in a look of confusion. She remembered Melissa had not recognized her. Evidently the same held true with Brad.

"You look like an angel." He smiled. "Are you going to take care of me, nurse?"

"Doctor," she corrected him. "Yes, I'm going to take care of you for the rest of your life." Alex returned his smile as tears of joy rolled down her cheeks.

Brad noticed the tears glistening on the tips of her eyelashes. Her emerald eyes glowed with emotion. His gaze took in every inch of her face. This woman seemed so familiar to him ... like he'd known her a long time ago. Yet, he couldn't recall ever seeing her until now. Perhaps he had known her in another lifetime? He would laugh if it didn't hurt so much. Maybe the accident had affected his mind. He didn't believe in that stuff. Still ...

He reached up and wiped her tears away. "Why do you cry for me? Do I know you ... beautiful one?"

Brad was just the way she remembered him. His face had been burned in her memory ... those hard-chiseled features and his ice-blue eyes. A small dark curl had fallen on his forehead, and she gently brushed it back. "Do you believe in destiny, Brad?"

He nodded.

"Good. Then I'm the angel who is going to take care of you now and forever." Why didn't he recognize her? It was probably one of those twists-of-fate Hattie threw in to make her life more interesting. But this time Alex didn't care. She might have to get to know Brad and Melissa all over again, but she didn't mind. She had her family back and that was all Alex cared about, because without a family, life wasn't worth very much.

Brad was surprised when the doctor leaned down and kissed him softly on the lips. His hand came up behind her head and pulled her closer. There was something about her that was so familiar. The softness of her lips were intoxicating and he found he wanted more than a simple kiss. Parting her lips, he deepened his kiss, but his aches and pains soon reminded him he was not well. If he didn't know this lady before, he would rectify that small matter when he was well again.

The kiss ended, and Brad stared up at the attractive woman. He watched as the burnished curls fell just below her shoulders. She didn't seem to realize just how enchanting she was when she smiled. Was it possible to fall in love with someone he had just set eyes on? It was a shame he had to break his leg just to meet her. God, she was beautiful. And one thing was sure ... he'd never had this kind of attention from a doctor before. "I like your bedside manner, Doc."

It didn't matter that Brad didn't remember her, because he definitely responded to her kiss, Alex thought. It also didn't matter that his leg was broken and she needed to have it set. Nothing mattered, not even the fact that she could be fired for her very inappropriate actions. *What did matter* was that she had Brad back and she loved him. Of course, he loved her, too. He had just forgotten, thanks to Hattie.

"Good, I'm glad you like my bedside manner, because I'm going to have your children, Brad Wentworth," Alex said huskily, staring down at him. Her twin dimples radiated, and once again made her face glow.

Brad chuckled that deep rich laugh she remembered as he reached up and pulled her down into his embrace. Folding his arms around her, he said. "Don't you think we should get to know each other first?"

"That might be wise," Alex teased.

"In that case, you'd better fix my leg, so I can get started." Brad didn't know where this lovely creature had come from, but one thing was for sure. He didn't intend to let her out of his life.

Yes, their life would be wonderful together and the passion strong. There was no doubt in Brad's mind about that point. He clasped Alex to him as his mouth sought hers with a promise of wonderful tomorrows. The future would belong to them.

Once more their lips met in an endless kiss that was a century old.

Epilogue

"Why don't they recognize me, Hattie?"

"Dey've just met you, cher."

"But before --"

"Patience, cher, patience. You really should learn to trust me more. Remember ..."

"I know Hattie. It's for my own good." Alex gave her that familiar, exasperating look.

Hattie's knowing smile made one wonder just what the woman would do next. An aura of agelessness radiated about her. Just how old was this woman? And how could she do the things she did? Alex laughed. Perhaps some things were better left unknown.

One thing was for sure, with Hattie taking care of her, how could Alex go wrong?

And, as Hattie loved to tell her ...

"When Tomorrow Comes, Alexandria, you'll understand everything."